Rekindling
THE
Flame

MADISON MYERS

PLAYLIST

the 1 – Taylor Swift
Lonely City – Mokita
Before You Go – Lewis Capaldi
Figure You Out – VOILÀ
Strangers – Kenya Grace
Live Like You Were Dying – Tim McGraw
Just One Yesterday – Fall Out Boy, Foxes
Beautiful Things – Benson Boone
I Want It All – Cameron Grey
exile – Taylor Swift, Bon Iver
Last Night – Morgan Wallen
Look After You – The Fray
Wish You The Best – Lewis Capaldi
What My World Spins Around – Jordan Davis
I Hope You Dance – Lee Ann Womack
Girls Just Want To Have Fun – The Maine, Adam Lazzara
Paradise – Justin Timberlake, *NSYNC
Five More Minutes – Scotty McCreery
Last Man Standing – Livingston

Finer Things – Post Malone, Hank Williams, Jr.
How Do I Say Goodbye – Dean Lewis
Wait For You – Myles Smith
Next Thing You Know – Jordan Davis

iv   PLAYLIST

Finer Things – Post Malone, Hank Williams, Jr.
How Do I Say Goodbye – Dean Lewis
Wait For You – Myles Smith
Next Thing You Know – Jordan Davis

For all my early readers who gave me a shot as a brand-new, unheard-of author, who left supportive reviews, made content about my books, and told their friends.

I'm keeping going because of you.

This one's for you.

NOTE FROM THE AUTHOR

Like with most of my books, these characters are flawed, there are toxic elements as well as explicit scenes, and this book may be triggering to some.

This book also focuses heavily on the loss of a parent (cancer).

As I always say, I write fiction, not self-help.

I hope you enjoy it. 💋

XOXO,
Maddie

1

Aurora

The mediocre sex is the one thing I won't miss about the city.

The loud noises, the infinite variety available on every block, the constant stimulation that keeps me from hearing my own thoughts ... that I *will* miss.

I know a lot of people would consider Smoky Heights an idyllic place to spend the foreseeable future, what with the small-mountain-town vibes, the endless woods that meet the horizon in all directions, the peace and quiet you hear so much about.

Those people didn't flee that town in their early twenties, to never return until now.

Tonight's scoop du jour rolls off of me, panting, sweat running down one side of his face.

Rude of me to call him the flavor of the day. We've been seeing each other on a ton of days when neither of us has someone else filling our calendar, on and off, for a while now. It sounds harsh, but we both know what this is. A shitty alternative to sleeping alone.

Tonight's a night I'll take any company over my own.

My last night in NYC.

His eyes squint in question, and I give him a half-hearted smile with no pretense behind it. I didn't even bother faking it, and we both know it. "A lot on my mind," I tell him in response.

It's not an apology. It's the truth. So would be saying that he's maybe a five out of ten, but sometimes a real cock is better than a silicone one, even if he can't use it that well.

But then again, when you start your sexual history off with an eleven out of ten, I guess everyone who comes after (pun sort of intended) is going to be a disappointment. It's had me grading every partner since on a curve. Haven't found anyone above a seven in all my years trying. And believe me, I've tried.

But that's the thing about your first, you don't have anyone to compare them to, so you don't even know if what you have is average, terrible, or—depressingly, in my case—the best you'll ever find.

Speaking of going back to my hometown, of all that's on my mind, all I'm freaking out about ... His ears must be burning.

For my own sanity, all I can do is hope to hide out at my mom's, avoid the reminders of my past, and somehow pray that I don't run straight into my past.

You'd think more than a decade apart would fracture the magnetic pull we once had between us, the electric chemistry that sparked up as soon as we were in one another's presence. Common sense says it probably has. But what we had defied common sense. A kind of attraction, an all-consuming need, that's never manifested with anyone else since. I guess I thought it would be the norm with other partners, but, turns out we were the anomaly, and I'm the one who ruined the best thing I'll ever have out of selfish fear.

I suck in quick breaths through my mouth, in and out, while my eyes bounce from object to object in my room, anything in the vicinity, until the thoughts stop spiraling. Until my head quiets a bit.

The guy to my right helps. So do the shouting voices from the street, floating up and infiltrating my sixth-floor window in the midnight hour, sandwiched by sirens and the occasional single horn blast.

Not sure what's going to focus me when I don't have these distractions to drown out the sound of my own thoughts, but I guess that's just one more cross to bear when I'm back in the Heights.

But when you get the call that your only remaining parent has months left to live, what else do you do? Maybe it's the guilt of leaving her alone all those years ago, never going back to visit since, maybe it's just what anyone with a heart and the financial means to pull it off would do, but I didn't think twice. I knew there was only one right thing to do after that news, and if I didn't follow through with it, I'd never forgive myself.

They may still never forgive me, but there's no way I'm not trying now.

I turned in my notice as an associate at the major firm I've been employed by for the past eight years (they didn't accept it, but I did *try* to quit), broke the lease on my studio apartment on the Upper West Side, and scheduled movers to be here tomorrow to pack it all up and put it in a portable storage unit while I head back to where I escaped from.

Never thought I'd be forced to face my fears at thirty-three, but I guess I couldn't run forever.

"Aurora?"

My eyes find Trevor's, and I see the concern shining in his.

"Mmm?"

"You good, hon?" he asks, that Eastern seashore accent poking through, despite the fact he's lived in Manhattan about as long as I have.

I let my fingers trail over his temple, push through his sandy blonde hair, mid-length nails scraping softly along his scalp. "As good as I can be," I promise him.

"Gonna be weird without you on the sixty-second floor." Trevor never passed the bar, so he's worked as a paralegal for years longer than he ever planned to. He's a good paralegal. A good guy. Just not the guy capable of passing his bar on the third attempt. And not the guy capable of holding my interest, at least not for more than the occasional office lunch or casual hookup. Though, to be fair to him, nobody does these days.

"Gonna be weird, period," I tell him, trying to keep my mind on the here and now, not let it drift and wander to what's waiting for me back home. Who. All the reasons I left in the first place. "What am I supposed to do when I'm craving Korean barbecue at two in the morning?" I joke.

"I suspect you won't have a shortage of barbecue where you're headed."

"A definite shortage of variety, though." In a town of less than five thousand? Barely got a Sonic and a Dollar General. "And restaurants open past 8:00 p.m.," I tack on, remembering the one local diner we had growing up used to close before the sun went down. Though, it's probably out of business now, like so much of the town, considering who used to run it.

"I'll send you some of your usuals from Goldbelly. Besides, you won't be gone forever, right?"

I scoff. "I'll be scratching my way back to the city tooth and claw the second my mom's affairs are in order and the dirt is on the casket." The words are more callous than I intend them to be, but they're still true.

That cynical voice in the back of my head tells me those sound like famous last words, and I let the bevy of sounds that accompany living on an island along with millions of others drown that voice out in the cacophony, the way I've found peace for the past twelve years.

2
Wyatt

The smell of motor oil and gasoline, an ever-present yet nearly invisible combination to my senses, is faintly registered by some part of my brain as I start up the 2001 Mercury Sable that Mrs. Dixon refuses to part with, despite the bi-monthly visits it has to take to my shop.

The ignition catches and the engine rolls over, and if I smiled, a small one would probably be on my face right now. But the hit of pride from another vehicle with a motor fixed is about as good as it gets for me. Add in a cold beer or a nice bourbon, the occasional warm body in my bed, and that's damn near the peak of my life.

In short? Can't complain.

A streak of something dark mars the tattoo that encases my forearm—a realistic cross-section of an engine—and I use the sorta, kinda, almost clean enough rag on the dash to wipe it off. A well-earned sigh leaks out as I climb out of the sedan, my knees creaking with the effort, the chief tell of another nine-hour day popping up and down beneath a hood, a chassis, anything that purrs or hums for me once I've fixed it up good.

Southern rock blasts from the boombox across the garage, one that's even older than Mrs. Dixon's car.

"Shit!" The only other human company I have in here graces me with his voice, somehow louder than Ronnie Van Zant's, and a heavy clunk follows it.

Ignoring him as usual, I wash my hands in the sink tucked in the back of the shop, using that granular orange soap to get the last of the grease residue off of my hands. At least what of it ever comes off at this point. Pretty sure my blood is a fraction motor oil at this point, but the doctor hasn't told me my time is around the corner yet, so I'm not too worried.

"Heading out," I call over to Gonzo.

His head pokes out from under the hood of the '73 'Vette he's working on, but he bumps into the hood strut instead of backing out smoothly and he hollers a few choice curse words that could use some creativity, if you ask me. His balding head shines with sweat in the dim light of the old garage as he rubs the back of it angrily. Impossible to miss that nose that got him his nickname in any light. "You coming back after you drop 'er off?"

I shake my head at him, hands in the pockets of my Dickies.

"See ya tomorrow then, Grady."

"Good luck with the missus." My usual farewell. Ninety percent sarcasm, but Gonzo bitches about his wife being up his ass enough that there's some truth to it. Mostly it's good luck to not piss her off. Like he's not lucky as fuck he pulled her all those years ago. She's still out of his league, and he knows it. He'd be an idiot to screw it up, and I'll be the first to remind him of that if needed.

Yank on the neckline of my shirt, pull it over my head, all the way off, and toss it straight into the shop washing machine, put on another coat of deodorant and a fresh, dark Henley out of the stack next to the dryer, pull those sleeves up a bit, and I'm back behind the wheel.

No point A to point B within the limits of Smoky Heights is more than fifteen minutes, but Old Lady Dix, as my boss likes to call her when no one else can hear, isn't even half that from Gonzo's Garage. Windows down, the comfortable end-of-summer breeze keeps me company as the trees fly by, the mountain view you can see from just about anywhere along the route never getting old even after thirty-four years in this town.

The population of a few thousand, where you know every single resident through some familial, church, or recreational connection? Yeah, that shit gets a little tired for me.

Alone time are two words most in this town don't know the meaning of. Just like privacy and boundaries.

Case in point, the socialization required when I come up to a stop sign a few blocks away from my client's house and one of my mom's neighbors strikes up a conversation through my open window. That's on me. I should've known better at this point than to drive up to a neighborhood with my windows down. Might as well walk down Main Street, whistling, arms wide with a shirt on that says "Free Hugs."

I do what I can to wrap the obligatory catch-up as quick as possible, offer a nod with a tight grimace and a hand raised in parting, and I'm back on my way, and so is the tiny buildup of traffic at the intersection we just held up for four minutes.

Unless I'm two-plus beers deep and it's Dallas, the usual bartender at my preferred haunt (Smoky Suds), a couple of the regulars there, or the one childhood friend I managed to make and keep through the years (Ronnie), small talk and chit-chat is pretty much a no for me. But tell that to the friendly folk in the South. That particular gene must've skipped me entirely. My brother Weston probably got my share of it, actually.

You might be starting to see how I've been volunteered as

the one to play the Grinch in the annual Smoky Heights Christmas parade more than once, but all that guy wanted was to be left alone, and honestly? I can relate.

When her baby and I roll up smoothly, no clunking noises audible anymore, Mrs. Dixon meanders on outside to collect her keys and get the lowdown on what we did to her this time. After filling her in and trading her an invoice for a personal check, she gives me her usual offer.

"Can I drop you off back at the shop, darlin'?"

"I'm good, ma'am."

"Are you sure?" she presses.

The head nod/sealed lips combo seals the deal.

"All right then, Wyatt. Thanks for taking care of ol' Bessie." When Old Lady Dix gave up on her dream of owning a farm after her husband passed away before they had the chance to start one, back in the nineties, she took to naming her cars like they were her cows instead.

Tilt my chin down at her. "Of course, ma'am. You let us know if she starts givin' you trouble again."

"See you around," she says with a smile, and waits on her front porch until I'm out of the driveway to head back inside her house.

The short walk to my nightly haunt stretches past several small craftsman houses that line the path to downtown, more churches than gas stations, and roads leading to the workplaces and/or homes of about half my graduating class. Nestled into the north side of Main Street, Smoky Suds kicks off the stretch us locals call downtown, though no one who's ever so much as seen a bigger city would probably acknowledge it as such. It's just a few central blocks, capped off with some "Welcome to Downtown Smoky Heights" archways on the north and south ends, splattered with most of the things we need to get by around here.

For me? That's this place. Suds, as it's usually known.

Rustic wood doors—the same unfinished look that all of the interior is decked out in—face the side parking lot and I grab the handle of the left one to avoid the chunky splinter poking out of the right-hand side, the damage it's waiting to give out to the sorry sucker who doesn't know the eccentricities that accompany Suds. Lucky for those folks, I guess, no one who isn't a local bothers to set foot in here too often.

The glare of the setting sun does its damndest to blind me on my way in. It's a few seconds of total darkness before the final brightness of the day is blocked out by the closing door behind me and my eyes reorient themselves to the familiar surroundings.

A dip of the head in greeting from Dallas behind the bar, like usual, possibly the only guy in this town even quieter than me.

If only everyone else in here got the memo too.

A chorus greets me instead of my preferred silence, but at least an icy longneck is also waiting for me at my regular spot at one corner of the square bar in the center of the room.

"Hey."

"Grady!"

"There he is!"

"Wyatttt."

"About time, young man."

"Guh-guh-guh-Graaaa-dy!"

The voices bounce off of the wooden walls and the inside of my skull, and I nod at the people they belong to all as one as I make my way over to my seat, grateful for the relief the first sip of cool liquid provides. It's a kind of peace I only find in alcohol, physical labor, and being outdoors, the way Southern boys grow up doing. Guess I found it one other place once upon a time, but we won't go there.

The voices blend and fade, drowned out by the buzz of the game that's on the TV behind me and the rhythmic bump of the country music playing overhead.

On my second beer, a hand claps my shoulder roughly and jolts my entire body in the process. I manage to salvage the beer, thanks to years of practice, and scowl to my right, at the grinning face waiting there like I knew it'd be. Deeply tanned, like mine, like all the blue-collar boys have around here. Ronnie works at the plant, not on cars, but he still spends a good chunk of his day sweating underneath the sun like the rest of us. The lines around his eyes are proof of that, and of the many horrible jokes he's cracked himself up with over the years. Guess that's why I don't have as many as him.

"There the fuck you are," he tells me, fool's grin still spread on his face, sandy brown brows waggling at me. "Didn't see your truck in the lot."

"Where the fuck else would I be?" I turn back toward the front and bring the bottle to my lips again.

When he doesn't answer me after a minute, I face him again. He nods to the standing bar that wraps along the front side of the building. The curvy blonde there, watching me with eyes full of sin.

"Better part of a foot inside of her?" His crass joke barely elicits a ghost of a snort from me. More like a sigh. I break the eye contact with her, not ready to commit to entertaining her for the night.

"Really wish you had some boundaries when it came to camping," I tell Ronnie, taking another swig as he settles in on the stool next to me.

"And I really wish my wife never saw your monster, but here we are." His wistful voice makes me shake my head at him.

"You're the one that opened the tent flap while I was chang-ing, fuckwit."

"You were in there for ages! I was checking on you, being a good damn friend." So defensive.

"Not sure how exposing me to half of our crew was being a good friend, but if that's what makes you feel better about it all, keep tellin' yourself that …"

"Well, now I know why it was taking you so long. Prolly had to roll that thing up like a Fruit by the Foot to fit it in your boxers and get all tucked away so you could actually zip your damn fly."

Times like this I almost miss laughing, but he keeps going, hands raised in front of his chest in innocence.

"Have I made that mistake again? No. But you still gotta bring it up every time, like it's my fault."

Ronnie taps the bar in front of him with his knuckles to get Dallas's attention and gets a jerk of the chin in response. I'm sure he knew Ronnie was here. My guess is he didn't want to hear this story one more damn time. Or maybe he just wanted to make him wait for his beer for being so fucking annoying. I wouldn't blame him if either were the case. Lord knows I take any chance I get to torture Ronnie. We all do. It's practically the local pastime.

Dallas drops off a Coors Light for the guy I begrudgingly call my best friend, but doesn't pop the lid for him before turning his back and heading to the opposite side of the enclosed square bar, tending to some other regulars with way more focus than usual.

Ronnie hollers after him, but Dallas doesn't turn back, and his voice drops to a mutter. "What am I supposed to do with this?"

I let Ronnie struggle for a minute before getting tired of his dramatics. I roll my eyes at him, grab his beer and pop the top for him. Dallas peers back over his shoulder and winks at me. Prick.

"Well," I proclaim, standing and taking my chance to jostle Ronnie's entire frame with both hands on his shoulders right as he goes for his first sip. Sweet payback. "Sounds like I have better places to be, don't it?"

"Seriously?" he whines. "I just got here, man. At least have a beer with me before I have to go back home and put the kids to bed. Grace's in a mood today and I need to get my energy up before I see her again. I can tell she's gonna ride me like a fucking barrel racer tonight."

I let the grimace show on my face. "That was way more than I needed to hear." Way more than I needed to visualize. Try to wash it away by tossing back the rest of my beer, and then I set the empty bottle on the counter with a clink. "You're on your own with that," I tell him.

Had I been planning on taking Hallie home before Ronnie threw it out there? Nah.

Does it sound better than sitting there listening to his dumb ass complain about shit all night? Yeah. If *she* gets talkative, I can fill her mouth with something that shuts her up every time.

Hallie sees me walking across the room to her and stands up before I'm even over to her, tossing her long, silky hair over a shoulder, straightening out her jean skirt, and eyeing me up and down like she's planning out a road trip on the map of my body, hitting every worthwhile spot on the ride, enough to take all night.

My balls don't tighten, my stomach doesn't drop, I don't get so much as a twitch anywhere in me. As per usual, I feel nothing inside. But I've got nothin' better to do. Gave up on anything better a long time ago. Like I said, this is as good as my life gets.

I nod my head toward the exit and lead the way.

3
Aurora

My stomach is in my throat, my heart is beating so fast that I'm shaking. I remind myself that I've dealt with some of the highest retainer accounts in all of Manhattan. I single-handedly sniffed out and dissolved the pitfalls and traps of the largest acquisition of the decade. If I can spot the loopholes and traps coming for my clients even when they're hidden in the finest of print and nail the verbiage that protects their asses in multi-billion-dollar deals, I can walk through this door and give my mom a hug, despite the rocky history behind us.

At least, that's what I'm trying to believe as I stand on the porch, bags in hand, asshole clenched.

Before I force myself to open the door and walk past that threshold, it opens for me and the face I hoped to avoid the longest while I was here—okay, maybe second longest—greets me there instead.

"Wow. Look who finally showed up."

If intuition, or the tone of her voice, didn't tell me that she couldn't be less excited if she tried, the fact that my sister's back is turned on me and she's walking away before she's even let go of the doorknob is a dead giveaway.

I grit my teeth, keep my eyes from rolling, and order my legs to move forward, one at a time.

"Lexi," I greet her as kindly as I'm capable of.

"Deserter!" she hollers over her shoulder without bothering to turn her head more than forty-five degrees.

I close my eyes and breathe deeply through my nose, out through my mouth, counting to ten and wishing like hell there were the noises of the city, the hustle and bustle that's distracted me from the cruelty in my own head all these years, but there's nothing to save me here.

"It's nice to see you, big sis," I whisper to the empty entryway.

My bags thunk to the floor just inside the door and I close it behind me, not bothering to lock it because my parents never locked their doors once that I can recall. I'm trying to avoid triggering any lectures right off the bat here, but I'm sure every step I take, every word out of my mouth will smack straight into an invisible laser in the maze of complicated emotions running between the remaining members of my family, apparently all here under this roof tonight.

Even Catherine Zeta-Jones in a catsuit wouldn't be able to avoid this shitshow, so how can I? Whether I can sense those triggers or not, I'm going to smash right into a ton of them either way. I know there's no helping setting my sister off, but I'm not here to make the rest of Mom's life any harder. I'm determined to make things better with her, for her, for however much time she's got left. Then Lexi and I can go back to hating each other quietly from seven hundred miles apart.

"In here," calls my mom's voice. It's raspier than I'm used to. I follow the sound of it, trepidation at what awaits me in every hesitant step. Hiding from this won't make it easier, logically, I know that, but no part of me is ready for what I'm about to come face to face with.

I round the corner into the living room and there she is. In the dark green La-Z-Boy that used to be my dad's. Her hair isn't falling out. She's got her teeth, as far as I can tell from here. She's wrinklier than the last time I saw her, and her skin is sagging a bit, probably from the rapid weight loss, but she looks surprisingly normal. She looks ... almost the same. Give or take ten years. Nothing that tells me she's in her final months on this plane.

That's not right, it doesn't seem fair that she looks so close to *normal* while she's dying right in front of my eyes, but my mind will dissect it later, when sleep is eluding me and there's nothing and no one to distract me from the worst of my own thoughts.

"Hi." That's what my brain comes up with.

Seven years of schooling. Passing one of the most stringent tests of intelligence in the nation. My entire career is navigating verbiage and wordsmithing for a rate of eight hundred plus an hour, and all I can think to say is *hi*. Genius. Truly inspired.

"You didn't have to do this." My mom's voice is a whisper, and if those are tears in her eyes, fuck me dead. I probably should've cried a dozen times over by now, and it might make me a horrible person that I haven't, but I can't take seeing her cry. Over me, or her ... situation. I'm not ready for any of this, but I make myself stand here anyway, knees locked, frozen in place so I can't turn back.

"We've been over this," I remind her quietly.

We've spoken more in the last three weeks than in the last twelve years. She couldn't talk me out of it before I turned in my notice at my dream job and abandoned my lease, she's not talking me out of it now. She was thrilled when my bosses counter-proposed a way for me to work remotely as time allows while I'm here, but *nothing* was going to talk me out of coming back to her. Despite the nerves my churning gut might indicate, I'm set on my plan.

"Of course I—" But I'm cut off by the scathing words of my big sister.

"Don't worry, Mom. She won't stay." Her brown eyes—the same hue as mine but so much harsher—slice over to me and cut me as sharply as her words do. "She never does."

Our mom cuts her a sideways glare and uses the same warning tone that always meant danger was near in our childhood. "Lexi …"

Lexi tosses her head to the side carelessly, hair swinging with the motion. "Tell me where I lied," she says defiantly.

"Alexis Marjorie!" Our mother does what probably would've once been a bellow but now sounds more like a harsh whisper. The reminder of the strength seeping out of her, all the parts of herself she's losing, how we'll lose all of her soon, it nestles beneath my skin and tries to find an open soft spot within me to burrow in and hurt on a deeper level, but I lock it out.

"I know I've missed a lot," I start, and see my sister physically (ostentatiously) pinch her lips shut with her fingers at a look from my mother, making a duck bill with her own mouth that should be comical but just serves to remind me of how much this trip is going to absolutely suck. "But I'm here now. To help however I can. I'm not expecting to waltz back in like I've been here all along. But don't shut me out."

"Of course we won't," my mother says, but I'm not sure any of us believe her.

Lexi doesn't dare voice anything in response.

But, kindly, perhaps more kindly than I deserve, neither of them point out how I've shut them out for more years than I have fingers.

"Do you mind if I go settle in? Then we can catch up, you can fill me in on your lives, your routine, what I can do to help, all of that?" I point to the hallway at the back of the living room, toward my old bedroom.

"Actually ..." my mother's voice trails off.

But Lexi can't keep it in. "You think you're staying *here?*" she scoffs.

My eyes shift between them and back to my mother again, but Lexi's scathing laugh breaks the silence before either of us do.

"As fucking *if.*" Chills erupt along my arms at the vitriol in her tone. How clear it is she thinks the worst of me, even when I'm standing right in front of her, as selfless as I've ever been. She continues her verbal assault. "No one believed you'd show up. Why would you start now?"

It comes out so callous. Like this hasn't changed *everything* for me. How could it not?

Her arms flail as she holds nothing back. "No one set the guest room up for you. No one wants you here."

The fire in my gut soars upward and threatens to spill out of me, but I knew what I'd be walking into. It was *me* who ran and broke all the hearts I left in my wake. It's me who never came back to clean up that damage, and it's me who's going to have to deal with it now. But I will not put up with her attitude if she keeps this up. I'm determined not to lose it on her on my first night back, but she remembers the girl who left, and she's about to meet the woman who returned.

I've spent the last twelve years, and the last eight especially, using my words on *way* scarier opponents than Alexis Weiss. Forget my clients and their competitors, just being a New Yorker demands a special kind of hardiness from those who survive there. Even my favorite bagel vendor gives me the kind of verbal sparring that Lexi could only dream of executing.

My mom's voice cuts into my thoughts. "There's no room

made up for her because I'm not letting her make me her entire life. She's built up her own, and she's not throwing all that away to wait on me twenty-four-seven like some hospice caretaker. Lexi, leave and do whatever you need to do to calm yourself down. You're not helping anything jumping down her throat. Your sister left her job, her life, to come back here and be with us."

Be with *her* is more like it, but I'm not going to correct her.

"Stop trying to scare her away," my mom continues. "I, for one, am thankful she's here."

My sister grunts, clearly struggling to withhold the rest of her thoughts, and she stomps out of the room like the incredibly emotionally mature thirty-five-year-old she is. "But you do need to find somewhere else to stay, Rory," my mom concedes.

My blood rushes at that name. "Aurora," I correct her quietly.

"I know your name, I'm the one who gave it to you," she tells me with rare bite that Lexi would find impressive.

Now that I say that, that's probably where she got it from. Not sure I've ever found too much Lexi's inherited from our mom before. She's always been a lot more Dad in the personality department. Less kind and level-headed, more asshole.

"Bye, *Rory*," Lexi calls out with as much disdain as you can fit into two syllables from the foyer before I hear a door slam and a sigh escapes me.

I turn back to my mother, reminding myself not to take it out on her. She's going through enough. The pillow in whatever shitty motel I end up in, however, that's probably going to catch these hands at this rate, unless I can find a twenty-four-seven kickboxing gym on my way. This rage is building up in me fast. I can feel the thoughts brewing, waiting to get me alone and begin their torment.

"So, what? I'm supposed to find an Airbnb in this town

that's just *chock* full of options at eight o'clock on a Thursday night?"

My mom doesn't miss a beat. "You're the smart one in the family. I'm sure you'll figure it out." She flashes me a sarcastic smile that tells me not to test her, and I'm smart enough to listen.

"Fine. When am I allowed to come back, then?"

Do you want some fries to go with that salt, Aurora?

I can only hope my inner monologue stays on the comical side of dark humor and doesn't tend toward the cruel when I'm alone again, in the pressing silence the mountains provide, nothing to distract me from the onslaught.

"Why don't we start by doing breakfast together tomorrow and go from there? You still eat waffles?"

My chin dips in a single nod.

"Good. I'll have them ready at nine, then."

"Great." It's a whisper that sounds far from it.

Feeling glad I left my bags in the entryway, because the only thing that could make this scene more pathetic is if I were dragging two suitcases behind me as I trail out of my childhood home, metaphorical tail tucked between my legs.

"Aurora," my mom calls softly.

"Yeah?" I turn back over a shoulder.

"Try Suds."

Suds. Suds. *Smoky Suds?* The one and basically only bar we have?

"For ...?" She's not wrong, I could use a pick-me-up, but I'm more worried about finding a place to stay that isn't an infected, negative-star motel within a half an hour of here. And this absolute piece of shit car I bought for the trip making it that far and back after the trek I put it through today. Pretty sure the noises it was making through the last two states weren't a good sign.

"I have it on good authority that the owner's apartment is available."

My brows dart up, but I nod in thanks and make my way out of the house, bags in tow. Reload them back in the trunk of the shitty gray Cutlass, and head toward downtown. Even gone all these years, my internal compass doesn't fail me, leading me there on the first try. I guess some things you just don't forget.

The lot at the north end of Main is pretty full, but I find a spot without any trouble. My stomach churns as I make my way to the wooden double doors that look more like you're heading into a barn than a bar. Try to give myself a pep talk on the way.

You're a bad bitch. You can walk into this bar full of the locals you left behind.

No one even remembers you.

Probably.

Likely.

Maybe.

Just don't yell "Roll Tide!" when you walk in and we should be good, yeah?

By the time I get to the doors, I have myself nearly convinced it'll be fine. I'll sneak in undetected, find Duke, assuming he's still the owner of Suds, and inquire about the apartment above the bar. I just need somewhere to stay for the night, and then I'm sure I can find something online for the foreseeable future when I have a little sleep and caffeine in my system. I'll be a better Aurora tomorrow, more suited to problem solving than bitching about how unfair it all is.

A deep breath, in and out, like the yogi I make it to once or twice a quarter always stresses, and I reach for the door on the right. My hand wraps around the rough handle and the handle fights back. A prick of pain and I yank my hand back with a curse. The door comes with it, and I prop it open with my foot so I can inspect my fingers and palm. There's a small gash in the meatiest part of my middle finger, with a little rivulet of blood already running down to my palm.

I can feel numerous eyes on me and the still-open door, probably wondering what kind of idiot just holds a door open and doesn't come in, and to answer their question, it's me. This kind of idiot. The one who cuts her hand open on said door and tries to lick the cut to quell the sting and the bleeding as she stands in the open doorway, wishing no one was paying her any attention.

I miss New York already. Nobody looks twice at you, even if you're bleeding out on the street. Too much going on for any one person to be anyone of importance. Here, where nothing goes on, everyone takes notice of everything.

And this is how I make my grand re-entrance into the hub of Smoky Heights. Ratty after a day-long drive, looking worse than I probably have in a long time, bags that wouldn't fit in an overhead compartment under my eyes, saggy ponytail, no makeup, kicked out of my family home, cussed out by my sister, and cut open by a fucking door as I try to find somewhere to get more than four hours of sleep for a change.

All so that I can help my mom through her end-of-life care in any way she'll let me. Which is looking less and less like I'll be able to do any of what I was planning and more and more like I'll just be getting my ass handed to me continually over what my twenty-one-year-old self chose to do.

And that's when I come face-to-face with what my twenty-one-year-old self ran away from. Who.

4
Wyatt

The voices in the bar quiet down until only old Ernie in the corner is still jabbering, telling no one and everyone about the two-foot trout he probably never actually caught, like we couldn't all tell the story word-for-word, anyway.

It's eerie, no voices aside from his. The country music overhead and the TV on behind me the only other sounds in the joint. Even the crack of the cue ball against stripes or solids has paused on the other side of the bar.

I give in to the temptation, turn my head to the right, back toward the door to see what everyone else is staring at, what's captivated everyone's attention so wholly. I hope someone didn't come in with a 'Bama shirt again. I'm not really in the mood to play peacekeeper with a few dozen of these boys tonight.

But when I look, the outside door—the one we all avoid, with the janky handle—is wide open, and there's soft muttering coming from just outside it.

I hear Ernie start to offer bets on what out-of-towner might've broken down outside of Suds and needed to come in for help, but a prickling on the back of my neck and scalp has all of my attention focused on the door and I tune him out, a skill I've evolved over years of nights like this, and the same six stories he's got on the tip of his tongue.

But then a body comes through.

A body I'd never not recognize, even if I haven't seen it since I was twenty-two.

The only body I might know better than my own.

The one that belongs to the best and worst thing that ever happened to me.

Once, when we were doing some metal work on an ancient jalopy together, Gonzo went off on a rant about his old lady and flung his hand, the one that was holding the heavy shrinking hammer. It pummeled into my abdomen, knocking the wind from me and nearly cracking my ribcage to the point I saw stars, fell to my knees, and barely retained consciousness.

This is like that all over again, but a bit further north. And maybe with two hammers.

Struggling for breath like it's a lump of metal lodged in my chest, not just the girl who I was always sure was the love of my life, I hear a collective gasp as everyone else in the bar registers who just walked in, before the whispers start up. They don't have the history we do, the one that allows me to identify her from a split-second glance. Could prolly have told you with a blindfold on who was at the door. They all had to study her face for a second to piece it together. My molecules reacted to hers, telling me who it was.

I can't decide if I'm the lucky one, or the rest of them are.

Speaking of her face, when my eyes finally make it there, fuck, she's as stunning as my memories like to remind me she is. She looked good when we were young, but damn, she's really grown into her looks. Oval-shaped face, petite features, delicate nose—can't see if that constellation of freckles is still across the bridge of it from here, but I hope it is—I think her lips might be bigger than I remember them, and her hair is lighter, too, but fuck me, she looks better than ever.

It only takes a second of gawking, of reacquainting myself with the finer details of how she's aged—of realizing how far out of my league she's gotten with time, or maybe it's me that fell out of hers—for me to see that her face is twisted in pain. She shakes out her right hand, fingers flying as her mouth screws up. When she stops flinging her wrist, she puts the underside of one finger in her mouth, sucking for a second—I ignore what that sight does to me on a visceral level—before pulling it out. She looks back down at it again, and even from here, I know it's a filthy curse she's muttering as she stares at it.

It's a reflex. A natural reaction, really. Before I can weigh it out, make a conscious decision about whether to say something or pretend I never saw her, I'm on my way over. She's hurting, and that took any question out of the equation. No room for indecision or thought. Regardless of how much pain she might've caused me when she left a lifetime ago, I can't not help her feel less of it here and now.

I clear my throat as I approach and say a name I haven't dared utter in an eon. One I wasn't sure I'd say again. "Rory."

Her head flies up, like her cells recognize me just as quickly as mine did her.

"It's Aurora," are the first words she's said to me since she ruined things for both of us.

Her face softens when she sees me though, the pain on her face replaced with shock, maybe fear, and then the look of hurt is back, maybe worse than before.

"Are you okay?"

Her eyes—still brown, still deep, still full of my favorite memories—bounce down from mine back to her own hand at my words. She shakes her head just a little, like she got lost in thought or something.

"I'm sure it'll be fine," she mumbles, rubbing the skin near a red spot on her hand.

"Is that—?"

I don't think about it, I just grab her hand, still it so I can get a closer look. Sure enough, yup, that's blood there. Bit of a nasty cut she got from that scraggly bit of wood, by the looks of it. It's filling up rapidly, pooling with more blood even as I stand here holding it.

"You're bleeding." I don't know why the words come out like a grunt. There were cavemen more charming than that.

My thumb trails over her skin, just below the cut, and she shivers and pulls her hand back.

"Sorry," I tell her.

"You shouldn't be," she whispers, and for some reason I'm reading into it. Like she's saying she's the one who should be. I'd given up on hoping to ever hear those words from her mouth around the time her area code changed to 2 1 2. My turn to shake my head and clear my thoughts.

"Let's get you cleaned up. And for future reference, nobody uses the door on the right. Now you know why." I tilt my head at her hand, still trickling blood.

She purses her lips together and nods at me wordlessly, probably still stunned at her fate, first with the door, then running into me. This can't be what she had planned for her grand re-entrance into the Heights.

I turn around to lead her to the bathroom along the side wall, by the office and the door that leads to the small kitchen, and I feel damn near every eye in the room on us. My posture stiffens a bit and I'm tempted to growl at Ernie, snickering on the far side of the bar, and anyone else who makes eye contact with me on the way, but I hear Diego, another nightly patron, loudly start conversing again, pulling a good amount of the attention back on them and I'm thankful for it. Grab Dallas's eyes with mine on my way past him and ask him for a first aid kit, and the way he tilts his chin says he'll nab it.

Try to ignore whatever the sizzling beneath the surface of my skin is. The familiarity of it. How *unfamiliar*, how alien the sensation is at the same time.

I push the bathroom door open and hold it for her so it doesn't break her nose as it snaps shut again, wait till she's fully inside the small room to let it slam closed, and do my best to keep my distance from her in the confined space.

"I wasn't expecting the door to be sharp," Rory—Aurora—murmurs, like she needs to justify what happened.

"Yeah, Duke really needs to take care of that. It's been a hazard for years. Sorry it claimed you as a victim."

The corner of her lip turns up, and my sore eyes don't want to look away from the sight of it in the mirror, but I force them down to the faucet, where I spin the hot tap and let it run.

"What are you doing here, Aurora?" My eyes don't leave the stream of water.

"I think I'm cleaning out my cut." The intended levity doesn't quite land, but I appreciate the gesture, regardless.

"And after that?"

She sucks in a sharp breath, and I close my eyes rather than let them follow the motion of her chest with the inhale.

"I'm looking for Duke. I heard the apartment upstairs might be available. I need somewhere to crash for the night."

Not sure my brain has had time to hazard a wager as to why she might be here, but that wasn't even in the neighborhood of where it would've gone, given the chance.

I've also heard the apartment is available, but I'm wondering how she did. I've got a guess.

Raise my brows at her through the mirror, squeezing in next to her at the sink again to test the water with a couple fingers. It's hot enough to remove skin, so I turn the cold tap on just a little to bring it back to the lightly-boil-and-sanitize setting.

"I just got here. Hadn't really warned anyone but my mom, but I'm ... back?" Her melodic voice raises on the last word, like she's not sure that's what she means. "For now, I mean," she clarifies. "For a bit."

I clear my throat and gesture to the running water now that it's ready for her.

"I hope that's not going to be weird for you. Us. Whatever." Rory stumbles over her words but makes quick work of rinsing off her finger and using soap to clean it off as best she can.

"Us was a long time ago, Ror."

"I know. You know what I mean. I'm sorry to spring this on you. Just. Show up to your town like this."

Interesting. The stumbling on words is new for her. Fierce little Rory Weiss struggling for what to say? Unheard of.

"The Heights is just as much yours—"

Her derisive snort cuts me off.

Yeah, okay, I won't go there.

She turns off the faucet and dries her hands with a paper towel, but keeps the wad pressed to her finger as we finally have nowhere left to look but one another.

The bare truth escapes me, as it's inclined to do.

"Fuck. This is weird, isn't it?"

She snorts and it's almost a real laugh. Her eyes crinkle at the corners. That's also new. I bet if my eyes were allowed to run up and down that body, they'd find a lot else that's changed too. I wonder if, underneath, she's still the same, or if she's as jaded and hardened as I've become with time.

"Yeah," she admits softly. "Not how I thought I'd be spending my night."

"So why are you here, Rory?"

Her eyes bounce around the room, but I've got no clue what

she's looking for. She won't find it in here. Four wooden walls, the sink, a toilet, and some questionable "artwork" about aiming when peeing, plus a sign reminding staff to wash their hands before returning to work. And me. The man, the future, she ran from all those years ago.

Nowhere to run this time.

5
Aurora

This tiny bathroom is even quieter than the bar was. My thoughts are pounding in my head, pummeling me, out of control with nothing to distract me from the onslaught.

My eyes seek out every inch of the room, breaths coming quickly, looking for some diversion, something to interrupt the pattern, that will quiet the noise that only I can hear.

But there's no reprieve in here. The only reprieve I found is six states away. I suppose I could always try taking home a random guy and seeing if that buys me a few minutes of distraction, but there's only one guy in the Heights I've ever been interested in. So much for not running into him for the whole eight months I'll be here.

Why I'm here is the million-dollar question. Why, indeed. Because I've lost the last twelve years with my mom, and when you find out she's only got nine months left, at most, it puts shit into perspective? Forces you to make the hard decision?

I know she hasn't wanted to break the news, but people are going to know sooner or later. And this is Wyatt. He's not everyone else. He deserves the truth from me at this point. Not hearing it in bar talk from Ernie, if he's still alive, or some old lady on the side of the street, spreading gossip.

I take a deep breath, command my eyes to focus, stop fluttering around and zero in on his. Green. Pines. Autumn grass. Fast cars. Adrenaline. Heavy breathing. Racing hearts.

His jaw's gotten stronger with time. The planes of his deeply tanned face are all angles and hardness, with a thick scruff along his jaw and chin. Like he should've shaved a couple days ago and was just too lazy. Not quite a beard, but more than a five o'clock shadow. Dark brown hair that's pushed back but looks like it might have a mind of its own from time to time, maybe it'll fall in his face later if it wants to. I can see the years on him, and it looks like they've been about as kind to him as they have to me. We both know who's to blame for that.

You know how they say it takes more muscles to frown than it does to smile? I think his face has had a lot of workouts in its time. Maybe that's how his jawline got so defined. All in all, Wyatt's got a face that would be just as easy to get lost in now as it was when I was sixteen and falling for him instead of paying attention in history class. I push the memories away as best I can to answer him.

"My mom is ... sick." It's harder to say those words aloud to someone who knows her. It felt much more detached turning in my resignation, telling the partners I report to and HR about the situation. But watching the only man I've ever loved as I tell him, watching his face fall, his expression crumple as my words settle in, I know he's pieced together what it means. How sick she must be for me to be here. His eyes dart to the door as it sinks in, and then they bounce back to mine.

"Fuck, Ro—Aurora."

"Yeah." What else is there to say?

"You said you're just here for the night?" he presses.

My eyes find the wall above the toilet. The sign there with a classy drawing of a stick figure taking aim. Better than watching his face as I give him the answer.

"I'm here until she's gone."

I feel more than see what that does to him. His eyes closing, body rocking just a bit with the bomb.

Silence presses into all the gaps between us, the years elapsed without a word and the voids those gouged in him and me both, until I break it, like I broke us.

"I'm just trying to find somewhere to stay for tonight until I can find somewhere more permanent tomorrow."

"Is there anything I can do?"

"The doctors can't. Guessing that means you can't either." He ignores the impolite words, doesn't even acknowledge how I'm far from full of Southern hospitality anymore.

"But you're back?" he presses for more. I'd want to know what to expect from me too. Can't blame him.

I shrug at him, eyes flicking back up to his. "Didn't want to regret not getting to spend this time with her. Not sure what I'll be able to do, but I'm gonna try for whatever she'll let me."

He whistles out a breath. "Brave of you."

I fold my lips in over my teeth and nod once. There's no sugarcoating how uncomfortable this already is, and it's not like it's going to get easier as my stay continues.

"I miss New York already," I mutter under my breath, lifting the paper towel off my finger to check on the status of the cut. It doesn't instantly fill back up with blood, so that seems good.

"It probably misses you already too," he says without thinking, and fuck me if that doesn't cut me deeper than that damn door did.

Just then there's an abrupt double knock on the bathroom door and it flies open, straight into my back, shoving me forward. Right into my ex's chest. I let out some sort of squeal as I fly into him, but he catches me without a struggle, bracing me easily. Chills break out along my torso where ours are connected, and he wastes no time peeling me off of him, using impressively minimal contact with that arm that's all tattooed now. I try not to look.

Getting his scent out of my nostrils, that'll be a bit harder. Masculine. A scent he didn't buy, like the guys back home, but one he earned through a hard day's work. A lifetime of days like it. It lights something up within me, and I'm back to hiding from the assault of my own thoughts, though of a completely different nature this time.

"Sorry," comes a gruff voice that sounds out of practice. I look over to the source of it, and the bartender I don't know doesn't look or sound sorry at all. Black hair, close cut on the sides, longer on the top, slicked back. Gorgeous face with just a couple days' of growth. His whole look is artfully styled, like he's straight out of Williamsburg. Eyes dark enough to scare me, something dangerous stirring in them I want no part of. He drops a white metal box on the counter and leaves again, the door slamming shut behind him.

Wyatt beats me to the counter, opening the grungy looking first aid kit and pulling out a Band-Aid, an alcohol wipe, and a single-use packet of ointment.

"Come on, then. Let's get you cleaned up and I'll help you find Duke. You could probably use some sleep."

I nod my head and swallow heavily as he hands me the alcohol and the ointment, letting me treat my own wound, which is only fair, I guess. I left him to lick his.

The wipe stings, but I can take it. I deserve worse. When the wound is covered in goop, he hands me the Band-Aid and I wrap it a little clumsily with just my left hand, but he doesn't offer to touch me again and I'm not going to ask him to.

This is all a little similar to another time he helped me clean up a cut—a day that led to a great night, one where I earned a new nickname—and I need to get off of memory lane before it's too late. I toss out the trash and yank the door in toward me, desperate to get out of this room, the space he consumes. Suck in a deep breath the second the bathroom door is open—that thick and heavy, suffocating tension hopefully remaining in the small room behind me—and I gulp down the air in the hallway, hoping to clear my senses, my entire system, of his proximity, the lingering effects he still has on me after all this time apart.

Wyatt's body, even bigger now than I remember it being then, pushes past me in the tight space and he ambles back into the main room of the bar, a dark Henley hugging his muscled frame, sleeves pushed up to the elbows, paired with Dickies and work boots. My eyes, and the rest of me, follow.

It doesn't take him long to track down Duke, the owner of Suds for as far back as I can remember. The look of understanding on his weathered, smooth-shaven face as I summarize my request takes me by surprise, but I'm in business mode, and no emotion flickers past the surface.

"I tell you what," he says when I'm done with my short (nondescript) spiel about being here to help my mom. Rather vague tale I told him, but he seems receptive. His husky voice tells me that if he never smoked, he spent decades inside a bar with patrons who did. "You can stay tonight on one condition."

My brows rise ever so slightly, encouraging him to go on.

"You don't look for somewhere else to stay."

Those tinted, threaded brows try to take residence in my hairline—as much as the occasional few units of Botox will allow—and I wait for more.

"You and I both know you're gonna end up a half an hour away, at best. Sounds like you're here for a good cause. She needs you. You don't need to commute an hour or more a day on top of everything else you're going to be going through." His pensive eyes flash to Wyatt's and back to mine again, earnest and almost glistening. "Stay here for as long as you need it. As long as she needs you."

I nod in acceptance of his kind offer. "Thank you. I'd appreciate that."

"It's still got some of my stuff in it, but I haven't really been staying here for a while, so I can make some room for your bags and stuff." He leads me upstairs, gives me a quick tour, and wastes no time moving the remainder of his belongings from one dresser into the other, freeing up some space for me. It's a small room, it's dated, but clean, which I appreciate. Not much to it, just a bed on the right-hand side, a nightstand, and two dressers framing the entrance to a small bathroom off the left wall. A small kitchenette with a mini fridge nestled in the corner. I'll have to figure out where to do my work from, but this will be fine otherwise. In most areas of Manhattan this would cost at least a few grand a month.

I make my way downstairs and am surprised to find Wyatt still waiting by the bar, beer in hand, which he puts down to follow me outside to help me with my bags.

"You don't have to do this," I tell him quietly, next to the junker I bought for less than a half of a month's rent back home.

"But you're gonna let me anyway," he says simply, tilting his head down at me knowingly.

"I mean ... If you wanna carry my heavy bags up a flight of stairs, be my gue—" My words are cut off sharply by him heaving not one but both of my giant bags over his shoulders in one move, barely a grunt leaving his mouth as he does, and I scramble after him to close the trunk and hustle to get the door for him.

"Use the—"

"Left-hand door, I know now," I mutter at him, rolling my eyes.

"Atta girl. You always were a quick learner." He winks at

me, somehow the rest of his face stays stoic as he passes through the doors and I can only stare as he goes, through the tables and chairs, to about three-quarters down the side wall, where the stairwell is, and I follow in his wake the entire way up, pretending like my heart is only beating double time from the stairs.

He plops the bags down next to the bed and I do my best not to gawk at him, where this evening has led. From being kicked out of my mom's house when I'm here only to help her, to running into the person I hoped to avoid for the longest, only to end up next to my bed with him by the end of the night.

This evening certainly could have gone more awkwardly than it did, but this is still a far cry from how I planned for it to go. Me, invisible, hidden deep inside my mom's house, never to have to see anyone else from the town I left behind, least of all, *him*. But here we fucking are.

I just wanna turn on some cityscape sounds on my iPad and hope to hell I can fall asleep tonight. Tomorrow is promising to be stressful enough, and I need any advantage I can get.

"Listen," he starts off, just as I say, "So ..."

I let out an awkward laugh and wave my hand at him to continue.

"I know shit's weird between us. But I want you to know that I admire the hell out of you and what you're here doing. Regardless of anything else. That took a lot of balls."

I dip my head down to the floor, then focus on the far wall. "I appreciate that," I say quietly.

"If you need a break from it all ... We still do bonfires most weekends down at the McKay property. Come by tomorrow, or whenever. Let your hair down a little."

My stomach drops into the vicinity of my freshly pedicured toenails at the thought of running into more than just him. Our old friends. Their spouses, partners, *lives* now. Like it isn't bad enough seeing *him*, facing everyone? All together? This trip is bad enough as is, thanks.

"I'll think about it," I tell him diplomatically, gathering my unruly, wavy (and probably frizzy) ponytail in one hand and redoing it more securely as I start to flit about the room, getting my bearings.

He rolls his eyes at me. "No, you fucking won't."

I stop in place and turn to face him again. "Well, what do you want me to say?" My voice rises on its own, annoyance clearly leaking into my words. Great. The two of us are already at each other's throats and all we've done so far is small talk. Can't wait to be trapped in the same tiny-ass shitty town as him for the foreseeable future.

"How about you try the truth and go from there?" His forest-green eyes narrow on mine, fuming.

"The truth isn't often pretty."

"I'd rather be blindsided by your ugly truths than your pretty fucking lies. At least I'd know what to goddamn expect."

I reel back at his harsh words before leaning forward, punctuating my words with flailing hands so he knows he's not the only one being wronged here. "You want my truth, Wyatt? Fine. Here it is. You were the *last* person I wanted to see coming here, and you're the first one I run into. I came back to help my mom, not to make things right between us." One of my hands flings back and forth in the air between us, gesturing. "And I thought maybe we've both grown up since then, maybe we can be civil, friendly, neighborly if we ran into one another. If I couldn't manage to avoid you the whole time I was here. But clearly I still get under your skin and you still get under mine. So, no, I don't want to go to a fucking bonfire where I can stare at everyone from my past, how their lives are still the same while there's nothing about me that's still the same as the last time I saw any one of you. I want to help keep my mom comfortable and make the most of however many months she has left, and the second she's dead and gone, so the fuck am I."

His nostrils flare, hands on his hips as he watches me silently until my rant is over.

He opens his mouth to reply, and his acidic words fill the room with disdain. "Thanks for warning me now. Would've been nice to know the first time, but I guess late is better than never. I won't expect you to stay when shit gets tough this time."

He turns on a booted foot and leaves, closing the door harder than necessary on his way out, and I hear his heavy footsteps clunking down the stairs.

Great.

I fall back onto the bed, hands covering my face as I replay my words to him. His to me.

I don't know what he wants from me. What he expects. It's been almost half our lives since we last saw each other. Surely he realizes we're different people now than we were then, that I'd hoped to never have to face our mutual history in the light of who we've both become.

Can't we just continue to pretend one another don't exist, live our happy fucking lives until I'm gone again?

What's the point of all the years, all the distance I worked so hard to put between us if he's just going to show back up in my life again, being kind and thoughtful and trying to help me adjust to being back in the Heights? What a raging dick.

I puff out a huge breath and sit back up to look around the room and spot my bags. Find the one that houses my iPad and MacBook packed in and amongst the clothes and toiletries and anything else I could fit in there.

I guess it was nice of him to bring my bags up. My hand plays with the bandage on my finger absentmindedly. And help me clean up my finger.

And it's not like word hasn't probably already spread

through this entire damn town like wildfire. I'm going to end up seeing everyone sooner or later. They'll start seeking me out like I'm some rare bird up for a sighting if I try to stay cooped up and to myself once word is out.

Maybe it wouldn't be so bad for the reunions to happen in a controlled setting, one designed for a good time, rather than a more stressful one, or even worse, an unanticipated one. At least I could plan for the evening, how I want to present myself, what I might say to everyone I left behind.

And it's with a heavy sigh that I realize once again, I'm the asshole here.

Maybe not that much has changed after all.

I quickly locate the necessities in my bags, use them to get ready for bed and tuck myself in, blasting the noises of the city as loud as my iPad will go. But nothing drowns out the voice in my head telling me I'm still the villain in this story.

6
Aurora

Nine o'clock sharp, I'm at my mom's for day two of what's already guaranteed to be the worst trip of my life.

Even worse than the four-night cruise I took with whatshisname out of Jersey where I ended up hugging the toilet the entire time, but he still kept asking me if he could at least hit it from the back as I was hunched over. (You know, so the trip wasn't a complete waste for him.) And I've barely hit the twelve-hour mark in Smoky Heights.

Ignore the ominous clicking noise coming from my car as I walk into the house, just like I'm ignoring the stream of consciousness telling me I did the wrong thing by coming here. I don't fit in. I'm not wanted. I'm only going to hurt the people I love by being here. I belong in New York. Why would I sacrifice my dream job, my incredible apartment, my life there to suffer *here*? And if I really love them so much, why did I leave them in the first place?

But we're tuning that out, remember?

Luckily, Lexi isn't here this time. Waffles for two, as apparently my sister has a shift at the lone little grocery store this morning, and I'm not mad about it.

My nose is actually pretty excited about it as I let myself in the front door and take a seat at the dining table, where my mom is already seated and waiting. Guess I know where I got my punctuality from. Back home, I'm inclined to be a good thirty-plus minutes early to anything that isn't being billed by the minute. This morning? Dread weighed me down, made me as late as I'll ever be to anything, what everyone else considers on-time. But in my line of work, every moment counts, none are to be wasted. That feels particularly true now that we're counting the last of hers.

"Morning," I say quietly, still gauging the air between us, how to act after all that has—and hasn't—transpired between us.

"Good morning, dove." That one takes me back. What has it been? Probably since the last time I was here that I heard that nickname. She drops a giant waffle on my plate and smiles at me pleasantly as I settle in.

"Did you sleep okay?" Wow. Resorting to small talk. Who am I?

My mom stops her motion, mid-lean, halfway across the table as she was grabbing the butter dish to look at me out of the side of both eyes.

"I slept as good as I ever do, these days. But let's not pretend we're strangers, okay? Why don't we get the awkward part out of the way now and be done with it."

She sits back in her chair and butters her waffle like it's any other day for her. It's a day I never thought I'd see. One I've been hiding from ever since I ran in the first place. A large part of me hopes I can still manage to hide from the past, even when I'm here, staring it in the face.

"I'm sorry." It's all I can say. Words won't make what she's going through any better. I can only hope my actions will, but what's the best you can even hope for in a situation like this?

Taking it from the worst-case scenario to *slightly* less shitty? So helpful.

"Are you?" She finishes buttering her waffle and then stares at me unblinkingly, familiar chocolate eyes on mine.

I breathe out through my nose. "I'm sorry for what you're going through. I'm sorry I didn't handle things better when I left, and that I didn't keep in touch more. I'm sorry I made things so complicated in our family. But I'm not sorry for pursuing a better life for myself, if that's what you're asking."

She nods at me, assessing my expression, the barest hint of emotion that shows through as I talk, and then she cuts into her waffle and takes a bite. Once she chews and swallows, she says, "I'm sorry you felt you had to leave to get a better life. And that there wasn't room for us in it."

I gulp down the orange juice that's in front of my place setting, eager to change the subject. Too deep, too fast, too early in the morning and into my trip for this shit. If I haven't had to face it in all this time, I'm sure as hell not ready in my first twenty-four hours back, and especially when I'm sober as a nun.

"Can we maybe not start with this? Can we talk about you, what you're going through, anything that'll make it better? That's what I'm here for."

My mom shrugs a shoulder and takes another bite. "Sure. A bit about me, let's see ..." She taps a finger on her chin, feigning thought. "Where to start. I'm fifty-four years old, I've got two grown daughters, and I'm dying. Incurable, inoperable brain tumor—doctors call it glioblastoma—I'm in constant pain that's only going to get worse, and before long my faculties will start to go, then my systems will start shutting down, and then I'll be gone. Not a whole heck of a lot to be done for any of it. Is that what you wanted to hear?"

My fork and knife clatter to the ceramic, floral-printed plate beneath them. The same ones I used as a girl. Take rapid breaths, in and out, and try to keep myself from exploding on her. This is her journey, her illness, *her* burden to bear, and if she wants to be cavalier about it, that's her right. It won't stop me from trying to make it better, but it's not my first choice for her attitude, either. I guess if I were the one on my deathbed, it would be my call, but it's not, so I bite my tongue.

I try a different approach. "I've been doing some research."

"Why doesn't that surprise me?" Her dry amusement still shines through, and I ignore the sass, push forward with my point.

"I know palliative care is limited in scope. The painkillers and medicines you're on can only do so much. But I've been looking into articles, studies, even anecdotal accounts of things others have done to ease the burden during end-of-life care, and I have some lists of things we might be able to do to make it a little easier for you."

"Wow. You've even made a list about me dying? That's the most Rory thing I ever heard."

Technically, yes, but I didn't even tell her about those yet. This is just about the things that can help her. But, yes, I've also got other lists of things to do, line up, wrap up, before she's gone. I roll my eyes at her instead of responding directly and tap my manicured nails on the table in a rhythmic pattern that soothes me marginally. I'll take what I can get. Control is never not calming, amirite?

"Look. This is a morbid subject. It's awful for me, and I can't imagine how terrible it is to be the one going through it. I'm just saying, I have some ideas, some things we might be able to do to make you more comfortable along the way. And I don't want you to hesitate to ask me for anything you might need or want, okay?"

My mom sops up the syrup on her plate with a bite of waffle on the end of her fork and chews it quietly before she looks back over at me. The hanging tail of the black and white cat clock on the wall ticks louder than any other noise in here. How do people live like this? I haven't heard a single siren since I got into town. It's disarming. If I listened closely enough, I could probably hear the seismic plates shifting with time beneath us. Where's the *life* here?

As if it's obvious to her even now how little I fit in here, how I don't belong, she says, "If it gets to the point I need help wiping my ass, just go back to the city, okay? Let me die with whatever semblance of dignity I might have left and go back to your life."

My competitive streak flares. "If you don't want me to wipe your ass, I'll hire a caretaker to do it for you. But I'm not leaving you, no matter how hard this gets. I'm riding this out with you, Mom."

She bites down, and I'm sure she's refraining from telling me she doesn't believe me, but we both know my track record isn't good, she doesn't have to state the obvious there. I'm the only one who can prove her wrong though, and I've never been more determined about anything before.

"All I'm saying is I'm here for you. For anything. If you wanna do something fun, if you need another pain pill, or you want Korean barbecue—"

My mother's face pulls in a highly unattractive way. "Why on earth would I want Korean barbecue?"

"Because it's one of the best foods I've ever had, and you want to try as much as you can before you go?" I roll my eyes at how literal she's being. "I don't know, it was what came to mind, just an example."

She hmphs, mutters, "Doesn't sound better than pulled

pork," and I continue like I didn't hear her, but my voice is nearing a yell, maybe even a shriek at this point. I can't believe I'm already going insane in under a day in this godforsaken town. Where is my carefully developed poise? I'm starting to worry I left it in my empty apartment on the Upper West Side, just a few blocks from Zabar's, Magnolia, and all the other best parts of my life.

"Fine, a chocolate chip cookie, then! I'm just saying that I'm here for you, okay? You're not alone in this. I want to help you however I can. And I don't want to waste the time you've got left."

"In all that fancy schooling you did, did they never teach you to take a hint, Aurora? For Christ's sake, you're going to make me cry into my waffles, and that would violate a staple rule of Southern life, never eat soggy waffles. I get it. You're back for me. Can you tell me about your life now? What other weird food y'all eat in New York? Anything that isn't depressing as all get out?"

A small smile pops one side of my mouth up at her candor. "Sure, Mom. Can I just ask you one thing first? Have you ever thought about making a bucket list?"

AN HOUR and three (sadly) virgin screwdrivers later, the conversation shifted from my life in New York back to my rude awakening of returning to the Heights.

"So you ran straight into Wyatt, hmm?"

"Yep. How'd you know that?" My eyes narrow in suspicion on hers. "Wait. Did you know he was going to be there?"

"Not specifically, but Suds is where most of the unhappy

men in this town spend their evenings, so there was a decent chance."

I raise a brow at her. "How'd you hear about that anyway?"

"I have my ways."

"It was Facebook, wasn't it?"

She nods her head in admittance, face screwed up as she takes a swig of coffee. "There was a post up in the Heights group within ten minutes of you leaving my house, dove. Mrs. Dixon saw you walking in."

I gave up on her Folgers roast after the first cup—even my poker face couldn't pretend to like it—and I'm absolutely desperate to find anything as close to a Starbies as possible on my way outta here.

My mom pushes her chair back, scraping the four feet along the ancient hardwood floor, and I do the same, scrambling to beat her to clearing the table and doing the dishes.

"You don't have to—" She tries to tell me off but halts mid-sentence when she sees the look on my face. "Right," she acquiesces. "Thank you, Aurora." She lets me take care of the kitchen and the table without a complaint.

"Got any plans for today?" I'm still trying to get a lay of the land, wrap my head around what her day-to-day life looks like. I know she's stopped working, I know she's not up for much most days, but it doesn't yet sound like she wants me here with her through most of her days, which isn't conducive to my plan.

I'm still working my way in, which, fair. I knew while this wasn't a hostile takeover, it's far from an amicable acquisition. More like a merger that's required to keep both businesses afloat, though neither is particularly thrilled about it.

I can't cut her out of my life then demand she grant me full access to hers just because I say so. Logically, I know that. Emotionally? It still stings to be shut out after everything I've done to be here.

It's going to take time to earn her trust. I'm willing to put in the work, but time is something neither of us have a lot of at the moment. Is there some sort of accelerate button when it comes to forgiving and forgetting? A cheat code I can find somewhere?

Guys have it so easy. Buy some flowers, say something sweet, spend a few minutes buried between your girl's legs and all is well again.

Soothing the pain from non-romantic relationships? Familial, friends? It can be so much trickier.

She answers me, and I can hear the exhaustion setting in already. "I'm going to take it easy today. Forgive me for saying it, but it's taken a lot out of me, this catchin' up we've been doing. I'm gonna see you out, then probably nap for quite a while."

My mind struggles to overlay the two images of my mother. The one that appears fairly healthy on the outside, who looks mostly normal and is still sharp as ever, with the one who I know has something killing her from within. Who is tuckered from a couple hours of chatting with her daughter, and who will need to recuperate and recover the entire rest of the day from it. I swallow down my sorrow and nod my head at her, drying off the last of the plates from breakfast.

"You'll let me know if you need anything?"

"I won't."

I start to protest but she talks over me. "I've been on my own for twelve years now. I appreciate what you're doing, but I'm not dead yet. I'm gonna keep taking care of myself as long as I can."

"Right." I dry my hands on the yellow and white dish towel and lay it flat next to the sink to dry.

Her kitchen is about a third the size of my entire apartment. I didn't bump into the oven or the fridge while doing the dishes, not even once, and she even has room for a dishwasher, even though I didn't think to use it. That was a novelty for me.

My mom speaks up again. "Take the day, get settled in. You staying at Suds?"

I nod at her, lips folded in over my teeth.

"Good. You're right around the corner if I need you." She winks at me, then starts walking to the front door and I take my cue.

"Uh oh," I hear the sing-song words before I make it to the door and rush onto the porch to see what she's staring at with that long face. There's a pool of dark liquid on the driveway underneath my car, and I'm feeling pretty sure it wasn't there when I got here.

I channel my best Geralt impression. "Fuck."

My mom lets out a low whistle. "You're gonna wanna get that straight over to Gonzo's if it'll start. If not, they'll have to come get it for ya."

If memory serves, that's the only car shop in town, and I'm also fairly confident it's not that far away. I guess nothing in this town is much farther than one Duane Reed to the next, really. Just by car instead of by foot.

Luckily—I use the word loosely—the Cutlass starts up for me, and my mom waves me off from her front porch as I say a prayer to whatever god might still be listening to me after all my years of neglect on the religious front.

It's not like I have some emotional attachment to this car, I'm just convinced this trip can't get any worse, and I'm not looking to tempt fate with a breakdown or spontaneous combustion. At least I don't have to worry about a theft or a carjacking if too much hasn't changed in this town. That's another perk of being out of NYC. Look at me, being all bright side and silver lining and shit.

Only eight more months until I'm back in New York, I chant to myself as I turn off at the third stoplight, just like she said to do, and putter up to the open bay at Gonzo's, just as the clicking noise I was hearing before gets even louder. Or maybe that was the sound of the last of my luck running out, because when the mechanic beneath the hood of the car laid out there turns around to see who or what is headed his way, I realize that any deity watching over me has a fucked up sense of humor and a weird concept of payback.

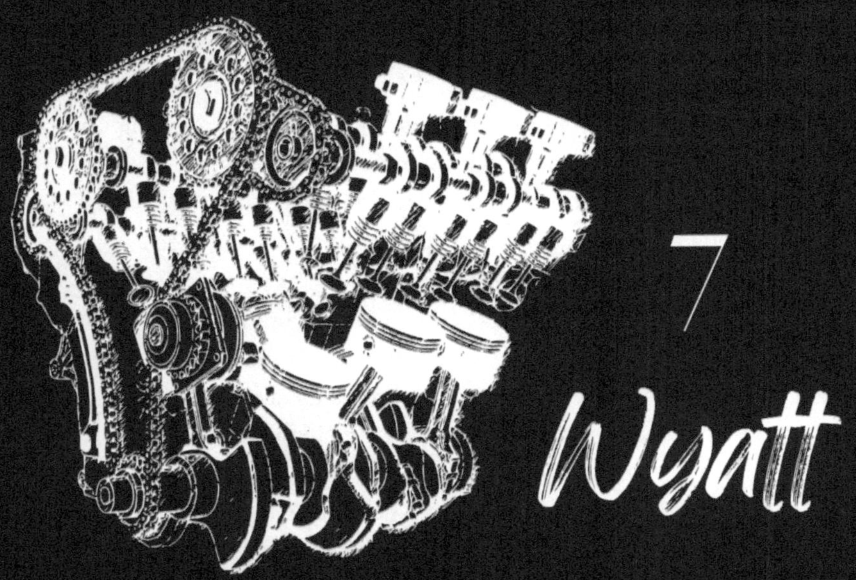

7

Wyatt

I can hear it before I can see it. An engine that's knocking around, like it's on damn near its last sip of oil. It turns my stomach to hear it—like, physical repulsion, chills and all—but if it's just a leak, they haven't been driving it around like that for an age, we might still be able to save her yet.

I back out from underneath the hood of the fixer upper I've been working on all day so far, trying to stay in my work and out of my head after the shit show of a reunion with *her* last night and take a second to stretch and crack my back as I stand straight and then turn around to face my next patient for critical care. The elective procedure—let's call it a hip replacement—is going to have to hold out for what's clearly going to be a life-or-death situation incoming. The one I've spent all morning on can take a backseat until this next one's out of the ICU.

And lo and behold. Why am I not surprised at who's behind the wheel, responsible for the death rattle coming out of this poor Cutlass.

I hope she's not back for round two. I don't think I have it in me to fight with her again. My head's still getting unfucked from last night. I forgot how she does this to me, how she twists me up from proximity alone. How she's either a bad trip or the high of a lifetime, but you'll never know which you're gonna get until she's in your veins, and it's too late to fight your fate.

It took ages to detox her from my system last time. I don't want to go down that path again.

Last night got out of hand. She's got a lot on her plate, it was a stressful day for her, and me snapping at her didn't make it any better for her. I'm vowing here and now to let sleeping dogs lie.

The past between us is in the past. It's long buried.

Like a landmine.

We can be mature adults and get through this short time together without stepping on any landmines.

I think.

At least that's what I've got myself nearly convinced of by the time she's out of the car and walking toward me, something between a grimace and acceptance on her face. If I needed a confidence boost, this wouldn't be it. Lucky for the both of us, I don't.

"Let me guess. She's lost a bunch of oil." The only thing drier than my tone is her engine right now.

Ro—*Aurora* tucks her cheek into her shoulder and raises it a little, not *not* coy. "Seems like it, but you're the one I'd trust on that front."

"Didn't I teach you how to check your oil once upon a time?" I'm not sure my tone can ever be construed as light, but at least give me credit for trying here.

She snorts, giving me that credit I was asking for. "Yeah, sorry to say I haven't had much use for that lesson lately. I'm a bit rusty."

I pop down on both knees in front of her car and give about a two-second inspection beneath her chassis. "So's your oil pan," I tell her wryly.

"I'm guessing that's not a good thing?" She fakes a smile,

blinking at me several times, and all it does is highlight the way the sun brings out a metric shit ton of hues in her eyes. Not one, flat brown, but a dozen or more different shades, all melted and blended together.

That buzzing sensation beneath my skin is back and this is fucked. I look away from her, squint into the sun on the horizon. A much safer view, staring into the sun—less potential damage to be had.

I shrug it off. "Nah, it's not a great thing. But good you brought her here before it got worse. Let me check it out and I'll see what we can do."

"I appreciate it," she says sincerely.

I shrug back at her once again. "It's my job."

She nods, lips between her teeth. "Right."

Now'd be a good time for a sigh, but I hold it in. Glad to see the awkwardness between us is in the past.

I hold my hand out for the keys, and she points with just her head back to the car, telling me they're still in there. If I wasn't so distracted by her, I wouldn't have missed the fact the car's still running, but what can I say, we've all got our weaknesses. For some, it's alcohol. Others, gambling. For me? A brown-eyed girl with thick hair and a hell of an attitude who gave me her virginity at sixteen and an apathetic outlook on life when she up and left me five years later.

I've got the driver's door open and a boot in the well when she calls my name.

"Wyatt."

Something like a hot breath blows down my back, causing my hair to stand on end, to say nothing of the tightening I'm feeling below the belt. Kind of fucked up that my head got the memo to try to get over her when she left, but the rest of me never did.

Take a split second to reel myself in, remind myself that it doesn't matter how good she looks, how good my name sounds rolling off her tongue, how good she looks rolling off of mine. When I've got it together, I look over my shoulder at her and wait.

She wrings her hands together, twisting her fingers and looking more apprehensive than I'd be willing to bet she damn near ever does.

"Can we ... start over?"

"What, like, from the beginning?"

"From yesterday."

My mouth shrugs as I weigh it out. "I mean, we can try." I do my part to lighten the mood. "You gonna use the left-hand door in this scenario?"

She shakes her head. "If I could redo it, I think I wouldn't go to the bar at all. Not run into half the town within an hour of arriving, sleepless and a total goddamn mess." She gestures to her head and face, waving her hand in front of it. If she's saying that's her on a bad day ... My cock thickens at the thought, and I bat the image away before I have to readjust myself.

Her voice is low and serious, that jest out of her tone when she speaks again. "Look, I know the only reason Ernie and everyone else in there last night didn't jump all over me was because of you. I should've thanked you for it."

I toss my head to the side, waving it off. "You've got enough on your plate, that didn't need to be any harder on you than it was."

"Or more awkward ..." She states the obvious, letting it trail off with something close to a half-smile. Still got that witty thing I always found so hot going for her, I see. If her tongue is still just as sharp, I might be in trouble.

Tilt my head from side to side a couple times. "Yeah, I dunno that you could've escaped that part of it, no matter how many times you got to do it over. Sorry. But it doesn't have to be awkward between us at least, 'kay?"

"Are you saying we can be ... friends?"

I could scoff at the word. Such an insignificant word for what we shared.

The hesitancy in her voice stops me. With what she's in for? She could really use someone on her side through what she's here to do, and I'm always a sucker for giving her what she needs. What am I going to do, deny her?

"Sure. Friends."

She nods decisively at me, and after a short pause says, "I think, if I could really do yesterday over, maybe I would just come straight to the shop. Before my car decides to explode in the middle of Main Street or something. And before my sister exploded all over me at the house."

My face screws up. I know her sister well enough to know how pleasant that must've been. "I dunno which would've been the better perk. I think your car might cause less damage."

She gives a sad laugh and shakes her head, headed toward the area Gonzo calls a waiting room along the side of the shop. Glad as shit he's out on a house call right now, I would *not* want to deal with his peanut gallery bullshit with Rory today. Or ever, really.

I pull the car up into the bay, shut it off, and get it raised so I can do a proper inspection. Below the chassis, beneath the hood, I check her out every which way and come to the same conclusion I had before I even looked her over. Busted oil pan, damn near no oil left, and luckily, no real engine damage just yet.

I feel her eyes on me as I go. Every time I look over, she's typing away on her phone, but if she thinks I can't feel her stare like a brand on my skin, she forgets what the two of us used to have. That connection doesn't fade with time, even when she tried to chop it off at the stem.

No helping it, that's not a choice either of us have in the matter. You can put distance, you can throw in time, but back in the same room for just a few minutes and I can feel it thrumming beneath the surface. All that shit we used to have between us, still hovering between the physical plane and whatever's beyond. It's in every word spoken, every look neither of us will indulge in, every thought left unsaid.

That *thing* that made us *us?* I'm so fucking sorry to say, that shit's still there.

No matter how much I've tried to dig it out and cauterize whatever's left behind over the years, with other women, alcohol, any distraction I could find. If I failed at it while she was gone, how am I supposed to ignore it with her back for the time being?

Rory must be done pretending she isn't paying attention to me, I feel her eyes again just before she calls, "Remind me when that bonfire party starts?" Her melodic, self-assured voice floats to me across the garage, confident as ever, something like teasing present in her tone.

I might be fucked.

8

Aurora

Wyatt was right. I'm gonna end up seeing everyone anyway. Might as well be on my own terms.

His scruffy, square jaw damn near hit the floor when I told him as much back at the shop earlier, but he recovered quickly.

We traded numbers in case I had any trouble finding this place—or my car failed me again after he fixed it up for me—and I think there's a sense of something like comfortable peace between us after we did our little reset.

Honestly? It feels nice to have someone that I know I can talk to about my mom's diagnosis, someone who won't pry for gossip, who has my best interests at heart. It feels ... mature of us to be able to be friends, or something close to it, despite our ... intense history. Friends.

FRIENDS

It's the word I keep repeating to myself as he heads over to greet me on the outskirts of the party on the old McKay property. Familiar stomping grounds, from another life. Familiar swooping sensation of the stomach, from that same life. Familiar territory all around, I guess.

We're friends now, I tell myself. Better than enemies. Better than exes who no longer speak. Friends is great.

Friends can notice how *good* one another looks. There's no rule against that. Trust me, I'm that bitch that would know if there were. The fine print is where I excel.

So I observe, admire, my new and only *friend* in Smoky Heights as I trek closer to him, and he walks across the giant grassy field in the last light of dusk to meet me. Behind him, a semi-dilapidated red barn is lit from within, several kegs placed in front of the open door, and a bonfire rages maybe twenty yards away, logs placed around the perimeter to sit and enjoy the ambience, the atmosphere, the Smokies just across the way.

Though this "party" is taking up what would be at least an entire city block back home, it doesn't hold an iota of the hustle and bustle, the madness, the unquantifiable throngs of rushing bodies I've come to expect and associate with an open space of this size.

The sheer room in between the clusters of people, the view, the endless horizon with those postcard-worthy peaks rising and falling against the purple, pink, and orange twilight sky—there's no towers, high rises or iconic landmarks blocking my view of what's beyond the next block, there's no vendors at their carts, a new scent hitting me every ten steps, no fray of madness, of people just trying to get where they're going, everyone else be damned. No honking and cursing everyone around them for being in your way, for simply *existing* and therefore wasting your precious time.

It couldn't be further from what I'm used to, but I'm

shocked to register that ... I don't hate it. In fact, there's an odd sense of peace, my lungs filling deeper than usual, some sort of calm overtaking part of me when I allow my eyes to take in the entire view.

It's not lost on me that *he's* the best part of that scenery. Wyatt's brown hair looks like it's wet, even darker than usual, near black in the low light, slicked back and to the side after what had to be a post-work shower. He didn't bother shaving—no surprise there—but he clearly cleaned himself up otherwise. His masculine smell washes over me as I step closer, and my knees nearly wobble when it hits my senses at once.

This is a man that's only gotten finer with time.

Granted, he looked great when he wore a smile back in the day, but I have a hunch as to why he's so stone-faced, judging from my recent dealings with him, and the hints my mother kept dropping during our breakfast conversation this morning.

If he had a reason to laugh again? He'd be deadly. Positively lethal in his handsomeness. And he'd make someone real fucking lucky then too.

That grayish-blue Henley, sleeves rolled up to show off his black tattoo I still need to sneak a closer look at. Dark jeans. Same brown work boots as always. The man looks like he belongs here.

Unlike me, in a long indigo dress, a merlot cardigan overtop to fight that nightly chill the mountains are privy to, even in late summer, even in the South, even in the Heights.

I look like I'm a long way from home, among these women I used to regard as peers, friends, my people, all in jeans, tees from car shows and rock concerts, or maybe a hoodie they stole from their partner.

My quick initial scan tells me I'm the only one to show up in sandals *or* a dress, but it's not like we're going hiking. Gross. Definitely not going hiking. This should be fine for standing, drinking, sitting. It's always been fine for those activities in New York. Yeah, this is a bit … grassier than the hangouts I'm used to, but—

"She give you any trouble on the way over?" His rich, deep baritone interrupts my internal monologue of overthinking as we finally reach a distance that allows for conversation without the awkwardness of trying to shout, like you're over-eager to end the god-awful phase of silent eye contact and eerie continued smiles as you approach one another for an eternity. If there's anything worse than that, I don't know it.

I shake my head no. "She was perfectly well-behaved, thank you."

"Bet no one's ever said that about you," he quips back, no reload time needed.

"Hah." I give him a dry snort. Very elegant. He's not wrong, though. I bet my fellow associates, the partners and my immediate team are the only ones who find my sharp mind and tongue to be an asset. In any other setting, they tend to be my downfall. Where I have patience for the pedantic, the details, in my work—one thing that makes me so good at what I do—I have only impatience outside of work. Yet another reason I drive everyone who gets to know me crazy. And away.

His voice cuts into my thoughts yet again, and my eyes wander from the mountains and the skyline back to his own green ones, this hue that nearly matches the shade of the tree line. "What'll you have tonight? A beer?" Wyatt gestures with a rough hand, thick fingers wrapped around a Solo cup to the kegs by the old barn where a majority of the attendees are standing around. "Or a beer?"

I tap my chin in mock thought, pretending to consider my options. "I think I'll take the house recommendation, whatever the locals like to partake in," I tell him seriously.

If I looked close enough, I might think the corner of his

mouth ticked in a distinctly not-downward direction, but I wouldn't dare look that closely at him when he looks and smells like *this*, so I can't be sure.

We walk a couple steps apart, leaving enough space between us to try to get some fresh air into my nose, my lungs, something that clears the unwelcome fog in my head, the one that's tainting everything Wyatt does or says in this pink haze.

No thinking with the bean tonight, I tell myself. This is just so I can dip my toes into temporary life back in the Heights in a way that won't make me feel like the one hairy goat at the petting zoo full of cute bunnies. Your mission orders are to unwind, relax, get settled into your time in the Heights and just let your hair down after the last few weeks of misery.

No matter that the way for me to *actually* unwind would involve a hot guy, preferably one who knows his way around female anatomy, a shit ton of cursing that's probably looked real down upon in this part of the country, a few positions that would most definitely get me kicked straight to hell in the eyes of most of this town, and about a half-gallon of sweat.

But, no, that's not on the menu tonight.

What is? This half-flat, not-quite lukewarm beer. Tastes like what I imagine cow piss would. I'm sure a number of people in attendance here tonight have taken the dare and could tell you for sure whether this cheap beer *actually* tastes like cow piss, but I'm not one of them, and I'd be willing to bet Wyatt isn't, either.

But alcohol is going to provide the only kind of release I'm getting here tonight, so I throw about half of it back when he hands it to me, without a grimace, because I'm a trooper. With time, I've learned when to make a stink and when to bad bitch up and suffer through it. This is one of those times to be grateful for what I've got. I don't see any Empress gin with grapefruit flavored sparkling water and fresh squeezed lime around, so I'm out of luck, I guess.

"Everyone," he gestures with his beer to the loose assembly of bodies, faces I vaguely recognize, some I'll never forget. "Aurora's back in the Heights for a while. Let's show her some of that Southern hospitality we're known for." His eyes are screaming that if they choose not to, they'll catch a free beer in their face, or maybe a fist, or worse.

A chorus of greetings, mostly friendly, a few lackluster, are shouted from nearly everyone within a fifteen-foot radius of us, and after I do my best to give a polite smile and nod, I'm thankful when Wyatt gestures with his head toward the glowing bonfire and starts to head that way.

I duck my head as I pass the strangers I used to consider kin, the thoughts a cacophony in my head, hammering me on every weakness and insecurity I possess as I go.

Everyone is just waiting to see how fast you take off again.

How's that better *you left to go find working out for you?*

Just as I get past the final ring of the seventh circle of hell, the toe of my sandal gets caught on something on the ground—a rock, maybe?

"Oof," I grunt out as I start to stumble, but quicker than I can process, a strong arm grabs my free one and I'm stabilized, not even a drop of beer spilled from the mishap.

"This isn't pavement," what used to be my favorite voice in the world says, and I swear there's something jovial in his tone. "Our ground is that organic, all-natural shit you New Yorkers are so into. Grass-fed, comes with dirt, and rocks, sometimes sticks and roots too. You gotta watch out for those surprises."

Again, coming in clutch with the levity. He looks so broody, yet he's navigating this treacherous ground—physical and metaphorical—so well. I go with it.

"Hey, I'm used to watching where I'm walking. Vents,

manhole covers, things I can't even voice in polite company ... trust me when I say I've tripped on worse than a rock before. At least I'm not in heels this time." I'm surprised to hear a small chuckle come out of my own mouth, as flashes of some of those times revisit me.

"Thank God for that," Wyatt says dryly, eyes flashing down to my feet as he walks by my side now, rather than a few steps ahead. "Do they not sell tennis shoes in New York?"

I roll my eyes at him and scoff, pretending his teasing, this distraction from my situation, my own head, isn't the most healing thing that's happened to me since I've been back in the Heights.

"If you think I was going to risk getting mud on my eight-hundred-dollar Gucci sneakers ... you're dumber than you look."

"If you paid eight hundred dollars for a pair of tennis shoes, I'm not the dumb one of us," he shoots back.

A laugh bubbles out of me, and I don't stop it this time. It's a sound I haven't heard in a while, and I know I'm not imagining the tick of his lips now.

We make it to the empty log in front of the fire, Wyatt rounding the end of it and holding out a hand to help me over. We're far enough away from the burn that the smoke isn't hitting us, but I can still feel the comforting warmth of it, pleasant in the evening chill that's setting in the mountain air, the promise of fall in the air.

I accept, gripping his free hand while holding my beer with the other, and swing one leg over the low-to-the-ground log, then the other. It's a little awkward with the dress, but I can admit that his assistance made it easier without giving up my feminist card, right?

Chivalry might be extinct on the dating apps I use back in the city, but it appears to not be completely dead and gone down here. That's reassuring, at least. For posterity's sake. Not mine.

He waits until I'm seated, my dress repositioned for comfort and modesty, before he eases down next to me with something between a groan and a sigh. I think I hear some things pop and crack as he does, and I look over at him, a brow raised in question.

"It was a long week," he tells me, taking a huge drink from his cup.

"Tell me about it," I retort with a snort I'd never let loose in NYC and take a sip from my own. I think the taste is growing on me?

Both of our gazes drift forward, to the last vestiges of the sun setting behind the mountain range. Laughter bellows out behind us, drowning out the other soft murmurs of conversation from anyone else within hearing distance. The breeze picks up, pleasantly cool and carrying the smell of old loam, pine trees, and something crisp but indiscernible, maybe from the nearby river that flows from the lake. It also brings a fresh influx of Wyatt's heady scent.

I gulp down another mouthful of the stuff in my cup to distract me from the unwelcome attraction brewing without a safe outlet. And actually, this beer's not all that bad. Down another couple gulps and I think I can almost feel the hint of a buzz, which is promising, so I throw back some more. When I lower the empty cup Wyatt is staring at me, a bit incredulous.

"Thirsty?"

My throat bobs as I swallow at the word he probably meant innocently, but all I can think is *yes*. I'm so fucking thirsty for a night of forgetting everything with him. Remembering what it's like to feel the height of bliss. Of someone who knows all the secrets your body has to tell and *uses* them. A flutter ripples up through my core into my lower stomach, and my nipples tighten.

"Yeah," I croak out.

My eyes drop down his frame, his built torso, that chest and those abs that I'd be willing to bet you could still do laundry on, and—my favorite—those thick, broad shoulders. My maverick eyes ignore all social protocol and keep traveling all the way down to his tattooed arm, hand resting on the log just a few inches away from my own, and I tighten my thighs in an attempt to fight the sensations stirring between them.

He holds that hand out for my empty cup, completely unaffected by me and my wandering gaze, so I pull myself together and pass it over. If he can keep this PG, so can I.

"I'll get you another one. Hang tight."

Wyatt swirls the last of the dregs of what's left in his cup as he stands, and I try not to watch as he strides away, the way those jeans hug his hips and legs, the way he fills them out with muscle and that fucking ass. What, does he just do squats all day at the garage?

Yikes, Aurora. What happened to pulling yourself together?

I force my eyes to the property, the skyline beyond it, and I take in the last of the shadowed mountains against the night sky as darkness settles in and falls around us. The campfire provides enough light to see by, as does the lit barn behind me, but this is a kind of dark I haven't seen since I left.

I tilt my head back, let my long wavy hair fall all the way down my back as I look straight up, at the stars starting to twinkle to life above me. A smile stretches across my face when I see just how many there are. How small it makes me feel. So inconsequential, but in a way that feels like relief. Like my problems, my issues, are so much *less* than they normally feel, when I get some perspective like this. It's a welcome vantage point for me.

Footsteps crunch on the ground behind me before his voice hits me. "See anything good up there?"

And then his face is in my line of sight. Scruffy, gruff, maybe even a little mischievous. That might just be the first wave of buzz hitting me, though. A hallucination from the cow piss.

I let out a sigh, a small, sad smile on my face. "Just remembering there are bigger things out there than my problems."

He extends a hand with a fresh beer for me, and my head comes back down to its normal position, and I find myself looking straight at his groin, right at my eye level. A flush heats my cheeks as I realize I'm staring, and I wonder how much stronger this beer is than I gave it credit for.

I take the drink from him and swig back another sip rapidly, averting my eyes, focusing on literally anything else at the moment, as he sits down next to me, and I swear there's a smirk on his face as he lifts his own fresh cup to his lips.

This cup is cooler than the first, maybe from a fresh keg? I kinda like the taste, actually.

After a second of slurping and silence, he says, "If I didn't already say it ... I'm really sorry about your mom, Rory. It's a shitty fucking hand she was dealt, and you're doing a really honorable thing by being here for her. I'm sure it's not easy. None of it. But not many people would do what you're doing. It takes guts. Regardless of anything else, our past aside, I'm really proud of you for this."

A knot forms in my throat and moves down to my stomach, where it starts churning.

A flurry of all of the reasons he shouldn't be proud of me ambushes my head.

"Wyatt, can I ask you something?"

He looks back over at me.

"Why do I feel like you're about to ask me if I'd still love you if you had a silkworm instead of a clit or some shit?"

I burst out with a laugh, and who is she? Same done-up face, same nails, same high-maintenance bitch that left NYC earlier this week, but there's a side coming out that I'm not entirely recognizing. At a party in a field, drinking beer, staring at the stars, an occasional laugh on her lips as she comes face-to-face with her demons in the place she once ran from. I don't think I know her tonight.

For a second, just a blip on the radar of time, I wonder what I was running from? What I was so scared of here, that had me hightail it away and never come back, not even to visit?

I shove that thought away and get back to the present. Present company. "Because you've dated some real winners since we last saw each other?" I toss it out there lightly, like it's not my fault. I know if I never left we never would've broken up. He never would've had to date some chick who asked him questions from some Buzzfeed quiz or some inane trend on TikTok. But if someone asked if he'd still fuck them if they had a silkworm instead of a clit, they deserve to be made fun of, I'm not even sorry.

"That I have," he says with a smack of his lips, and another pointed sip of his beer.

I don't know how much longer we'll be able to tiptoe around this Claymore between us without setting off the tripwire (again), but I appreciate that we're both trying.

The chatter behind us turns into more raucous laughter, and a smile curves my mouth for them. For this happiness these people have found. Despite how shitty and sucky life can be, they've found something that they enjoy, people they care about, and like spending their time with.

We should all be so lucky.

When I get back home, it'll be back to thirteen-hour days, sprinting down Amsterdam in a Reformation dress under a blazer and whichever Valentino Garavani heels I could sneak in the budget that month as I hustle to or from work, unsatisfying nights with Trevor (or some other unlucky schmuck who has to go to bed with me and pretend I'm the girl of his dreams while I convince myself he's half-decent in the sack), and a sea of unfamiliar faces, none of whom give a single fuck about me.

But that's why I love it. Me and my problems disappear in the sea of random motion. Endless opportunity, unlimited variety, infinite choices. Impossible to get bored, nothing is dull in New York. If it is, it doesn't survive the frenzy of the free market. And, perhaps most importantly, enough insanity to make my own feel less significant. The way the incessant noise calms me. So much for me to focus on, so much to hold my attention on the world around me, that the assault of my own thoughts falls into the background. My problems don't compare to the whirlwind around me.

That would never have been my life here.

But I can't get the question out of my mind. I have to voice it, it'll eat away at me until I do, and the alcohol is making me a lot braver than I maybe should be, than I deserve to be with him. But it slips out of me anyway.

"Could you ever forgive me?"

The silence that follows might be the worst one I've heard yet.

9
Wyatt

Jesus Christ. There's not enough beer in the kegs by the barn for this. Definitely not enough in my system.

Could I ever forgive her?

Do I even have an answer to that?

I thought we were being friends. Do friends pick at old wounds, scabs with little corners sticking up on the sides, ripe for tearing off and gouging the skin that had been trying to heal and creating even worse scar tissue than what was there before?

It's taken me years and years to form these scabs, even shitty as they may be, but in she comes, ready to just pull at them all, scrape away and scratch them off rather than let me keep doing my slow healing?

Nah.

This is a conversation I'm not here for. Not tonight.

Rory breathes out a heavy breath next to me, cheeks all puffed out as she looks the other way.

"I'm sorry. You don't have to answer that. I ... I shouldn't have asked."

"Damn, girl. What happened to starting over?" My tone is more strained than I was shooting for, but I think I've done pretty well tonight, all things considered. I should get a little slack here.

That gets me a watery laugh, and she shakes her head. "You're right. I was out of line."

I nudge her body with my elbow and wait until she turns back and meets my eye again.

"Friends, yeah?" I offer. "I meant that. While you're here, if you need a friend … I'm here."

She's always been my soft spot. No matter the turn my life took after she left, the damage she caused, all I can feel for her now that she's back is empathy. That's a sentiment I'm not too familiar with, being a bit of a surly fucker myself, but like I said, she's my weakness. Always has been. She's hurting, she's in pain, she's here, facing her fuck ups to do the impossible, and I can't not try to make it easier for her. Giving her what she needs, I spent so much of my youth, my formative years, focusing on it, I think it became part of my DNA, some sort of evolutionary shit.

"Friends," she says with a nod and what might be a sniffle. She takes a big gulp of her beer and looks back at the bonfire. "So, how's your brother?"

I huff out some sort of snort and she looks over at me, eyes wide. "Another sore subject? Damn, this is like Battleship, trying to talk to you, huh? Direct hit after direct hit?"

My beer is dangling from my hand by the lip of the cup, and I raise it in front of my face to down some more. Hopefully it gives me the ability to talk to my one sore subject about the other.

"Think I've only got the two," I mutter with a look that tells her I'm not being cruel. Most other topics should be safe. "Weston … he's Weston," I add on with a shrug. "Same old irresponsible little shit he always was."

She laughs, looking back at the fire, lost in some memory of him that's much happier than mine are. "I always liked your brother," she says fondly. "Like we're kindred in some ways."

"Yeah, you're both bougie as fuck, and expensive to keep happy, and neither of you cared to stay in the Heights."

She pulls back with a start. "He left the Heights too?"

I shrug back at her. "He left, came back, left again. In and out whenever the urge strikes. I'm sure he'll be back. Flaky bastard that he is, it'll probably be when he needs something."

She makes a noncommittal noise, something like disapproval, and I realize we need to change the subject before this turns into a sad sack fest. That's not the break she needs tonight.

I ask her about life in New York, and she tells me all about the amazing apartment she scored, how she finished school up there, and the firm she got a job with and has since moved up the ranks with. Her favorite bagel vendor, the various bakeries and grocers she frequents. Her face lights up when she talks about all of it, and for a minute I'm jealous of the city for giving her that light that this town and I couldn't. But I'm happy for her. It's good to see that she followed her dream and it worked out.

I fill her in on what she's missed around here. Not a whole lot. I'm still working on cars, obviously, just like I was when she left. Give her the recap on my family, Ronnie's, the general gist of the town at large, at least the better parts of it.

"Sounds like everything's more or less the same then?" She tosses out with a quirked brow after my updates.

I suck in an offended breath through my teeth. "You take that back, ma'am. We got a Buc-ee's. It's basically a whole new world out here."

The sound of her tinkling laughter warms my insides even more than the beer, and I manage to prompt her for more about her life, despite the thickness in my throat.

She tells me how the partners she reports to wouldn't let her fully quit, insisted that she go on a hiatus, and possibly do some remote work on contracts and other legal documents while she's away. How she's been trying to figure out how to make that work in that tiny apartment she's living out of while also doing what she's here to do.

"I'm sure Duke and Dallas would let you use the bar during the daytime," I throw out. "There's never anyone really other than Ernie there until the plant and the factory close."

She waggles her head back and forth. "Yeah, that's true. Definitely would be more room down there at least. If I could set up a printer somewhere it'd probably be a lot easier to review documentation on a larger surface than whatever tiny desk would fit upstairs." She smiles at me, and it feels like a prize I've earned. "Thanks, Wyatt."

Her eyes—those dangerous, wavering little bastards of mischief—they float to my lips, not for the first time tonight. My cock takes note, and I fight readjusting myself. I tip back my beer for another swig instead. "Of course."

She licks her lips and looks away, and I wonder if she'd still taste the same. Wonder how crazy I'd have to be to try and find out.

I'm nearing the end of this cup, my third beer, when something unexpected leaves her mouth again. She's still facing the other way when she asks, "Do you ever think of me?"

I toss back the rest of my cup. Fuck it. She wants my truth, I'll give it to her.

"Only when I'm coming." It sounds like a growl, and I can feel her reaction next to me, without giving in to the temptation of looking over at her. The sharp little inhale she takes when she registers my words.

I bet her cheeks are pink, her nipples pebbled, and her pussy wet.

I wonder if *that* still tastes the same.

Now there's no helping it, I'm gonna have to readjust. I rest an elbow on a knee, drape my arm across my lap, and sneak the other hand down to free up some space inside my pants, my underwear, try to let my boner breathe until I can talk it down or rub it out, whichever comes first.

"Oh," she finally says, and I dare it. I look over to my left and she's staring at me, that mouth of hers in a perfect O, one that I could easily see stretched around my dick, because I've already seen it hundreds of times before. After all, it's what I usually see when I'm coming in some other girl's mouth.

"I think about you too," she admits softly, and I give in again.

I let my eyes run over her face, those lips even plumper than I remember them, down her neck, follow that flush to her chest, those perfect tits that look even bigger than they were the last time I got to see them. She's breathing faster, and I follow the rise and fall of that chest, let my eyes fall down her dress, picturing what's happening underneath it right now. Is her underwear soaked? Are her thighs clenched? Is her clit puffy and begging for my tongue, my lips, my teeth?

If she looks at me with those needy eyes—begging for things her mouth won't say aloud—when she's fully sober, I'm gonna do something about it. That's the kind of friend I am, I guess. You need something, I'm your guy. As long as your name is Aurora Rose.

And it's when my eyes are on her legs that I see something *else* by her legs. Something she surely hasn't noticed, because as much as Aurora Rose Weiss has changed, she's *definitely* not any more outdoorsy now than she was when she lived here. And the creature creeping toward her exposed toes, feet, and legs is not going to be a welcome one.

I OPEN my mouth to warn her, but the critter gets to her first. It wends between her ankles, beneath the extended calf there, and brushes up against her, tail winding around her lower leg, eliciting an ear-piercing scream.

It actually makes me feel a bit safer—if she's got that set of lungs on her, I don't think she needs a whistle for muggings or any of the other thousand dangers I've spent hours researching the statistics of on Google in her absence.

In an instant, she's jumped up, back, and away from the thing, but I was ready. I'm with her, next to her, bracing her as she tries to jump on top of the log, like that's going to help her get away from the friendly barn cat.

"WYATT!"

This would be a great time for a joke about her screaming my name, if I still did those. That was Wyatt 1.0.

"I'm here, you're fine," I tell her placatingly, but not patronizingly. Her irrational fear of cats isn't as irrational as it might sound, actually. She had a bad run-in with an overprotective mama kitty when we were teens. She's still got the scar on her arm, and the nickname to boot.

Aurora is still dancing on top of the log, mostly behind me, holding onto my shoulders for balance as she wipes the offended leg on her other, trying to remove the feeling from her skin.

Like I said, I know the girl. Dedicated a huge chunk of my life to knowing her, her needs. Understanding them.

"Hop up," I tell her, gesturing toward my back, and she doesn't think twice. Her lithe body, tall, pretty average build, soft in all the right places, leaps up and attaches itself to mine. Those arms of hers wrap around my neck, strangling me.

"You might like to be choked, but I don't," I grunt out, peeling her forearms from off of my windpipe.

"Not the time for jokes, Grady!"

Ooh. My last name. She means business.

I grasp her lower legs to make sure she's secure and then I reach down to the cat, who's now pacing the log, purring by my ankles, and scratch behind his ears.

"This is Boots," I tell Aurora, trying not to focus on the way her heavy breaths are hitting my ear, her breasts pressed into my back so tightly I'm pretty sure I can feel her rapid heartbeat through them. Is there an ulterior motive at work here? Me, leaning down, her being pressed further into me as I do? Might be. "Puss in Boots, in full. He's the barn cat here."

"That's lovely. Please get me away from Boots." Her death grip on me tightened when I leaned down, and she doesn't ease up until I've walked around the log, toward the majority of the other people and her senses seem to come back to her when we're far enough away from the danger.

"You can put me down now," she says stiffly, and I drop her down carefully, hands bracing her as best I can from this angle as she goes, trying to ignore all the curves I end up feeling by default as she dismounts.

I turn to face her and she's hugging herself, arms across her body. "Thank you," she says as dignified as one can be after just having been terrified by a furry little friendly cat and scaling your ex for safety.

It's a good thing I'm not prone to excessive smiling or laughing, because I can tell that would *not* be the right move based off of the look on her face, her posture, her demeanor.

"We can hang out over here?" I gesture back toward the barn and the bulk of the other people, many of whom are now staring at her, some even snickering or laughing at her display. Knowing them, it's probably just amusement at what just happened, but knowing her—for as much as she says she's changed, I'm quickly seeing she's still a lot of the girl I've always known—she's probably taking it as something worse than that. Her mind always worked against her when she got stressed, and I'd say that probably hasn't changed.

She shakes her head in what I think might be horror. "No, no, I think I'm good. Thanks again for the beers, and the invite. And, you know, saving me."

Her attempted fleeing is interrupted by the arrival of my best friend. "Is that Rory?" Ronnie's brash yell reaches us from where he's just parked. "Is that Rory Weiss I see?"

"You might've missed your chance to go peacefully," I whisper to her as he crosses the field, nodding and waving his hello to most of our friends as he does.

She grumbles, shifting from one foot to the other, but doesn't make a break for it.

When Ronnie gets to us, he walks straight over to Rory, leans down to hug her, and then lifts her up and spins them around.

Something acidic turns in my stomach, and I have the most unusual impulse to crack his spine. Honestly, I could punch him on a good day, but the specificity of the spine cracking is what's new there.

He puts her down and I think she'd be laughing once again if she weren't still shaken and a bit mortified by what happened with the damn cat.

I can tell she's back in her own head again, after all the work of getting her out here, back into nature, what's always calmed her, and those benefits have already faded away.

"It's Aurora now," she tells Ronnie instead of the million

other ways she could've greeted him, and I see his face fall just a fraction before he gives her a big grin.

"You'll always be Rory to us," he tells her jovially, but it doesn't land.

I glance between them and can see her shutting down brick by brick. Great.

"And seeing you with Grady? Just like old times!" He keeps going, because he's a fucking numbskull who can't read the room if it were in a children's picture book with hundred-point font right in front of his damn face.

Aurora's face falls even further, and she backs up away from both Ronnie and me.

"I was just leaving, actually," she says, jerking a thumb over her shoulder, back toward the makeshift lot.

"Are you good to drive?" I ask her. "I can take you," I offer before she responds.

She shakes her head. "No, no, I'm good. That sobered me right up. Thanks."

I glare at Ronnie for a split second, then back to her. "At least text me when you get home?"

"Home is seven hundred miles away," she corrects me quietly. "But I'll text you when I get to the bar."

And she's gone. Again.

The silence of her absence makes me realize that, for once, I didn't mind all the talking tonight.

My sharp glare returns to Ronnie, a crestfallen look on his face.

"What did I do?"

10
Aurora

Feathers flutter in my face, and it sounds like an entire flock of birds taking flight around me.

A horrible smell, and my life flashes before my eyes.

Squawks—whether from me or the beasts, that's TBD—abound, and my mother's stifled laughter makes it to me from her spot in a chair on her back patio.

My hands close tighter around the firm, feathered body, and it tries to take off, again.

I scream, again.

A cackle rends the air, and I squeeze my eyes tight until my head is over my shoulder, in the direction I'm fairly confident my mother is laughing at me from. When I feel marginally safe, I open my eyes, trying not to rethink my entire trip and plan in the process.

"This?" I ask her, the chicken still grasped firmly in between my hands, held out as far from my body as possible, even in these overalls and rubber boots she leant me. I refuse to let this thing get close to me. My underwear alone cost more than anything my sister owns, and I have no interest in getting *bird* all over them. "This is the priority on your bucket list?"

This is *not* the kind of cock I'm used to wrangling.

"Seeing you get your hands dirty? Yeah, it's pretty high up there." Her voice is cool amusement. Not unkind, but that no-shit attitude that the apple didn't fall far at all from the tree on is definitely present.

"I'm surprised you even trust me with your precious babies," I say sarcastically, but only a small sliver of the statement is a joke.

My mom's silvering hair catches a glare in the sun and I let myself watch for just a second, trying to appreciate the moment, the way she stirs the glass straw—the one with the ceramic bee attached to the side of it—in her mason jar, clinking the ice against the sides of the glass, before she takes a sip of lemonade that's probably spiked, if I still know her.

A weird time to be reminded, but her hair glinting jogs something in me that it's almost time to get mine touched up. My nails, too, now that I've been here for two whole weeks. On that note, before long, my lips will need touching up, too, but we'll freak out about the options for those later.

"Closest thing I got to grandbabies, you can humor me," she calls out after she's wet her whistle.

Arms fully extended in front of me, face screwed up and head scrunched as far to the side and buried between my shoulders as my neck will allow, I carry the beast to the separate enclosure my mom apparently stores them in while their hen house gets cleaned out.

By me.

I'll say one thing (and one thing only). The only thoughts going through my head have been oh my god, ohmigod, *oh my god*, so I haven't had time for my usual mental harassment of self, and I guess that's not the worst thing ever.

But moving these birds, cleaning out the facility where they lay their eggs, do ... whatever it is that chickens do?

Absolutely fucking disgusting.

I'd rather be forced to power wash the streets of the Meatpacking District.

If I hadn't accompanied her to an appointment with the oncologist last week—heard firsthand how the tumor is progressing, her prognosis, the lack of options, the dimness of it all—I'd say this was the worst thing I've done in years.

It's a solid number two, and please don't make the obvious joke there.

But if she thinks she's going to get me to quit on her, to give up on my plan to help her through this time by giving me a difficult task, she forgets how hardheaded of a daughter she raised.

THREE HAUNTING, sweaty hours later, the birds are back in their coop, locked away, thankfully, and I'm in front of my mom on the patio.

I blow a strand of hair that's plastered to my face—well, I try to blow it using all the force my bottom lip can muster in an upward direction, but the bottom half of the lock just flops around, the top refusing to budge.

I bring the back of my less offending forearm up and swipe at it, trying to keep as much dirt and grime from my face as possible, and a shudder rips through me at the visceral realization I was unsuccessful in that.

I knew this trip wasn't going to be *fun*, but today has been a special kind of torture. If there was a decent day spa within an afternoon's drive, I'd say I'd earned one hell of a spa day. Alas, the nearest five-star resort is probably a *ways* away.

Only seven and a half more months until I'm back in New

York, I remind myself. Think of all the spa days waiting for me then. And the lack of chickens, unless you count the ones on the roof of the next building over, but I don't have to clean up their shit, so I don't count those.

"Having fun?" My mom waggles her brows at me from her spot in the shade, refilled glass next to her, condensation dripping down its side, and I snap.

My gloved hand lurches out for her glass and I gulp it down from the rim of the glass, straw pressed against my cheek as I guzzle it.

Yep, vodka.

I swallow every drop of the refreshing blend and don't stop until the glass is empty of anything but ice, tumbling in a cool rush toward my face, and I don't even stop then.

When I finally do put it back down, she's watching me with an amused gleam in her eye.

"Your doctor approve of all that alcohol?"

She scoffs at my nerve. "What's he gonna tell me, I'm dying? I'm not dead yet, dove. Gonna get my kicks where I still can."

I have to press my lips together to keep from laughing at her morbid sense of humor.

"Nice job today, Aurora." My mom nods her head toward the chicken coop and then stands from the rocking chair and heads inside, me trailing her with a grunt. Rendered fairly speechless by the day's activities, too exhausted for thoughts, too worn out for words. I guess there's a silver lining after all.

Lexi is sitting at the dining room table when we come through the back door, swiping the screen on her Android, but she looks up at our entrance. One look at me and she's doubled over in laughter.

And the day just continues to get better.

"I didn't realize y'all had wrestling in the pig pen on the list for today," she gets out between heaves.

"Hardy har har." I roll my eyes and yank the gloves off my body as I head toward the laundry room off of the kitchen, where I strip out of everything I borrowed and throw the clothes in the basket waiting there, ignoring the tittering I hear coming from the two of them in the main room.

When I head back out, it's in nothing but what God gave me, a cami, and my undies, and I stride past them pointedly on my way to my mom's room. "I'm taking a shower," I call without looking back, and I grab the clothes I arrived in from where they've been waiting for me to finish playing Old McDonald.

"We could just hose you off in the backyard like the rest of the livestock?" My sister can barely control her hoots of laughter, but between you and I, it's nice to have something between us that isn't seething hatred, so I ignore the jibe. This is the first time since I've been back that we've seen each other and it hasn't been just straight at each other's throats, so I'll take the growth where I can get it.

"Use mine," my mom calls out. "It's got shampoo and all already in it."

I emerge thirty minutes later a brand-new person. Soaking wet hair rolled up in a towel, the corduroy coverall dress I came in looking a bit more revealing without the cami on underneath, but that thing will be lucky if it doesn't get burned after what it's been through today. Showing a bit of extra skin is just going to have to be the vibe. Luckily the bralette I wore here is cute enough it might just pass for something intentional.

Strolling into the living room, I find my mom and sister seated in the La-Z-Boy and the mismatched loveseat, respectively. I hold out the men's razor I found in her shower.

"What's this?"

"That's called a razor. It's what us plebeians use to remove body hair when we can't afford fancy waxes or whatever your people do when you're too good for shaving."

I roll my eyes at my sister. "It's called laser hair removal, look into it, Lex. That mustache doesn't have to be a permanent fixture on your face." I turn back to my mother while my sister feels her upper lip self-consciously. Hah. Point one for Aurora. "My question is why is a *men's* razor in your shower, Mom?"

My mom's turn to roll her eyes. We're a sophisticated bunch, I guess. "Well, dear. We're a little late for this talk, but I suspect you know by now that sometimes women have *needs*, and sometimes they choose men to fulfill those needs."

"Gross!" Lexi shouts, covering her ears.

"That's uncalled for, Mother," I say with complete disdain, in concert with my sister's outburst.

"Oh, please. Lexi, you've been walked in on by half of our family. Rory, the number of times we had to pretend not to hear you and Wyatt Grady in your room—"

I let out a shriek that doesn't drown out enough of her words.

"—can't handle the fact that you're not the only ones under this roof who enjoy male company."

"Fucking disgusting, Mom!" Lexi continues protesting loudly. "You had sex twice, when you got pregnant with me, and again with her, and that's it!"

My mother swats the air with a hand at the both of us. "Like you don't need a good dicking from time to time, the both of ya. It'd probably fix a lot of issues for each of you, actually. If you need recommendations—"

"Seriously, just stop!" I shout this time.

"That should be illegal," Lexi spits out.

But the twinkle in my mom's eye makes this gross-out—this entire day—almost worth it.

11
Aurora

The top of my Swarovski pen bounces atop the paperwork I'm dissecting and reconstructing at a wide table down in the common area of the bar.

Wyatt was right. This was much better than trying to work off of a nightstand upstairs. This allows me to lay out close to ten pages across and several deep as well, perfect for projects like the one I'm currently working on, a thirty-pager.

My pink AirPods Max do wonders for noise canceling, not that there's any real patrons here—Ernie doesn't count, he's more of a bump on the log that never leaves, and Duke and Dallas are always around, but never loud—but the headphones help to keep me focused on the task at hand. Would you laugh at me if I told you I was playing cityscape noises as I work?

The haptic tap, tap, tap of my pen focuses me, and my eyes fly through line by line, seeking out any discrepancies, inconsistencies, or items that would be contrary to our client's best interests.

My four colors of highlighters sit less than six inches from my right hand, just within reach for times like *now*, when I need to use the blue one to mark this *joke* of a stipulation that wouldn't even hold up in court.

Who did these people *hire* to put this agreement together?

Fucking amateurs.

I snort in a mix of self-satisfaction and, okay, slight derision at the opposition's weak-ass counsel as I write the amendment in the margin.

Yeah, yeah, I know. Pride is a deadly sin. But stupidity should be too. At least I don't have that.

A hand—a male hand, and a not-unattractive one at that—drops down atop the papers I'm staring at and I jump back with what I hope isn't an audible scream.

I yank my headphones off and instinctively hit the pause button on the software tracking my time on my laptop.

When I look up, Wyatt is standing over me, an amused smirk on his face that tells me that scream probably wasn't only in my head, his brows ever so slightly quirked as he watches me scramble.

"Jesus H. Christ, Grady."

Those thick brows of his rise further along his forehead.

"Warn a girl, why don't ya?"

"Thought that's what I was doing with my hand on the table?"

I roll my eyes at him and blow out a heavy breath, before tightening my ponytail for maximum control.

"Why aren't you at work?" I ask him with a scowl.

He pops a shoulder casually. "It's not my favorite thing to do to stay after hours."

After hours?

I check the time on my laptop and see that it's nearly six o'clock. The software we use says I logged eight-plus hours this session, between both projects. That flew.

And now that my headphones are off, my adrenaline is

cooling down, and my heartbeat quieting so I can hear other noises aside from my own blood whooshing in my ears from that jump scare, I'm aware of quite a few voices around me.

"Shit," I murmur. "I didn't realize it had gotten so late. Dallas didn't …"

"I'm sure you're not in anyone's way yet," Wyatt is quick to reassure me, already knowing what I was worried about. "But personally, I wouldn't wanna be this close to the dart boards when the regulars have had enough time for a few more beers to hit their systems."

I give him a wan smile and start to pack up my papers, laptop, and various office supplies.

"Going well?" His eyes shoot to the table between us, the organized mess scattered upon it.

"Yeah, actually. It's been working out down here. When I'm not at risk of ruining a multi-million-dollar deal with stray darts." I gesture at the table, the bar. "And I'm making good progress on this contract."

He shakes his head a little in disbelief but pulls out a seat and drops down in it, two bottles of beer in one hand.

"That's a lot of *whos* and *whoms* there." He tilts his head at the pile of papers. "Look at little Rory Weiss, all grown up and a badass with her pen and highlighter. Probably making grown men cry with your words, like you always have."

He gets a low chuckle from me on that. "Let's just say it wouldn't be a first."

His mouth doesn't move, but his eyes light up, maybe even twinkle with something like pride and amusement.

"That doesn't surprise me." This time, the corner of his mouth *does* tick in a way that—on anyone else—would indicate something of a smile.

"That for me?" I point with one finger at one of the beers he placed on the table.

He makes an awkward grimace. "Actually, they're both mine. Sorry."

I laugh at him and reach out with one leg to kick whatever of him I can reach under the table. Pretty sure I got a shin. He doesn't even flinch, the jerk.

"Nah, here." He pushes the base of one bottle, sliding it along the empty side of the table, keeping it away from the work and electronics piled on the other edge.

"Thanks." I take a sip and it hits me that I haven't had any alcohol but beer since I've been back. Woof. I should really try to get a bottle of my favorite gin here, get a little stash upstairs for nights like these, when I've earned a treat.

We both sip our beer in relative silence for a few. It's more comfortable than you'd think it should be between exes, and I blame that on him.

Finally, he asks, "Have you done *anything* fun since you got here?"

I don't miss a beat. "Does wrestling a few cocks count?"

He sputters on the sip of beer he was trying to swallow, eyes wide as the Saks window display on Fifth Avenue, but collects himself.

"I really wanna hope you're talking about your mom's chickens, but all she's got is hens, Hellcat." Been an age since I've heard that nickname. I don't hate it.

Chin pressed into my chest, I smirk up at him. "You caught me. I was playing with her peckers."

He shakes his head, the tiniest of what could technically be referred to as a grin on his breathtaking face. Maybe it's only breathtaking to me because the last time I saw it, he admitted he thinks of me when he comes. Maybe every time he comes? I haven't exactly tried to clarify with him, but the wording I've replayed over and over in my own head each time *I* have come on my own hand—picturing him doing the same—since that night leads me to believe it was, in fact, meant in the present indefinite tense. Sloppy wording that would never get approved in any document for a client of mine, but amazing spank bank fodder.

My face flushes.

Blissfully, he doesn't bring attention to my reddened cheeks, the way I'm ready to fan myself with the top sheet from my stack of papers.

He just keeps talking about the hens.

"Aside from what I can only imagine was a rip-roaring day I would've paid to have seen with you and the ..." A poignant pause. "Chickens ..." Those piercing, deep green eyes find mine. "You done anything to give yourself a break since you've been back?"

Let's see ... Run through the mental checklist real quick. I've been with my mom as much as she'll allow, taking her to appointments, working through the few bucket list items she's thrown on the list so far, doing my actual work whenever I'm not with her ... The answer *not really* is on the tip of my tongue, but that's not entirely true, now, is it?

"My ex took me to a bonfire the first weekend I was here."

He pulls a wince. "Oof. Sounds like it could've been awkward."

I shrug, looking up at him from beneath my lashes. "Eh, could've been worse."

Those eyes, something dark in them, flash at me again. "Got any plans tomorrow?"

I scan through my mental calendar. My mom doesn't have any appointments over the weekend, I have no mandatory tasks for work. This contract isn't due until late next week, and it's the only time-sensitive one currently on my plate.

"Not that I know of. I was gonna stop over at the house again, but considering my mom's been kicking me out of the house at every opportunity, I'm starting to get the idea she wouldn't hate some alone time away from me ..."

He snorts the closest thing to a laugh I've heard from him since being back—my stomach dips in response and I ignore it—and his eyes travel the room, catching on something on the far side of the bar. "I bet she would," he mutters.

"Did she put you up to this?" My suspicion sensor blares at me.

Her sending me to the bar my first night. Knowing I ran into him immediately after the fact.

Him trying to take me off her hands both then and now.

Are they tag teaming me for some reason?

He shakes his head a single time. "No, Rory. You've just been staying awful busy since you got here. Haven't even seen you around since the bonfire the other week, and I thought you might use a little mental break."

Truthfully, my time here has been way less intense than my usual life back home, but the added mental strain of watching my mother slip down the irreversible slope of terminal illness, on top of what just being back here has done to me, he's not wrong. A mental break is more than a little tempting for me at this point. That, or a mental break*down*.

"What did you have in mind?" I ask him.

"Do you still own jeans?" Wyatt asks in that low voice of his.

I scoff. "Of course I own jeans." I don't. "What, do you think people on the East Coast only wear power suits and gowns?" I hope he didn't get a peek inside my pathetic excuse for a closet.

He tilts his head and shrugs with just his eyebrows. "Haven't seen you in 'em since you been back."

"It's called style, Grady. That's something I got in the city."

The back-and-forth barbs, the bantering, it's more old territory for us. A familiar landscape. And he falls back into it as easily as I do.

"Yeah, well, that style's gonna get dirty real fast with what I got in mind."

I don't miss the way his eyes roll down my body as he says it. I hope he misses the reaction in me as he does. The attraction, the flirting, that's as familiar as territory gets between us.

"What do you have in mind?" Did my voice turn into a whisper?

Did his throat just bob?

"Oh, I've got a lot in mind for you, Hellcat."

My turn to swallow, eyes wide.

"In fact," he continues, "when it comes to you, there's not much that *isn't* on my mind."

Dear God. My stomach definitely just fell into my pelvic region.

"But my dirty mind isn't what's going to get your clothes all messed up."

"No?"

"Nah, that'll be what we're getting up to when you're wearing those jeans tomorrow."

"And what's that?"

"That? That is called blue balls." Ronnie's voice is accompanied by his body dropping onto a backward chair that he drags up and straddles next to the table we're occupying. The spell between us snaps, the moment—whatever was in it—broken.

Wyatt's face, that was bordering on not-not-amused, drops flat, back into his normal dry expression. He levels his gaze on the new arrival, his messy sandy brownish hair, the beer gripped in his hand, arms rested on top of the back of the chair.

"What the fuck are you talking about now?" Wyatt's voice is practically a growl. "And tell me it wasn't my junk ... again."

Ronnie gives a casual shrug. "I figured Rory was asking what your problem was."

"Jesus fucking—" Wyatt breathes out, but Ronnie keeps going.

"If I had to guess, his balls are bluer than an indigo bunting right about now. Speaking of his balls, *you* already know this, Roro, but it still baffles me. They're shockingly *not* massive for how big the rest of his package is. Isn't that weird, though? I dunno, I guess I always thought the bigger the dick, the bigger the balls."

This is both better and worse than watching a train wreck. I couldn't—or wouldn't—stop his verbal diarrhea if I had magic Pepto Bismol of the vocal cords for him.

"Maybe balls are all, more or less, the same size, regardless of length and girth of the rest of the equipment?" Ronnie hypothesizes, like he's on his own scientific podcast with no guests and no audience, and that doesn't deter him in the least. His arms wave wildly as he discusses with himself. "But maybe that's a good thing in his case." Eyes on mine, he (not at all discreetly) jerks his head in Wyatt's direction in the least subtle move I've ever seen.

"Ronnie." The threat in the growl is as clear as his Mamaw's famous Jello salad, but Ronnie somehow misses it.

This is a kind of entertainment I've never seen on Broadway, and I'm eating up every word his trap is letting loose. Wyatt, however, looks like a cartoon character right before steam comes out of their ears and they fly through the roof. Ronnie ignores both of our reactions, enamored with the sound of his own voice. Or perhaps it's Grady's cock he's obsessed with. Could I blame him if it were the latter? How many years has it been since I've seen it, and I'd be lying if I said it wasn't on my mind ... frequently.

Ronnie keeps rambling, despite the imminent danger to his

right side. "If the berries matched the twig, he'd have a pair of peaches in his pants, you know what I mean? I'd say they were more like plums if memory serves. Anyway, I'm getting off topic here. His plums have gotta be so blue they're purple by now. Hell, plums *are* purple." He shrugs but doesn't slow his roll for a single breath. "I guess that works. My point is, the man hasn't been hooking up since you've been back. I ain't even seen many girls in this bar since you showed up. You must've scared 'em all away. And I don't need to tell you how big of a snake he has that needs to feed regularly."

He makes a pointed look at me, then glances completely obviously, faux-surreptitiously, to Wyatt's pants and back to me.

"Ronnie." The warning turns into more of a hiss on that one, and even I can tell Ronnie's about to get a free realignment of his jaw, courtesy of Wyatt's fist.

"I know I'll never forget the size of that anaconda." He winks at me in a ridiculous gesture that no one in this entire bar could possibly have missed. "Actually, Rory—"

"Don't call me that."

"I have a question on that front. How did that work between you, physics-wise?"

"RONNIE!"

"I mean, I get that you can push babies out of that thing, so I know that it, theoretically, it *should* work. A rubber band and a watermelon, and all that. But I mean, I saw the thing, and in my professional opinion, I don't think it would fit. Did he tell you? Yeah, he showed it off when we were camping one time. A little rude, if you ask me, my wife was right there—does he have no boundaries? Gracie hasn't looked at me the same since. But anyway—"

Wyatt's hand claps over Ronnie's mouth, cutting off his words, but not stopping him from trying. Mumbles and grumbles are still leaking out from beneath Wyatt's palm, and it's taking more effort than I'd care to admit not to laugh at the scene in front of me. Looks like Ronnie is one move away from getting his neck snapped, judging from the expression on his best friend's face.

"Shut. The fuck. Up." I've never heard Wyatt's voice so dangerous.

Ronnie's eyes widen, bouncing to Wyatt, then me, before going back to his best friend's. Wyatt must be convinced Ronnie got the message, because he drops his hand, wiping it on his Dickies.

"Did you have to lick me?"

Ronnie tilts his mouth up in a boyish grin and shoots me an overdone wink.

"Figured someone at this table ought to."

"Leave." The word was more of a low rumble than a syllable, but Ronnie hops back up off his chair, finally sensing that his own balls might be in danger, and backs away from the table.

"Good to see you, Ror."

I tilt my head at him in a small nod, stifling the laugh that's been aching to break free this entire encounter. "You ..." You know what? Fuck it. "You too, Ronnie." Can't say it wasn't a good time. An awkward time, sure, but not a bad one.

"He is such a fucking ..." Wyatt lets the muttered insult trail off, hanging his head before shaking it, seemingly unable to think of anything bad enough to describe his best friend.

I'm sure he wants to sink into the earth right now. Or maybe just bury Ronnie six feet under it. But I'm still fighting a chuckle. Nobody back home would bust my nuts like he just did, and I don't hate the warmth in my gut right now.

"Aurora Weiss, care of Smoky Suds, question mark question mark. I'm guessing this is for you," Dallas calls out dryly, reading from a label. He steps over to the table I've been stationed at all day, bearing a fairly massive box. It's got a giant red sticker on the side, an open mouth with *perishable* written on the tongue, along with a name that sends a thrill through me. *Goldbelly.*

Fuck, I can't believe it. A taste of New York, here in the Heights. My mouth is watering at the thought. What it could be.

Zabar's? Junior's? Fuck, tell me it's bagels. Oh, but I'd do unholy things for Gray's Papaya at this point.

Hell, I'll even eat carbs today, and it's not supposed to be a cheat day. Three weeks away from my favorite city in the world has turned me into a fiend.

I jump up from my seat and accept Dallas's outstretched offering. "Thank you, thank you, *thank you!*" That was way too close to a squeal for my liking, so I reclaim my composure and try again.

Dallas raises his dark brows at me, and Wyatt watches on, something like amused curiosity.

"What the hell is that?" Wyatt manages to point with only his eyeballs at the box I'm holding like it's a winning lottery ticket, clutched to my chest.

"Good food."

Dallas rolls his eyes and walks away, but Wyatt's forest green eyes narrow on me, or maybe on it.

"What?" I ask him.

"Where's it from?"

I point to the label, the branding that's all over the box. "This site. Goldbelly."

"Who's it from?" he amends.

I busy myself with opening the packaging, and he whips out a pocketknife to speed the process along.

The lid pops open after a couple of slices and I'm pretty sure what comes out of me would be described as a moan that Trevor's never pulled out of me any other way before.

Beneath the dry ice, the box is full, and I mean *full* of Korean barbecue. Everything I need for a complete feast, it'll be just like I was back home, crammed in a corner table, arms pressed up against a stranger's as I shove bulgogi, kimchi, and meat down my throat. I'm too hungry to even make a joke out of shoving meat down my throat in public right now. Guess that's what I get for working eight hours straight in a blackout.

When I look up from Christmas in almost-October, Wyatt is still staring at me, waiting for an answer.

"My favorite Korean place back home," I tell him.

"They sent you a box of food? They miss you that much?"

His voice is almost teasing, if this version of Wyatt was capable of it, but I know what he's asking.

The ding of a small bell being rung twice in rapid succession flits through the bar, and the growing post-work crowd continues to get louder the longer we sit here.

"No," I roll my eyes. "It's from Trevor."

"Trevor?" Ice rolls through those two syllables. I try not to roll my eyes.

"A guy back home."

"Hmph."

He could be a grumpy horse in a Disney movie, with how low his brow is right now, that long face. If he were, his upper lip would've fluttered in the wind with that sound.

"Stop," I tell him.

"I didn't start anything," he quips back.

That time I *do* roll my eyes. Think I'm starting to get cranky, because that attitude in his voice is about to set me off.

"He knows I miss New York. This was as close as I could get to feeling at home while I'm here. And, damn, I didn't even realize how hungry I was until I saw that kimbap." I cover my rumbling stomach with one hand and point back behind me, to the stairs that lead up to my apartment. "I'm gonna heat some of this up, I think."

Before I can stand, Dallas is approaching the table again, this time with a red oval plastic basket in his hand, a red and white paper liner peeking out from all sides, and the smell of something distinctly fried seeping into the air around it.

He places the basket on the table—grilled chicken sandwich and fries, and a side of mayo—and heads back behind the bar wordlessly.

"Wha—we didn't order this," I call out uselessly to his retreating form.

"Yes, we did," Wyatt tells me quietly.

My eyes jump to his, and the look he gives me makes my stomach drop, but not because it's empty.

"You haven't eaten all day." It's not a question.

"Did Dallas tell you that?"

"No, my eyeballs told me that."

I grab a fry—food for thought—dip it in mayo (can't believe he thought of that), and start munching while I eye him suspiciously. I *did* say I'd have carbs today, after all. Strangely, my mood spikes on the first bite.

"Your leg was jumping a mile a minute, you were tapping your highlighter on the table, dead giveaways that you're about to enter the danger zone, and you're clearly wrapped up in whatever—" his arm waves at the paperwork I set to the side "—this is, and probably have been all damn day. I know you, *Aurora*, and I know you haven't eaten in way too long. So eat. And wear jeans when you meet me tomorrow."

The warmth in my center is from more than the hot food.

DO I STILL OWN JEANS?

Do I own boots?

The voice in my head scoffs. Of course I do.

Did I have to order them after the barn cat episode, as it shall henceforth be known (not to be confused with the feral cat interlude)? Perhaps. But the point is, I *do* have boots and jeans.

Not a chance I'm going anywhere in this town where the wildlife has a shot at assaulting me with bare legs again.

Preferably, I can just avoid the wildlife, period.

Logic says if I can avoid the rats in NYC all this time, I should be able to dodge most of the wilderness here too. But if I were operating entirely off of *logic*, would I be meeting my ex alone in the woods?

I look from the pin he texted me, the map on my phone, to the location I'm in, and wonder for the fourth time in even fewer minutes if I ended up in the right place.

A small field that leads into some woods, whose trees are dancing in the first cool wind of the season, branches bouncing with the occasional gust. I know October just started but fall seems to have rolled in overnight. Before long, it'll be sweater weather, the perfect season in New York. But I guess these fog-kissed mountains are a pretty good backdrop to autumn too.

The loud hum of an engine sounds a moment before a large navy truck pulls up next to me. My mind runs away from me briefly, convinced it's a serial killer who's trapped me out here, but when I turn and see Wyatt's profile in the cab, I breathe a sigh of relief and turn the Cutlass off.

He's out of the truck and headed around to the back by the time I'm out of my car.

It's not until I'm out of the car and looking his truck up and down that I realize it's towing something, a whole trailer on the back of it. Two small vehicles on top of that.

Loud clunking sounds, maybe a lock or a chain coming off, a ramp dropping down off the back, and I follow around to see what the heck he thinks he's getting me to do out here. Compared to the alternatives my mind is coming up with, I almost hope he needs my help hiding a body.

Four wheelers.

Son of a bitch.

My mouth dries and my throat clogs with something thick when I see what he's wearing, his Southern boy on full display today. Jeans, his usual boots, and a dark green T-shirt that is absolutely glued to his biceps, those incredible shoulders of his, showing off a tattoo that runs about halfway up his left arm. It's caught my eye every time I've gotten a glimpse of it so far, but this is the first time I've had a clear view of it. Something mechanical, beautifully shaded in a way that fluctuates every time his tendons flex. Not that I'm staring close enough to see or anything. All that, paired with a tan, backwards baseball hat, just to be sure I'm rendered speechless, estrogen spiking with my heart rate.

He glances up for just a split second, then goes back to the four wheelers in the trailer, working on getting them freed and out for us.

"Sorry I'm a few minutes late," Wyatt says through his teeth. He grunts at something he's loosening, and it pops free with an audible noise. "Had to stop last minute for an extra can of gas. Think Weston drained mine last time he showed his face." He scowls, but I don't think it's at the trailer.

"No problem," I say quietly, and use the time to get my bearings. Turning in one spot, I take in the scenery, not dissimilar to where we held the bonfire, maybe just a little muddier? Really, a lot of the fields and wooded areas around here look the same, and it's been too long since I could call these my stomping grounds to identify them by sight alone.

Tire tracks run off one side of the dirt lot, through the grass and into the woods beyond. A chill runs down my spine at the thought of going in there of my own free will. This is something Aurora Weiss, senior associate, would *never* pick for a day for herself.

Did you think he was taking you shopping and to a spa?

The voice like acid in my head trolls me.

Well, no, but I didn't think four wheeling was going to be the theme of the day, either.

I turn back around until I'm facing him again, and I don't think the perspective really helped. I'm still close to speechless, seeing those arms flex as he rolls one ATV down, and then the next.

Consciously, I knew the attraction between us—at least on my side—hadn't gone anywhere. I think I thought there would be so much hostility between us, that the physical want, that old familiar need that's never hit me with anyone else, wouldn't have a chance to really flare up. But here we are, being mature, friendly adults about the whole thing. He's been a perfect gentleman, not holding my past actions against me like I expected him to. Accepting my request to start fresh, offering to be friends for as long as I'm here. I won't be the one to mess that up with my hormones and libido at the helm, even if it's all I can think about when I watch him work with his hands like he's doing now.

After all, just because I'm still attracted to him on a visceral level doesn't even mean that a hookup would still be anywhere near as good as it used to be. I've probably built it up in my head, for one, and for two, surely all of our emotions and the love we had for one another was a part of that, too, wouldn't you think?

It'd probably be a borderline hate fuck at best if I gave in to anything with him now, and I certainly couldn't blame him if that's how he felt about me. Most of the time it's how I feel about me.

So, no. I'm not going to ruin this tentative, temporary friendship we've found between us with my horny lusting after this man who I've put through enough. My hormones are probably just a bit haywire with all the added emotional stress lately. Like I'm not enough of a mess on a good day, anyway.

He finishes unloading the two vehicles and turns back to look at me, arms wide. "You ready?"

I shake my head slowly at him. "We both know this is not what I'm cut out for, Wyatt. Unless you're going to tell me you're taking me on some scenic, flat route to a secret metropolitan deep in the Smokies where they have the finest gastropubs that serve only the most delicate floral gins, and every door has a designer store behind it?" The hope in my voice has all but disappeared by the end of that mirage I painted.

Wyatt wants to laugh; I can see it on his face. But he's a strong man, and he doesn't. Instead, he kicks the dirt with the toe of his boot. "Today, Aurora Rose Weiss, we're reminding you of your roots. A little one-on-one time with nature." He waves a hand at the skyline, the mountains, and the horizon beyond. "A little adrenaline, a little adventure with the ATVs."

No one else could make it sound as appealing as he does, I'll give him that. Exploring nature couldn't be much further from the top of my list, unless perhaps you added live jazz music to the experience somehow. One Hinge date at a jazz club in Greenwich Village was all I needed to know that's for sure a tactic the devil is going to use on me when it's my time for eternal torture.

But exploring nature while seated, marginally comfortable in these clothes, with Wyatt Andrew Grady as my tour guide and protector from the wild things ... I guess it could be worse, that's all I'm saying.

If I *had* to go out there ... this isn't the most awful way to do it.

I push my tongue into my cheek as I think it all over and withhold a smirk when I see his eyes track the motion, the way that one motion visibly affects him. At least I'm not suffering alone here.

I shove my hands into my back pockets, elbows out to the sides, and my chest pops out a little with the movement, this shirt I chose just form-fitting enough to make the most of my assets as I do.

Wyatt's eyes shift to the side, to the trees, where there's nothing else to see, and clears his throat, and I have to bite my lip to hide my smile.

Today's gonna be fun.

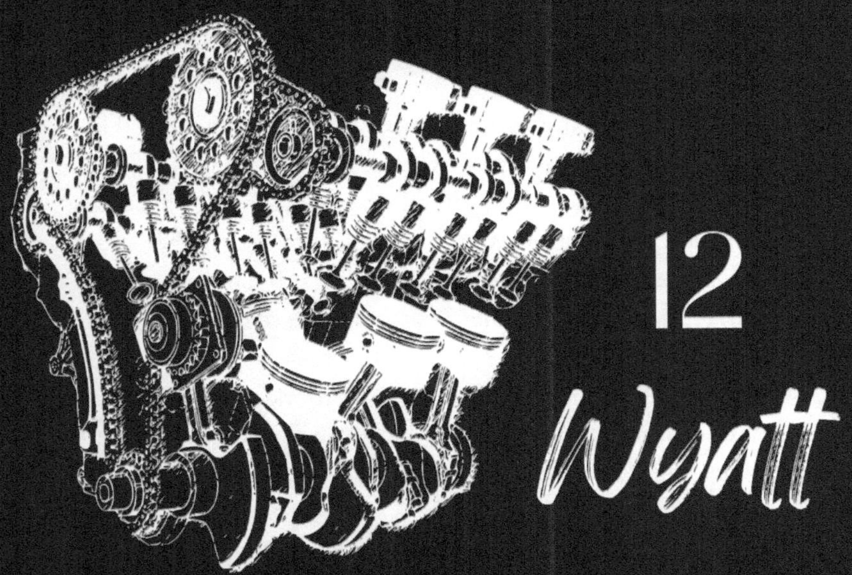

12
Wyatt

What right does she have to show up here looking like that?

A pair of jeans that aren't the tight little skinny ones I was used to seeing her in before, but these are higher-waisted, looser around the legs, and somehow she looks even hotter in them.

That shirt that's tight enough to remind me what I'm missing.

Like I'm not reminded every time I close my eyes the past few weeks she's been back—and, fuck, if we're being honest, a hell of a lot longer than that.

This is bullshit.

No way OSHA would let her in our garage like that. It's a goddamn safety hazard how doable she looks right now.

Like I could unbutton those jeans, pull them down past her hips, shove her over the bed of my truck and take her from behind, hard, how I would've if we were still together. Whenever, wherever, just because she's hot as hell, and that pussy was made to have my cock inside it, and we're way better together than we are apart.

At least, that's how it was before.

Deep breath, eyes on the woods, the mountains, we're here

to let nature do its thing. For her, mostly, but for both of us. This is one of the very few places life doesn't suck for me.

Keep that in mind, rather than how tight she'd feel if I were buried inside her, as it takes me a few minutes to get the ATVs started, moved over to the trail, and to refresh her on the controls, let it come back to her how to ride these things.

"Why do they look different?"

Seated atop the red ATV, next to my dark gray one, at the end of our impromptu lesson, she moves her head between our two rides, their handlebars, the drastic differences between them.

"Yours is an automatic. Mine isn't, it's got gear shifts and extra shit on it. Yours is simpler, it'll be an easy ride for you. It's the one Weston always uses when he's in town." I almost wish he were here just to hear that dig at him. Bite back my smirk at the thought before I'm back to her. "You just gotta hold the throttle to go, squeeze the brakes on the right to stop."

Her engine hums, then roars as she gives it a go, and then she's ripping off, her entire upper body jolting backward as the ATV lurches forward, and it doesn't stop.

I race after her, the cool early October air whipping past me, standing upright on my machine to try to keep a better eye on her, ready to jump off as soon as I'm by her side and mount her ride like a bronc at a rodeo, get it back under control.

Before I can catch her, laughter reaches my ears through the wind. Rory tosses her head back as she keeps driving down the open trail, and she *laughs*. I don't know how to explain what that sound does to me.

I drop back down into my seat as she slows down to turn her head back to me, asking me wordlessly if I saw her, and I sure fucking did. Give her whatever kind of smile I'm capable of mustering these days.

Eyes on her, not the path, and I miss the pretty big rock that

I hit dead-on, and both my four-wheeler and I bounce over it, which isn't ordinarily a painful thing if I'm ready for it.

And I'm not at half-mast.

As it is, my body bounces painfully, and in the commotion my poor dick gets strangled in the too-small tent in my pants.

I let out a grunt as one hand comes off the handlebar and falls to my crotch, face screwed up in pain, and what does Aurora do? She laughs. Again.

If it wasn't a sound I'd been waiting half my life to hear, I might realize what a valuable life lesson this is for me.

Get distracted by her, focus on her instead of where you're going, the path you're *actually* on instead of the one you wish you were, and you wind up in pain. Bruised balls, or worse.

Schmuck that I am, I miss all of that deeper meaning, and I just soak up the fact that I made her laugh not once but twice so far, and the day's only just begun.

The sun shines down on my face, and I feel a genuine smile break out for more reason than one, despite all the dozens not to.

A LITTLE UNDER AN HOUR IN, and more than just the freckles across the bridge of her nose have returned to her face.

There's a lightness to her that I thought she might've lost for good.

She's sun-kissed, pink cheeks and forehead already, and she's laughed more times than I can count as we rode the trails.

Something primal inside of me is satisfied and settles at the knowledge I did this for her. I gave her what she needed. Even if I'm not enough, even if she deserves more, at least I could do this much.

A bit of nature has always done her good, and if you can add adrenaline into the mix? It's a surefire combo. You just gotta work around her aversion to the outdoors, wildlife, and getting dirty.

She's got the most beautiful mind I've ever known, but it's never not going at six thousand RPM. She's constantly red lining, and nobody can survive like that.

I think she forgets what it's like to have balance. What it's like to have a break for her mind. Hopefully today is a kill switch that stops her from burning out and running herself to death.

Stopped side by side, staring across the valley and at the peaks beyond, the view couldn't be any better.

I look to my side and see her there, squinting against the sun, nose crinkled up in a way that's entirely too close to adorable for someone as fierce as she is.

But I guess even a hellcat purrs if you know how to approach it, where it likes to be stroked and pet. And if there's anything I know about Aurora Weiss, it's what she likes. I'm confident that's a muscle memory that'll never go away, not even after more than a dozen years, not even if I went into a coma and woke up with amnesia. My body will never forget what hers likes.

After a moment, she looks back over at me, and her serene smile falls as our eyes meet.

"What?" That attitude comes back to defend her the second she feels any scrutiny.

I sidestep the question with a non-lie, non-truth. "You're burning." I swing a leg over my seat and dismount, walking over to her. Pull the backwards hat off my head and place it down atop hers, facing forward, to keep some of that sun off of her.

She's frozen in place for just a second, then she pulls her

hair through the opening in the back, so the ponytail is hanging out.

"Thanks." It's spoken as quiet as the first couple of leaves are when they fall, but I catch it.

The feel of her head beneath my hands, as I placed the hat there just now, and all the hundreds of other times I've touched her less innocently—held those unruly strands as I've fucked her mouth, fucked her in every known position and a few new ones —it burns in my memory and I shake my hands out, stretching my fingers to try to chase the feeling away.

Fat chance.

I've been trying to forget how good she feels for as long as I can remember.

Memories overtake me, and for just a moment, while I can still breathe her in, I give in. The soft, warm feel of her enveloping my cock as I push into her. The gasp she'd always give me when I bottomed out. The way her eyes would roll back in her head, her back would arch, and those perfect tits would press out, just begging to be sucked and bitten as I withdrew to the tip and pushed in all over again.

My eyes fall down her frame in the here and now, catch on those same tits, and I wonder if she still likes her nipples played with when she comes. I'll think about it some more in the shower tonight, when I'm painting the tile with my cum. If I think about it any more right now, the way she keeps eyeing me, I'm liable to do something about it for both our sakes.

I roll my head from side to side to crack my neck and try to get the situation beneath my belt under control.

We should really get going again before my dick takes over my entire body here. It's already getting reckless ideas in its head.

Turn my back to her so I can readjust on the way back to my four-wheeler. "Let's head back."

Is my voice always that gruff? Why am I just noticing it now?

"Wyatt?" There's something like trepidation in her voice and it snaps me out of it. Is she in danger? My blood freezes in my veins, and I turn back to face her.

Her eyes are darting around our environment like they often do, but there's nothing panicked or neurotic about the way she's doing it now. They aren't bouncing, they're seeking something.

Our path back? She doesn't need to worry. I know where we're going. I won't let anything happen to her, let her get lost.

"What am I supposed to do about ..."

About *what*? Rising crime rates in New York City? That piece of shit car she's driving that she won't take my advice on trading in for something more reliable, because it's bound to leave her on the side of the road in the middle of the night some-where someday soon? What can she possibly be worried about solving out here, in the closest thing we'll get to paradise?

If I can't keep her mind off her problems with a view like this, with her adrenaline kicked up like it's been all morning ... I can't do anything for her.

Those brown eyes that captivate me anytime they look my way are looking anywhere *but* me and I realize she really doesn't want to say whatever the end of this sentence is. And I thought we were having such a good day. I sigh, shoulders dropping, and ask the question.

"About what, Hellcat?"

She whispers the words, self-conscious and a little pissy, but with nothing else out here but a light breeze, I hear them.

"About a bathroom!"

And then, I tip my head back, and a laugh roars out of me for the first time I can remember in an age.

"Wyatt!" It's part whine, part reprimand, and it only makes

me laugh harder, my shoulders shaking in a way that's bizarrely familiar when I'm with her.

She's worried about where to pee?

With all the problems in the world, while we're surrounded by woods, where every animal known to man relieves themselves since the beginning of time. Where, for thousands of years, this is as sophisticated of a restroom as *Homo sapiens* had.

This is what has her freaked out?

I'm laughing so hard I can't even tell if this is funny or not anymore, but it's like the dam burst, and all the years I missed of laughter are coming back to me in this one instant.

I hope it's not permanent.

"Stop laughing at me!" Rory wheedles from across the short distance between us, but there's a break in her words, like she's starting to laugh too.

I extend my arms to the sides, gesturing to the endless woods on almost every side.

"We're literally surrounded by more places to take a piss than even Buc-ee's. Take your pick, Aurora."

She protests, but I guess she eventually decides the only thing worse than peeing in the woods is talking to me about it when there's no other option.

I offer to keep her guard while she goes, but that gets me the dirtiest scowl yet, so I step back and wait about fifty yards away, turned away from the section of woods she chose for modesty— like I don't remember every single inch of her bare skin, anyway —but ears tuned in for those impressive lungs of hers in case she sees a squirrel or some other threat to national security.

When she's back, looking like she's seen things Jack Bauer would be scarred by, patting her lower half down repeatedly, then hugging herself, I hold out a bottle of water I took out of the trunk on the back of my four-wheeler as she approaches.

She shakes her head, wrapping her arms tighter around her upper body, stepping away from me.

"You crazy, Grady? You think I'm gonna take a drink and risk having to … do *that* again?" She shudders, and I can't tell if any of it is a joke or not, so I withhold the urge to laugh again.

"You at least wanna rinse your hands off?" I ask her dryly, and she unwraps her arms instantly, running over and cupping her hands in front of me like an orphan in a Dickens novel we had to read in school.

"Oh, fuck yeah," she says eagerly, and why does that sound sexual to my poor dick? It's not like he doesn't get any action, although he hasn't seen anything but my own palm and five fingers since she's been back. Still. He needs to settle down. Even if giving her more of what we both know she needs is starting to sound better and better.

I tip the bottle so water pours out onto her hands, and she rubs them, doing the closest thing she can to a full wash out here in the wilderness. Once she's shaken out her hands like a dog coming in after the rain—I'll never admit to her I said that—and dried them as best she can on the sides of her jeans, we hop back on the trail to continue the only kind of relief I can offer her these days.

THE SUN SINKS below the distant skyline, rays of light darting between drifts of clouds and mist and streaking the sky in watercolor, the Smokies hazy in the blue shadow being cast by it all.

"Don't have sunsets like that in New York, do you?" I have to shout a bit to be heard over the roar of the engines, but the exhaust silencers on my ATVs cut out a lot of that noise, and I know she catches the question.

"I wouldn't know."

"Got a shitty, tiny apartment that doesn't even have a window or what?"

She doesn't answer but tilts her head back for a second as she rides, letting the wind grab her hair. My hat looks good on her. More of me would look good on her too.

"Or does it overlook an alley and all you can see is straight into another window, nothing but a view of your neighbor's hairy ass as he bends over to pull his muffins out of the Easy-Bake Oven, or what?"

She looks over her shoulder at me, a *come the fuck on* expression plastered all over that gorgeous face, but at least I get a response out of her.

"No, asshole."

"Ooh," I joke. I *joke.* "I see we're both back to our cutesy nicknames. It's like you never left."

She looks over at me and snorts but shakes her head and faces ahead again as she navigates the rocky path. Her voice reaches me above the hum of the vehicles when she speaks again.

"I don't know what the sunsets are like in New York because I'm usually in my office when it's going down, or if I'm lucky, maybe grabbing something from Duane Reed or the bodega by my building that legally passes as a meal before I pass out and do it all again."

I can't even imagine. To not even appreciate the best Mother Nature gives us? They say it's the simple things in life, and I'd wager a guess there's not anything simple going on in that woman's life, but to not even be able to take a breath and reset with the passing of time ... She deserves to appreciate the natural beauty in her life.

"Come on, Hellcat. You seriously have never watched the sun set since you've been in New York? Is the only thing you do work?" Rory's superpower has always been her focus, her determination, how when she puts her mind to something, she gets it done. I can only imagine what she's like when she unleashes that at the job she spent so many years working to secure. But she deserves to enjoy life, too, and I'm starting to wonder if she does.

She thinks about it for a minute, takes her time answering as we round a curve, taking a fork in the path that leads us the right way. I'm surprised she remembers how to get back. We did a hell of a lot of forking off earlier—and I was glad for the extra time it added to our day—but it's not like she's run these trails recently, if ever. Seems there's a little Southern in her, yet.

"I do kickboxing sometimes. Maybe even a yoga class or two."

"Kickboxing, huh? You got a signature badass move?"

"The nut shot."

I think that's a vein of humor in her voice, but my balls twitch anyway. Or maybe that was my cock, at the thought of her getting near it.

Her eyes slide to the side to find mine again, and she cracks a smile. Earning her smiles today feels better than anything else I can remember in a long, long time.

I make the decision a good tour guide would, and pull us off at the next clearing, which happens to be on top of a cliff that overlooks the range. She might've had everything she thought she wanted in Manhattan, but she's forgotten the simple things that are worth enjoying, and I'm gonna remind her of those. Show her she can have something almost like a good time while she's here. Starting with this sunset.

"FINE," she sighs the word out on a weighted exhale, but it's a good one. "That was worth spending my time on. Are you happy?"

"Fuck yeah, I'm happy. If you could use one word to describe me, I bet you'd pick *happy*, wouldn't you?"

She rolls her eyes at my dry line, but I smirk at her and then stand up from the ground, extending a hand to help her up as well, before turning to head back to our rides. She dusts her bottom off, and I do my best not to look, with her backlit like that in the post-sunset glow that'll last another hour or so. Plenty of time to get us back to the cars before it's too dark for her to feel safe out here on the trails.

Throwing one leg over the single seat of my ATV, I straddle the machine and start 'er up. The same rumble doesn't echo from my left, and when I turn to check on Rory, I hear the tell-tale clicking with no turnover as she tries to get the machine going. The sign that a vehicle won't start.

A lead ball forms in my stomach and drops down, something inside me just *knowing* it's not something that's going to fix right now.

That same shrewd instinct also tells me my brother had something to do with this.

How?

I don't know.

But I do.

She dismounts and steps aside while I inspect the four-wheeler and attempt to diagnose it on the fly. It takes some impressive moves to diagnose (that, were I in a less shitty mood after this wrench in the works, I'd be pretty proud of), but I manage to find the problem, tucked deep inside the heart of the four-wheeler. A crack in the gas tank, and it's not new from the looks of it.

What gives it away, you ask?

The bit of flex tape—you know? From the infomercials, and the memes?—still holding on to one side of the crack, that appears to have flapped loose and is just barely hanging in for dear life there. Unfortunately, it's no longer holding the *gas* in the tank.

This has Weston written *all* over it.

My blood pressure reaches dangerous levels, and on instinct I reach for my phone to send a threatening text about the safety of his nuts next time he's within arm's reach of me. But my back pocket is empty because I left my phone in the truck. Why would I need a phone when I'm out on the trails? Short of a medical emergency, but I know she's got hers on her, so why would I bring mine?

Thumbs in my front pockets, I drop my head and shake it side to side, a dark chuckle that I hope he feels from wherever the fuck he is this month and starts running before I find him.

He took that ATV out last time he showed his face around here. Not only did he drain my can of gas, now I know why. He cracked the tank, probably rode it like a damn baboon and got a stick stuck up there or something, and drained the gas. Somehow he slapped some flex tape on there—God knows how he got up in there, honestly—and then refilled it with my spare can, and left my ATV broken, my can empty, and didn't even bother to tell me.

This is such a metaphor for his janky ass life, it makes me snort what twenty minutes ago would've been an actual laugh. Now it's something derisive that makes my blood boil.

Weston *is* that guy from the meme.

Got a major issue?

Slap some tape over it, ignore the root cause, and move right along!

It's his approach to anything in life.

Rory draws in closer to me cautiously, probably worried for my sanity, I must look like a Disney villain over here, plotting how to make my brother pay in the most painful way as I stare down the out-of-commission unit.

"Did you figure out what's wrong?" Her voice is kind, but strong.

Some part of me vaguely recognizes that this is already growth and change from our former selves. Used to be when one of us got mad, the other did too, instantly, no matter what the circumstances. But here I am, losing my cool, and here she is, keeping hers.

What chance might we have had as kids if we weren't so toxic? If we were a little more mature and less volatile, at least some of the time? Without a Time-Turner, I'll never know, but it's bittersweet to know we might've had the capacity to work out if we were more like this back then. That maybe she wouldn't have left if I'd grown up sooner.

"Wyatt?" Her voice brings me back, reminds me of her question.

What's wrong?

What's wrong?

What's always wrong?

"Weston. That absolute fuckup. That's what."

Her eyes move slowly between mine and the four-wheeler, like she's looking for Weston to appear and start laughing, revealing some prank he pulled on the two of us, like this is fifteen years ago.

"Is Weston here with us now?" she whispers in a ridiculous

voice, like I said I talk to the ghost of a Victorian girl who lives in the attic or something.

You know what, fucking bless her, it actually breaks the tension for me, and I shove my hands in my pockets, turning to face her fully.

"No, smart ass. But he used this ATV last time he was in town, and he damaged the fuel tank. Badly." I shake my head. "I don't even know how he managed to do it." Blow out a heavy exhale. "I'm gonna have to come back later with Ronnie and try to fix it or else tow it."

Look between the two ATVs again, like I don't know exactly what I'm looking at, and scratch the back of my head, putting the inevitable off for just a few more seconds.

This is worse than having to share one horse. My four-wheeler has a trunk on the back, and there's just the one seat. No room behind it for a second body, thanks to the gear there. She's going to have to wedge herself in front of me, sitting on top of the fuel tank, and I'm going to have to hold her there to try to keep her as safe as possible the entire way back. It won't be a comfortable ride pressed up against that thing, but it's our only option.

And us? That close? Historically that only ends one way.

I take a deep breath and prepare for the worst as I tell her our fate.

13
Aurora

He *had* to mention choking me that night at the bonfire.

Does he know how hard it is to find a guy who knows how to give a proper hand necklace?

Most of the Wall Street types I hooked up with never initiated anything a shade beyond Tahitian Vanilla. Not even Stracciatella, and *definitely* not anything close to Rocky Road, where I'd like to think I hang out on that scale.

And if I asked for it? They'd either grip my neck lightly, clammy hands too scared to do more than a feather touch, or they'd try to choke me out right then and there, cut off my air flow in a way that's more serial killer than sexy-kinky and I'd have to break out a self-defense maneuver I learned in kickboxing to even have the wherewithal to get the safe word out. And by then, the evening—and my distant orgasm—were always ruined.

How hard is it to put a firm hand around the throat, possessive, claiming, and still respectful while you dick a girl down good and give her what she needs?

Or maybe *he's* what I need, and the taste I developed from a young age was one no one else could ever quench?

Those hands of his have clouded my vision more than should be allowed ever since that reminder. The way they used to hold me *just* right, tight enough without making me fear for my life. How his thick fingers felt pushing into me, stretching me out as he ate me out, prepping me for more.

I've had those hands on—in—just about every inch of me.

Most recently, on my mind, damn near constantly.

And now those hands are in my line of vision, for the next hour or so.

Where I can imagine them back on my throat, my neck, my breasts, further down.

I swallow heavily, watching as they grip the handlebars, fingers clenching, tendons flexing as he accelerates, shifting gears, steering us through the wooded trail with expert skill that's sexier than it should be. The way he works the infinite buttons and switches on this thing with a dexterity that shoots a thrill through me.

I'm mesmerized by every motion he makes to control this machine—gotta be a thousand pounds with us on it—the sheer competency he demonstrates, whipping us past trees, around corners, and across treacherous ground with no hesitation, no faltering in his driving despite the unexpected turn of events and the dimming remnants of daylight.

There's such raw, unapologetic masculinity in everything he's doing, and it's a complete fucking turn-on. Try as I might to ignore it, my body refuses to.

A day like this? Where we've both let loose, relaxed, *joked*, even laughed? Undoubtedly flirted, multiple times. And now his arms are caging me in, extended around either side of me, keeping me secure in my precarious, makeshift seat atop the gas tank, his body warm and solid pressed up behind mine.

My heartbeat flutters in my clit, or maybe that's the vibration of the ATV beneath me? Final verdict: it's both, and my core clenches in response, already starting to ready itself for him at the feel of his torso against me, his legs bracketing mine, those arms engulfing my frame.

How many kinds of fucked up does someone have to be to get turned on from *this?*

I try to tell her that's not what this is, that's not what his body up on mine means in this case, but my kitty says our history says otherwise.

There's not a lot of room for personal space up here, sharing this thing made for one, but he does what he can, keeping his head held out to the side of our bodies, rather than resting it near or atop my shoulder as would probably be more comfortable for him.

I appreciate the gesture, but also, why is his consideration for my comfort with this situation turning me on even more? My body is taking it as some kind of modern chivalry, the fact that he isn't using this as an opportunity to be as all over me as he could be. And fuck me for wanting him to *be* all over me as a result.

There's a burst of some sort of extra rumble through the vehicle as we change gears, probably muffled some for him by the comfier seat Wyatt is on, but with my legs straddling the front of the chassis, wedged right behind the handlebars, in front of the only seat behind me, hips and pelvis directly on top of the fuel tank, I *feel* it.

I close my eyes, try to fight the added sensation it's bringing to the moment, pretend I'm not hornier than I have any right to be for a wholesome day out with a friend, like my nipples didn't tighten at that vibration, like I'm not halfway to coming from this fucked up situation already.

And when he revs again, switching to a lower gear to take a rather rockier portion of the path—I remember feeling like a pioneer on the Oregon Trail as I navigated it on our way out this morning—I'm embarrassed to say, a moan slips out.

If I'm not careful, I'll find myself wiggling my hips, grinding against his toy to try to get mine, like I'm not a civilized, educated woman, just a walking sack of estradiol. But even that has gotta be better than grinding against him, moving my hips and ass against anything I can find behind me to try and relieve this building need, what's turning into a pulsing ache deep inside me. Neither of these options are part of the plan, and I am determined to stay strong here. Just because I'm in front of the most intense addiction I've ever had doesn't mean I have to partake, does it? Or is being in his proximity enough, am I reminded on a visceral level of what I had and lost, and desperate to get any sliver of that back while I have the chance?

My fingers flex into their perch in front of me, nowhere to go, but seeking a stronger hold on what's keeping me tethered to my boundaries, any sort of social propriety that separates me from a wild animal who knows no wrong in following instinct, humping his leg until I come all over it, swiveling in this seat so I can grind my pelvis overtop his until we both shatter and our pleasure takes over everything else.

The hard plastic doesn't give underneath my nails, but my biceps strain with the motion, arms extended in front of me, and Wyatt notices, pulling his head in closer to mine, even as we continue trekking across the trail more smoothly than I'd have thought possible after riding it solo earlier.

Wyatt's left hand leaves the grip, and he uses one finger to softly trace the bright white scar on my left forearm, shining intermittently beneath the streaks of sunlight as we weave in and out of the canopies of tree cover. I think it's probably the most intimate touch we've shared since my return.

"You've still got that scar." It's not exactly a murmur, as it makes it over the roar of the engine and the crunch of the first fallen leaves we're flying over, but it's something close. "Hell-cat." The word sounds almost like a purr in his voice, so close to my ear that I suppress a shiver.

It brings me back to the day I got the scar, and the nickname.

We were hanging out deep in an abandoned field as horny teens are wont to do in the country, with few places to go, and little to do but one another. He'd gone to do something—take a piss, get more beer, I can't remember at this point—and while he was gone, I was attacked. A feral cat, mama to a new litter, we later discovered, must've thought I was some sort of enemy predator, and she launched at me.

Can't say I was ever a fan of wildlife, but I promise you I've been even less of a fan since that day.

Wyatt came running when he heard me shrieking, but I'd already fought her off, gotten all eighteen of her claws out of my arm, and flung her far enough away for me to get somewhere a bit safer before she could retaliate again. But it wasn't before she sliced me pretty good with one of her dewclaws and left a fat gash in my forearm that was bleeding rather heavily.

He was traumatized by the incident—possibly more so than even I was—but he tried to make light of it. Said that feral cat didn't know she was messing with a hellcat, and the nickname stuck.

Of course, once he got me back home and cleaned up, and he was reassured there was no permanent damage or stitches required, he made me feel *much* better, and that scar may have a couple of other memories attached to it after how the rest of that day (and night) played out.

Feeling his finger run across it now? No stopping the chills that break out up and down my spine and move their way down south. I clench my core against the desire pooling there, try to tell myself to ignore how good he feels, that I'm stronger than this, and we're just a couple hours away from my favorite vibrator combination. I can tag team the two of them until both they, and I, are fully drained.

A dark chuckle hits my eardrum, and I give a metaphorical gulp.

He knows what he's doing to me. What this closeness, these memories, this ride is doing to me.

I feel Wyatt's chest move in closer to mine, encroaching on that tiny bit of personal space he'd worked so hard to save me, and then he's pressing forward, so I'm forced to lean forward with the motion too.

The new angle puts me in even more contact with the source of all those vibrations beneath me, and my eyes roll back in my head at the feel of it, but I bite my lip to prevent any more unwanted sounds from betraying me.

He backs away slightly, letting me sit back up for just a second, then he pulses forward again, and again. The rhythm is a taunting preview, the start to a very promising buildup and potential release, and my teeth dig into my lip harder, but I'm nearly certain he hears the noise I make anyway.

"Come on, *Aurora*." His voice is a tease. Just like the rest of him. "Spent the better part of my formative years learning all your tells and signs. You think I can't tell when you're turned on and wetter than the river?"

He drops down to a lower gear again and slows our pace but gives an extra rev to rattle my entire frame from the force of the horsepower between my legs. My thighs tighten around the thing, but it doesn't exactly help.

"You've prolly soaked those hot little jeans, haven't you?"

I shut my eyes and pray to whatever gods haven't abandoned me after all my sins for the strength to not cross this line with him. To not put him through any more torture when it comes to me, when we both know where this will end. Again.

Or maybe I'm praying for him to keep going. Because it's been so long since I've felt the kind of *alive* I am when I'm with him. Where fire and need courses through my bloodstream, and it defies the laws of physics the way I feel like I'll combust if we don't give in to the pull.

We drift to a slow crawl and his voice drops quieter with less competition to be heard.

When he speaks again, his voice is damn near a growl against the shell of my ear. "I bet you'd come if I grazed that clit right now, wouldn't you? Just one little fingertip would probably make those legs shake and that pussy gush. I can tell you're close, even without tasting you, without having my tongue, my fingers, or my cock inside you. I'll never forget what it feels like to make you come, Hellcat."

And at that, I whimper. I can't help it.

His filthy words, his perfect brand of ownership, the way he always delivers just what I need, it's too much for me to resist. But still, I remain wordless. My body is screaming *yes*, and I'm praying, for my ego's sake, he doesn't make my mouth echo the word. We can dissect that fucked up little piece of Aurora lore later. For now, I hope he's listening to my silent pleas for more.

Wyatt's teeth graze my earlobe, which is an oddly personal, sensual touch when no other part of him is directly touching me. His hands are still on the controls, and the rest of our bodies are only flush where we can't help it, and through clothing at that.

I feel what those teeth on my skin do to me on a base, instinctual level, and I can only hope he can't see my thighs flexing, my core clenching around the hollow vibrations, the closest thing to relief it can find. Desire burns deep inside me, stoking a fire of need in my low stomach that spreads deliciously out to every erogenous zone I possess. My breasts, my peaked nipples —practically chafing against this bra and thin shirt I wish he'd tear off me at this point—my pussy, so desperate to be filled and worked over by someone who knows what it needs, and beyond.

I feel his head hovering over my shoulder, in full view of said nipples, which would give me away even if I'd tried to deny everything he's accusing me of.

He *tsks* in my ear in disapproval, or maybe a reprimand, and I nearly drop my head back with another groan.

"Still staying silent, hmm? That's a shame. I always loved to hear you scream for me."

I know he hears the way I suck in a breath at that, and I can *feel* his smirk, even if I refuse to look over and see it for myself. Let him see what he's doing to me. The fucking mess I'm turning into, straddled in between his legs, legs held open by this ATV, no way to hide from the pleasure, already on the edge of exploding from what he's doing to me without even *touching* me. The way he's closing in on me, forcing me to lean forward, make more contact between my clit and the rumbling parts of this four-wheeler, which he's controlling with his very talented —and sorely missed—hands.

I watch those hands for as long as I can until my eyes flutter shut as he revs the machine just once, higher than before, and another whimper sounds from my throat. Deeper than the last.

He presses his next words into my shoulder, and there's no missing them. "Lucky for you it goes against everything I've always known to not give you what you need, Rory, so if you're gonna be stubborn and not ask me for what we both know you're dying for, that's okay. I'll still take care of you, Hellcat."

And then his hands are off of the controls, letting the machine idle at a steady rumble, and one of those hands comes down on the top of my thigh, and the other on my low back. He presses me forward, forward, and I let myself give in to the sensations, how good it all feels when it's him in control. When I'm not the one who has to be, for once. My eyes close, refusing to watch what he's doing to me, but I feel it all twice as intensely for it.

That hand on my thigh wraps around the top of it, fingertips licking the inside of my inner thigh, and I know he can feel the heat emanating from just north of there.

He pulses his hand on my lower back, pressing me down, letting me up again, and pressing me down, over and over, in a rhythm that's going to send me over the edge in no time flat. Probably break some sort of speed record for ATVs even.

"You're still a fucking brat, I see."

His teasing tone is so unexpected and so fucking welcome. My body knows what to do when he talks like that to it. Another rush of wetness soaks the inside of my panties, and when he presses me down on the next rhythmic pulse, I feel my legs start to shake. But I manage to keep my lips pressed together. At least the ones on my face.

"Still trying to pretend like you don't need this? Need what I can give you? That's a shame, Rory. It would be my *honor* to scratch that itch anytime you need it. All you have to do is ask."

His hand tightens on my leg, and I know he's as tempted to put a couple fingers as deep inside me as I want him to, but I think I'm not the only one who's aware I will *not* be the one to cave and ask for it, either.

Do I want him to stop? No.

Do I want to be the one of us who gives in and makes that move? Also no.

But am I strong enough to not beg him for it with my words? Barely.

My body is doing enough begging for the both of us, though. And he's always spoken its language fluently.

Wyatt puts the one hand back on the grip and starts to rev the engine in time with the rhythm he's moving my hips to. He's using his own hips now to guide the motion, and I feel just how much *he's* enjoying this too. That dick of his, that I've dreamt of a thousand times or more since I last felt it against my body. In my body. What I wouldn't give to feel him inside me again. To take my mind off of how shitty the rest of my life is, just once. Just one sweaty session of pure fucking bliss, the way I used to be privy to on the daily. That's all I'd need.

I'm lost in the fantasy of it, imagining how good it would be if he'd take me here, back at the bar, anywhere, really, as long as he could get in good and deep, and ride me hard. We used to be pros at sneaking in quickies, staying nearly silent while we got what we needed from one another. I think we could probably ace it again.

His voice breaks my concentration and brings me back to the present.

"I know you're dying for some part of me inside of you, but I'll give you the next best thing."

Those words tear a noise out of my throat, but my attention refocuses on my center, the way the release is building, just out of reach, but definitely visible on the horizon. Like the glow of a sunrise after an endless, twelve-year-long night.

He removes the hand that's been on my lower back and uses it to fist my ponytail where it peeks out of the hat, holding my head exactly where he wants it as his frame presses into mine from above and behind. My eyes fly open at the pressure on my scalp, the sure grip he has on my hair, the feel of his hardness digging into my ass, all the rest of him, and I know I'm right on the edge now.

"Fuck," I finally whimper.

"That's right. I want your eyes open, right here with me when I make you come, Aurora."

I let out a strangled moan and keep them open but refuse to look over my shoulder at him and give him that satisfaction. Wherever he's paused our journey back to the cars, there's an opening in the trees and I can see the Smokies there, the peaks not far in the distance, one row after another, bathed in shadows of dark blue and black in the twilit sky.

He uses that hand on the throttle to give it more gas, even though we're in neutral and not going anywhere, and the four-wheeler revs in response, the hardest one yet. His hips flex into mine in a fast pattern, forcing me into the vibrations in time with how he's revving it, and I hate to admit that my collection is going to have a hard time keeping up with what he's doing to me right now. I don't think they have quite the horsepower he's putting to work for me.

The smell of gasoline hits my nostrils from how he's revving the engine, a scent I've long associated with the man behind me. Combine that with the fragrance of fresh pine, the early autumn leaves and the inescapable, ever-present scent surrounding me today that's *purely* Wyatt, and my senses are overloaded. It's a weird fucking thing to be turned on by, the smell of gasoline, wilderness, and my first love, but I'm self-aware enough to admit that's what's doing it for me.

With every breath, I'm surrounded by him, breathing him in, straight into my bloodstream and it's inescapable. The air in my nostrils, the peaks along the skyline, even though I'm not looking at him, everything around me screams Wyatt. My system is inundated with everything *him*. The sights, the sounds, the smells are everything Grady.

This entire scene is just so *him*, the way he's gripping me by the ponytail, driving his hips into mine from behind to control my motions, to give me exactly what I need but can't bring myself to ask for—not a single bit of his flesh touching mine, but still making sure I get off just the same—the mountain view in the distance, his masculine scent and gasoline overtaking my senses, that there's no stopping myself from toppling over the edge.

And at this point, I don't think I could even think of a reason not to. Giving in to this man sounds like the best idea I've had since I've been back.

I free fall, adrenaline pumping, no parachute on as I let myself pass go without collecting two hundred dollars, and the start of an orgasm ripples through me.

"This is fucking familiar," he purrs into my ear. "Think about you coming every goddamn night, Rory, but it's so much better to see it again." And I'm a goner.

My sensitivity skyrockets to new levels, my nipples begging for some sort of touch, a little tug, a pinch, a rough nip as my release barrels toward me, full speed ahead. My inner muscles tighten, my ass and thighs clench, and my entire body stiffens as the pleasure builds beyond anything I've had back home, finally cresting, peaking at an impossibly high level. It flares throughout my system in a high that I can now confirm nothing in my impressive toy collection will compare to again, and then dissipates slowly, the waves receding gradually, taking forever to see themselves out.

My breaths come in shaky pants as I come down, and his hand eases off of my ponytail, his body backing away from mine. Sadly, his erection leaves me as he does, and I'm left shivering from the aftershocks, still needy as I've ever been to be filled by him, but speechless when it comes to what to do about it.

Well, shit.

This was not how today was supposed to go.

14
Wyatt

Downshifting gears as I coast down the foothills in the heart of the Heights as the leaves start to change colors is something that's just hard to beat, objectively.

The crisp fall air, the caramelization of the trees—the oaks, maples, beech, and birch—signaling the cooler weather to come, the changing of the climate guards. It's the perfect temperature, the perfect weather, the perfect scenery, just as good as it gets in the Smokies.

Something that tops it?

Making Rory come.

Feeling her legs shake.

Watching those cheeks flush, her nipples taut and begging for things her mouth refuses to.

The rare deep reds, the occasional golden orange, those pops of bright yellow amid the ever-present dark greens of the hectares of forest as far as the eye can see give me something else to focus on for a change.

A rare moment where my fingers don't recall the way they gripped her thigh, her thick hair, dying to slip inside of her and make her fall apart from the inside out.

Lord knows that's all that's been playing on repeat in my mind in the six days that have passed since.

I mean, truthfully? She's always been easy to get off, but maybe that's just because hers is the body I learned all my tricks on. She was my teacher and the altar I prayed to in one.

Rory wasn't just the whetstone that sharpened my knife, she was the smithy where it was forged in the first place.

But for her to come that quickly, without even a single touch from me ... That tells me at least one part of her misses me the way I can never outrun missing her.

Was it temporary insanity on my part, or was this supposed to happen between us? If she missed me the way I was so certain of, would I have had nearly a week of radio silence?

My phone buzzes and I break a law or two to check it, stupidly thinking maybe it's *her*. Breaking the silence between us, what's becoming a pattern since her return.

We hang out.

Nothing for weeks.

Hang out again.

More silence.

Maybe I should learn to take a damn hint?

She couldn't have been much clearer when she up and fucking left you. What do you want from her this time? To tell you to fuck off to your face?

So, no. Of course the text isn't from her.

Does that stop the glimmer of disappointment from settling in my gut at that knowledge?

Of course not. Because clearly, I don't learn.

But it's just my mom responding to my text from three hours ago.

MOM

No. We don't need you to bring anything. Just yourself. Please hurry but be safe.

Something else that's likely to give my newest homemade mental porno a break before I burn out the tape is where I'm headed. Who I'm headed to see.

I heave a weighted sigh as I take a hairpin turn around the base of the mountain we ATVed on the other day, the one that's very definitely on the long way to get to my parents' house. Well, my mom and stepdad's, Daniel.

This could've been a ten-minute drive, but I've turned into a twenty-minute one.

I'd make it even longer if I could get away with it.

I'm already pushing the six o'clock start time of the family dinner-slash-reunion as it is, and not looking for a dressing down from my mama over it.

But as little time I spend with Weston tonight is in everyone's best interest.

Not sure why the wind blew him into town this time. A handful of callous suggestions roll through my head, like one of those cages that spits out the balls with the numbers down at the rec center on bingo night. I don't let any of those bitter ideas past the filter that keeps me from being a complete and total asshole. But I can't promise that'll hold all night.

Shit, it'll probably vanish the second I see his happy-go-lucky face, like he's living the best life in the whole world, hopping from place to place, not a trouble in sight.

Smug isn't the word I'd use for him, but it always feels like he's rubbing his happiness in my face, no matter how humble or charming others might think he is.

To me, he'll always be the smarmy little teenage shit who was more concerned with sneaking out and getting his dick wet than whether or not Mom would be able to put food on the table for the three of us that week.

By the end of my mental tirade, I've rolled up to the house we grew up in. Dusk is hours away yet, it's still full daylight, but the front porch light is on just the same, a welcoming beacon to her favorite boys in the world.

Grabbing the six-pack of Coors by the cardboard handle, the bottles clink in my right hand a bit as I hop down from my 2018 Ram and close the door with my left.

I treat this thing better than my imaginary wife since I'll be stuck with it for the rest of my damn life. Don't get me started on how they discontinued making these in manual transmissions. The fact that it was done at the same time the truck spiked in popularity thanks to a little show called *Yellowstone* isn't lost on me. Folks wanna look like they walk the walk of the country life, but put 'em in the mountains for a few days, put 'em to work on a farm and let's see how long that lasts.

Sure, we've got unbeatable views out here, but it comes with a price. Lack of convenience or proximity to just about anything you'd find in a big city. A tiny community that is your only resource for the things you might need. Reliance on that tight-knit network to get you through the tough times. A hard day's work just to make ends meet, every day, for the rest of your life.

It's not for everyone.

But it's for me.

WHO IT APPEARS it isn't for? Weston.

Despite our mother's numerous attempts throughout the evening thus far—seven at my latest count, in the past hour and a half since I arrived—he doesn't seem to be budging on coming back home for good.

"Life's good."

"I'm good for now."

"Thanks, but things are good."

What I have lost count of is all the ways he's made my blood pressure surge so far tonight, all the ways he's contrasted our existences without even trying.

He's the golden boy, our green eyes the only thing the same about us. Where I've got dark hair, he's got light. Where I've spent the last twelve years as a grumpy, lonely bastard, he flies by the seat of his pants, following his heart or some shit, wherever the hell it takes him, chasing his latest whim.

Good?

Can't remember the last time I used that word to describe my life, or me.

As good as it gets, sure. Not as bad as it could be, also fair.

But just *good?* Nah.

He can take his good and shove it up his—

"Right, Wyatt?" My mother's sugar and honey voice breaks through my mental tirade.

"Yeah, Ma," I grunt, agreeing to whatever she's asking rather than admitting I wasn't listening, and she looks pleased as peach pie.

"See, Weston, we'd *all* love it if you were around more." Her soft beam of a grin turns back toward the child that can do no wrong, despite all his wrong decisions, a never-ending stream of them over the course of his life.

I take another swig of my longneck rather than open my mouth for something less productive. I doubt that self-control will hold for much longer, but I hope I at least get brownie points for trying.

It'd be hard to miss the pointed ring in her voice on how we *all* want him back.

Weston's eyes meet mine briefly, so similar to my own, but softer, friendlier, less poisoned than mine. But something catches my attention when he does. There's a glint of something there I've never noticed before. Pain, possibly? Regret?

Maybe we're more similar than I give us credit for. Or maybe these beers are adding up.

"Yeah, Wes," I tease, knowing he hates that shortened version of his name. "We're all just dying for you to stick around." My tone couldn't sound further from sincere or genuine. "Please, come break my shit on the regular instead of once in a while."

"What did I do now?" Credit where it's due, he sounds more amused than affronted.

"Oh, I dunno," I start sarcastically, "do you remember taking out one of my ATVs last time you were in town?"

"Yeah, and I didn't take your precious Grizzly, I took the bitch mobile. Ronnie's ride." The side of his mouth pops up into a smirk at the dig, and fuck it, mine does too. That shit's funny.

"And did anything *happen* to the Honda when you were out?"

He rolls his eyes while taking another bite of dessert, washing it down with sip of beer, like he's got all the time in the world to answer me, as usual, not a care in the fucking world.

"Yeah, and I fucking told you about it when I got back. Said I'd work on it next time I was in town."

If I try really hard, I might remember him buzzing like a gnat I couldn't get rid of next to one ear, but nothing distinguishable came out of his mouth. Huh, weird.

"Like I'd fucking let you near one of my vehicles."

"Oh please, you know as well as I do that up to 450 CCs,

I'm better than your crotchety ass." He waves me off with a careless hand and my eyes narrow at him.

Our mom shakes her head at us and gathers up a few plates to join our stepdad in the kitchen while we do something a lot more sophisticated than bicker.

"Is that why my Honda broke down on the trail last weekend then? Because you took such good care of it? Because you're some fucking engine whisperer? That's why the fuel tank was held together with damn duct tape and the thing died on Rory an hour away from the trailer?"

I realize my slip but it's too late to take the words back. This. This is why I don't usually say more than six words at a time. I can't be sure what comes out is what should be said.

A golden-brown brow raises. "Rory?"

He gets something close to a *harrumph* from me before I turn away to glare at the wall.

"*Rory* Rory?"

My stony silence doesn't dissuade him.

"Your Rory?"

"She's not *my* Rory," I seethe, turning back to him. "But yes, *that* Rory—Aurora—was on the bike and she got stranded, thanks to you."

Weston fills his cheeks with air and lets it out in a *whoosh*, wide eyes on me, but I refuse to find anything about this situation comical, even the way he looks right now.

"Well, now I get it," he finally says, like it's some sort of epiphany.

"Now you get what?" I snap irritably.

"You're jumping down my throat 'cause you clearly aren't getting down hers." Weston barely keeps a straight face, finishing the line with a small hoot, and he jumps back away from me before I can get my hands on him.

"Get fucked," I growl out.

"You clearly need to," he quips back.

"Fuck. Off." My eyes dart to the kitchen, hoping our mom isn't hearing the arguing between us. She'd probably threaten to whoop my ass with the wooden spoon for upsetting her dear son while he visits.

"I'm just saying. You were way less miserable of a prick when you were getting inside of her on the reg—" His words get cut off, suspended midair like he is, flush against the wall, my forearms against his chest, his toes an inch from the ground.

"Watch what you say about her." I don't need to lace my words with anything but the truth for him to get the threat, the promise behind them.

His body slides back down to the floor slowly as I back off of him and he raises his hands in self-defense. "Whoa, bro. I was just messing around. Point taken."

I force back the impulse to bare my teeth at him. "Next time don't touch my shit if you're just gonna leave it broken when you're done with it."

Weston mumbles something under his breath in a singsong tone, and I might not hear him correctly, but I'm pretty sure he says, "Sounds like you should tell Rory that," and somehow I don't think he's talking about my ATV, but just then, our mom comes back into the room and glances between us, almost nervously.

When she sees the expression on my face, she does her two signature moves in one: try to play peacekeeper between us and try to get my brother to come back, all in one. "Now Weston, you got any pretty girls in your life to bring home to us?"

"Please," I scoff. "The day Weston settles down's the day I'm done working on cars. He will be hopping bed to bed, town to town, until he's in a nursing home."

My mom covers her mouth from my view and whispers loudly to Weston. "It might be time to think about a long-term future with one of your lady friends before you end up an old, hopeless pessimist like this one here. Crotchety was a good word for it." She jerks her head toward me in a super subtle nod, and I pull a sarcastic face at her in response that doesn't do much but prove her point.

"Hey," I bark out with a modicum of offense. "I'm not that old and hopeless. Ask Hallie." Throw a smirk at my mother just to drive my point home. I've still got moves where it counts, even if I'm not a golden fucking retriever who shits rainbows and uses my tail to paint with them like her other child.

"Oh please," my mom says with a roll of her eyes. "You're one bottle of Tums away from sitting on your porch all day just to yell at kids to get off your lawn."

Something hot and unsteady runs through my internal organs at the thought of my home, the porch and lawn in question, in relation to Aurora's renewed presence (or lack thereof) in my life. The same sensation I get regularly since she walked into Suds that first night.

But I do what I can to help my mama out and lighten the mood, since it seems Weston has moved past talking about Rory and I can too. "Oh, so now my life goals are problematic?"

Weston lets out another hoot, and my mom joins him, hunching over the table in laughter, leaning on West for support. Pretty sure they're laughing with me not at me, which means another Grady family night is in the books.

15
Aurora

Ten days.

An orgasm, then ten days of nothing.

A hands-free orgasm, at that. He didn't even give me the courtesy of feeling *him* while he made me come.

That day is where my mind wanders, now that it's back to its usual mode of all things, all the time.

That lone day of mental stillness and quiet, out on the trails with Wyatt, it was something I didn't know I needed.

A stark contrast to the one setting I have: always on.

I wish I could recreate that peace in some other way, without giving in, asking him for another round and starting more than I think either of us might be ready for, but this week has proven that's a feeling I'm not getting without him.

And it's not just the sex that did it.

I don't know what it was, to be honest. The environment, the activities, the ... company? I couldn't tell you what specifically did it. Just that that one day, despite the hiccups of the day, was the most at ease my mind has been in a *long* while.

I wish I could capture that feeling, bottle it, take a snort of it whenever I needed it. Like today. When I'm hoping to get my mom to put some actual thought into her bucket list and tackling some of the other end-of-life concerns. A special sort of hell I wouldn't wish on anyone, but I'm doing what I can to make it ... can I say fun? When it involves her being removed from this plane all too soon? I'm not sure that's the word I can use, but I really am trying to bring whatever joy is possible to her life and this stage of it.

"Are you sure you're okay?" I ask her for at least the fourteenth time since we returned from our attempt at a paint and sip. "We don't need to call your doctor's emergency line or anything?"

"I'm fine, but if you ask me one more time, I won't be."

I roll my eyes and give her some classic Aurora salt. "Excuse me for giving a shit."

She doesn't miss a beat. "You're excused."

I can't help but laugh at her retort, and the tension is broken. But my care lingers. "Well, you can't act like fainting isn't cause for concern."

"And I told you, shit happens. It's brain cancer, Aurora, it's not a bachelorette party. But I'm fine."

She's not. She'll never be *fine* again. But if she wants me to ease up, I'll try. After all, this is all to be expected, according to her oncologist. Fatigue, weight loss, fainting, and eventually the possibility of seizures and even paralysis before the end. It's not the way I'd choose to go if it were up to me. Nothing glamorous about it. But it's a chicken and the egg question. Is it better to have the time to prepare, to be able to say goodbye? Or is it better to always wonder *what if* or carry those regrets, but not have to live with the weeks and months of misery, all those tough times, leading up to their passing?

Tonight's goal was to let Mom live out her younger self's dream to be an artist.

I look at our paintings, in the corner of the room, unfinished.

Mine, a night sky, moon shining bright, the waterline bisecting the composition, but the ocean below untouched.

Hers, so similar to mine, but a heavy streak of bright white running down the canvas where the brush made contact as she collapsed. Not sure we can say she got to check off being an artist tonight.

"We could still finish those," I tell her.

Her eyes travel to where mine are still focused. "I'm not sure mine can be salvaged."

"Or we could do new ones?" I'm sure I could find an instructor willing to do a private in-home lesson. If my mom is going to faint in the middle of a painting, I'd rather it be in her recliner than from a barstool three feet in the air. We're lucky she didn't break her nose, or worse. I barely caught her before she hit the ground. Though, now that I think about it, I can't remember the last time I saw her without a smattering of bruises all over. Has this been what her life has been resigned to? Fainting randomly, everywhere she goes? Could explain why she's treating this as no big deal.

"Sure," she appeases me. "We can try again."

"I'll set it up."

Mom takes another sip of sweet tea, using it to down her next dose of pain pills—with an extra one the doctor said she could take as needed—and I do my best not to let my reaction show as I watch. I try a change of subject.

"So, what else is on this bucket list of yours? You ready to finally make it for real?"

She gives me a mouth shrug and lifts her shoulders. "I guess we could do that."

The Notes app might as well be the background on my phone, I've opened it so many times, trying to compile this list for her.

How do you fit decades of life into someone's remaining

time? Can you ever feel like you've done enough so that they can pass peacefully? I know I won't ever hit that point where my last remaining parent is concerned. But this list isn't about me. It's about making it worthwhile for her. Whatever she wants to accomplish while she's still here with us, I will make sure she gets to experience.

"Okay, so can't check off painting a masterpiece yet," I murmur.

"But I got to see you take care of the chickens. That was somethin'." Amusement colors her voice at the memory of me fighting for my life with those accursed birds, and at least I've given her a half a reason to smile since my arrival.

"Watch Aurora fight for her life and survive the avian flu. Check," I read off in a monotone voice. "What else have you wanted to do or see?"

"Always wanted to visit Thailand."

My jaw drops.

She bobs her head a few times, agreeing with her own statement.

"Thailand?"

"What, did you think I've never seen a globe? That travel is only for the rich folks you left in high rises back up in New York?"

I fight to not roll my eyes at her jabs. "No, Mom, I don't think you're ignorant, or not worthy of seeing the world, you just threw me there. I can't believe I've never heard of this before. How long have you wanted to go there?"

She thinks to herself for a second before answering. "Second grade, I think it was. We watched some video on geography in my class, and I wanted to ride in a tuk tuk. Try the food, see the sights, hit the markets."

I force my jaw to close, try to look like I haven't been trying to catch flies. "See Thailand," I murmur, narrating as my fingers type into the note. As if typing it into my phone was the key to unlocking the best idea I've ever had, a plan forms. An *insane* one, but I think I love it.

"Anywhere else you wanted to go?"

It takes the better part of an hour to get all the answers she has to give me, there was a lot of thinking to be done, like these thoughts were buried somewhere deep inside her, like she hasn't had the luxury of dreaming for herself in a very long time. But by the end of it I feel like I know my mom better than possibly I ever have before.

They were largely divided into four categories.

Try new things.

Recover lost items.

Repay misdeeds.

Spend time with loved ones.

And I'm determined to make as many of these happen as possible. Whatever it takes.

I scroll down to the section of the note I've been working on in between morose Google searches that make cyanide sound like a better alternative than what she's in for.

These paragraphs are for the stuff that's even less fun than watching your mother die: Preparing for it in a logistical sense. Making an itemized list to organize an orderly passing. As gruesome as it is, I'd never want to leave this for her to do alone, or for it to fall to Lexi. And that's why I volunteered for this in the first place, right? We're all better at some parts of life than others. The fine print is mine.

"There's a few other things to consider," I say delicately, the voice of a woman who's negotiated countless terms that meant the difference of millions of dollars for her clients, but perhaps never literal life and death before.

"Like what?" she asks.

"I'm not sure what you already have in place, but I wanted

to help take care of any affairs that might need to be put in order."

She stares at me, waiting for more.

"A will and last testament would be a lot of it. Financial matters. The boring stuff life has to offer." I shoot her a cheesy smile. "Those are where I come in. Aurora Weiss, reader and writer of legal jargon at your service. But also any other ... *things*," I try to put it delicately, "that you might want to have a chance to complete, while you still can." No one knows this woman's limited remaining time frame better than she does, I don't need to rub it in. "Remember that research I was telling you about?"

She makes a noise that says she does.

"There can't be an easy way to discuss this topic," I try to ease into it. "But I want to make whatever time you have left the best it can be. And from the research I did, one major advice that kept coming up was to help your loved one get their affairs in order, not just the paperwork and the financial bullshit and whatever else, but also giving them the chance to right any wrongs. To not leave things undone, or unspoken. Try to get closure wherever possible, and not leave this world with worries, but at peace."

"At peace," she echoes, matter-of-factly.

My head bobs delicately. I know we've made a lot of progress this past month, gotten closer day by day, and she clearly trusts me more than she did before, but this is a line to be tread carefully, respectfully. I'm not yet in a position to tell this woman what to do about anything, and I need to be cognizant of remaining helpful, not just be a constant reminder that she's dying. Feels like my presence is that omen in itself.

After considering the advice, Mom finally shares something. "I stole a dollar from the rec center when I was a kid. It's been bothering me ever since."

A bubble of laughter bursts out of me. Something that would bother her even in death is a dollar she stole decades ago? I have opponents of clients back home who routinely gouge their customers, thieving in much larger sums than pennies, impacting lives, taking away people's means to support their families. But a dollar is what she wants to make restitution for, and so we shall.

"You're a cold hard criminal who should be locked up, woman."

That one goes under the *repaying misdeeds* category.

The other items that she eventually names off are much more innocuous and less exciting, believe me. But eventually we've laid out all of the ones we can think of between us, including telling friends, which she says she wants to hold off on until she has no choice. And we've added a fifth category that most of the new additions fall under.

Loose ends.

"Anything else you think needs to be taken care of while I'm here to help?"

A lull. Uncharacteristic quiet. I sense the shift and peer up at her. When she speaks, it's so quiet I have to strain my ears to hear her above the buzz of the last of the katydids, out unseasonably late this year.

"Sure would be nice if my girls got along again. If I knew you two would be okay and have each other, even if I'm not here."

And if that doesn't stop my heart.

Because that's one thing I don't know how to promise her.

BY THE TIME I make it to my temporary home, it's a surprisingly welcome sight. Somewhere I can let my shoulders droop, the mask slip, and not worry about looking strong.

It's late enough that even most of the Monday night crowd has gone home for the evening, the bulk of the noise inside of Suds is coming from Ernie as I make my way through the large open room toward the stairwell about three-quarters down the side wall that leads to my studio hideaway. I catch something about a trout, but do my best not to.

An angry eruption stops me in my tracks. "God dammit! Motherfuckers!" It's a voice I've never heard raised before, which is what stops me.

My head swivels until it finds the hole in the wall Duke calls his office. I backtrack and poke my head in the door there to find him standing over his desk, arms outstretched on the edge of it, head hung low. Stress, worry, and outrage roll off him in waves, palpable even from the doorway.

"Duke? What happened?" I ask him gently, not trying to startle him.

He turns to face me, normally kind eyes rimmed in red, like that anger I heard from him is about to pour out through any possible opening, but not at me. At the paper on his desk, I'm guessing.

"These motherfuckers at the bank, that's what."

"May I?" I ask, gesturing at the offending document.

"Have at it." He sweeps his arm, inviting me in further.

A lot of unnecessary vernacular in my professional opinion, but the words that stand out as most important to me are *ninety days*, *final warning*, and *forfeit*. The logo at the top is mighty familiar to me, as well. Brown Stone Bank.

"Have they sent you anything before this?" I ask him when I'm done looking it over.

"Sure they have."

"Would you let me look it over?"

Duke digs around in a drawer attached to the dingy metal desk for a minute and produces a handful of earlier letters, stored in their respective envelopes.

"May I take pictures to look these over more thoroughly?"

He nods and I take them all out to scan with my phone.

"Do you have representation?"

Duke looks at me like *what do you think* before shaking his head, lips pursed. That's what I figured.

"Something about this isn't right. Give me some time on this, okay?"

"I appreciate it. Take all the time you need," he says, hands dropping back down to his desk with a loud slap. "As long as it isn't over ninety days."

16
Wyatt

She looks stressed. Can't say I'm a fan of that bunched up thing her brows are doing as she slowly stomps up the stairs to her apartment, nose practically pressed to the phone in her hand, clearly absorbed in worries.

Doesn't take but a split second for me to decide my course of action.

Who else is gonna make that girl feel better if it isn't me?

Am I just supposed to stand by and let her head spin, her shoulders cave in, her spirit drop, when I'm right fucking here?

Naw, not when she's doing the hard thing, the right thing, that the lucky majority of us will never have to even consider. She doesn't deserve the weight of the world on top of that.

Besides, that jean skirt she's wearing deserves an audience who'll appreciate it. And that's not her mom, or Duke.

I drop the pool stick on the felt and step back from the table, which doesn't make my opponent too happy. "Aw, come on, Grady. At least finish the game," he whines.

I've already beaten him at four in a row tonight. "What, are we gonna make it best of eleven? Give it up. We'll add it to your tab, my beers'll be on you another time. Call it a night, old man.

Go home to the wife. Be grateful you have someone waiting for you." I would be, in another life. But that's not what Fate had in store for me.

I follow Fate, up the stairs, to the room she's staying in, haunting me from above my favorite haunt.

There's noises coming from beneath the wood door. Muted, but loud enough for me to hear them. It sounds like ... pneumatic brakes and cars honking? Is she watching a movie? Something set in NYC, maybe?

I knock before my head tricks me into thinking there's someone else in there with her and my blood pressure spikes.

Shuffled footsteps and then the door cracks open, just enough that her face, worn and exhausted—still fucking beautiful—peeks through.

"Wyatt," she breathes, and maybe I'm crazy, but I think she looks a little lighter than she did when she walked up these stairs a minute ago. It solidifies my plan.

"Saw you come in, thought you might be avoiding me when you didn't come say hi." It's a lie. She didn't even see me. But I need an in, and that's mine.

She shakes her head, opening the door wider. "No, no, I'm sorry. It's been a weird week. Between Mom and work, I've just been really wrapped up in my own world." She runs both hands through her hair, scalp to tip, and fuck do I wanna feel it for myself again. Feel how soft it is, then wrap my fist in it. Twice, even. Always had a thing for her hair.

"You're good," I comfort her. It's my default setting.

"Come in, come in," she repeats herself, not quite nervous, just maybe unsure, that head of hers is still spinning, I can tell. My turn to step it up, give her a distraction, break that pattern she's stuck in right now. Only a couple ways I know how to do that, and there's no nature around right now that I can take her out in, so ... I'll work with what I've got.

Aurora steps back into the room and gestures for me to come in. Her bedroom probably isn't the safest place for the two of us to be alone, the way she's been on my mind lately, what we shared the last time we were together, and the way she looks right now. That's a combo that's only leading one way if my lower head has anything to say about it. And shit, I might still talk myself into it, it's an effective distraction for her—always has been—but maybe I should at least *try* something else before convincing myself I'm jumping in her bed to save her from herself. Like it wouldn't be the best fucking thing to happen to me in years.

"Actually," I drag the word out, toe the floor of her threshold with the front of my boot. "I was downstairs, looking for a partner to play a game of pool with when you walked in. You busy?"

Her face visibly clears from the stress of a moment ago, and heated flirtation swims through her gaze instead. Much better. "Pool? I could play a round, I guess. It's been a minute since I've played. You might have to refresh me on how to hit a ball to save my life." Her eyes wander down my Henley, to my jeans as she says it, and I bite my lip at the thoughts written across her face. Fuck, how I'd love to show her some things she's forgotten.

That's it, Aurora. Come play with me.

"I got you," I promise her.

She leads the way downstairs, my hand on her lower back out of habit more than anything—slipping right back into all our old habits—but she doesn't seem to mind it.

Dallas is breaking down the bar—we must've missed last call while we were upstairs just now—but he watches me out of the corner of his eye as we make our way to the game I left abandoned, the nosy fuck. And Duke, from his office all the way across the bar, gives me a scowl that might as well be a neon sign screaming at me not to do anything stupid.

Neither of them realizes I've never had a choice when it comes to Rory Weiss.

I've been under her spell since I was seventeen. I've never had a say in that. Even twelve years of a broken heart can't keep me away from her, so how the hell is a look from one of them supposed to?

Bottom line is she needs me right now, and I'm not gonna let her down. It's me that makes her head stop spinning, that tilts her lips up in a smile, that makes her cheeks flush with life. And right now? This girl could use a reason to smile. So I'm gonna give her one.

"First to land the eight ball in the pocket of the other's choice?" I toss out.

"That doesn't seem fair." Her nose crinkles in distaste, but so much of that heaviness I saw on her before is already gone.

"If you're saying you need a handicap, I'm sure we could work something out ..." I let the taunt hang there, deadweight in the air until she takes the bait.

She scoffs and goes on the offensive, ready to negotiate, such a good little lawyer. "You're the one that probably plays pool every day of his life. You think I hang out in a bar like this back home? You clearly have the advantage here."

"You could have my advantage, if you wanted to." I'm such a sucker. Always so quick to offer myself to her. I would've never stopped if she hadn't left. Woulda thought it'd be hard to go that route again, but here we are.

The tip of her tongue comes out to lick her lips. "How so?"

She quirks her brows, drops her eyes down and lets them roam over me, and it's not the wooden cue stick or any of the balls on the table next to her on her mind when she does. I might not be the kind of book smart she is, but I'm smart enough to know things when it comes to her. The only subject I studied in my high school and college years. She wants more than what she got last weekend on the ATV, but she's gonna have to show me she wants this before I go any further with her. Even if I know with one hundred percent certainty it's what she wants, hell, it might be what she *needs* right about now, I need her to show me this isn't one-sided.

"I'll help you hit your shots," I offer.

That face of hers is so expressive. She screws it up at the offer, clearly not good enough for her. Don't I know it. "That's all you got? You're already hitting your own shots. Barely even a level playing field, much less a handicap."

"You don't want a level playing field? You want a leg up over me?"

"Of course I want a leg up over you. I don't play to get my rocks off, Wyatt. If I'm gonna play, it's to win."

I know exactly how she likes to get her rocks off. With me on top of her, in control of her pleasure. If last Saturday was any indication, that hasn't changed, even if so much else has.

"You want more from me then? You want a better offer?"

Her brows drop back down, and those plump lips tilt up, giving me some of her trademark sass I've always been hard for.

"What else you got?" she taunts me, that perfect pout staying open after she says the word, enough for me to stare at her tongue as it finishes making the sound, remember just how good she uses it.

"All right," I concede, like it's a hard thing to give into her. Easiest fucking thing I've ever known. "I'll help you make your shots *and* you get to name the pocket."

"I'll tell you where to put it, and you'll help me sink it?" It's a clarification, but it sounds more like an order coming from her lips. The confidence in her tone makes my balls tighten, but I keep it together on the surface.

"Deal." Seal it with an extended hand, offer a shake, but she turns her back on me instead, flipping that long brown hair that didn't used to have all this blonde in it over her shoulder, and facing the pool table instead. The way she does it, her ass sticks out in invitation, begging my body to mold to hers from behind, move with hers, and she looks back over a shoulder at me impatiently.

"You coming?" Oh, she definitely knows what she's doing to me, but she'd better not forget I know just what I can do to her too.

"After you." I gesture to the cue stick for her to grab it off the table, and when she leans forward to do so, I step in behind her, closer than I could've had she stayed standing straight up. The front of my thighs to the back of hers. My pelvis to her ass. Denim to denim, or mostly denim to skin with how short that skirt is with her bent over like this.

I hear the breath she sucks in when she feels the contact, and I don't give her time to adjust as I reach around her to grab the cue that's in her hands, taking control of the long wooden stick and lining it up against our bodies. My other hand trails up her thigh, all that bare skin beneath the hem of her skirt, and goosebumps break out beneath my touch. It's enough to get me past half-mast.

Rory doesn't miss a beat, though. She tilts her head in a quick glance around us to make sure the partial wall that's behind the stairs leading up to her apartment is hiding this side of the table from the view of the rest of the bar before she encircles her fingers around the stick in our hands. She pumps it a couple of times, bringing her hand back to rest on mine, making sure I felt what she just did in more ways than one.

A low growl rolls in my chest, and I press in even closer, until my scruff is catching on her silky strands, my lips next to her ear. "Careful, Hellcat. You push me, I'll push you right back."

"Is that a promise?" Her throaty whisper wouldn't even

make it to my ears if I weren't consuming the same space as she is right now, but the way my cock stiffens against her ass in response should be her answer.

"Is that what you want?" My voice rumbles in her ear. I part my lips just enough for my teeth to grab onto her soft lobe and pull on it gently. She moans louder than she thinks she does. "You want me to push you down on this pool table and make you come in front of everyone in this bar?"

It's more of a whimper that leaves her this time, and I feel her legs part ever so slightly before she shifts her hips back and forth, looking for more than she's got. She's stubborn, this girl, but there's only been one time I haven't known how to give her what she wants, and it's not tonight.

"Name a pocket," I order her.

She leans further forward, stretching herself on top of the table, her ass presented to me, nestled against my hardening dick, as she points to a top pocket, obscured by a half a dozen balls. A difficult shot, but I can hit it.

"That hole," she says playfully, then she leans back just a bit, in position for me to lean over her and take the shot.

"Are you trying to make this impossible on me?" I ask her, and she shrugs against me, our bodies pressed together over the felt.

I guide the stick, our hands atop it, pull it back to aim for the cue ball, and she lets out a noise that still haunts my alone time most nights. This purr-moan hybrid that goes straight to my cock, and my concentration shatters. The cue ball cracks against the other balls, scattering them, but the 8 ball rolls off to the side, no closer to the pocket.

"You realize you just sabotaged your own turn, right?" I ask her, standing back up and allowing her to do the same.

"Oh no, you're going to have to press up against me again for another shot?" she asks sarcastically, with a pout I know is there even without seeing her face. Her hips back up into me, rotating over my lap and turning this into a show for no one else's eyes but mine.

My right hand still holding the cue, hers on top of it, I bring my other hand around the front of her body, wrap it around her middle, and grip her just underneath the soft flesh of her breast. Listen to the way her breath catches and quickens before I let my fingers ride the curve of her chest to one of her most sensitive spots. I tug at her nipple over her shirt, over her bra, but she feels it. The way her hips back into mine even harder, her ass rubbing against my dick, tell me that.

"What you got from me wasn't enough, was it? You're greedy tonight, aren't you, Aurora?" I whisper against the side of her head, letting my fingers continue exploring her. "Greedy for a distraction? Or greedy for what I can give you?"

"Why can't it be both?" It's a whisper and a plea.

"Is it my fingers you want? Or is it my cock you think about the most?"

My hand wanders, tweaking, teasing along her skin, and she brings her hand on the cue further back up the stick until she's holding my arm, squeezing me. Her hips rotate against mine, seeking, searching for contact, for friction I can't give her from this angle. Her fingers and those claws on the tips of 'em, they dig into the skin of my forearm, marking me even through my tattoo there, making me wish her death grip was on a different appendage altogether.

"Which do you want right now, Hellcat? My fingers or my cock?"

"Surprise me."

I'll fucking surprise her, all right.

I yank her body backward with me as I take a half a step back, putting just enough space between her body and the edge of the pool table. Use a booted foot to kick her feet apart, spread those legs a little while my eyes do a quick round, make sure no one that's still in the bar has moved to where they can see us. When my left hand comes back down to press against the front of her pussy, overtop her jean skirt, firm enough she feels it, she takes in a sharp breath, her knees jerk at the contact, and I bite back a smirk.

My lips find her ears so I can whisper to her and her alone. "You should know by now, I'll give you whatever the fuck you need, all you gotta do is ask me for it. Is that so hard?"

She sucks a breath in between her teeth and manages to slip her left hand in between our bodies to graze my dick, which is now rock hard.

"Feels like it to me," she murmurs with satisfaction, and it's time to remind her that I'm the one to come to when she needs her fix. The fun sharing an ATV clearly didn't do it, but a full night together might just refresh her memory.

My hand closes around her wrist and peels her arm from between our bodies, and I place it on the edge of the table before removing my hand, leaving hers there. She keeps hers in place, like the good girl she can be when she's got the right inspiration. Bring the pool cue up so it's vertical and use both hands to place it between her spread legs, firmly. My hips push hers forward until there's resistance, and I watch over her shoulder as the wood pushes that skirt up, up, up, until it makes contact with her black, silken underwear, and more importantly, what's beneath it.

The groan that leaves her mouth could be the only thing they play on the radio and I'd tune in twenty-four-seven, as loud as my truck's speakers can go. It's throaty, breathy, and there's something taboo about it.

She's gonna play this game with me, be too coy to admit to me what she really wants, well, I'm gonna give her everything *but* what she so desperately needs. I use my hips to move her pelvis back and forth, over the cue stick, rhythmic pressure that drives her wild. The way her hips are starting to gyrate, her legs trembling, those little mewling sounds she doesn't mean to be making right now, they're giving away just how badly she wants more than what she's getting. She's so fucking turned on right now, she might surprise me and come before I even get her to give in and ask for my cock.

"You ready to give in? Stop being a tease and just admit you want me to take you upstairs and give you what you've been missing? This is the only thing we ever got right, Rory, and we might not know how to do to anything else good together, but this? This we know how to do."

I use my top hand to hold the stick steady and my bottom one to twist it against her, move it against her sensitive little clit as best I can without being down there myself. Must be working, because her head drops down between her shoulders, one hand gripping the stick for dear life, the other using the edge of the table to support her weight as she gives in, riding the stick, my hips as her guide. The pressure and friction against my cock is torture as I roll our bodies, grinding her into the hard surface, side to side, then switch it up when I feel her getting too close.

After one too many near misses, she speaks up again. "And you call me a tease?" It's more whiny than playful, but this is one area I've always known how to give her what she needs. A mental break. Some physical relief, and a release that blows everything else out of her head for now. That's what I can give her. Nothing else that she deserves, but at least I can do that much for her.

"You want more, Rory, use that mouth of yours and ask."

She grits out a response through her teeth, and I can barely catch it, but points to her for effort with that sass. "You'd love that, wouldn't you?"

"Fuck, look at you right now. A shaking mess for me, in the

middle of this bar, and you're still running that damn mouth like you're getting paid for it. This ain't your day job, Hellcat. It's not your smart mouth I'm after, it's your cunt."

Aurora whimpers, and her movements get more frantic, more desperate for release. She's trying to get what she needs without giving in, but she's gotta feel so empty right now, those tight walls clamping down around the *nothing* that's filling her when it could be me there instead. I hold her close, keep my lips moving against her ear, beard scruff catching on the soft strands covering it as I whisper, "All anyone has to do is look over and they'd see you, about to come before you even got me inside you. You're probably dripping all over this thing, huh? Fucking needy for me, aren't you? I wouldn't even have to spit on this pussy to get it ready for my cock right now, would I?"

"Jesus," she moans out the word in disbelief. Like she's forgotten what we're like together. How well I know this side of her.

Her hips start rocking faster, my dick pressing into her ass, wishing it could slip inside of her, anywhere, really, while we maintain the rhythm.

"You're really gonna come right here, aren't you?" I mutter in her ear. "Not even gonna let me take you upstairs and fill you up first? Let me feel you squeeze my cock this time?"

"Shit," she whispers the word, sounds like she's panicked. I know that tone. She's close. Practically gone already. So I push her over.

"If you're going to come down here in the middle of the bar, the least we could do is let Dallas watch." She moans, head flopping even further back on my shoulder, body slumping ever so slightly. Guess she still likes the thought of being watched.

"All I'd have to do is call his name, and he'd be able to look over here and see how fucking needy you are for it. That you couldn't even make it behind closed doors before you had to get off."

Her body starts to tremble against mine, hips picking up their frantic pace. "You want his eyes on yours as I make you come out here, fucking you with this cue?" Her eyes flutter shut, too far gone from the thought, already breaking.

"Too fucking bad," I growl into her ear. "When I make you come, Hellcat, it's for my eyes only." I bite down on her shoulder, my lips pressed against her warm skin, teeth marking this woman as mine once again, in whatever way I can have her, even if it's just this moment, even if it's just in my head.

With my lips and teeth on her, my cock pressed into her from behind, she throws her head back against my shoulder and lets go.

She's fucking beautiful when she comes.

Time hasn't changed that.

I didn't get this good of a view last week, but this is one I'm gonna remember on a lot of lonely nights to come. The way she looks, the way she feels against me as she falls apart.

She starts to slip down with those shaking legs struggling to hold her upright, so I press into her harder, holding her up steady against the table as she shatters. If I had use of my hands, I'd be holding her neck, her throat, pinching her nipples, or her clit, but they're too busy keeping this lucky fucking stick between her legs, giving her what she needs to ride this out. Her sharp gasps turn into choppy breaths against the fabric of my shirt—those warm puffs of air hitting my shoulder through the Henley—then longer ones as she begins to come down, and my imagination couldn't possibly do justice to what's happening between her thighs right now, but fuck do I wish I was feeling it for myself.

I slow the motion of my hips and hands, pull my teeth off of her delicate skin and kiss the spot there, those indentations, before pulling back entirely. She turns to face me and where I expected her to withdraw from me, for regret to shine there, for her to flee once again, all I see is fire. Her eyes are molten as her chest heaves, face and neck flushed with her high and come-down, determination printed across her features.

Aurora doesn't spare a split second, just grabs my wrist and pulls me toward the stairs. The cue falls to the ground behind me with a clatter and I barely have time to readjust myself—make sure nobody else in this bar gets to see what's behind my tent flap, Ronnie's enough—as I run behind her, all the way up the stairs and into her apartment. She slams the door behind me the instant I cross the threshold, then pulls me around in one motion to stand in front of her, her back pressed against the door.

Her voice is guttural, something out of my dreams, when she speaks, full brat on display. "You want me to use my mouth? I'll use my mouth, Wyatt, but I'm not gonna ask you for shit. You're gonna be the one begging here."

She drops to her knees before I can even form a coherent thought and she has me unbuckled and pulled out in seconds. My jeans and boxer briefs get shoved to just below my ass, legs spread enough that they're held up, and her face is so close, not even inches from where I need her, for the first time in *so* long. She's stationed herself slightly to the side, so she can watch closely as she teases me with her touch.

Her grip on me, the way her fingers wrap around my length, nice and tight, the way I like it, I'm liable to blow as fast as she did. Fucking embarrassing, really. Her hands are smaller than I remember, she can barely wrap me in her fist, and after watching and feeling her come between my legs not once but *twice* in the past week or so, my balls are ready to spill at the first suck of her warm mouth on my shaft, I can feel the release building already.

"Jesus." She breathes the word out like it's a compliment, awe all over her face. If she's not careful, that'll be my cum. "You weren't *this* big before, were you?"

I chuckle darkly. "Looks like I need to refresh your memory."

An evil smile turns up the corners of her mouth and she leans forward, maintaining eye contact with me. "Allow me the honor of getting reacquainted," she whispers, and then she starts in on my payback.

The tip of her tongue—just the tip—reaches out and licks the spot where my shaft meets my balls, pressing into the skin there and lighting my nerves on fire in a flash. She's the spark to my fuel chamber, and it's instant combustion. My hips buck into her hand, jerking me in her grip, sliding me through her fist as my knees buckle and I catch myself against the door behind her.

"Fuck, Hellcat. Warn a guy, would ya?"

All I get in response is a wicked grin, and then her hands start working me. Up, and down, the occasional twist and flick of her wrist, varying pressure from her fingers that keeps me on my toes, and my jaw tics at the way she's pumping me, how my balls are tightening and she's barely even begun.

"This is your warning," she breathes out against the skin on the underside of my dick. And then she's tonguing my balls.

"Oh, Jesus, fuck, Rory."

Her mouth pulls away from me, but her hands keep working, sliding, gripping. "Don't call me that," she whispers, and then her mouth is back to work again.

She licks the underside of my balls, tongue sliding up the center of my sac, using a pressure a notch above what would be deemed polite or gentle to separate my boys with just her fucking tongue. They practically jump up in an effort to blow their load, but I talk them down, coax them into waiting as long as they can, because I've been waiting over a decade to feel her mouth on me again and I need this moment to last.

"I'll call you whatever the fuck you want if you keep doing that," I barely grunt the words out.

"Mmm," she hums in approval against my clean-shaven skin, lips closed and pressed against my balls before she opens her mouth and sucks an entire nut in her mouth. Her head bobs below her hands that are still jerking me off, the pressure is insane, and that tugging thing she's doing between her cheeks, teeth, and her tongue, I think I'm going to explode before I even get to feel her mouth on my head or shaft. Who the fuck does this? She used to give me a little tug back in the day, but this? It's filthy. It's fucking mind-blowing. A blowjob will never be the same again.

One hand is on the door for balance and support, so I don't slip forward and knock us both out. The other, I tangle through her hair, finally getting to run through those strands from roots to ends, no ponytail in the way today. She groans around her mouthful as I pull on her hair, her head tugging back with the motion, creating the most insane pull on my package. She switches to the other one, giving my boys equal attention, and I'm not gonna make it inside of her before I blow my load if she keeps this up.

"Fuck, where did you *learn* that?" It comes out as more of a growl, but between what she's doing to me, those rhythmic strokes with that perfect grip, and the pressure she's using to lick and suck my balls as she goes, added to the red hot flare of jealousy that went through my gut at the thought of her learning this from anyone— *for* anyone—but me, you can't blame me.

Aurora doesn't answer me—thank God, my fist would end up through the door if she says some other fuck's name while it's me who just made her come, me who's in her mouth—but she does pull back, maintaining eye contact as she uses her tongue to trace a line down the entire length of the underside of my shaft.

My knees tremble and threaten to give out, but I lock them, not about to lose this moment, even if I have to pass out to finish this. Mama didn't raise no quitter. (Well, she raised one, but it ain't me.)

Aurora's eyes stay on mine as she licks that path, and I know the second she wraps those lips around the head of my cock, it's gonna be all over.

"Fuck, yes," I groan. My hand in her hair tightens and her eyes flare with heat in response.

Aurora uses the flat of her tongue to tease that spot on my shaft, just below where it joins the head, and then she works her way backward again, down toward the base, never giving me the attention the sensitive tip of my cock craves.

I nearly come just from the tease of it, how she made me think she was going to give it to me, then took it away at the last second. Her nipples are peaked beneath that shirt right in my line of vision, she's just as turned on from this as I am.

I let her have the W.

"You're not gonna give me more? Not gonna give me that mouth, that throat?"

Her hands are back on my dick, circling me, pumping me, sucking that release from me like her mouth wouldn't. "Mm mmm," is the only verbal response she gives me because she's using that mouth again on something else. Two somethings.

My eyes narrow on hers, her blown out pupils and that look in them that says she wants me a lot deeper than her mouth can take me.

"You waiting for me to ask you for it? Fuck, Aurora. I want to feel that hot, wet mouth on me. Want your throat to take every drop you earn. You gonna give it to me?"

She laughs cruelly around my balls and it's the hottest

sound I've ever heard. She pulls back with a final lick and looks up at me, challenge flaring in her gaze.

"You're gonna have to do more than that to prep me for this thing." Her eyes point to what's barely contained in her hands, and it stiffens further under her ministrations, her implication.

"Aw, come on, Hellcat. You've always been able to take me before," I chide her, as she keeps stroking me, hungry eyes giving away how badly she wants just what I want too.

"It's been too long," she says between languid licks of whatever she feels like, as long as it's not my tip, or the precum leaking out of it.

She's making sure this is both the best and worst blowjob of my life—the hottest thing I've ever received, while never giving me what I really want, what I've been waiting years to feel again, what would finish this, finish me, in a moment—and I hope it never fucking ends.

She laughs throatily. "I'd choke on you in a second, and you know it."

"Now you're just trying to make me come, aren't you? Making me picture you, pinned up against this door, can't breathe cause I'm halfway down your throat while your eyes start to water and spit runs down your chin."

She makes almost a squeak and leans forward to suck my balls back in her mouth to hide that heat in her gaze.

"Fuck, I think you'd like that as much as I would, wouldn't you? Are your thighs slippery right now, Hellcat? Is this pussy making a mess for me already?"

Aurora shifts in place, giving herself away, how drenched she is for exactly what I'm describing. Shit, she's probably taking it farther in her head than I am. She always liked to be held down, a firm grip, a touch of domination. But I've always been the one on my knees for her.

"You win, Aurora," I give in. "This is me begging for your

mouth, your pussy, any hole in your body. I'll fill them, wreck them, remind you what it's like to be thoroughly used, to have your body owned and say thank you at the end of it. I'll take your face, your cunt, or your ass, just let me fuck you wherever you want it most and give us both what we need right now."

As I talk, I twist my wrist to wrap her hair in my fist again, getting close to the scalp to apply the right amount of pressure, begging her with my hand as much as my mouth. She moans incoherently around me, and the vibration, that sucking motion she's doing where she's *tugging* my nuts into her mouth, stroking me with her tongue, this entire fucking display, it's more than I can hold out against.

"Too late." The words are a grunted rumble, but I think she hears them. "Gonna have to save that for the next round. You and that *mouth* are gonna ruin my plans. God, fuck, I'm close, Hellcat. I'm coming. So much."

She urges me on with her tongue, the determination in her grip on my dick as she pulls the orgasm out of me, forcing the release before I wanted it to happen, but there's no way I can stop it. This girl on her knees for me. Sucking me down like she's missed the taste of me, the sight of me coming undone for her. Her long blonde-ish hair in my fist, her spit pooling in the corners of her mouth. The second I can get hard again, I'm going to fuck her so hard, so deep, she'll never leave the Heights again, and if she does, she'll *still* feel me between her legs.

Her eyes flutter shut as my balls clench and tighten with my release, like she knows what she's doing to me, and relishing in it the way it feels.

"Ah, fuck, coming," I pant out in warning.

"Mmhmm," she nods, encouraging me from that angle she's at down below me, watching intently, and her grip gets even tighter, my cock impossibly harder.

She jerks me, strokes me, once, twice more, swallowing around my balls, and I'm done for. My cock twitches as my release spurts up and out, straight onto the door in front of us with a heavy splat. The waves of release keep coming, my entire body locked up as ropes of cum shoot out and mark a pattern on the faux wood. Her eyes stick to it, mesmerized to watch it drip down, as she breathes heavily out her nose, puffs of air against my cock and upper thighs.

Aurora sits back on her heels, shifts her hips around once more, readjusting herself like she's as turned on as I am right now. Her lips pop off of my balls with a loud smack and I let out a noise that's somewhere between a thanks and a threat. Barely coherent after that torture, but I know exactly what I want next. Her begging for it.

"Get on the bed," I tell her in a deep voice.

She watches me, her eyes wide and innocent—way more innocent than she is—her knees spread further apart on this carpeted floor, probably rubbed raw from rug burn, and I just know her pussy is drenched all over again. She keeps her eyes on mine as she takes a finger and wipes it through the mess on the door, then puts that fingertip in her mouth, licking my cum off of it in a private show I'd pay to see again.

"Get on the fucking bed," I repeat in a growl. "Now." My cock is already twitching back to life, and that hasn't happened this fast since ... probably since she left.

Aurora's eyes twinkle and a self-satisfied smirk she can't hide peeks through, but she gets up off her knees and rises back to her full height, staring me down in challenge instead of doing what I told her to. Awful sassy for someone I'm about to split in half.

With the same hand she just used to wipe the door with, she reaches between her legs, up her denim skirt, and she swipes through the mess I know is waiting for me there beneath those wet little panties. The mess I've earned, the one I'll be glad to clean up.

She brings her hand out again and holds two fingers in front of my face. Two soaking fingers, rich and heady with a scent I could *never* forget. My favorite nectar.

"Your turn," she tells me in a throaty voice, offering me her hand.

I grab her wrist and open my mouth, tongue eager and ready for the challenge ahead, when there's a sharp rap, a knock at the door that stops us both in our trajectory to an entire night of well-earned bliss.

17
Aurora

Both of our eyes dart to the door to the studio apartment, knowing there are very few who could be on the other side of it, at the top of the stairs, pounding at the door like I wish he were pounding inside of me right now.

Whoever it is, I'll fucking end them.

I may not have biceps from a lifetime of labor like the man in front of me, but I've got a razor-sharp tongue, and that motherfucker can be just as deadly. Probably more so, because inflicting damage on others with my weapon of choice doesn't tend to lead to as many arrests as his would.

Wyatt's fingers don't loosen their hold on my wrist.

"Grady. Need to talk to you," comes the husky, muffled voice of Duke.

"Old fucking bastard," I grit out.

Wyatt scoffs in agreement. "That he is."

He doesn't *need* Wyatt. He could've seen him all fucking night while they were both downstairs. What he *wants* is Wyatt not upstairs. Not with me. Because I'm the bitch that ruins everything in this town. Especially Wyatt.

My eyes zero in on the man in question, the burning gaze he

has on me, my hand that he's still got captured in his vise of a grip. Making sure I'm watching him, he brings his head forward until he's directly in front of my hand—held up in the air, frozen—opens his mouth, and closes it around my fingers I've been holding out for his inspection.

He sucks my fingers like I wouldn't do to his dick, using his tongue to swipe up and around, teasing me, letting me know exactly the treatment my clit would get from his mouth if we'd remained uninterrupted. The way his eyes drill into mine is so intensely personal, I flush. Flutters erupt throughout my core and my heart beats between my legs, both sensations I can't remember *ever* getting from one of my partners in New York. And this is from what he's doing to my *fingers*.

Wyatt pulls his head back, back, back until my fingers pop free of his lips, all evidence of my arousal gone, nothing but remnants of his saliva in its place, glinting in the shitty, low light of the room. I'd say it's one of the hottest things I've ever seen, but my spank bank is *full* of insanely hot shit this man has done.

Still, I may have just flooded my underwear. Again.

"Grady!" Duke's voice booms throughout the small room, causing us to jump apart, and Wyatt to curse under his breath.

"Hold your fucking horses," Wyatt grumbles as he redoes his pants, and I take a second to adjust my skirt after everything it's gone through tonight, try to look a little less guilty of whatever crime he's here to accuse us of.

Wyatt stalks to the door and yanks it open just enough for his large body to fit in the open space, blocking me and most of the room from Duke's searching gaze. The owner of the bar doesn't try to lower his voice, making sure we can both hear every word he says.

"I don't know what you two think you're doing, but we all know it's not nothin'. There's enough hardship in this town right now without you two causing another meltdown for everyone involved like you did last time."

"Mind your business, Duke," Wyatt grumbles.

Duke brushes off the rebuke and keeps going in on us both. "Think with the head on your shoulders, not the one in your britches, and maybe talk some things out between the two of you, like mature adults, before you start desecrating my bar again. This place means something to these people. You can at least do me that much, both of you." There's a pause for a few seconds before I hear him speak a little quieter this time. "I don't wanna know what you did to that pool cue or why it's on the ground, but you'd better clean up your mess."

Now would be a great time to be swept away in a flash flood, thanks so much.

His volume is even louder when he speaks again. "Also, you look like you haven't shaved in two weeks, Grady. It's called a razor. Use one. The ladies like a smooth face against their softest bits." I see Wyatt's head flinch to the side ever so slightly as Duke taps his cheek a couple times and is gone.

And with that, the door closes again, a little sharper than necessary, leaving the two of us in the kind of awkward silence I expected when I first ran into him, my first (awful) night back in the Heights, but strangely, haven't felt with him until this precise moment.

The years of history, the eon of cruel silence that followed, they swallow me now. Swarm in, rushing to fill every gap, every iota of space in this small room, and press in on me. I'm left gaping, grasping for a way to fill the silence—the unanswered questions he must have—with anything that makes sense, makes what happened all those years ago any better, makes what we just did okay after all of it. For the first time in all twelve years, I'm faced with the pressure of having to explain myself, having to face the damage I caused to this man's life, to his very soul. At least try to apologize for the scars I left behind.

Duke is right.

We need to talk.

The fact Wyatt didn't ambush me for answers the second I walked back into town, stumbled into Suds, it speaks to his maturity, his strength as a person. The fact that he hasn't held our past against me, hasn't pushed me for anything beyond what I can give him here and now, but he's just been here for me, giving me what *I* need to get through this shitshow of a time ...

He deserves more from me than what I've given him. Time to bad bitch up.

"We should probably talk about the elephant in the room," I say, pointing at the only piece of furniture in here that's big enough for two. We both head over as my head spins to try to find words.

"Eh, that elephant, she's kinda my roommate at this point," he cracks, but it cracks something in me. That I've left him with this burden to bear, all this time.

"I'm sorry," I start quietly, clearly, as I sit down on the edge of the bed that takes up most of the square footage in this room.

His solid frame follows me down, and the bed shifts and settles under his added weight next to me.

"You don't need to apologize," he rebuts automatically, something softer than normal already present in his tone. That better not be pity. Or understanding. Ugh, understanding might be even worse.

How could he understand? I'm the asshole that left him in the middle of the night with nothing but a note after we were together for five years. He *shouldn't* understand. If the roles were reversed, I would've nut-punched him when he strode back into the bar that first night, and probably thrown him outside and let the rest of the locals have at him too.

He's clearly grown and matured well beyond the young man I fell in love with. The one who was as hot-tempered as I am, and almost equally as selfish. There's nothing selfish about the way he's been there for me since I got back. Being my buffer from this town, all the feels that come with it. Keeping me out of my head as best he can when he owes me nothing. Just protecting me because that's his nature.

I wonder if he can tell I'm still the same self-serving girl I was when I left. The one who expects too much and gives too little. Who's never fit in this small town, who had to go to the biggest city in the country to blend in, and still struggles with living with herself there, even amongst millions of other people who probably have more trauma and bigger problems than I have the right to claim I suffer from.

If anything, I'm a bigger mess now than I was when I left, and he deserves better. Everyone here knows it, too, even Duke, who is nicer to me than anyone else in the Heights, but still knows I'm bad news. Hell, he's probably counting down to me leaving and being out of his precious bar almost as much as I am.

My chest heaves with a sigh and I resign myself to the truth. "I do. I need to apologize because you didn't deserve that ending after what we had."

More than the best sex I've ever had. *He* was the best I ever had. Best I'll ever have, I know that now. My—maybe our—issues kept us from working past our youth, paired with my burning need to get the hell out of Dodge, but being around him again this past month, there's no denying my memory didn't even do him justice. He's an eleven out of ten across the boards, only gotten finer with time, grown into one hell of a good man, and I'm the girl who broke his heart and never even told him why. My leg bounces as my mind races.

He lets out a heavy breath and looks at the ground between

his booted feet before he answers me. "If you hadn't left then and there, you might never have. I get that now. I don't love it. I'll never like it. But I see it."

His maturity, that objectivity he's showing about my well-being instead of focusing on how I wronged him, it could take my breath away if I let it. This is the worst thing that ever happened to me, probably to both of us if I may be so bold, but at least I had a say in the matter. He was blindsided, not even a warning we were on the rocks. It's damage I inflicted on myself, on both of us, and I still hate me for it. How he doesn't stuns me.

I had no intention of running into him, had hoped to defy the odds and not be forced to see him by sheer proximity for my entire stay here. It never occurred to me that just weeks in, I'd be *trying* to see him, *wanting* to spend time with him, or God forbid, hook up with him while I was here. The guilt should've eaten me alive by now. But I guess that goes to show you what kind of person I am. Willing to hurt him all over again because it makes me feel good (or more accurately, less shitty) to be around him.

I should be better than that. Not because I have some great aspirations as a human being, but just because the last thing I owe this man is more pain. So I try to apologize, my best effort at making things as right as they can be after what I did to him.

"I'm sorry for getting ... physical with you after the way things were left between us."

"Don't give me that shit."

My mouth pops open at his harsh tone.

"I'm just saying, it probably wasn't the right thing to do." I can feel, more than hear, the defensiveness in my voice, the acrid taste in my mouth of how sour things can get between the two of us when we start in on one another.

We weren't oil and water; we were fuel and a match. We went together perfectly, but when one of us lit up or went off, so did the other. Now … now I don't know what we are, what we might have the potential to be, but clearly it's still something explosive. Is it any more stable than what we were before?

Wyatt gets up off the bed and starts rummaging through the kitchenette in the corner of the room.

"When's the last time you ate?"

"What?"

"Your vocabulary is a lot more impressive than mine, Aurora, don't act like you didn't understand the question. When did you last eat?"

My head pulls back in shock from the random divergence.

"Um, I don't know. Lunch, I guess?"

"Lunch." He huffs out the word, lazy hand on a trim hip, staring at me in disbelief. "It's almost nine, Rory."

I bite back the impulse to correct him. "I was with my mom." That defensiveness has crept back into my words, and I make a concerted effort to drop it before I say, "She had a medical emergency."

"Shit, what happened?" In an instant, the accusation in his glare shifts to concern, worry for the woman who was damn near his second mother for a number of years too.

"She fainted while we were out together. Fell pretty hard, got bruised up, but the paramedics said she was fine to go home. She didn't hit her head, miraculously. But I stayed to watch her for a while."

"So you haven't eaten since before all that," he mutters under his breath, back to digging around through my kitch-enette. He finds something in the mini fridge he deems viable after a sniff check and pops the biodegradable plate in the microwave. "You're too busy taking care of your mom to take care of *you*." He says it more to himself than to me, but I catch the disapproval in his voice. The hum of the ancient appliance fills the silence as he watches the door with determination until it finally dings. Wyatt brings the plate of leftovers to me with a new disposable fork he found on the counter, and hands it to me.

"Eat," he commands me.

When I put the first forkful in my mouth and start to chew, he does this tiny nod of satisfaction, and then he starts talking.

"You can be sorry for a lot of things, Aurora, but don't be sorry for giving in to what we both wanted. We're adults. We're not kids anymore. If we need to scratch an itch, there's no reason you can't scratch my back and I scratch yours. You wanna talk shit out so we can keep doing that without feeling bad about it, I'm all ears. But don't you try to fucking give me some shit about not doing it again when we both know you damn well want to."

"How do you not hate me, Wyatt?"

He shrugs. "A lot of water has gone under that particular bridge. Can't say I would've reacted as well if you'd come back ten years ago, or five. But I've had time to process. And it's not like you're here to rub in my face how well you're doing. You're here because your mom is dying. Come on, what do you think, I don't have a heart? I know you don't want to be here a second longer than you have to be. Couldn't be plainer on your face that you can't wait to get the hell out of the Heights again. But is it really such a terrible idea to make your trip a little less shitty by spending a few nights together, here and there?" A shoulder bumps up into his cheek again. "It'd make my life a little more rewarding, at least."

"Do you really think that's smart? Do you think we can get involved again?"

Lord knows it's hard for me to even see him, much less be around him, without being attracted to him. Wanting the physical aspect with him. Kinda thought time would've taken that out of my system, but it's only intensified, apparently. All the ways he's evolved are apparently exactly what some huge part of me has been looking for (and not finding) in NYC.

"I don't see any reason not to. Might as fucking well."

"Not to sound pessimistic, but I think any semblance of a repeat of last time would be a good enough reason not to."

"I'm not saying we should date. Plan our future together, name our kids." Again.

The cozy cottage-cabin combo we were going to build ourselves out in the woods. (Okay, he was going to build it while I admired him from the sidelines, there to thank him for all his work for our future after a long, hard day of physical labor, and make sure he felt inspired to keep going on it the next day.) With a yard that's just a meadow full of flowers in the spring, where we'd do a bonfire in the fall. The house with the windows I could open outward anytime it snowed and put an arm through the opening to catch snowflakes while still staying warm, drinking my hot apple cider. Where we'd raise our one son, Axle, with his cousins from Lexi and, eventually, Weston.

My eyes sting, so I blink away the thought.

"Definitely not," I agree.

"I know you had to leave. You had your reasons, whatever they were. I'm just happy you found what you were looking for."

Hah. Found what I was looking for. I'm still running, is the pathetic truth of it. Still haven't found a way to stay still without feeling like everything is crumbling in on me, but that's my burden to bear, not his. He doesn't need my shit, he's probably got his own. It takes a moment to swallow the final bite, and I stand up to throw out my plate and fork before turning to face him again, somehow feeling more even-tempered already.

"So what are you proposing, exactly?"

Another careless shrug, but I see through it. He wants this. For some reason, he wants to keep seeing me.

"We keep hooking up, trade some Os while you're here."

I actually laugh a little at him. "Make it sound more clinical, why don't you?"

His eyes twinkle at me as I step between his legs. "What do you want me to say? I'll get you off, if you wanna get me off, I'm down for that too?"

My head tilts back and a real laugh bursts out of me. "So fucking romantic."

The corner of his lips tilts up in a rare sighting of humor. "Don't bullshit me, Hellcat. You don't want romance from me. You want my cock."

"You make it sound cheap and dirty."

"You like it dirty," he throws back. "You just also like it expensive." A genuine smile breaks out across my face.

"I mean, I wouldn't hate banging you while I'm here."

"Gee, thanks," he mutters, with zero offense taken, as I keep talking, unbothered by the interruption.

"But we both need to know what this is. I'll feel guilty till the day I die about what I did to you last time. The only way I'm agreeing to this is if we stay clear on what this is."

"Clear as the Heights River to me, Hellcat. I get your pussy, not your head, not your heart." He holds his hands up in front of him. "More than I've had in a long time. I can live with that."

I push my tongue into my cheek, watching him closely as I think it over.

"How is this going to work?" I ask him.

"You're the contract whisperer, the professional negotiator. Isn't this your specialty? Don't you get paid to make deals and lay out terms? You tell me."

"Hmm." I tap my finger on my chin in mock thought. "A mutually beneficial arrangement. I think I can draw up something agreeable."

"I consent to an oral arrangement, if you do."

I reach out a hand and shove his shoulder playfully, and his arms come up to catch around my waist as an excuse to hold himself in place. The tips of his fingers trace the curve of my back as he opens up.

"Look, the past is the past," he tells me seriously. "I can keep it there, take what I can get while you're here. I think I'm man enough to act like an adult about this, if you are."

It's worth taking a second to consider the potential pitfalls and downsides to the arrangement before jumping in with my kitty doing my thinking for me. My ovaries have always wanted this man. I need to be sure the rest of me can handle this too.

Truthfully, there were good parts to us. There were *great* parts. But there was toxic shit too. We had our issues. The way we fought. The way we would never put one another ahead of our own wants. Am I naïve enough to think that none of that will rear its head this time? Or have we possibly outgrown that?

By setting boundaries, maintaining clarity on exactly what this is and isn't, are we really able to enjoy one another's company while I'm here, and both come out unscathed the next time I leave this foggy, sleepy town nestled in the Smokies for the hustle and bustle of the Big Apple and never look back?

Maybe it's the lack of good sex I've had since him, and this giant carrot (pun intended) dangling in front of me right now. Maybe it's the lack of anything halfway decent in this season of my life. Facing all my demons to say goodbye to my mother, while eating shit for decisions I made as essentially a child from just about everyone around me.

Wyatt might be the only one who's treating me with dignity, kindness, decency, and appreciation. He is rapidly (okay, tonight moved him *way* up the list) becoming the best part of my stay here. Why shouldn't I get more of him?

Without the feelings, the emotional side we would get so wrapped up in, we can do what we do best. Fuck each other's brains out, give each other some dopamine hits, and go our separate ways again.

For me, it'll be something to look forward to, something to take my mind off the hellhole that is watching my only remaining parent slip away a handful of cells at a time, while being surrounded by everything I sacrificed my entire life to escape.

It'll be a way to stock up on a fresh batch of the kind of memories I'll need to rely on to get off when I'm back beneath Trevor, or any other of the lackluster suitors I've had back home.

Maybe it's selfish of me to give in so quickly, to see all the ways this could serve me, instead of the potential of hurting him, but I never claimed to be a good person. Just one trying to get through this mess I call my current reality.

"You've got yourself a deal," I tell him, hands on his firm shoulders. "Your cock is mine, for as long as I'm here. Then you can have it back."

"Shit, Hellcat, I'm not gonna have any use for it when you're not around." He's got a teasing smile on his face, but I can't tell if it's a joke.

We discuss the terms until we reach an agreement. Very mature of us. For all my prowess in conference rooms, my personal life has never been put together in quite the same way. There's something satisfying about all this. Having precise expectations, what will be offered and what will be gained from the pact.

This arrangement is not to exceed the end of Aurora's stay in Smoky Heights.

No feelings are to get involved, only genitals.

We both continue our normal lives and routines, no expectations other than the occasional physical release when our schedules align. My mom is my priority, so is keeping up on my work from afar, and those will always come first.

No other partners during this time. (Obviously, but we're being thorough here.)

And lastly, we leave the past dead and buried.

It's near midnight by the time we've laid out the "terms," and Wyatt tells me he's going to take care of the cue stick and "some other things the bar needs done." We say good night, goodbye for now, and agree to text later this week about when to meet up next. It's the first night I fall asleep without the cityscape noises playing on the iPad, and I don't even realize it.

I spend the bulk of the next day diving into my project for Duke, and I tap in some resources from back home to help me with some specialized research.

But the next time I enter the bar, later that evening, my nose is tucked into my phone again—as per usual—reviewing the response I got, and I don't think about it. On instinct, I use the right-hand door when entering Suds. Except, I don't get a splinter. The handle is completely smooth, freshly sanded.

18
Aurora

Red and white lights.

Mechanical clatter.

Wheels rolling over pavement.

Voices, questions I struggle to answer.

I'm shaking, but that's not what's important.

I haven't stopped shaking since twenty minutes ago, the second worst phone call of my life. At least she has.

"911, what's your emergency?"

"My mom, she's ..."

For someone who remains composed and able to put words together in stressful situations for a living, I'm really failing at this.

"Ma'am? What's going on with your mom?"

A strangled cry leaves my lips, and I hold the mouthpiece of the phone away from my face so the operator doesn't have to hear it. I take a quick inhale to compose myself, remember who I am and why I'm here.

I'm the best chance at helping my mom through this.

I'm the one who doesn't get emotional and fuck shit up when things are on the line.

I'm the one who's going to help her remain as comfortable as possible for the rest of her life.

That clicks my left frontal lobe out of neutral and into first gear, and I'm back.

"My mom needs an ambulance."

At least my mom's stopped twitching and jerking, where she lies on the gurney. It won't stop replaying in my mind, though. I doubt it ever will.

The EMTs lead the way into their entrance at the ER, and I follow behind, numbly.

A slew of nurses, technicians, and other medical staff are waiting and join our entourage as soon as we make it through the swinging doors of the bay, which is where the pace picks up and we start to jog.

"Female, fifty-four years old. Grade four brain cancer. First seizure, according to the patient's daughter. Fell and hit her head, in stable condition now. Heart rate still high, blood pressure one-thirty over eighty-six. Vitals are still coming back to normal. May have a brain hemorrhage, needs an MRI if the patient's oncologist authorizes it." I barely register the words the staff are saying, my mind preoccupied with replaying the clip of her, not even a half an hour ago.

Lexi's squawk breaks through my haze, it reaches me before my eyeballs can even try to locate her body within the buzz of the chaos in this hallway. "MOM! Is my mom okay?" Her voice is fevered chaos, pure distress. I know because it's exactly how I feel. I recognize it instinctually, by vibe alone.

"How did she even get back here?" one of the EMTs mutters.

One of the techs who is now trotting next to my mom's stretcher, a guy I grew up with who hasn't looked at me once so far, by the name of Shawn, answers them. "She's got connections here. The local hookup. You're still new here, but you'll see it in action the more you're around.

"Lex," I call out. Not Alexis. My throat barely cooperates. Now that my mom is under medical supervision, someone else is responsible for saving her, my faculties have almost entirely abandoned me again. That brief moment where I felt the pressure of not letting her slip away, not letting her pass on my watch, it's gone, and without that burden of responsibility, so is my ability to be the person Mom needed me to be.

Since then, a whole new level of fear has set in, facing a future without my mom. Not in some far-off, distant time, but imminently. Those remaining seven months feel a lot shorter since I watched her collapse. It all seemed so esoteric when she's looked (and mostly acted) fairly normal up until now. A little sleepy, a little bruised, a lot more pills to take. But mostly still the mom I've always known.

Seeing her frail, nearly lifeless, completely helpless as to what was happening ... For all the ways I thought I could do this, after today, I'm wondering if I really can. Sit by and try to remain strong and unaffected while I watch the woman who raised me—despite our estrangement, despite the space I forced between us—to have to watch her lose her capacities, her faculties, her life force? I might be strong in a lot of ways but getting a glimpse of what this will look like as she worsens has given me a lot to rethink as soon as we're past this moment.

Lexi's eyes fly to mine in a panic that is echoed throughout my entire being right now, but I can't let her see it. She needs me now, more than Mom does, which brings back some of my steel determination, my need for composure.

"Rory, thank God. What the hell happened?" Lexi—still in her work uniform—grabs my arm, short nails digging into the soft flesh there like I'm her anchor, keeping her from floating into the abyss of panic, and I brace against the wince that wants to show. She needs me to be strong. I can do that for her. That's why I'm here, after all.

My armor chinks back into place, the facade I'm so used to wearing. It's never been this difficult to put it on before, but I do it for them. For both of them.

"Mom had a seizure. She's fine, Alexis."

"She's clearly not *fine*, Rory, she looks half dead!" Lexi's arm flails and points to our mother's ashen body, rolling through the halls of the only hospital in the region, medical staff swarming her, doing their job of keeping her alive on the way to the room she was assigned en route.

"She's not half dead, she's just passed out from the seizure. This is what the oncologist warned us about. It's expected with her diagnosis. She's better off than she looks." That last part might not be true, I can't vouch for it, but Lexi freaking out won't help her wake up any faster. If anything, it'll stress her out, annoy the staff, and get us kicked out. And I'm *not* not staying by my mother's side right now after what I just witnessed. The way my stomach bottomed out, dropped down to my feet and then kept going. How she fell to the floor, for the second time in recent memory, but *so* much worse than before.

The twitching, the jerking, the way her eyes rolled back and she lost consciousness. I thought it was the end for her. And in some ways, I think it would've been a kinder end than what she's in store for. Another six-ish months of slowly escalating torture on her body, mind, and spirit. And, much less importantly, on that of those of us who love her.

But I've never been so thankful to see eyes just like my own staring back at me as nearly three hours after she got admitted to the ER, when she finally opens them.

"Girls," my mother croaks out, her voice wispy and crackling in ways it didn't used to. I pretend it's only because she's parched.

Both Lexi and I jump up from our chairs and are by either side of her in an instant. Since I go straight for the remote to call her nurse, Lexi takes her left hand before I get the chance to pick up her right, and she grabs it a little too forcefully. I can see Mom shrink back in pain, so I speak up on her behalf. "Don't break her bones, Lex, they're gonna make her stay an extra week if you do that. She's already gonna have to be here for days as is." Lexi scowls at me, face pinched up like she's trying to skin me with her laser stare, but she loosens her grip and Mom's face relaxes.

Instead of holding her hand like I want to and risk hurting her out of my own need to assure myself she's really still here, she's some form of okay (for now), I run the back of my fingers up and down her forearm soothingly, while grappling with the other hand for the damn remote. I press the call button as fast as I can find it and turn the entirety of my attention back on my family.

"What's today?"

"It's Friday, Mom." Lexi beats me to it, again.

"Remind me what happened?"

Lexi and I trade unsure glances. Does she not remember? Or is she just foggy from the blackout? If she has a lapse in memory, is it from the fall? The seizure itself? Or the glioblastoma? I'm not ready for her condition to worsen to the point she loses her short-term memory. After that, it might be her long-term memory. If the day comes where she doesn't recognize me? I don't care how strong I've tried to be for her, that's something I wouldn't survive.

"We were at the rec center, Mom, do you remember that?"

"The rec center?"

"Yeah, you were giving them back the money you'd stolen," I say gently.

Lexi's worried gaze on mine reinforces my determination to

not make this harder on either of them. After all the pain I've caused them, this is something I can make better. Calm, cool, no trace of panic evident. Emit the energy we need here, and they'll match it. That's the theory, right? I shoot for breaking the solemnity.

"You gave everyone there a good laugh with your story of how you stole it by distracting the attendant with a possum you'd snuck in the building and let loose." Can't tell if my attempt at jogging her memory is bringing anything back for her, but I keep trying. "When the poor woman up front screamed and ran for help, you took the only dollar they had in the collection box, grabbed the possum, and ran back out. Then you told everyone this morning how you'd tried to keep it as a pet, named it Dolly Possum, hid it under your bed for weeks, barricaded in there, until the smell got so bad your dad tore apart your room and tanned your hide so bad you couldn't sit for days."

She chuckles, and Lexi's face lightens a bit, as does my heart. "You had a whole crowd enraptured this morning. And on the way out," I remind her tenderly, "you had a seizure and fell to the concrete floor."

"Right, right," she says, nodding her head in tiny movements, like it's all familiar to her, but neither of her daughters are convinced.

Selfishly, my heart drops even further at the realization the big surprise I've been working on isn't going to be possible now. I don't need someone in a white coat to tell me she's taken a turn for the worse at this point and that she needs to take it easy.

Putting her through the physical strain my plan involved would be too chancy with how quickly she's deteriorating. The risk would far outweigh the benefit, and accepting defeat on bringing one of her dreams to life is going to be a tough pill for me to swallow. Almost as difficult as realizing she's slipping down this slide faster than I'm ready or able to deal with.

"Mrs. Weiss, you're awake!" The chipper nurse assigned to Mom walks in, rubbing sanitizer on her hands, smiling brightly at my mom in the upright bed.

"It's Laura Lee, dear," my mom corrects her, and I bite back a smile. That sounded more like her normal self.

"Okay, Miss Laura Lee, I'll write that on the board over here. How are you feeling?"

"Higher than I was at Woodstock."

Something resembling a guffaw bursts out of me, and Lexi shrieks, "Mom, you didn't go to Woodstock. You weren't even alive then."

"Okay, then, higher than I was when I got pregnant with Lexi." Both Lexi and I pull faces of disgust, and our mom makes an apologetic frown. "I was trying not to paint you a word picture, but you had to call me out, so you're getting specifics."

The curvy nurse with the radiant smile chuckles at the three of us. "I bet you're feeling pretty good right now, Laura Lee. The ER doctor consulted with your care team, and since pain management is the current objective of your treatment plan, they went ahead and gave you the okay for some of the good stuff so you wouldn't feel too many effects of that little spill you took today. You're also on something to reduce the swelling in your brain after all that, mmkay, and hopefully we can keep you from having another seizure anytime soon. For now, you're on concussion protocol and we're going to be keeping you under observation for a few days just to be extra safe, all right? Your oncologist wants to make sure nothing else flares up after that fall, but the doctor will come in and explain that to you and answer any questions you may have shortly, mmkay."

Mom doesn't show any further memory difficulties or other concerning behavior while the nurse is with us, and when the doctor comes in later to talk things over with her, discuss her results from the scans they did and explain why they want her to stay in the hospital for at least seventy-two hours for observation, possibly longer, she doesn't even put up a fight. She just looks between Lex and me and says, "You girls better keep them chickens alive while I'm here. Between the two of you. Lexi knows what to do."

We both just nod, our eye contact after her request surprisingly uncharged. This might be the first time she and I have agreed on anything, the afternoon spent in Mom's hospital room the longest we've gone without nasty barbs at one another or trying to annoy the other. Both willing to set aside long-standing issues, petty ones, too, in the name of more important things.

The first sign of peace, perhaps?

A temporary treaty, at least.

We break that eye contact when the doctor does her best to answer our biggest question. Why did Mom have a seizure, what can we do to stop it from happening again?

"Truthfully, no one really knows why seizures are a common part of this path," she explains. "All we can do is hypothesize as to what interrupted the electrical impulses to trigger the seizure." Her kind brown eyes bounce from Mom to Lexi to me. "One possible explanation is that as the tumor grows, it's compressing other areas of your brain. There is only so much room to expand, the skull is rather immovable, as you might imagine. So the soft tissue is what gives. In this case, it's possible the neural network within the white matter was affected by the growth for some reason. I'm sure your oncologist has prepared you for what to expect as this progresses. Personally, I'd say you were lucky to go this long into your journey without suffering from them, but we're going to do what we can while you're here to try to keep you stabilized."

After the ER doctor leaves with a final order for her to rest up, Mom makes Lex and me agree to go home and rest ourselves, not be (and I quote) "helicopter daughters by her side for the rest of her stay," and as much as I want to fight her on it, to show up anyway—for my benefit, if not hers—I see the look in her eyes. The fire that is so often present in my bathroom mirror back in New York on the mornings before a particularly high-stakes contract negotiation. And I know not to push her on it. So I agree, even if it kills me to do so.

I don't know how many days I really have left with her, and I won't be taking any of them for granted again. I've got a lot of life to fit in whatever time she has left. Maybe it's how frail she looks in this bed, the indelible change I scent in the air after this morning—like I can feel on some innate level her worsening by the hour now—but something tells me it won't be six more months we get together.

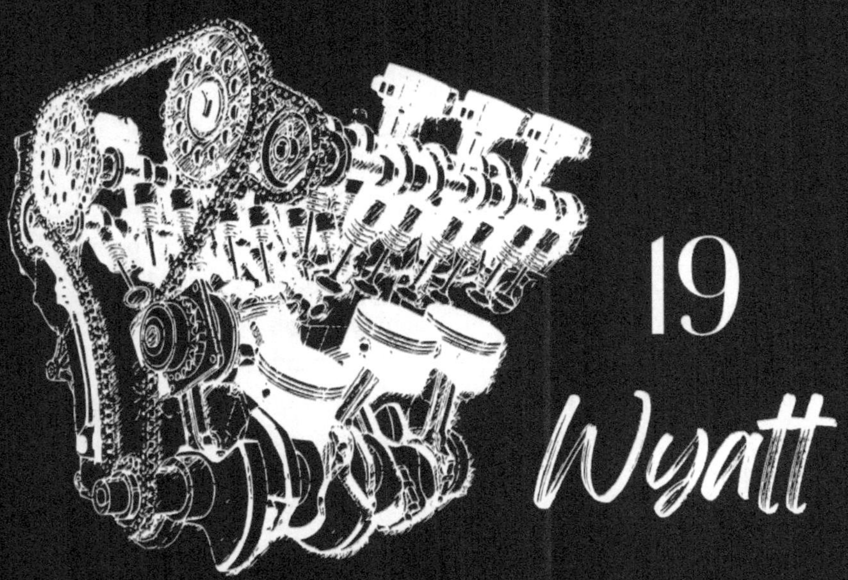

19

Wyatt

The logs in the bonfire pop, crackle, and hiss as the flames rise higher into the night.

Aside from the soft whistle of the occasional gust of autumn air, the voices of old friends—mostly acquaintances I'm stuck with for decades and have been since grade school—surround me, raucous laughter and the sounds of enjoying life everywhere I look. It's a bit salt-in-the-wound if you ask me. The inescapable reminder that everyone else got to enjoy themselves beyond their early twenties. I'm the only sad sack who's been walking around this town half-miserable since then.

Though, admittedly, a lot less miserable these past weeks. And, okay, this past week most of all. The sight of Rory Weiss, on her knees, my cum spraying all over the wall right next to her flawless face as she stroked and licked me ... It's helped a lot.

Except she hasn't reached out to initiate another round, and call me idiotic, but I was convinced she would when I left her place that night. I know she felt better after what we did, even the tough talk after we got interrupted was a success.

With how high strung she is normally, how over-the-top stressed she's been, I know she could use another release like that. One that she's welcome to access any time she wants, thanks to our new pact.

Kind of surprised it's been seven days of radio silence. I could understand during the week, between her mom's appointments, their outings together, plus her workload. But I thought maybe Saturday might be our chance to get together, and I didn't even hear from her yesterday. I've even been avoiding the bar a bit, trying to give her some space so I don't come off like a needy fuck, but she's holding out longer than I thought she would. If I wasn't there, hadn't seen how hard she came, I might get a complex wondering if she didn't enjoy herself, but I know she did.

Bring my Solo cup up to my lips and take a deep pull of the borderline tepid liquid as I take in the turning treetops along the ridge of the Smokies. That vibrant green is already damn near gone, soon they'll be nothing but yellow, orange, just a couple pops of red, and then brown. This view is the best part of these nights, especially as the seasons start to change. Sure beats the rest of the surroundings.

Man, are we really still drinking shitty beer on a weekend night in our thirties? I guess most of the married ones, those with kids, especially, aren't here tonight. It's mostly those of us who never settled down that are relegated to this tradition of meeting up for a bonfire whenever the weather permits. Bigger ones, like some Friday nights, most of our old crew shows up. But nights like tonight? Just makes me feel pathetic for not having anything else better to be doing with my life.

The conversation drifts in and out of my awareness.

"You think it'll close?"

"Suds?"

"Yeah."

"I fucking hope not."

"Nah, no way ol' Duke will give up. He'll go out swinging before they take Suds away."

Another voice pipes up, changing the subject. "Anyone heard from Lexi?" My ears perk up on anything Rory-adjacent, as usual, and my attention homes in on the guy who asked the question. I take a few paces in his direction, eyes on the distant tree line so as not to look interested or commit myself to engaging in their conversation.

"Yeah, she was at work today," a girl we went to school with answers, sadly. "She's a wreck, though. She wasn't up for coming tonight."

"You should've seen her at the hospital," another guy we grew up with, Shawn, says, brows raised, the expression he pulls saying more than his words did before he lets out a long whistle. "Or seen her sister, yikes."

I thought I'd be able to hear better over here, but now it feels like maybe there's cotton in my ears? Some sort of ringing sound? And is the ground moving beneath me? We aren't supposed to get earthquakes in the Smokies.

Hospital?

"Why was Rory at the hospital?" My voice is gruff and croaks a little on the question (from disuse, nothing else). A chill crosses my skin that has nothing to do with the dropping temperature that's accompanying the way the leaves are more golden than green these days.

All the eyes around the fire shoot to me, some looking guilty, some alight with scandal, fresh gossip waiting to pour out, others are just interested, watching to see what happens next.

What's gonna happen next is I'm gonna get violent if someone doesn't start talking. Is Rory okay?

"I heard their mom slipped and fell."

Fuck.

When I meet Shawn's eyes, I know that's not the real story. He might be able to tell I know too.

"When was this?" The words are more of a grunt than anything, but Sophia, who works as an administrator at the hospital, same as Shawn, speaks up. She can barely restrain the delight in her eyes at the focus from the entire group, being the center of attention, the one who gets to spill the tea. My stomach threatens to spill the half a cup of beer all over this grassy field if she doesn't spit this out.

"She was admitted Friday."

Two fucking days ago?

And Rory didn't text me, didn't tell me, didn't ask for help? Jesus Christ, she's probably a complete mess. Was this the thing that broke through her outer shell—those incredible defenses she has—cracked her and let that softness she works so hard to hide feel the damage for once?

Shawn pipes up again. Why, I have no clue. "She had no emotion, I'm telling you, it was like watching a mannequin controlled by AI sitting in that room. She's so cold, it was creepy."

Sophia joins in, and soon half of the people around the fire are talking out of their ass.

"I heard she wouldn't even hold her mom's hand."

"She probably didn't want to mess up her nails," one girl scoffs.

"Or get hospital germs on her designer clothes," another one cackles.

Sophia takes the lead again. "Why is she even back anyway? She clearly hates it here, she should just go back to wherever she's been." Like she doesn't know where Rory's been all these years. I think it was at the last bonfire of the summer two years ago when she gave an entire dissertation about how brave Rory was for going to New York, how that's something she's always wanted to do, but she could never.

These motherfuckers are treating her life like it's their personal reality show to look in on, observe, and comment on, like she's not a living person, like she doesn't still have half my soul.

I toss my red plastic cup into the trash can to the side of one of the logs we use as benches and spit on the ground at the feet of those who are still running their mouths.

"Judgmental pricks," I seethe. "No wonder she never comes back, when this is what's waiting for her. None of you have even *tried* to talk to her, make her feel welcome for coming back home, you all just couldn't wait for the chance to play Regina George—" Yeah, that's right, Rory made me see that movie once upon a time. Got to second base during it, if I remember right. "—and talk shit about her. You have no clue what that girl's life is like, the hardships she's facing, and what even brought her back here. She's a better person than anyone here, myself included. And fuck every one of you who knew what happened and didn't think to check on her, or at least tell *me* so I could, and just sat here using it as fodder for your own fucking entertainment. *You* are the problem."

Those same voices call my name, whimper and protest at my retreat, but they can talk to my ass for all the fucks I give. I throw a middle finger up over my shoulder, they can all sit and spin. It's Rory they should be apologizing to, anyway, not me. Hop in my Ram and peel to her place, thankful I'd barely gotten any alcohol in me and didn't have to wait for it to get out of my system first.

Jog straight into Suds, the Dodge still running in the parking lot one building over, only to find the place fairly empty. Dallas is restocking the bar, and he looks up as I run past.

Duke, however, sees me from his open office door. "She's

not here, son." He looks haggard and weary, but I don't have time to check on him. "She ain't been here in days. At her mom's, I reckon."

That makes me stop in my tracks, turn around on a booted heel and bolt back the way I came. Not five minutes before I'm at her mom's place, and this time I *do* take the second and a half to turn off my truck, and race up to the door. Get a brief flash of all the nights I snuck in and out through her window ages ago, but that's not fast enough tonight, it'll have to be the last resort if I can't get in some other way. Knock quickly before opening it, thankful as fuck that our small town is still safe enough that the old-timers who grew up here don't lock their doors.

"Laura Lee?" I call out, slowing down to a walk instead of a rampage. "Aurora?"

There's some sort of noise from down in the hallway, and I follow it. "Rory?" I call again.

"Wyatt?" Her voice is thick, like her throat is obstructed. I'm back to a run again, checking every door I pass until I arrive at the bathroom and the scene there grasps my heart in its claws.

Rory is crumpled on the floor, on the bathmat in front of the tub. Her hair is a mess, it could be a bird's nest at this point, and if I had to guess she's been in those clothes for going on seventy-two hours now.

But none of that is what's causing this sharpness in my ribs, this shortness of breath. It's the look on her face. Defeat. Despair. Red-rimmed eyes, puffy skin underneath them, and that slumped posture, held up only by the ceramic bathtub and the wall behind her. Like even her will has left her.

Behind her, inside the tub, is ... a chicken.

It looks almost as rough as she does. Hunkered down, neck pulled in, feathers limp, and eyes droopy. Clearly unwell.

But I'm only here for one of them.

I drop to my knees in front of her on the linoleum floor and put a hand to her face, cup her jaw in my palm. I want to ask how she is, I want to ask if she's okay, but I know the answers to those already. If reading Rory Weiss was offered as a degree, maybe I woulda gone to college. Or maybe I could've tested out of it. So instead, I say, "I'm here."

She slumps forward, head falling until her forehead lands on my shoulder, and her body wracks with sobs as soon as the contact is made.

My arms come around her back to hold her in place, taking more and more of her weight as she gives in. I'd be willing to bet she hasn't as much as let someone else see her cry, much less lean on them throughout it, since we were together. My stubbled cheek is pressed to the top of her head, catching on her straggly strands, but neither of us moves to readjust. I sit there and take every ounce of pain she shares with me wordlessly.

After a while, her sobs quiet, her hiccupped breaths slowing back down to a calmer rhythm, one that matches mine. Our chests rise and fall together in the echoing silence of the small room. Just the occasional ruffle of the feathers we hear as the hen let us know she's still disgruntled.

After another couple minutes, Aurora is collected enough to pull back from me and go back to leaning against the wall, with a tiny bit of backbone this time.

"You came," she croaks out in what almost passes for a whisper.

"Of course I did. I just heard. I'm so sorry, Aurora."

Her eyes well up newly, but she doesn't let the tears spill this time, averts her eyes to the bathtub instead, the hen inside of it, some shred of determination in her gaze.

"She asked me to keep the chickens alive. I'm failing her, Wyatt. Lexi's had work all weekend, it's all on me, and I can't even keep her fucking chicken alive when she's dying. She's *dying*, Wyatt. Nine months sounded so far away when I got that first call, but I'm watching it happen, and it's way too soon, and I can't even do this for her? I can't let her down again, I can't."

A tear does break free at that, and Aurora covers her face with both hands, trying to get her composure back.

"Hey," I try to soothe her. "This fluffy girl looks alive to me, unless you know something I don't and she's somehow dead and moving around at the same time. So you're keeping your word to your mom. This girl isn't going anywhere on our watch."

She hiccups again, I think it might be a scoff, or maybe even a fraction of a laugh, and wipes her cheeks with her palms as she tosses her head back up again and I get to see that face I used to spend my life waiting to stare at. "Something was wrong with Henrietta the Eighth. I tried googling it, and chickenmama4lyfe on Reddit said it was heat stress, and to give her honey water and to keep her somewhere away from the rest of the flock and isolated. This was the only place I could think of."

"How long have you and Henrietta been in here?" I ask gently. It's not a setting that comes naturally for me, sounds a little rougher than I mean it to, but she's never been one to flinch or recoil from the more callous parts of me, and she doesn't now, either.

"Friday," she says simply, numbly.

"Hellcat, it's Sunday night."

"Is it?"

"Have you slept?"

She wobbles her head side to side a bit in a noncommittal response.

"Have you eaten?"

She shakes her head, sullen.

"Have you left this room at all?"

"For the birds, yeah. Pellets. Water."

Her hand kind of flops with the explanation. I can see the tiredness around her, like squiggles coming off of a cartoon character, but really fucking depressing ones. She must be beyond exhausted. I don't know how she isn't delirious at this point.

"Okay, new plan," I tell her. "I'm on chicken duty."

Aurora tries to argue, but she's so tired, so emotionally and physically drained even her ability to perform her favorite pastime, verbal MMA, is hindered, which is really saying something.

I persist. "I'm going to make sure Henrietta gets her honey water, right after I get something to eat in you, and once you get some sleep, and I'll stay up on chicken duty tonight."

"You have work," she grumbles, and it's mostly to her own shoulder as her head lolls. She must be real exhausted if that's all she's got.

"Not anymore. I'm taking the day off. Gonzo doesn't need me." Not as much as you do, is the quiet part of that sentence. "Let me do this for you. For both of you."

She gives in with a small nod, eyes closing already, and I take that as my cue to pick her up and carry her to the couch. She's asleep before I'm back with a glass of water and some eggs to eat, so I wake her up with a gentle nudge to the shoulder.

"That's cruel," she says sleepily when she sees what I brought her.

"It's all I could find that could be made quick, and it's not like it's a damn chicken breast. Henrietta won't even hold it against you."

I'm surprised she hasn't accused me of having a feeding kink yet, but I know this girl. The way she gets consumed by her work, her thoughts, her stress. She hasn't been taking care of herself, too focused on her mom and trying to keep up with her workload to boot. Can't let anyone down, even if it means running herself into the ground.

Her lack of self-care is going to bite her in the ass sooner rather than later. Can't run a car on no oil and no gas, and when this girl doesn't eat, doesn't sleep enough, doesn't get outside and touch grass once in a while, her battles get harder.

After the time we've spent together these past weeks, I can see it now. When she's out of fuel, the way her temperament shifts. She starts to get cranky, annoyed at damn near everything, even if she tries to hide it with those masks she wears—the ones that say nothing gets to her. But every single time I've checked with her when she gets that shift, sure enough, she hasn't eaten.

What she's going through is hard enough. She barely sleeps as is, she never thinks to eat, or even drink her water. Of course she's gonna be snappy and shit's gonna suck even harder. You can take the sanest person alive, and if you deprive them of food, of sleep, they're gonna turn into a goddamn psychopath on you. It happens to the best of us. Hell, it's a torture technique they use on opposition for a reason.

If she doesn't take care of herself, she has no chance at winning the battles she's fighting. But I'm here not just to take care of her, but to give her every possible tool, build out her arsenal so she can win her own battles every fucking time.

And now that she's passed out, fast asleep, stocking up on her other chief line of defense against her demons, I'm gonna go save a fucking chicken's life.

20
Aurora

My eyes struggle to open, giving me a millimeter of daylight and then shutting heavily again. Or maybe they didn't open at all, because that sight I thought I saw had to have been a dream, right?

It takes a few seconds, but eventually I coax my eyelids to try again and they part for me. There, directly in my line of vision, is Wyatt, in the same dark Henley he wore last night, a pair of khaki-colored Dickies, hair rumpled, jaw extra scruffy and looking fine as hell. And in his arms is a towel-covered Henrietta the Eighth. Her brown feathers look normal again, not limp and droopy, but healthily ruffled. She's alert, swiveling her head on that lithe neck of hers to look around the room, and blinking rapidly.

I've woken up to the sight of random men countless times in New York, none have made my insides warm like the scene before me does. They didn't come with this hazy glow behind them, either, but that might just be the sleep in my eyes.

"Good afternoon," Wyatt says in that gruff voice of his. It's hard to tell when he's so dry most the time, but I think … I think that was a dad joke at how late I slept.

I rub my eyes but that glow around him is still there. Shit. "Time is it?" I ask with a yawn, sitting up slowly. I can feel my hair flump across the top of my head in whatever is left of the bun I put it in days ago.

"About two," he says, standing from the recliner he's in, still holding Henrietta.

That wakes me up. "Shit," I say. "You have work."

He shakes his head. "Told you I was taking the day off."

"You should've woken me up," I argue, my sass coming to life before the rest of my consciousness does.

"You needed the sleep," he says mildly.

"You shouldn't have skipped work for me," I insist.

"I did it for Henrietta," he humors me. He lifts the bird up a bit, and she really does look much better.

"She's okay?"

"You did all the hard parts," he tells me with a wink. A dimple even makes an appearance underneath all that scruff. A freaking *dimple*. "Just took a little time for the honey water to kick in, I think. She should be good to go back to the coop now."

I nod at him, slightly starry eyed. Now that I've slept, I think I might feel like a whole new Aurora. A good cry, some food in me, and enough sleep might just be a magic combination. Other parts of me are starting to wake up too. More physical needs that haven't been met yet. My eyes fall down his tall frame, how good he looks right now, wondering if he's been thinking about our little pact as much as I have been, at least before the emergency. I clear my throat and say, "Give me a minute, I'll take her back and give the ladies, eh, we'll call it brunch."

When I locate and unlock my phone I see a string of texts from Lexi, sent earlier this morning.

ALEXIS WEISS

Came to see Mom before work

Doc is keeping her for one more night. Said
she can go home tomorrow if all's well

She kicked me out

So rude

Can you believe her?

She takes after you like that

Anyways she told me to tell you you'd better
not show your face here today either

That was a direct quote.

I don't blame her for not wanting to see your
face. Your eyebrows are getting out of control.
They're starting to look like those fuzzy
caterpillars we always used to see in the yard.

And about an hour ago, another string of texts from her.

Feels weird, you not having a mean comeback

But then again, I guess silence from you is
more familiar at this point

Thought you'd at least answer me about Mom

wtf "Aurora"

Giving me the silent treatment or something?

If I didn't drive by and see your car at the
house, I'd think you were back in NY again.
But now I see. Grady's truck is there too.

The reassurance on Mom drastically lightens the lead ball in my stomach. I think I can just about take a deep breath again. But of course she had to hit below the belt. I blow out a big breath and starting composing a text back.

ME

Sorry, last night was the first night I've slept in a while. Apparently I needed it, I just woke up. Wyatt stayed to watch one of the birds who was sick. I wish she were coming home today, but I'm really glad she's doing better and at least you got to see her. Jealous. 💋 I'll be there in the morning to help with the discharge.

Gross. I've heard a lot of nasty names for a cooch but a sick bird is a new one. Don't tell me that again.

And in the same sentence as discharge.

No.

I'm blocking your number.

A laugh bubbles up out of me, and I shake my head at her. Sisters will be sisters, I guess.

I remember when you begged for details of the dirty shit he and I used to do in your lonely virginal days. How the turntables.

This number can no longer receive massages

Nice try

See Mom's getting her money out of that community college degree

*Messages

Fuck you

After I use the bathroom and wash my hands, I make the mistake of looking up into the mirror hanging above the sink, and I shriek.

If I were a better woman, I'd put a ring on Wyatt Grady right now and lock that shit down for the fact he hasn't run screaming from this house yet. Were I in New York, my scoop du jour would've tossed me off the fire escape, thinking me some sort of Sasquatch that escaped the northern mountains, hopped the Canadian border, and began breaking into apartments looking for treats from Zabar's.

My hair is knotted in a mat about six inches high on the top of my head, and the bags under my eyes would definitely require additional fees if I tried to board a plane right now, to say *nothing* of the rest of my appearance.

Wyatt appears on the other side of the door as soon as I open it.

"What's wrong?" He and Henrietta look ready to fight whoever's attacking me in here.

I grasp my chest in fright from his sudden appearance, then remember what I look like and immediately slam the door in his face.

"Aurora?" he calls through the closed door. "You okay?"

"Mmhmm!" I call back in a falsely positive intonation.

Absolutely not! I was hoping today might lead to me getting railed within an inch of my life when I look like *this*? His dick is probably negative inches right now, burrowed up inside of his abdomen after having to watch this hot mess express of a train wreck. Like the snotty sobbing on the bathroom floor last night wasn't enough.

It takes a good ten minutes to work through the cluster fuck that is my hair—I'm so overdue for a cut and color and my hair is *punishing* me for it, but where am I supposed to go out here? I've barely been able to stay on top of nail appointments out here in the middle of nowhere, and don't even get me *started* on when I need to touch up my lip filler. I might have to fly back for that or make a day trip to the nearest metro with some decent options.

Eventually, the Goody paddle brush that's probably been in

this drawer since the '90s is able to make its way through the disaster that is my locks, and I put it into a slick-back ponytail with the help of a lot of water and some hair gel that's older than the car I'm driving. Not much I can do for my face here, but I splash some cool water on it and, maybe it's an illusion, but I swear I look about seventy percent less terrifying already. That's a good start.

I come back out of the bathroom with a faux-chipper smile on my face and Wyatt is still standing there, brows raised, wondering what the fuck is wrong with me.

"You look ..."

I wait for the compliments.

Gorgeous.

Hot as hell.

Like a sight for sore eyes and blue balls.

Bangable.

Any and all will do.

"... terrifying with that smile. Can you get rid of it?"

My jaw drops.

"Yeah, that's better," he says with a shudder. "That was the most unnatural shit I've ever seen."

My mouth still hangs open, my entire face surely radiating a death warning at him. How dare he?

Wyatt holds Henrietta the Eighth in one arm and uses one finger from his other hand to push my chin up and close my mouth.

"That thing stays open, I'll find a use for it." There's a glimmer of something mischievous in his eyes that makes him that much hotter, and now I want that picture he painted for my mind. The shimmer of desire in my lower belly is turning into a ball of need that's dropping even lower and taking on a pulse of its own.

"Don't make promises you can't back up, Grady," I taunt

him, my confidence largely restored after the updates from Lex and that quick little refresh.

I take the chicken out of his arms and take her back to her sisters, open up the coop for the day, and give them a little extra food to make up for being late this morning.

"Now I know we had a deal," I tell Henrietta as she pecks at the ground, scavenging for her meal, all back to normal after some TLC from that fine man back in the house. "You held up your end of it. You pulled through. I'll keep my word, you just gotta give me some time, okay?" She clucks in between pecks and I take that as a verbal contract. Good enough to be considered legally binding in the state of New York is good enough for me.

When I get back inside, Wyatt is leaning against the avocado green wall of the dining room, right beneath that black and white cat clock, with his arms crossed, those sleeves pushed up to his elbows and showing me a delicious glimpse at all that ink on his left forearm.

"Let's go," he says casually.

"Go where?"

"I've got the day off. Let's make the most of it."

My eyes—without my permission, I swear to you—glance down the hallway to my old bedroom, and he doesn't miss it. He chuckles at me, but it's a dangerous sound.

"No, Hellcat. We're not staying in this house, where you've got nothing but memories of your mom."

"I've got memories of you here too," I tell him, the corner of my mouth sliding up into a smirk that lets him know which memories are being recalled right about now.

"Well, right now, no matter what you look at in this house, you're going to think of your mom. We're going out."

I sigh because he's right. As much as I'd love a good distraction from him, I can feel the heaviness in this place, without her presence here. It's a constant reminder that she won't be here that much longer, and my eyes sting at the thought.

I try to divert my attention, focus on the man in front of me, the day ahead of us. At least I can still flirt with him; even if so much of the rest of me is damaged, that appears to still be intact. My number one coping mechanism: Distracting myself from my real issues before they cause a mental breakdown, or as I call it, ol' faithful.

"Are you at least gonna make it worth my while?"

"If you're good," he says with another deadly smirk that shoots a bolt of desire straight down south. Just as I think my kitty can't flutter any more, as I'm walking by him to get to the door the motherfucker slaps my ass. I nearly come on the spot.

WE PARTED ways with his instruction to shower, change for the outdoors, and—his new favorite thing to tell me—to eat, and he'd pick me up in a bit.

"I can't drive where we're going?" I asked with a bratty pout.

"In that piece of shit? I'm surprised you can make it the couple minutes to your mom's and back. You're really going to have to let me help you pick out something better. No way that thing makes it the rest of your stay. I'll be driving today, Hellcat."

I gave him a glare but didn't object to him picking me up after that.

"Bring a jacket, or whatever is in your wardrobe that will keep you warm," he said.

"I'm from New York," I retorted. "I know when I need a coat and when I don't. How to dress for cold weather is in my blood. And by the way?" I added, hand lifted in the air to further articulate my point. "This? Isn't it. I'll be fine."

So I wore athleisure. Hot pink yoga pants, an active bra with underwire for all the boost I can get in that department, and a soft, stretchy, white short-sleeve shirt with a pair of white and pink New Balances.

I wanted to *not* eat, just to spite him, but I was actually pretty hungry. And I know this sounds weird, but I swear, the last few times we've been together and he's made me have something, things were just a bit better after that. So I followed his direction on that, too, but I'll deny it if he asks me about it.

We make it about a half hour into the hike before I start to get on his nerves.

I'm kinda surprised this is what he planned for our afternoon together, actually. He's got free rein to fuck and flee, without any emotional attachment or obligation for the couple-y shit. It's basically the jackpot in the dating world. Bonus points, I already know what he likes. Or, what he used to. He could've just fucked me a time or two, ran me hard and put me up wet, then gone to have some beers with Ronnie and the rest of the Monday night regulars at Suds. But no, he wants to spend time together even when we're not getting down? He might be about to regret that choice.

Is he doing some sort of strategic holdout on me so I'll go feral on him when he finally gives me what I want? Cause I'd promise here and now to earn back my nickname in a whole new way if given the chance.

I guess my grumbling wasn't just in my head.

"Exercise is good for you, Aurora," he says.

"Not my preferred form of cardio," I reply, nose scrunched. "I'm more on Henry Cavill's level when it comes to that."

"What's wrong with hiking?" He doesn't sigh, but it's

implied from his tone of voice alone. An implied sigh was definitely present there.

"We're outdoors, Wyatt. There could be animals, I could get attacked again."

He stifles what I'm pretty sure would've been a laugh if he weren't so quick to catch it.

"We're nowhere near Boots, I think you're safe from cuddly cats today."

"There's—" my hand flies around everywhere, gesturing at everything all at once, even though he's walking in front of me and can't see me, "—dirt *everywhere*. It's basically my worst nightmare. Add in a broken nail, a missed deadline, a three-star hotel, and a saxophone, and it couldn't get worse for me."

"Fresh air, Aurora. Get that heart rate up. Enjoy this place before you're back to that concrete jungle."

"I prefer air that's been processed through some refrigerant first, thank you."

"You know this shit's good for you, right?" He's definitely getting exasperated now.

"You know what else is good for you? Sex three times a week." He can't argue with that, can he?

"Jesus Christ, Aurora. You're acting like I'm dragging you through an electrified mud pit. We're walking a beginner trail in one of the most scenic spots in the entire country, the weather couldn't be better—"

"It's a little chilly, actually," I butt in. It's only in the low fifties today, but something about this mountain air, it hits different than the same temperature in the city would. It's brisker, more refreshing.

"Oh for FUCK'S SAKE." He turns around from where he's been leading our little expedition, an outdoorsy backpack slung across his broad shoulders and hanging down to his trim hips. A few leaves crunch under his feet as he turns suddenly to face me and I bite down on my lower lip to stop from smiling. My cheeks actually hurt from the resistance; it's trying so hard to break out. It's so fun to get him riled up like this.

Wyatt pulls an arm out from the strap of the backpack and then slings it off the other shoulder to place it on the ground next to his feet. He shrugs out of the black Dodge hoodie he's wearing and pulls it off his head, leaving him in just a dark gray Henley that was beneath. It goes *great* with those lighter gray joggers he's wearing. I can practically trace the skin beneath those clothes with my eyes already. I want to do it with my tongue.

He shoves the hoodie at me, arm extended, but I don't take it.

"Put on the damn hoodie, Rory."

My body picks a horribly inopportune moment for me to give into the shiver that's been brewing for several moments now, and he doesn't miss it. So it's a little fucking chilly out, so what? His eyes darken and he steps closer, garment between his hands. Wyatt puts his hands through the bottom, opens the hole at the neck, and places it over my head, yanking it down over my torso. It's way too big for me, hanging down past my ass, but God, is it warm. It's cozy, it's delicious in here, smells like him, and I think my skin is *tingling* in response.

"You're still such a goddamn brat," he says through clenched teeth, inches from my face.

"What are you gonna do about it?" I ask breathlessly, hoping to bait him into some sort of life lesson I won't forget.

His palms come around my sides and down on my ass, just a little firmer than a tap, but he grips my cheeks there, fingers grazing teasingly low as he pulls on me. He lets his fingertips slide further, further, until they're approaching my entrance from behind. My knees threaten to buckle, and I fight a whimper that wants to make it out of my throat. One, two of those large pads of his fingers stroke and swipe at my pussy, overtop the stretchy fabric of my pants, and the response he creates within me is instantaneous.

"Gonna remind you why you like being on my good side, Hellcat."

The mewling sound does make it out that time.

He smirks in response, picks up his backpack from the ground, slings it back over his shoulders, and starts walking again.

Looks like I'm in for some punishment here.

I DON'T WANT to admit it out loud, but my mind hasn't been this calm in weeks. It's *never* this calm at home, actually. Whether it's Wyatt, this stupid fucking hike he's making me do —the trail covered in a thick carpet of pine needles and leaves, either side of it hemmed in by shoots, stalks, sprigs, and stems taller than I am, some tipped in feathery yellow, white, orange, and purple, others with bulbs and spheres of every imaginable color—or maybe it's just the expanse of the Smokies, the endless peaks that rise and fall with the shadows of the slowly sinking sun that are calming me down, making my mind stop racing.

There might be something to this self-care shit he's been harping on about lately. You get some sleep in me, a little bit of nutrition, and a solid walk in, and I'm a brand new bitch. Wonder what I'd be like after some six-star sex? I vote we find out in the name of science.

We're paused on our trek back to the car, taking a little breather, sat atop a grassy field that's serving as an overlook to the range. Haven't run into a single other person out here this entire hike—he says this is a section of the trail nobody ever comes to, it's too far removed from the tourist spots, and the locals don't go out this far, either—but we have seen a *disturbing* amount of wildlife. Lucky I haven't been attacked yet, the man is putting my life on the line out here.

Aside from the rabbits, various birds, and one possum who didn't respond to Dolly, I think I counted something like seventy-three squirrels, harvesting acorns and anything they could find for the cold months ahead. I can relate, honestly. I, too, am using this season to stock up on good memories before I'm back in a waking slumber-like-state, in a cold place without the things that make me happy.

My last chance at time well-spent with my mother—as soon as she's discharged tomorrow and I can go back to being a helicopter daughter.

These brief rendezvous with Wyatt, where even when he never even touches me—like the ATV, or the pool table—he blows my mind far beyond anything I've felt back in New York.

These next months will be the best ones I'll ever have; I know that now. The transition from stranger to daughter, sister, friend, it's been gradual over the weeks, but we've gone from awkward and practically at each other's throats to working together and I think even *enjoying* our time together. The hospitalization, that was my wake-up call. Now is the time to soak the good moments up while I can, make the most of what I'm being given before it's gone again.

Wyatt opens up the backpack for the first time and pulls out a large Thermos, like we're in elementary school together and he's about to have soup for lunch.

"What did you bring?" I ask him.

He stays silent, working the cap until it loosens, then flicking it with the tips of his fingers repeatedly to unscrew it rapidly. It's strangely mesmerizing. I think I could watch him work with his hands forever. When he pours the liquid from the tumbler into the lid and passes it over, I get a deep whiff before it's even in my hands.

"Hot cider?" Why does my voice sound so tender? I'm expecting him to make another joke about it not suiting me, but his eyes just flash to mine, looking warmer than usual too.

The fact that he remembered this was one of my favorites—we used to dream about the day I could drink it at our future home together, watching the snow fall through that open window—thought to get some, then made it and brought it for our hike ... I'm speechless. A rarity, for sure.

At the first sip, my mouth could cry. Sweet, crisp apples, spiced with clove and cinnamon. Makes me want a slice of homemade pumpkin loaf to go with it. It tastes like nostalgia, like everything good that I used to have. Everything that I left behind because I'm an awful person.

"Damn, Grady," I breathe out, in lieu of a thank you, but he hears what I'm not saying.

"What? You think I'm not gonna take every chance to spoil you while I have you?" He tosses it back like it's nothing, but my stomach flips. Something between us feels so *different* this time. Is this what growing up looks like? Maturing as individuals, to be better partners?

"What else do you have in that backpack of yours?" I ask, instead of giving in to the mushiness brewing inside of me.

He pulls apart the sides of it so I can peer in, the sound of the zipper sliding further down as he does. The bag is mostly empty, but I see what looks like some packaged snacks in there.

"Did you pack us a picnic, Wyatt Grady?"

He snorts. "Fuck no. I brought you some cider, and I put some beef jerky in here in case you got cranky." I punch his shoulder. "Or in case you got us lost, and I had to play Bear

Grylls and survive on what's in my backpack for a day until I can get us back to civilization."

"You're being a dick," I reprimand him.

"I've always been a dick," he replies, shrugging a shoulder. "That's not new."

"True," I concede with a chuckle, and the crisp, chilly breeze on my face refreshes me as we both look over the expanse of the peaks for a moment, watch the sun reflect off of the fog that's hanging out among the mountaintops, and admire the gorgeous colors in and amongst the hectares and hectares of foliage.

From somewhere to our left side, a strong breeze whisks countless leaves from their former homes and blows them right in front of us, letting them tumble midair, chasing one another as they float by us, before falling to the ground when the wind dies down.

I take a deep breath, letting it fill my lungs with the kind of replenishment you only get from nature, then speak. "I was gone so long, but stepping back into the Heights, into my old life, it's like everything and everyone kept going just as they were before. It's tough for me to try to pick up where I left off when nothing about me fits in here anymore."

Wyatt twists his head to the side, not loving that. "You fit in just fine, Hellcat. And it might look like things continued here as normal, but I can tell you, for a lot of people around here, life stopped when you left, Rory. For at least three of us, but probably a lot more than that, by extension. You're not the only one this whole thing is hard on."

My mouth dries up and a ball forms in my voice box that I can't swallow around.

"Anyway," he moves on, clearing his throat. "A lot is the same, really. Ernie is still telling shitty stories down at the bar. Mrs. Dixon is still keeping the town stocked on gossip, bouncing between the post office, coffee shop, nail salon, and laundromat to make sure everyone's heard. But some things are changing." He shrugs. "You saw what downtown looks like these days." I nod. "A while back, we had a bit of a recession. This bank swooped in, helping some folks out when the mine first closed. Opened up an office here, and looking back, I think they might've been targeting us. Taking advantage of how trusting the folks here are, and how we weren't as book smart as them. They'd bought out a bunch of mortgages in the town from other banks, and they offered refinancing to those who'd been affected, and a lot of people jumped on it. But before long rates started going up, families have been struggling. Businesses too. It's been tough for a lot of us. Downtown has really dried up."

"That's the same bastards who are hounding Duke, isn't it? Brown Stone?" I voice the realization out loud.

"So it's true," he muses.

I nod, taking another sip of cider. "They're up to some sketchy shit. I've looked into as much as I can from here, but I had to tag in the team back at the office. Got permission to put some of our research team onto it, actually. There's too much that doesn't make sense about them, something is very *off* where they're concerned. I was just trying to get to the bottom of Duke's situation, but maybe I should have them expand their parameters, see what else we can dig up on these fuckfaces."

"Do it. I hope you nail their asses," he murmurs in a low voice.

We pass the cider back and forth until, eventually, it's gone and he puts the Thermos back in his bag. Finally, I have to say it. "Thank you for last night. And for today." It's hardly above a whisper, thanks to the emotion behind it. I guess today is full of rarities for me.

"Don't mention it," he says gruffly.

"A hike sounded like the worst thing in the world, but this

has actually been one of the best days I've had in a long, long time."

"You always needed reminding there's bigger things out there. Put life into perspective."

It hits me that he's right. Out here, everything around me is bigger than I am, bigger than my problems, bigger than my grief and my failures. The issues I've been running from ever since I left. Everything is less shitty out here, and with him.

"I know you, Rory. Always known you. What you need."

The mood shifts with his words, and his eyes fall to my lips.

"Are we finally going to hook up?" I whisper the words against his mouth.

"If that's what'll shut you up," he mutters against my own, the brush of his lips a ghost of a tease as they move with his words.

And then he's taking my breath away, capturing my mouth with his and kissing me like my taste is what's going to keep him alive. Like he's rediscovering the secrets my lips have been keeping, and has only this moment to learn them all.

His body leans into mine, pressing me backward, crushing me to him. Any extra space I had in this hoodie is eaten up by the proximity of him, the way he folds himself into my personal space, invading, dominating. I yield instantly.

Wyatt's lips continue to move against mine, and my own respond in kind. His week or so of scruff burns in the best way as it drags roughly against my skin, and my skin lights up at the scrape of it. My thighs want to know what it'll feel like next, if there's a signup sheet somewhere.

He moves to deepen the contact, meshing lips instead of nipping at them, and I bring a hand up to hold his face, looking for something to steady this free fall in my low belly, in my chest, maybe even in my head too. He growls at the scrape of my long nails as they push backward into his hair, and he presses me until I'm flat against the ground, his frame hovering above me, lips still on mine.

If we're being honest, this could be enough. As much as I've dreamed of this man since losing him, as many times as my mind has wandered to him in the most inopportune of moments, nothing my memory has offered me has compared to this, the feel of his mouth on mine, the weight of his body atop mine, our hearts beating together, the sharp bite of the chilly air surrounding us in a light breeze as he *owns* me, consuming me with nothing but a kiss. It's so much better than anything I remember before. And still, I want more.

I open my mouth for him as his tongue sweeps, and relish the reentry, welcome him home after so long apart, like a soldier coming home from war. Back to his safe haven, the port he'll always be welcome in.

"Fuck," he whispers against the line of my jaw as he peppers kisses along the delicate skin there. "You're going to kill me, aren't you?"

Wyatt's lips gravitate to the most sensitive part of my neck like they're a pair of magnets, meant to be touching always, and I whimper his name, the way I used to. His tongue flicks out to tease the skin there and my body responds the way he trained it to over years of moments like this. Hips buck off the ground, core clenching, wet already, and so fucking empty. Painfully hollow without him inside me.

When he pulls back to look me in the eye, I see it reflected in his own gaze. How painfully empty he is without me too. I throw my head to the side, break the eye contact, and do my best to convince myself that there's nothing more to this than release, for either of us. There can't be. But sex, we can do.

He sits back on his heels, watching me writhe beneath his stare, the anticipation of what comes next, but I refuse to look back. Instead, I raise my upper body enough that I can unhook my bra—thank you yoga, for the core strength for this maneuver —and pull one arm out, then pull the garment out of the other arm hole of the hoodie and toss it to the side, several yards away, where it won't be in the way.

I can feel the warmth of his gaze, even if I refuse to give in and see it for myself. His breathing gets heavier, and I see his chest rise and fall from the corner of my eye as I lay back down, spread in front of him like his own personal meal. It's just a question of where he wants to start.

"Your turn," I tell him, trying to break that concentrated stare he's focused on me. The one I'm not willing to meet.

"Just deciding what I want to do first," he says thoughtfully, palms running up my thighs so slowly it lights my nerve endings up and scatters goosebumps along my skin. My nipples are so stiff they almost ache, and I wish he could see them right now, pay them the attention they're so overdue for. "My fingers, stretching that tight pussy out, prepping you for the rest of me?" I nod my head and bring my eyes back to him, let myself focus on his hands, the ink on his left forearm, the tendons and veins running down it that I could watch flex and move as he uses those thick fingers to spread me, ready me for more. My inner walls clench at the thought, thighs shifting, and his eyes home in on the motion.

"Or, I could treat myself to a feast. Aurora's cunt." One hand comes up to his mouth, rubbing his lips in thought, but it serves to remind me of what his lips, his beard, his tongue, feel like against my flesh, and a chill breaks out along my flesh. "Rory's always was my favorite flavor. I'd love to see how Aurora's compares."

My clit *jumps* at that. Jolts from just his fucking words. And he says I'm the wordsmith? Something tells me he'd make a lot more than a couple hundred an hour if he spoke like that for a living.

He continues, "Or, maybe we skip the foreplay, since you were such a brat today, and I just take mine? Shove my cock in as deep as you can take me, no warning, no prep work, fuck you until you can't take it anymore, until you feel like you're being split in half—like you're so full you're going to burst—and then and only then I could pull out and finish on your tits?"

The words are conversational, like he's weighing his options for which path we should take back to the truck, river or mountain, but they *hit* me like a truck. My eyes flutter and roll back in my head from that visual, him using me, taking what he needs, not even letting me come, because part of me knows I don't deserve it. It would be my penance, my atonement, letting him use me like that.

And it turns me on. The sharp pinch and painful stretch of me trying to take all of him, without anything to warm me up first. How he'd be pulling out and slamming in again, before I'd even adjusted to his size, that insane girth. Just when I think I couldn't take any more of it, he'd draw back and plunge in again, and I'd scream, but I'd beg him not to stop, even if it hurt. I can feel my underwear soaking already, and he hasn't even touched me yet.

How does he do this to me? How does he get me so ready, so wet for him, practically frothing at the mouth for him before he's even begun? This man gets me, my mind, my body, what *all* of me needs. Being with him is more than a physical experience, it sates me on every level.

Where my mind is so often my worst enemy, Wyatt teams up with it, turns it in both of our favors, gets it working in a direction where it's running with what he's saying, the visuals he's painting, getting me desperate for the scenes it runs away with.

He continues laying out his options, deliberating aloud in a way that has me close to panting. "Could also come all over your ass. I'd say your face, but I know better than to ruin that perfect hair. Maybe I should stick to wrecking your pussy instead." His eyes land on my thighs, and he uses both hands to part them, opening my knees and letting them fall to the sides for him, staring at what's in between.

"Your pants are soaked already, Hellcat," he purrs, and I let out another one of those embarrassing whimpers. My legs try to close again, but he holds them open with a hand on the inside of each knee and shakes his head at me, just once.

"No, I think I wanna play with you like this," he says in a drawl that's just toeing the line between confident and cocky.

My eyes slam shut, and I tilt my head back as far as it will go on the ground. When I open them again, a grayish blue sky, a scattering of thin clouds fill my vision, with that gorgeous foliage the Smokies are known for this time of year just framing the edges, like my own personal painting. The stunning background to a mental memory I'll never let myself forget.

When I look down again, he's repositioned himself in between my legs, and that look on his face is positively lethal. I'm certain he's violating at least a dozen laws with that thing, if you'd let me consult my volumes of legal codes I could probably list them out for you.

Wyatt waits until I'm watching and then he brings a hand forward, placing it on my lower abdomen, flat against my stomach, pinning me in place. My body jolts from the contact, the sensuality of it. He brings his other hand to the hem of the hoodie I'm wearing—his hoodie—and slides the hand up. He lets the fabric bunch up, slipping out from under his other hand that's still on my stomach, and that other hand drifts further and further up, tracing the skin beneath both layers of clothing until he's cupping a breast.

I suck in a sharp breath as his finger and thumb play with me, rolling my nipple between them, tugging on it in a way that pulls directly on my clit with each motion. He watches closely, intently, to see my reactions, gauge my response to the line between pleasure and pain that he's playing jump rope with.

I must be a sick fuck, because all he's doing is making me needier, more desperate for him and his particular brand of torture. My pussy floods my underwear with a fresh rush of desire, and the fact that my legs are wide open, he's got me on display like this, not knowing what he's going to do next, it just makes me hotter.

I'm pretty sure if he keeps going, keeping me pinned in place, his legs forcing mine to stay open as he tugs at and tweaks my nipples, I think he'd give me my third orgasm without touching my pussy directly in the last few weeks. And fuck, do I want him to touch me directly. Enough that I'm finally ready to ask for it.

"Please," I whimper, as he gives a final, sharp tug on my nipple that leaves it stinging, almost burning with pleasure, still feeling his touch even after he's abandoned it to pay attention to the other.

My eyes flutter shut as he starts to play with the other one, making up for the lack of attention it got while he tormented my other breast.

"Please what?" he asks, pinching and twisting.

"Fill me," I beg.

"Oh, you'll be filled. Is it my cock you want to be filled with? Or my cum?"

The thought of him spilling inside of me, pumping his release halfway to my throat as my walls clamp down on him, begging him to stay longer, to come harder, to give me more, it makes me moan. Seeing him come all over my bedroom door wasn't enough. I want to *feel* it leaking out of me. I want to be soaked in both of our releases. Treated like the dirty girl I miss being. The one only he's fulfilled the needs of.

"Yes," I answer, and he smirks.

Wyatt releases my other nipple with a final flick, and my body hums in arousal, pure need for whatever he wants to do to it next. Whatever it is, my answer is *yes*.

He folds down his fingers of the hand still on my stomach, slips them down below the waistband and jerks it down, yanking in a couple of quick motions, pulling my pants down over my ass and peeling each leg off, underwear, socks, and shoes along for the ride. My bare ass lands on the grass, and he must see the discomfort on my face because he brings the pants back up and lifts me up by the hips to put them beneath me, protecting me from the direct contact with the ground.

Just like that, I'm back in the moment. The way he knows me, knows what I need, it could melt me if I let it.

Wyatt's forest-green eyes dilate, flare and flame with desire, staring down at me, wearing nothing but his hoodie, bare legs leading to a bare pussy, spread wide and on display for him.

His hands run up the insides of my legs, up my thighs, until he's got a hand on either side of my pussy, and he pulls, spreading me further apart so I'm fully exposed to him, nothing in the way of his view this time. The cold air hits my hot center, my sensitive clit, and he smirks as I squirm beneath his hands.

"Dying to know how tight this thing is these days," he murmurs, letting the fingers of his right hand drift over to my entrance, where he swipes up some of the arousal there and spreads it around the entire area. He brushes past my clit too quick to give me what I need, but my body jerks at the contact just the same. "Mmm," he hums. "You *are* wet for me, Hellcat."

"Yes," I gasp. "So stop fucking teasing me and just fuck me already," I snap at him. "Why are you still dressed? Why are you not—" my words are cut off with a sharp gasp as he plunges two huge fingers inside of me with no warning.

"What was that you were saying?" he teases, curling his

fingers, stroking my front wall, pressing against the muscles clamping down on him. *"Fuck,"* he breathes out roughly. "This pussy get this tight from yoga? Or is this witchcraft?"

Words have left me as all of my awareness, my entire existence slow zooms in on the feel of him inside of me, the force he's exerting to get his fingers to spread within me, stretch me, but my body isn't giving. I'm so wound up, the tension so tightly wound within me, my walls clamping so hard, he's not getting anywhere.

"God*damn.*"

I don't have anything to add to that statement, I just push my upper body off the ground and hold myself up, arms extended and locked behind me, my legs wide open around Wyatt's body so I can watch. The two of us stare, mesmerized at the sight, the feel of his fingers pushing in and out of me, sliding in so easily thanks to all that slickness, scissoring inside of me, rotating in there. And when he curls those fingers, finding the spot that no one else seems to know how to activate, how to turn into the pleasure center it's always been with him, I fall back to the ground with a loud moan.

Wyatt's face pulls tight with desire, and he takes his other hand to rub himself once, twice, overtop of his joggers, the tent there growing ever more noticeable. Starting to look painful, actually. I bet if he pulled those gray pants down for me, I'd see a fat bead of precum leaking out the tip. My mouth waters, and I decide on what I'm going to try first when it's my turn.

"Nah," he groans, finally making up his mind. "I'm not fucking this pussy until I've tasted it." He dives forward, launching himself onto his stomach between my legs in a motion that nearly startles me in its suddenness.

It's when his face is just a few inches away from my center that the self-consciousness hits me. Memories resurface of the hike we just finished, the way I sweat through the more arduous parts of it, the feel of the fabric sticking to my legs, and I realize now is *not* the time for him to go down on me.

My legs try to close around his head, and he looks up at me in question.

"Another time," I tell him in a pleading voice. "When we didn't just finish exercising."

He practically glowers at me. "You might have gotten used to the pretty city boys who are scared to get their hands dirty, but out here, it's a way of life. A fucking honor, and a privilege. So, please, Hellcat. Let me get filthy like a good little country boy." That smirk on his face alone is a danger to female libidos everywhere.

Once again, I am *speechless*, but the flutters that went through my center, up into my core and my lower stomach from that tell me I love the idea after all, and my legs fall back open.

He doesn't wait for any further permission or give me a chance to think it through. He lurches forward, face nestled in between my legs, nose pressed against the top of my pussy as his tongue darts out and parts me. Wyatt sinks his tongue into me for the first time in over a decade, and I moan, a fresh wave of arousal coating his mouth. I can feel it even without watching what's happening down there. He laps it up, and he's not quiet about the way he's enjoying himself at it, sliding that tongue up, up my center until he finds my clit, teasing it with the tip of his tongue until I'm mewling.

Wyatt finishes that thorough taste test and draws his head back to look me in the eyes again. "Goddamn, Hellcat. You taste even better than I remember. I've come to the memory of your scent and taste more times than I can count, but I think it's gotten even better with time," he says, and then he disappears again.

My head lifts up to follow him, and I look past the hoodie that's still covering my top half to where he's crouched between my thighs, eyes on mine as his mouth absolutely *feasts* on me.

He presses his entire face in against me, devouring for his own sake, not even focusing on my pleasure, like a man given one-night access to his favorite drink after it was discontinued years earlier. This isn't for the bartender, it's for the alcoholic.

His rough stubble scratches against the delicate skin of my bikini line, and since that entire area is completely bare thanks to laser hair removal, it's extra susceptible to beard burn, and I hope I can feel the scrape of it with every step I take for *days*. Each one will give me this visual to accompany the twinge.

Those gorgeous green eyes that have haunted me for years close with a moan as he sinks his tongue into my core again, exploring, soaking up as much of me as he can. The sight nearly pushes me over the edge, the pressure that's been coiled in my lower belly since he started playing with my nipples threatening to burst and spill over.

He opens his eyes, and it looks like it takes effort, like he forces himself to pull back from my center, but when he does, he licks a delicate trail up to my clit.

I can't decide what I like more, when his mouth is spitting filth in my ear, using anything in our vicinity to make me come, or when it's too busy licking my cunt to be able to.

Wyatt closes his mouth around my clit, and starts sucking, pulling on it with alternating pressures, first gentle, then firmer. It shoots blazing pleasure pulsing through my nerve endings, my entire body responding to what he's doing.

"Oh God, Wyatt," I cry out.

He slips a finger back in my center, but he doesn't start fingering me. Doesn't seek out those spots that he could press on and end this in a second. He slips the finger in, and then back out, like the cruelest form of teasing.

That mouth of his keeps sucking, pulling on my clit, the

barest hint of teeth getting involved, just enough to skim over the bud and set my nerve endings on fire. A small scream comes out of me the first time he does it, and when he pairs it with that finger, in and out, in and out, I'm close to breaking.

The tremors start, my legs shaking around his body, and he removes his finger once again, that tongue, those lips still working my clit.

There's a pressure below my entrance, my ass cheeks being separated, and then his wet finger is at my *other* entrance. The wrong entrance. Somewhere I haven't let anyone go before, not even him. His eyes are on mine, and though panic courses through me at the unknown, sensation of it, how dirty it feels —it's always been forbidden for me—a thrill rushes through me at the same time. Excitement darts through my system, lighting me up, cranking my sensitivity up to a whole new level, several notches up above the max setting it was already on.

He must sense it, or maybe he feels his chin get soaked, because he presses the tip of his finger in, breaches that tight hole for the first time. Adding that extra dose of forbidden to this already risky session is all it takes. His tongue flicks my clit in a rhythmic pattern that my most expensive vibrator could only dream of emulating, and when he seals his lips around my clit to give the next pull of suction, pulsing in a cadence that unlocks a new level of decadence for me, I shatter.

My orgasm rips through me, back bowing off the ground as I cry his name out, along with a slew of curses that are sending me straight to hell, if the sex in a public place with my ex didn't already do the trick.

He keeps doing the same thing, not changing the rhythm or the pressure as I ride it out, letting me fall and fall, further than I normally do, the waves of pleasure taking their sweet time receding.

When my eyes open again, it's to find his locked on mine, then darting over my shoulder, and back to mine again.

I'm still shuddering with aftershocks as he withdraws his finger, and slowly pulls back from my pussy.

"Jesus," I groan, voice barely working. "Not to be dramatic, but I think I'm going to die if you don't get inside me right the fuck now. Take those clothes off, Grady. Hurry."

He doesn't move to pull his pants down, doesn't push inside of me, doesn't even peel off his shirt.

"Not to kill the mood, but I think we have a better chance of dying if I *do* get inside you right now."

I turn to look at what he's been staring at, and his hand covers my mouth to muffle the scream. To be fair, he's muffled my screams hundreds of times, but only ever out of carnal pleasure.

Never because I was scared for my life.

21
Wyatt

"Hey, bear!" I call out.

The adolescent black bear I've been watching the last couple minutes gets a little closer than it has up until now. About fifty yards out, give or take, and moving in on us.

Not full-grown, but not young enough to be with its overprotective mama either. Its first couple months on its own, I'd guess. Mildly dangerous if it gets close enough to attack, but not the worst scenario I've encountered hiking or camping in the Smokies.

Rory is shaking in my arms, probably still from the aftershocks of her orgasm, but very likely also in fear. There's a lot of creatures and critters she wouldn't want to run into out here, but a bear is pretty close to the top of that list. If you thought she was afraid of cats ... I mean, she'd probably take a cute bear over something crawling on her—or, God forbid, slithering near her—but if that cute little bear starts clawing at her and trying to eviscerate her, she might change her order real fast.

"Put your pants on," I tell her, withdrawing my hand from her mouth now that she's had the chance to gauge the situation for herself. "And we're going to back away."

She stands, still a bit shaky, and hops around on one leg at a time, trying her best to get her pants back on, and I'm pretty sure they're on backwards but I'm not going to try to get her to do more aerobics to fix that now. While she pulls them up over her hips, I stand, grabbing the backpack, then take her hand with my other. She holds her sneakers in her free hand, and we aren't waiting to put them on right now.

The bear comes closer still and I holler at it, louder this time. It doesn't stop its approach.

"Walk backwards with me, Ror." For once, she doesn't correct me for calling her the wrong name.

I glance behind us every couple of steps, making sure we aren't going to trip on anything, leading us back toward the trail we came from, the one that takes us back to my truck.

The bear follows for a number of paces, but loses interest, wandering back into the woods across the clearing, nose high in the air, sniffing.

As soon as our backs are past the wood line we turn around and make a break for it, dashing for the truck. The sun is just starting to set, sinking beneath the peaks on the horizon, but in late October that doesn't give us a whole lot of daylight left to get somewhere safe.

As we run, she finds the breath and the mental wherewithal to start yelling, which is a little impressive, I have to say.

"Did you really eat me out with a bear behind me?"

"Not the whole time," I say, leaping over a log and gripping her hand in mine to make sure she's secure with those bare feet.

"We can probably stop to put your shoes on now," I offer.

"Probably?" she screeches. "We're *probably* not going to die if we stop to put on my shoes?"

Hard to shake my head while jogging for our lives, but I manage to make it work. I try again. "We're fine to put on your shoes now."

"I'd rather survive, thanks," she shoots back, but I can tell it's hurting her. "Can we go back to the part where you let me lay there getting tongue fucked while a fucking *bear* considered making a meal out of us both?"

"That's an exaggeration," I tell her. "It wasn't that big of a bear. It might've eaten one of us, no way it was gonna get both of us. I mean, it might've *attacked* us both, but no way it was going to *eat* both of us."

"WYATT!" she shrieks.

"Bad time for a joke," I admit. "Listen, I had my eye on it. It only showed up around the time your legs started shaking, and I took my chances. I'd rather face a black bear than you if I didn't finish what I'd started there. I don't regret my choice."

"You're—ow—such a fucking—ow—jackass—ow."

It really doesn't hold the same punch when it's punctuated with all those noises of distress.

Aurora tries to keep going, but I wrap my arms around her waist and lift her from the ground, stopping her mid-stride. She wiggles and grumbles, and somehow my dick didn't go completely flaccid from the bear incident—the taste of her still on my tongue is probably to blame—so what she's doing isn't very comfortable for me.

"I'm a jackass who has his priorities straight, now would you mind not breaking my dick while I'm rescuing your feet?"

"My feet don't need rescuing!" she says indignantly.

It's not lost on me how the younger version of me would've taken her bait any number of times today, gotten heated, gotten pissed, and blown up over at least one of the ridiculous arguments she's started (or tried to). The version of me that's lived twelve years without her isn't taking her for granted. I know how special this connection between the two of us is, not just the physical one, and yeah, she might be high-maintenance, and she has a bratty streak that's a mile wide, but she's fucking magnificent, and completely worth every ounce of trouble she brings to my life. Wish I realized it back then, showed her a little better the lengths I'd go to for her.

"I am not letting you get hurt on my watch. If you aren't putting these shoes back on your feet, Aurora Rose Weiss, I'll carry you."

"Sure," she grumbles. "Now you're worried for my safety, just not when there's a literal bear behind me, ready to strike."

"Believe me, I wasn't gonna let that thing eat you." I pause, then add, "Only I get to eat you." My mischievous smirk isn't winning her over, so I hike her up so she's wrapped around my front and start to carry her back to the car, chuckling at her mumbling as we go.

This woman is beautiful—more so than ever—headstrong, so damn brilliant, capable, witty, and a mouth I love just as much when she's using it to start shit as when she's sucking me off with it. She's a custom creation, all her finishes are after-market, no one else like her, not in the Heights, not in that city of eight million she's so fond of, nowhere. I used to think she was custom made for me, but now I see how high she flew, all the ways she grew without me, and I know there's someone much better for her than my grumpy ass. Some other lucky asshole who will get the privilege of maintaining her. With a job that allows him to afford the things she deserves, the life she wants. He won't be a mechanic from a small town whose best years are behind him, I know that much.

If I'd known what my future would've looked like without her in it, I would've grown up a lot fucking faster to be the man she needed way back when. But I didn't. So all I can be is the man she needs now. For the next however many months she's in town. And then let her go again because she found what she was looking for. A life without me.

She lived out her dream, she got the fancy degrees, the job she always prayed for, she's doing everything she set out to. Me? I'm still the same schlump I always was, just seventy percent more miserable now. But I'll be damned if I'm not gonna put the effort in while she's here now, even if it's the equivalent of signing my own death warrant. I've seen what else is out there, I've lived both sides of the tracks. Going back to the other side might suck, but for now, I'll take what I can get from her, while I can get it. And right now, that's rough sex, the dirtier the better.

As for when she leaves, well, we'll cross that bridge when we get to it. I survived once before. I can do it again. As long as I don't lose sight of the fact that this is just sex for her. I'm just being what she needs. Her escape, the distraction she needs to stay safe from her mind doing those cruel little things it does to her when she's alone with it for too long.

And if some nosy fuck like Weston were to ask, do I feel better when I'm with her? I'd say, maybe, but that's not important and fuck right off, thank you kindly.

By the time we make it back to the truck, her arms around my neck, legs slung around my waist, she's shaking in my arms, her rapid breaths hitting my neck. She still smells like cider. I crane my head back to try to see her face, gauge what's happening right now, but she buries it further in my shoulder. Her sounds go from muffled and muted to full-volume as I watch her, assessing, and soon I realize it's her laughter that is raining around us, filling the empty dirt lot with the mirthful, tinkling sound.

Leaning forward I put her back down on the ground, but Rory doesn't stop laughing. She backs against the truck for support and howls, peals of laughter splitting the night sky. It might be the best thing I've ever heard.

Unrestrained, uninhibited, unencumbered by how difficult

these last couple months and the next ones will be. Just the pure sound of someone enjoying the life they're living. More carefree in this moment than I've seen her, even since before she left, probably.

It's infectious, contagious, and I've shared in everything else with this girl, I might as well share in this too. My head falls back, and a sound I haven't heard in so long I don't even recognize it comes out.

Laughter, uproarious, uncontrolled, wild, and robust, the kind of sound I didn't know my soul still had enough juice left in me to make.

Minutes, maybe longer, we spend in the moment. Doubled over, eyes streaming, cheeks hurting, neither of us able to get words out.

"My—" she finally gasps, "—bra!"

I realize what she's trying to say, that her bra was left behind, still in the field back there, and the idea seems funnier than usual, sending me into another round, a fresh burst that kicks the whole thing off all over again.

They say it's medicine for the soul, and I'm not sure I ever knew what the great, all-knowing *they* meant until this moment.

You can seal over an open wound that won't (or can't) close. I've heard about it being done, Shawn's told us more than we wanted to know about patients who've had the procedure. A sterile covering that goes over the gap in your chest after open heart surgery. Sure, it protects the insides. But you can't walk around like that and pretend you're whole. It's a surrogate for the real thing, a temporary fix, but you won't be able to truly *live* like that.

That's what it's felt like these past twelve years.

This might be the first moment it's felt like my chest is whole in all this time.

I knew it was there, knew the handicap I was living with,

but it's been part of me so long, I forgot what it felt like to live as a whole person.

To enjoy life, the one you're with, to fuck, and laugh, and run for your life. The shit all the best memories are made of.

We've checked two of the three off.

Time to make another core memory with this girl. Lord knows she's in all my best ones already.

As the laughter dies down, the tension between us, ever-present, crackles to life, the heat rising.

We're two of those substances we learned about in chemistry (when we were flirting instead of paying attention) where they're room temperature on their own, but you put them together and it's instant heat. They start to boil and bubble over from proximity alone, and will ignite if left close to one another. Lightning sparking in a jar, the shit that defies common sense.

She is what makes me this way, it's only for her that I get like this. There's something in our molecules, something in our chemical makeup that makes us respond to one another in the way we do. That makes anything with her so much better than it's been with anyone else.

When she wipes her eyes, dries the second set of tears I've seen of hers in recent memory, and our eyes catch, she feels the shift in my mood, the way I need her. It's inexplicable, and consuming. I need her body, the connection to life that I get only from her, I need it more than I need this oxygen surrounding me. So I take it.

I grab her face with one hand, grasp her cheeks to hold her in place while I sweep the other around her back and pull her in for a deep kiss. My tongue probes her mouth, plunging, searching, claiming. The spicy flavor of cider greets me, and she groans when she registers what *my* tongue tastes like. Her. Still my favorite flavor.

One arm still holding her up, I remove the other one from

between our bodies and use it to unlock the truck and then open the back door clumsily. I toss the backpack in first, which thumps against the footwell, cushioned by the mat. Precious cargo in there, couldn't leave that behind. Grab her shoes from her hand and lob those in too.

We fumble, not willing to break apart, but trying to get inside the backseat all the same. It takes us a few tries, finally I hoist her up so she's perched on the upholstered seat, legs spread, me between them. She's tall up there like this, nearly my height, and it lets us keep this kiss going, but I need more. We both do.

I step up onto the side bar, never breaking contact between our mouths, tongues still dancing, lips and hands roving restlessly, until I can fit the rest of my body into the cab with hers. Too tall to kneel upright in here, but I can work with this, hunching over her. Takes some work to make it all happen while never parting our lips, but I get her pushed up, further across the bench seats, manage to close the door behind me and lock us in using the key fob in my pocket.

Finally pull my mouth away from those swollen lips of hers to kiss down her jaw, her neck, that throat, until the hoodie blocks my path further down. She shivers from the scrape of my beard against her soft skin, so fragrant with that scent that's only ever belonged to her. Feminine, musky but soft—like a less concentrated version of how she tastes—I hope I never forget the way it lights me up again.

Manage to pull the hoodie up and over her head, she helps me disentangle herself from the long arms of the thing, and it lands in the footwell. Her shirt is next, and then (with some effort), those pants of hers that I'm still pretty sure she put on backwards during our great escape, along with her underwear.

Then I get to take a moment to soak in the sight of her. Bare beneath me, she's so much more *everything* in person than she's been in my mind when it gets to remembering her. Gorgeous, soft, alluring. She's changed, with time, some bits are bigger—like her tits, those lips that are calling to me—and some are a bit softer. I want to dive in and get reacquainted with all of her. Cover her body with mine until neither of us can remember what it was like to not be merged as one.

Reach back to grab the collar of my shirt at the back of the neck and peel if off with one hand, toss it down with the rest of her clothes, and it's tricky as hell to get these pants and boxer briefs off in this tight space, but I manage to kick my shoes off and do it.

Her eyes lock on my chest, my stomach, and then they fall down, past the V that's gotten more carved out with time, down to my cock, reaching out for her, needing to be inside her.

"Fuck, you're hot." The words come out like an objection, like she'll be speaking to management about that, maybe draft a formal complaint, or even propose legislation.

"You're one to talk," I tell her, gripping beneath her thigh and sliding her back down toward me just enough. Her long hair, still in that ponytail, fans out behind her, around her head, like spilled light in the dark truck, teasing me. "Look at these tits, like the rest of you wasn't enough. Had to go and remind me what perfection looks like."

Her brown eyes heat, promise and intention leaking out of them as she watches me. She brings her hands up, running them up the slight curve of her stomach, testing my patience. My eyes follow as they go up, up, over her ribcage and scaling the peaks of her breasts. Her fingertips toy with the stiff buds there, rosy and ready for my mouth, my firm grip.

She's had enough fun. It's my turn.

I lean forward, sucking the soft skin around her nipple into my mouth, teasing, grazing as I circle the bud there, her squirming beneath me. Let the torment get to her, kiss and pull at everywhere but where she wants me to until she's whining unintelligibly, shoving at my shoulders and head with her hands, and then I give in with a dark chuckle. Wrap my lips around her nipple, use my teeth to scrape the sensitive skin there and relish in the way she writhes beneath me when I do. The tip of my tongue flicks out across her pebbled skin, and she squirms again, legs spreading wider with a moan.

"Fuck, Grady." Damn. Rory only calls me that when she's worked up. Good sign.

Using my mouth for suction, I pull on her nipple until it releases with a smacking sound. I can feel my dick leaking, but he needs to wait his turn. Knowing how wet this is making her, how needy that cunt is right now, the way she's crawling out of her skin, ready to explode as soon as I give her the first bit of pressure she's craving, it's *exactly* what I need right now. What can I say? I like to play as much as I like to watch her legs shake, sometimes more.

Swapping sides, I pay equal attention to her other nipple, teasing, nipping, and pulling at her most sensitive parts. Her hips buck at first, and then she starts to roll them, wrapping her legs around my thigh and grinding against it. The feel of her slick pussy sliding against my skin is the breaking point for me. It's what makes me snap.

"You're ready for me, Hellcat. As ready as you're getting," I grind out.

Sitting back up as much as I can, my ass rests on my heels, still hunched over her a bit. Aurora follows me, sitting up with me, running a hand down my chest, the smattering of hair there. She lets it drag down, across my clenched abs, and I lean over to grab the backpack with the condoms. Couldn't leave those behind in the wild bear mauling, as she'll undoubtedly refer to it from here on out.

Fumble around with the zipper, my hand digging around

in the spacious compartment to find the single foil floating somewhere at the bottom. Around the same time my fingertips make contact with the square package, her fingers make contact with *my* package. I hiss through my teeth on a sharp inhale as she circles my cock with one finger, teasing me. Aurora drags the tip of her finger through the wetness on the tip of my dick, swirling it around, then encircling my cock with her entire hand. My hips jerk suddenly, pushing into her fist, and she groans at the way my cock forces her fingers to widen as it moves through them. When I make it back to her with the condom in hand, her lips are parted, gaze dripping with need.

"That's enough foreplay," I tell her. "I'm going to wreck your pussy now." I have a promise to live up to, after all. "Gonna wreck you for all those pretty boys back in New York."

"God, please." Her breaths are heavy in my ear, the hot little puffs driving me almost as crazy as her hand is. "I'm on the shot," she pants out, fingers wrapped around me and working me in wicked ways already. "And I'm clean."

"I'd fuck you anyway," I tell her honestly. "Nothing other than the word *no* would stop me from getting inside of you right now. But I'm clean too." I press the words into her shoulder, eyes screwed up from the feel of her tight fist around me, needing more, and fast. "And in the spirit of honesty, I can't get you pregnant."

She stops stroking me, eyes finding mine in confusion.

"I had a vasectomy."

The words hang. We don't unpack it. There are no follow-up questions. She thinks it over briefly, then takes the condom from my hand, ripping it out of my fingers. I watch, waiting for her to use her teeth to open the foil, make a show out of pinching the tip and rolling it down my shaft like she always would back when we used condoms. Instead, she chucks it to the side, lets it fly somewhere in the front seat, and says, "Bareback it is."

Then she lays back, pulls her knees to her chest, and uses her fingers to spread herself for me. All that perfect pink wetness is ready for me, waiting. Fuck the sunset, she's gotta be the Lord's best work.

Instead of letting out the groan brewing in my chest, I fist the base of my cock and stare at her, open and ready for me. "Think you can still take all of me, Hellcat?"

"Let's find out," she moans.

"Gonna make sure you take it all," I promise her, and then I'm moving forward, fitting the tip into her waiting center.

Our hands brush, hers parting her lips, mine guiding my cock into her, and somehow it feels so personal in that touch, the way our knuckles skim one another's as I slide through the wetness waiting for me there. Our eyes catch, and so does her breath as I push the head in, past the resistance, and notch myself in as far as I can go.

"Stop clenching," I force out through a tight jaw.

"I'm not," she pants.

"Let me in, Hellcat, relax," I try again.

"Yeah, because telling a woman to relax has worked exactly NEVER out of the infini—JESUS!"

Her bitching at me gets interrupted when I pinch her nipple roughly right as I flex my hips forward, able to push a good halfway in on that one thrust thanks to her body's immediate response.

"Oh God," she moans, legs falling open, muscles finally relaxing.

With a final tweak, I pull my hand off her nipple and move it up to clasp around her throat instead. I can feel her hum and groan against my hand, the vibration there, and sure enough, there's less resistance when I piston my hips forward, finally able to get all the way in and bottom out inside her. There's that gasp I've been waiting for.

Her brown eyes go wide, thick brows stretched high as I stretch her out for me, remind her what it feels like to be completely, thoroughly filled. I can see the thousand unsaid words in them now, all the things she wants to moan, wants to scream, wants to beg me to do to her, but she doesn't need to ask. For now, she can soak it all in, the way I'm trying to. I'll do my best to short-circuit that incredible mind of hers, keep it from taking away from this moment for her.

Leaning forward over her, I pull my hips back until just the tip is left inside of her, and then slam them forward again, filling her completely, wrapping myself in the best kind of warmth on this planet. Better than a stomach full of whiskey or sitting in front of a bonfire when you're camping, being sunk inside of Aurora is as good as it gets. Her walls tighten around me on the second thrust, and I let out a noise against her chest to tell her what that feels like.

Her throat flutters against the grip of my hand as she struggles to take in enough air to keep up with her heartbeat. I kiss the spot where her heart is doing overtime and release her throat to let her get the oxygen her body needs to withstand what I'm about to put it through.

"Isn't this how we did this the first time?" She barely gets the words out, but if she's still able to joke, then I'm not doing my job right. She's not wrong, though. The back of my truck. Out in the woods somewhere no one will find us. Me, balls deep inside of her. That was a first for both of us. All these years later, she's still the best I ever had. Now I'm gonna make sure she feels the same.

"I think you screamed a lot more the first time," I tell her, deadpan.

"You split me open, then gave me my first vaginal orgasm. What did you expect?"

"Kinda thought you might be screaming by now," I say through clenched teeth.

"So make me," she taunts me.

"Fucking hell, woman." Always gotta give me a hard time. There's never an easy route with her. But if she wants me to make her scream, I'll do her one better. I'll shut her up for once.

I pull back and slam my hips forward again, but she's so damn tight I can hardly keep my focus.

"Did you get bigger?" Aurora asks in a strained voice.

"Did you get tighter?" I shoot back.

"I'm—" she pants, but the words don't come out.

I pull back and push forward into her again, but I can feel it already. What she's trying to say. She's close. I knew she'd be like this. So turned on by the time we got started, she'd be milking me within seconds.

She arches her back, those taut nipples staring at me, begging for the little bit of attention they need to finish her again already.

Her pussy grabs me as I pull out of her again, and push my way back in, tilting her hips up with my hands to give me the angle I need to hit her front wall on the way.

Aurora screams out a curse and her eyes roll back, and I can't decide which I prefer. Getting to fuck her the way I've been craving or watching her come again. Guess it's a good thing I can do both at once.

Wrapping a hand under her thigh, I hitch her leg up and bring it to my hip, and she wraps it around me, pulling me close with it.

"You gonna come again?" I grunt out, and she tilts her head a fraction of an inch in a nod.

My hips slam into hers again, her heel pressed into my ass,

my pelvic bone flush against her, rubbing her clit with each thrust. Maxed out, but she still wants more, this greedy woman. Tilt my hips, grind into her a bit more and when I feel her start to tip over the edge, I slap the side of her breast. Give it a sharp clip that glances off her nipple as I do, watch it ripple through her, and I can see what the jolt of it does to her. Feel it for myself with how she clenches down.

Rory gasps, eyes wide as the sensation hits her, and it topples her over. Her eyes close, mouth wide, chest heaving in bursts of heavy breaths as I continue to work myself in and out of her, up and along that front wall with each thrust as she free falls. Don't let up, keep my hips working, driving into her as she shudders, as I feel her walls tighten and clench, trying to suck my own release out of me, but nice try. I'm gonna make this last a hell of a lot longer for the both of us than a minute or two. Her pussy floods me as she keeps coming, and I do what a good man does, and don't fucking stop.

One hand reaches out to play with her nipple, while the other holds the top of the seat for support. She gasps and moans, but seems like that speechless thing is working as I keep pulling and tweaking her nipple, harder than most women can take it, and she shudders through the rest of her orgasm.

"Goddamn, you're a dirty fuck, Rory," I tell her.

"Don't," she starts to say, but she struggles to get the words out, even if her eyes are open again. She can't even tell me not to call her that, and I'd call that a job well done on my part.

"When it's my cock inside of you, I'll call you what I want," I smirk at her. "Aurora. *Rory*. Dirty fucking girl."

Her eyes roll back again at that, and I can feel the tremors still rocking through her. She likes that more than she wants to.

"Is that what you want to hear?" I ask her. "How bad you are?" She moans again, her pussy clenching down on me yet again. "So proper for everyone else, Aurora, but such a filthy girl for me. Imagine if everyone in New York could see you now, knees to your ears in the back of my truck, covered in sweat and cum. My cock halfway to your ribs. Pussy dripping all over these seats for me and the nasty shit I can do to you. They don't know that this is where you belong. But I do, Rory. And I'll fucking remind you. You might belong in a boardroom by day, but at night? You should be on your back, beneath me."

She nods, eyes, face frantic, desperate for more from me. So I give it to her. Pound into her, hand around her knee, holding her wide for me as I show her what it feels like to be fucked by the one that got away.

My movements are rough, jagged, filled with a dozen years of resentment, and what ifs. Of knowing that we could've worked out, if she'd just tried. If she'd told me what was going on instead of never giving me the chance to make it right. My hips slam into hers, my balls smack against her ass, and it's rough, it's an ugly sound, but it's what we need. Her whimpers fill the cab, the slapping of our skin, but I don't let up on her.

"Make sure that every fucking time you even think of the Heights, of where you come from, it's me you feel, still lodged inside you. My cock splitting you open like this. How hard you come when it's me that's making you."

"Oh God," she moans out in between staggered breaths. "Harder, Grady," she demands, pleads with me.

"I'd love to. It'd be easier if your pussy wasn't strangling me."

"It's just self-defense from that monster of yours impaling me," she claps back. I'd laugh at her determination to start shit with me no matter where we are or what we're doing if I weren't so busy, sweat dripping down my brow at the concentration it's taking to not fill her up with my cum already. She huffs out something like a scoff at some realization she's had. "Jesus we can't even fuck without fighting," she says tightly, in between thrusts.

"You call this fighting?" I ask her, heavy breaths between the words. "Nah, Hellcat, this is just what fucking is supposed to be like. It's called passion. Fire." I illustrate my point with a sharp slap of my hips against hers, and she grunts involuntarily in response, walls clenching around me. "You'd rather have boring missionary with some wet noodle who gets hard over spreadsheets and calls you pumpkin, you know where to go. You wanna feel alive, get what you need, it's me you come to."

Her eyes meet mine, and she tilts her head away almost immediately.

"This is too personal," she whispers. "Too much like old times."

I withdraw, pulling out of her and missing the heat and tightness of her instantly, but I've lived without it for this long. I can last a few seconds.

"Fine by me," I mutter, turning her over so she's on her knees before shoving her forward roughly. She falls forward and catches herself on the door, but doesn't look back, just pushes her ass back toward me, waiting for more.

Shake my head at her efforts to keep me out, like it's gonna help if she isn't watching me. She'll feel me so deep inside her I'll be imprinted in her fucking soul for another seventeen years, the way she is on mine. But I'll humor her, and I'll get my second favorite view while I'm at it.

Use both hands to spread her ass cheeks apart—take in that image to keep me warm on lonely nights, both her holes on display for me—and line myself up with her entrance again. She's had enough warming up, now it's my turn to take what I need.

When I slam my hips forward, fronts of my thighs slapping the backs of hers, Aurora screams out at the feel of me invading her from this new, deeper angle and falls forward again, but my arms wrap around her to catch her this time. Both of us leaned a bit forward beneath the roof of the cab, I drive into her over and over again, holding her in place so she can't help but to take every inch I'm giving her. No mercy for how hard I'm fucking her, just like she had no mercy on me when she fucked us both by leaving.

I tilt my torso back a bit to make sure I capture a visual to go with this moment, the way she's so tight around me I can barely hold out. Turns out, watching her stretch and mold to the shape of my cock makes it even better, because that image nearly sends me over the edge.

"Fuck, Aurora. You should see you, trying to take me."

She whimpers, and I feel her pussy flutter around me. I wrap myself around her torso once again, left arm slung over her shoulder so I can grasp a breast in my hand roughly as my right hand sneaks around her hip and holds her pussy from the front as I continue to pound into her. Her moans encourage me, like the audience singing along at a concert, she feeds me the fuel I need to give her my best performance, all of my energy going into this moment.

"Should you get to come again?" I ask her, lips against the shell of her ear. Her sweat-soaked hair invades my nose, my mouth, and I couldn't give a fuck. Give her nipple a firm pinch and relish in the way her walls clamp down on me as it hits her. "The way I see it, you've been a fucking brat the whole time we've had this little arrangement between us. Seems fair to me if you're the one who gets left on the edge this time. Leave this pussy soaking, clit begging for more with my cum dripping out of you. That way, even if you give in and finish yourself off, it'll still be me you feel there."

Her unintelligible moans and whimpers grow louder and she moves her hips faster, more frantically, chasing her next release, like the insatiable fuck she's always been. The threat of not getting more enough to make her work even harder for it, prove she deserves another orgasm.

"So eager for my cum, so fucking thirsty, aren't you, Rory?"

Her torso is pressed to mine, back to front, our skin slick with sweat, and she nods against my shoulder, the back of her head rolling in her delirious state, nothing but need right now, high on my dick, this magic shit that we make together, so desperate for another fix while she still has the chance.

"What will you do for it?" I ask her. "Will you get back on your knees and suck the taste of you off of my cock until my cum is down your throat?"

She whines, and I move my fingers from her nipple to shove two into her mouth, as far back as they'll go.

"Show me," I growl into her ear, my punishing thrusts maintaining their brutal pace as I get closer and closer.

Rory sucks on my fingers, using her tongue to tease me, show me what a good girl she can be when you give her a reason, and I yank them out again, use the spit on my fingers, spread it around her nipple and keep plucking at it harder as I fuck her.

"Or maybe I should pull out and come all over your back?"

More noises from this girl, meaningless, mindless babble instead of a tongue lashing, from the one who has words for days, even in the worst of times.

"Fucked the lawyer right out of you, didn't I, Hellcat? You got nothing to say now? That pretty tongue too busy to give me hell?"

My name seems to be the best she can do. "Wyatt," she moans, and it's in that panicked tone that's her version of a warning. She's going to come whether I want her to or not. Might as well join her. Stop holding it off and lean into the pleasure, the way she's gripping me as I slide in and out of her, her soft heat the best thing my cock's ever been privileged to.

"Gonna come so hard you're gonna feel it hit the back of your throat, Rory. You ready?"

She turns her face sharply, finally looking back at me, and she doesn't second guess her instinct. Aurora leans in and captures my mouth with hers, nothing demure about it. Her mouth isn't closed, it's not sweet or cute, she sucks my fucking tongue into her mouth as her first move, and the feel of her mouth on mine, the way she's sucking on my tongue the way I'd love to feel her just about anywhere on my body, it's all I can take.

I make sure she falls with me, using my arm that's still around her chest to pinch her nipple the same time the calloused first finger and thumb of my other hand pinch her clit. I'm about as gentle as she's being with her mouth, and I can feel her soft scream that's absorbed by my mouth, but the result is instantaneous. She's shaking, coming, falling apart at the seams, and if my arms weren't holding her up, I'm all but certain she'd melt into the cushion of the seat itself. As it is, I hold her up, keeping our pelvises aligned as I thrust into her, letting go myself.

My balls tighten, tingles shooting up from the base of my spine and throughout my system as I pump her full of my load when I thought I'd never get the chance again. The feel of both of our releases embracing my cock—hers slick and mine sticky— as I continue driving into her is a memory for the mental safe deposit box. Her tongue in my mouth, lips pressed to mine, tits in my hand, pussy gripping me for all its worth, those are all getting stored right in there with it.

We pull back, ending the kiss as I pull out of her and she shudders, goosebumps all along her skin.

"Okay, I think that might've been a little better than our first time," she admits breathlessly, and I'm shocked to hear myself laugh again. Even after she's drained me, run me dry, she's managed to put another rare hint of a smile on my face.

"Yeah," I agree. "Just imagine what it'll be like when we're not out of practice together."

Now I just get to convince myself I won't miss the way this is with her, that Hallie at the bar feels just as good, that I can live without sex like this every night for the rest of my life. Only took me how many years to convince myself of it the first time? Should be able to do it again, right?

22
Aurora

"Be here at nine," Mom said when we parted ways after I got her settled in back home from the hospital yesterday. "We have some things to discuss."

I could scoff. Does she even know me at all?

No, the asshole inside my head says. *No, she really doesn't, and it's your fault.*

If she did, I reason, she would know that *be here at nine* translates into *be here by eight-fifteen* in Aurora-ese.

Wyatt might've said he fucked the lawyer right out of me a couple nights ago, but it would take a lot more than one night (even with him) to fuck the over-preparer out of me.

It's also possible that I was just worried my POS car wouldn't make it here (no, I still haven't let Wyatt talk me into swapping it out for something better), and I'd end up walking the last mile in my Valentino Garavani heels and had to account for that in my commute time. Ten blocks in the Upper West Side goes a lot faster than a mile walking through the untamed wilderness, wandering the barely paved backroads of the Heights. Especially since every neighbor you pass would insist on catching up along the way. I'd be lucky to make it by nightfall.

Either way, it's barely past eight when I push open the front door to my childhood home and find a naked man in the kitchen.

The Heights has really gone downhill.

From no crime to a peeping Tom with a B&E kink? Not on my fucking watch, asshole. My mom's going through enough. You can go wipe your junk on the dish towel at some other unlucky bastard's house, it won't be my mom's kitchen you desecrate.

I've seen *plenty* of his type back home—I've seen more unsolicited penises in my decade as a New Yorker than a stage-hand working quick change Off Broadway—and I know just what to do. Hoist my cognac leather tote bag over my shoulder more securely, and like a good New Yorker, I run *for* him, not away from him, screaming at the top of my lungs, brandishing whatever I have in hand as a weapon. Walking to my apartment after dark in the city, that's usually mace and maybe claws made out of keys, depending on the path I'm walking for the night. But today, in the Heights—and still on a high from being fucked within an inch of my sanity—my guards were (stupidly) down. So today, that weapon of choice is my fluffy pom-pom keychain that my ride-or-die lip balm is attached to, but I'll make it work. My scrappy attitude is really my secret weapon, after all.

"Get out of my mom's house, asshole!" I scream at the intruder, flying up behind him and attacking him with the pom-pom. I brandish it like nunchucks, whapping him over the back of the head and shoulders, all I can (or am willing) to see of the stranger, doing the kind of damage I hope would make my kick-boxing instructor proud.

The naked man's mug of coffee sits abandoned on the

counter as he brings his arms over his head and covers himself from the onslaught of my attacks.

What kind of intruder makes coffee? *Naked?*

One that's about to eat shit, that's who.

"You sicko!"

Whack.

"Get!"

Whack.

"Out!"

Whack.

"Motherfucker!"

"Well, you finally got something right," comes a husky voice that's too familiar.

I gasp in recognition, but my arms don't get the memo and they keep thwacking him with my deadly keychain. My bag lands with a thump at my feet, my arms too busy besieging this bastard with imminent doom to catch it as it falls, and still I continue my "best defense is a good offense" themed ambush.

"Would you mind stopping assailing me for long enough to cover myself and maybe find a towel?"

"I sure do fucking mind, you perv!"

Thwack, whap, smack.

"Come on, Aurora," he pleads.

"You clearly didn't mind the whole naked thing when you came in here. You know, you made your bed and all that," I gasp out between laborious strikes. "I am seriously rethinking that whole *good man* category I had you under, just so you know."

"What's all that racket, honey?" my mom's voice calls down the hallway.

Honey. A word I haven't heard her use since my dad left. And I realize she isn't asking me. She's asking *him.*

He's ... here by invitation? The magnitude of all of this hits me, and I'm too stunned to keep the assault going. My arms fall to my sides, pom-pom puff in hand. She ... *knows* about the exhibitionist intruder?

"Laura Lee," Duke calls out dryly in response. "I don't wanna alarm anyone, but I *think* Aurora knows about us."

The emphasis on *think* would make me laugh if my jaw weren't halfway to the cracked linoleum floor right now.

Sure enough, my mom rounds the corner into the kitchen—dressed in a robe with cartoon chickens on it, hair in a towel turban—and witnesses this *man* backed into the cabinets of her kitchen, bare ass glinting like the full moon in here, and she doesn't even thank me for coming to her defense. For my efforts to *rescue* her. Nope. She looks affronted and chastises me instead.

"What on God's green earth do you think you're doing, dove?"

"Me?" I sputter, hand to my chest, pom-pom hanging at my side. "ME?" It's more of a shriek than a word.

"Yes, you. Barging in here and, what? Buffing Duke's back with that thing? Seriously, Aurora, what are you doing?"

"If I may speak up," comes Duke's wry voice. "I think she was trying to run me out of the house."

"What are *you* doing here?" My speech is coming back to me slower than I'd care to acknowledge, but at least it's still chock full of barbs.

"That's really none of your business," my mom shoots back at me.

"I've seen the man's ass, in fact, I *still* see the man's ass, so I don't think I'm being particularly unreasonable by asking why. But I'll go with my deductive powers of reasoning at this point—please, if you love me at all, don't answer the question—and I'm just going to go wash my eyes out while you put on some clothes. Remind me, Mom, where do you keep the bleach?"

Duke harrumphs and reaches a hand out toward my mother,

his body still facing the kitchen wall for whatever modicum of modesty he can still preserve. My mother leans forward, tousling her hair with the towel it was wrapped in seconds ago, and hands him the thin yellow towel. From the corner of my eye I can see him wrap it around his waist and turn around to face us for the first time.

I've never once in my life used the term silver fox about anyone who wasn't Timothy Olyphant, but as Duke glares at me, glowering as he turns around, only his most necessary bits covered, I can't help the eyeful I get, and I think he might make it into that category. Come to think of it, he looks quite a bit like Timothy.

I'd congratulate my mom on the pull if I wasn't too busy losing my fucking mind about this development. This secret the two of them have been keeping. For how long?

Mental acuity is normally one of my strengths, but between the lack of coffee and the bare old-man ass I was faced with when I opened the door—not to mention, how that was followed by the second biggest shock of the damn decade—I am *not* firing at all cylinders this morning, to use a metaphor that would make Wyatt proud.

My mom's eyes catch on my bag, slumped over on the floor by my feet, and before I can move to pick it up she's leaning forward to grab it herself. I mean, yeah, it wasn't a cheap bag, but it's fine on the floor for a minute. Hopefully my laptop survived the fall, but really, it's the least of my worries at this particular moment.

But it's not my laptop my mom reaches for.

Her fingers close on a pink envelope, *Mom* written in elegant script on the front. "What's this?" she asks, voice a whisper.

That envelope has been in there since last Friday. It was going to be my surprise after repaying her life's biggest regret at the rec center, had that day not taken a turn for the awful. Haven't been able to bring myself to toss the envelope yet, even if what it represents is more than dead to me now.

"Nothing," I say automatically, hand flying for the envelope, but she's quick for an old lady on the downslope of life.

I feel two sets of eyes on me and Duke makes a move to block my path, him and that too-thin yellow towel I don't want to go near, as my mom settles in at the dining room table to open the oversized envelope.

"Seriously, Mom," I try again. "Just give it back."

"Oh, is this for your other mom?" The snark in her voice has bite, but it's not mean. It's more me than Lexi whose bite is usually meant to take your legs out from under you.

"It's not ..." my voice trails off, because what do I even say?

She slides her finger along the top of the envelope beneath the flap to rip it open and there's no going back now.

Mom pulls out the giant custom card and gasps at the picture on the front. A photoshopped image of her and me (had to get her picture off of Facebook, but I got it), in front of the Grand Palace in Bangkok.

"What is this?" she asks in a small voice, but she's already opening the card and I know she knows.

Two thick, glossy rectangular pieces of paper with rounded edges slip out as she opens it, and she catches them.

"Tickets?"

Technically, they're printouts I had made on Etsy to represent the digital tickets I'd bought, but close enough. It doesn't matter now anyway. Not a chance she can travel that far with how quickly her cancer is progressing.

I shrug instead of answer.

"Oh, Rory," she whispers, and fuck me, her eyes are glinting abnormally bright beneath this chandelier from the '70s.

I hear a sniffle from Duke at my side and turn to face him

right as he's wiping a fist across an eye, like he got some dust in it or something.

"Can we go back to what he's fucking doing here?" I point at him for emphasis.

"What I'm fucking doing is your m—" Duke doesn't miss a beat, but I cut him off.

"NO. We aren't doing that, thank you." My hand in his face should shut him up, but it doesn't.

"I assure you, we most certainly are," he says with a wink to my mother and just *gross*. But she grins back at him, looking twenty years younger and not fatally ill, and why is that almost cute? She never looked at my dad like that, as far as I can recall. The bags under her eyes don't look so large, the twinkling in her eye adds some much-needed life to her appearance, and somehow it sparks hope deep inside me. That maybe I could have that one day too.

The door swings open abruptly and all three of us turn to face the front door, Lexi barging through it, sunglasses high on her thin nose, attitude all over her face, wild hair tumbling all over the place.

"Thought I'd beat Rory for once in my life," she singsongs as she steps over the threshold, and then comes to a dead halt when she meets all of our gazes. "But apparently not. What the fuck did I just walk in on?" she asks, pushing her glasses up to hold her hair out of her face, and pointing between us all with a judgmental finger. Her brown eyes, identical to mine, narrow on the pom-pom still clutched in my hand. "Are you into tickling now, Aurora? Rory would've never," she quips. "But I guess we all develop new kinks as we age. I don't even wanna know what woke this one up. Do us all a favor and keep that to yourself, thanks. If that shit's contagious, I don't want to risk it."

I glare at her silently, tongue pressed in my cheek, willing her to register the scene in front of her, what's *way* more important than my keychain.

"Well," my mother says quietly, gesturing to the dining room table. "I invited you girls to be here at *nine* this morning," she stresses the time, still a good half an hour away, "to sit you down and talk to you about what to expect from here."

"I didn't expect to walk in on a naked Duke in your dining room," Lexi says, huffing out a breath like she's got a heavy load on her shoulders. "But I guess it was only a matter of time."

"You knew?" I accuse her, more than ask her.

"Of course I knew," she screws up her face at me, like I'm as big of an idiot as I was when we were in grade school. "I mean, duh, the man hasn't left the bar since Reagan was in office, and all of a sudden his room is just *open* for Rory. Mom kicking us out of the hospital every night. There's been dozens of clues, you two aren't as clever as you think you are. You've been about as subtle as Rory trying to sneak Grady in and out of her bedroom window when the whole house could hear her bedsprings creaking."

Cheap shot, and my scowl tells her so.

Lexi continues dryly. "I'm just glad I didn't have to hear your headboard squeaking, Mom. You're probably smart enough to put pillows behind it. Rory's hormones developed before her brain did."

I change the subject as rapidly as possible. "How long has this been going on?" I ask my mom and Duke.

"Long while," he says quietly.

My mom watches him, adoration shining in her eyes, and something inside me softens, melts into a puddle that Wyatt started, he's been working on warming up—made some pretty good progress last weekend, with staying here, helping the chickens, that hike we took, the cider, and that memorable night in his truck—but this might've done it. That ice around my heart might finally be nearly gone now.

"We started ... prioritizing it more when the diagnosis came," she adds softly.

"Well, thank God you finally said it out loud." Lexi rolls her eyes and drags a chair out from the table, scraping along the old, dark hardwood floor loudly as she sits down in it. "Worst kept secret in this town. Gracie said Grady told Ronnie he suspected it months ago. It was only a matter of time before everyone else figured it out too."

Figures that Wyatt is the only one who put it together. All the times he might have known, the times he might have spilled their secret but chose to respect them instead flash before my eyes. And where that would normally piss me off, it warms me that he chose to protect their peace.

My mother sighs, but it's not a heavy one. "If the cat's already out of the bag, you may as well stay for this talk, then, Duke."

He pulls another chair out from the table, across from Lexi and next to my mom, and Lexi's eyes on his naked upper body speak volumes, but her mouth still says it anyway. "I get that you're, like, built and whatever, but would you mind putting on some clothes? I don't want to stare at my future stepdaddy's nakedness at the breakfast table, thanks so much." She shoots an acidic smile that's zero percent authentic at him to try to sugar up the words, complete with several overdone blinks.

Duke mutters, shakes his head, and walks away, leaving the three of us alone. I take the fourth chair, the one across from Mom, and stare at her expectantly.

"We're going to start telling people," she says. "About my diagnosis."

"Yeah, we got that much," Lexi says, a little more scathingly than I appreciate being aimed at our mother. But I think it's her way of protecting herself from the reminder. That mom has a diagnosis, and it's not a good one. But not saying it out loud doesn't change the fact it exists.

"Like Aurora has been saying," Mom gestures at me, "it's better to wrap up loose ends than leave things unsaid. So I'm going to not leave this as a surprise for people, or leave them to speculate and gossip as my condition worsens—" her eyes cut to Lexi's, who doesn't even look rightfully ashamed at her loud-mouth reputation. "—and I'm going to start telling people, give folks a chance to get some time in with me before it's too late. Plus, you know how this town is. It'll be all anyone talks about until the next new thing, but I wanted you girls to know first, so you can be prepared for people comin' to you about it, or the things you might hear."

"This mean I can finally tell Gracie?" Lexi asks. "She knows I've been lying to her, and she'll probably give me an 'accidental perm' next time she does my hair if she hears it from anyone else." I snort a laugh.

My mom nods. "Yeah, you'd better, but maybe you can let me tell one or two others first. We all know that girl's got the biggest mouth this side of the Mississippi after a couple sips of anything stronger than a light beer."

"Hey," Lexi snaps. "She's kept quiet on your little tryst," she says, pointing at my mom.

"Ooh, that's a four-dollar word for you, Lex," I tease her. "You learned that one in *40 Days and 40 Nights*, didn't you?" She had a strong Josh Hartnett phase for a while there.

Duke steps back into the room, preventing the spat from escalating, and thankfully he's dressed in his usual jeans and a checked shirt this time, gray hair styled back from his face, weathered cowboy boots on his feet. He takes his seat next to Mom and his hand closes over hers, atop the table where we can all see it. When his thumb runs across the top of her hand, the backs of my eyes sting.

Unfortunately for me, that motion calls Lexi's sharp eyes to the table, the card and tickets lying there.

"The fuck is that?"

Just like Mom, her hand darts out before any of us can stop her. She picks up the card, the tickets laying on top of it, and scans them with impressive speed, putting it together rapidly.

"For the two of you?" The acid in her tone is unmistakable. I could feel that chill from halfway across the country, were I still there.

"It wasn't exactly a cheap trip, Lex," I start, somewhere between defensive and soft. "Not like offering to cover a meal for you or something. It's first-class, international tickets and an entire itinerary in a foreign country."

"Right. For you and her. Something you knew I couldn't join you on. Because why would I want to share in my mom's final time alive? I'm just the bitchy older sister you left behind. I'm not even dying, so I'm not enough for you to care about, I guess."

This kitchen just became a pressure cooker, and there's nowhere for the steam to vent. We're about to boil over into a very dangerous explosion if anyone so much as breathes near this room the wrong way.

"It wasn't meant to leave you out, Alexis. I was just trying to get some time in with Mom. Do something fun together." My voice is softer than usual, trying not to step in any snares she's left lying around.

Alexis puts a hand up in my face, bitter anger and hurt across her features. "You can't just come back here and throw money around and expect to buy back your place in Mom's life. I've been here, been with her even when I had a choice." She slams her pointer finger into the table, emphasizing her point. "You show up only when it'll eat you alive for the rest of your shitty, lonely, pathetic life if you didn't, and use your money to try to make up for it. But that doesn't change the fact you don't give a shit about any of us, anyone who isn't named Aurora." That one slices deeper than I'd like it to. To add insult to injury, she throws the tickets at me, and while they don't go far, the sight of them fluttering down in the streaky light will take permanent residence in my mental replay of all my worst moments for years to come. "Fuck you," she spits out at me. "We don't want your money. All she wanted was *you*, and you wouldn't give her that. Now all *I* want is you to leave again." She sneers at me, disdain rolling off her thickly, in waves. "Thailand wouldn't be far enough if you ask me. Maybe we can make this a one-way ticket? You can fuck off for good this time."

"That's *enough*," my mom tries to roar the words, but it comes out as more of a croak.

Duke speaks at the same time. "Alexis." There's more gravitas in his voice than I've heard before, and I'm impressed with the authority he commands in the name of harboring respect for my mother.

Me? My head is spinning, thoughts getting more violent than they have in weeks, like an angry sea, they slap against the sides of my skull, crashing into me repeatedly, no safe harbor, nowhere to escape as they assault me.

My mom's words, the last thing she added to her bucket list, mock me as Lexi's words echo through my head.

Sure would be nice if my girls got along again. If I knew you two would be okay and have each other, even if I'm not here.

Not only is Thailand not happening, looks like she won't get that wish either. For all the ways I wanted to help make this transition easier on my mom, I'm feeling like one hell of a failure right now.

The tears start to brim, nose and the backs of my eyes stinging, and I stare into the light to try to chase them away.

I hear Alexis arguing with both Duke and my mother as they continue to chastise her. "I'm only speaking the truth." I don't have to look at her to see the cool indifference she's sporting. I can picture the exact face she's making.

"Go cool off," he tells her.

"Leave," my mom's brittle voice cuts off any other arguments my sister tries to throw out, and I hear the sounds of her chair scraping back, her stomping off, the door slamming, and two heavy exhales. Maybe three?

I focus on the one thing that I'm able to right now. The thing that pisses me off instead of breaks my heart.

"I can't believe you hid this from me."

"I'm sorry, remind me why my love life is your business, *Aurora?* When's the last time you shared anything about your life with me?" I don't know what's in the water supply in this house, but every woman who's ever lived here came out *spicier* than the garden variety normally found in the Heights. Or maybe it's just genetic and Lex and I both got it from the woman in front of me.

"I moved back here for you. I quit my job for you. I gave up my entire *life* to come be with you and help you through this. And you kicked me out because you didn't want me to know he's here?"

Duke leans back in his seat, eyes bouncing between my mother and I, but he looks like he's ready to jump in the moment my mom asks for a tag team, and right now, I fucking dare him to.

"Oh, don't pull that on me," my mom scoffs at me. "I never asked you to come back. That was your call. And thank God your bosses had more sense than to let you quit over me. We both know when this is all over, you're going to go right back to that place you call home, and dive back in right where you left off."

Not sure why that gouges a path in my gut. I think this might be the first moment I'm realizing I haven't been counting down to that picture she painted lately. That some part of me has been warming up to the idea of more time with Wyatt. This interim life I have going here has become ... nice. It doesn't sound as crazy as it used to that I could be happy here.

"And you and I both know you staying here when we haven't so much as seen each other since you were twenty-one would've been like holding a magnifying glass to an ant hill. Whether it was me, Lexi, or you that blew up, that was never going to end well. I appreciate you being here, doing what you can to make up for lost time, but you can't just expect to be treated like the last twelve years didn't happen, Aurora. You left a lot of damage in your wake, and I'm trying to look past it in light of what we're all going through, but just because you feel different after all these years, it doesn't mean everyone else sees you that way. To us, you're the same Rory who left without a word and never came back. Going by Aurora, having a new hair color and a degree—" probably not the time to correct her, it's actually three degrees, "—with some fancy clothes doesn't change that for us."

"I'm gonna take off, Laura Lee. Let you ladies talk this out." Duke stands with a somber face and leans in to kiss my mother's cheek. His mouth twitches into something of a chuckle at whatever thought he pops into his head. "Guess I don't have to wait until Rory's back to the bar to come over tonight."

My mom tilts her head and produces a small smile for him. "You sure don't, handsome. Guess you can come over whenever the hell you feel like it now. All our secrets are gonna be public property soon."

With a smack against her lips, he takes off, and my mom and I stare at each other in the uncomfortably quiet home.

"Let's hear it, then," my mother says, resigned, and lets her arms fall to the table with a slap.

I stare at her in question, my best *you're gonna have to do better than that, opposing counsel* face in place.

"Have at me. Now's your chance." She tosses her arms up and lets them fall down again. "You're thinking it. You've been thinking it for all these damn years, you might as well say it, Rory. All that resentment you hold for me. And your father."

My sharp inhale gives away how precisely she just hit that nail on the head.

"You think I don't know that you've held it against me all this time? That it's my fault you left? You're the one who wants me to tie up loose ends while I'm still around, now's your chance to duke it out with me. So do it. Lay it on me."

An alarm goes off in the kitchen—what timing, like now *is* the time, regardless of what the gurgling in my stomach has to say about it—and we both look over to it. My mom stands up, takes a couple pills of varying sizes from her plastic pill planner, downs them like a pro with the mug of (surely cold) coffee that's still on the counter there from when I came in earlier this morning.

When she comes back and reclaims her seat, I'm not looking forward to this any more than I was when the words first left her lips, but this is probably a talk I can't avoid for another dozen years. So I remove the filter between my brain and my mouth.

"He left, and you did nothing. He left us for *her* and you let it happen." The first tear falls down my face, a lifetime of anger, betrayal, and hurt in that single droplet. I swipe it away, pissed that it broke through the barrier.

"What, did you want me to have her taken out?" Mom tosses back at me. "Thrown in the river with a bunch of rocks?"

I roll my eyes, swallow the sardonic chuckle that tries to escape, despite the somber setting. "God, you're a tough old broad."

She raises her brows at me. "About time you noticed. Where'd you think you got it from, anyway, huh?"

I blow out a big breath and tell her what I should've way too long ago. "I didn't leave because of *you*. I left because of *him*."

"So, to get back at him for leaving your family, you left your family? How'd that work out for you?" The way this woman busts balls as a hobby, she'd make a hell of an attorney if you ask me. All my best traits that make me such an asset for the firm surely come from her, after all.

"I left because I couldn't go through that, Mom. It hurt enough to have my dad do that to my mom. The man I'd trusted most my entire life. If it happened to me by my own husband? I wouldn't have survived. I don't know how you did, actually."

If it could happen to the best woman I've ever known, what the fuck chance did my shitty ass have at finding and keeping love in this town? Lord knows the pattern Wyatt and I were in back then wasn't healthy. We had good parts, yeah, but neither of us were willing to become the people we needed to be to make it work long-term, and neither of us had the balls to call it off either. We would've gone down the exact path my parents did. The one his parents did. Heartbreak. A broken family. All I did was pull the plug before it got pulled for me years later, when it would've hurt way more.

"It wasn't a surprise to me, Rory. You think I'm as dumb as Ronnie looks?"

My head pulls back at that, and I shake it a couple of times, stunned. "You *knew*?"

"What, you think he was some brilliant son of a bitch about cheating on me for half our marriage? Of course I knew."

Whatever remaining esteem I've held her in all these years just bottomed out, crashed through the floor, and dug itself deep into this rocky soil beneath every building in this town. It was bad enough that she *didn't* know, that she was as blindsided as I was by him leaving our family for a woman barely older than Lexi was at the time. But for her to *know*? I don't know how to respect her at all after that bombshell.

"If you haven't bothered to talk to me in all these years, I know you haven't been talking to him," my mom hypothesizes, already knowing she's right. I give her a tiny nod to confirm.

I cut almost all the ties to the life I left. The occasional text with my mom was about it once I was gone. Definitely didn't give my new number to my dad who bailed on us. Cheat on my mom, abandon your girls? You're dead to me.

"But growing up, that man was your hero. You and Lexi both. Sure, he was a shitty husband, but he had value in some areas." She looks around, at the walls of the house we're in. "He provided for us, above and beyond what my income would've allowed for with two young kids. But we could've done without his money. More important to me was the way you two loved that man. You're both so headstrong, having him around was good for you. Flawed as he might be, he wasn't a bad father."

Until he ran off with a girl barely older than his daughters, if you count that sort of thing. I bite the retort back, but my mom's eyes narrow in on me like she knows what I was thinking, and hell, she probably does. She leans forward, from across the table from me, elbows on the wooden surface.

"Listen, Aurora. One day, when you're a mom, you'll understand. Or maybe you never will. But when you're a parent, all you can do is what you think is best for your kids. It's the *only* thing that matters when you're a mother. You'll make some mistakes, you're bound to. Lord knows I did. But you'll try to do your best, and that's all you can do. I'm sorry you think I failed you by staying with him despite the sort of husband he was. But I'm thankful you had a father for those additional years. It was worth it to me to keep him around for the two of you, even if my marriage was nowhere near perfect. And when you were good and grown, ready to move out on your own, I kicked his ass out."

My jaw slackens at that. She kicked *him* out?

All these years I spent judging her, pitying her, for what she went through. The way she was made a fool of. How what she went through convinced me not to give the best years of my life to some man who was going to string me along like an absolute idiot, and it wasn't even true?

My mom keeps going, dropping more truth bombs on me. "Your daddy isn't every man in Smoky Heights, Rory. He's just one man. Duke isn't your dad. Wyatt Grady isn't your dad. There are good men here. I know because I've had one for a long time now. And Duke is the kind of man on his worst day your father could never dream to be on his best."

There's a foreign sensation in my chest, and I realize it's the final *drip* of the last of that ice that's been thawing around my heart.

The love in my mom's voice. The warmth when reflecting on how well Duke treats her.

It cinches it for me. Makes it clearer than the Hudson could ever hope to be that I was so fucking wrong. Maybe Wyatt and I were idiots way back when, but we've both matured. We could absolutely work out now. I think this has been dawning on me for weeks, maybe longer, but this has solidified it for me. Staying in the Heights doesn't seem like a punchline anymore. It's more like the fuzzy light flares on the beautiful shot at the end of a movie, when you see the happily ever after. Mine just might be here after all.

So after my mom and I finish laying it all on the table, clearing the air and hugging for a long, long time, I head for the one person that somehow doesn't hold my past against me. The one who has more of a right to than anyone else, and still chooses not to.

23
Aurora

If I only have six months left in the Heights, I need to use my time wisely. That's a specialty of mine, if you didn't know.

Which is why, at 4:02 p.m., I'm pulling up to Gonzo's Garage, just as its namesake is pulling out. Something I hope Wyatt doesn't do tonight.

Gonzo waves at me as we pass one another turning in and out of the gravel lot, and the knowing smirk on his face tells me Wyatt's gonna get an earful tomorrow, but I'm too focused on why I'm here to let it deter me.

Managed to push past the way my mind was racing for the better part of the day, clocked a decent chunk of hours on my latest assignment, the Puffin Press merger, and sent off the final file, finally. Spent a little time on my pet project, too, Brown Stone. But spent all of it—the entire day—counting down to now. When Wyatt's off the clock, somewhere I can have him all to myself.

His truck's still here and I park next to it in my clunker, amazed it hasn't quit on me again since my second day in town, almost six weeks ago.

Do a quick check in the visor mirror, smoosh my lips

together, flick over them with my teeth a bit to make them extra plump, extra pink. It's time to refresh my filler, but we're not going to worry about that today. I'd kill to have my brows laminated and find a decent place for a full set of lashes while we're at it, but it's a big enough ask to keep my nails done while I'm here, and please don't remind me about the state of my roots. I've cried enough today. I gotta work with a more natural Aurora at the moment, and I know he'll like exactly what he's getting from me just fine, no room for self-doubt.

Glance down at the short dress I'm wearing, the maroon one that buttons all the way up the front, and I undo a couple more from the top, make sure the girls are nice and visible. Eh, might as well just open 'er up down to my belly button, keep that flimsy lace bra on full display so there's *no* question as to what I'm here for. It doesn't give the lift of a push-up, it shows the effects of all the years since he knew my body better than I did, but it's hot as hell just the same.

Is the late October chill a little much for this tiny outfit? Perhaps, but I'm counting on Wyatt to warm me right up.

If we were in New York I'd worry about cameras on the building, or on the street. But back home? I should be safe to go unrecorded just about anywhere. The knowledge adds some extra swagger into my saunter as I approach the open garage bays.

Sure enough, Wyatt is bent over a car, just like I hope I will be in about thirty seconds. The hood is popped, his head is beneath it, and I get to take in how fine he's gotten with time. He's always been good-looking, but he's aged in a way that is *very* promising for his older years. He's thicker than he was when we were together, a slim waistline, with built shoulders, arms toned and streaked with grease. That tattoo that covers his forearm. After our night in the truck together, I now know it's not his only one, and my heart picks up its pace at the memory.

He's back in his usual today, dark Dickies and a Henley with the sleeves pushed up to his elbows. Steel-toe boots that probably have more miles on them than most of the cabs in NYC.

Today, his dark hair is slightly mussed, but still pushed back, out of his tanned, rugged face. I can imagine the intensity in those forest green eyes as they stay focused on whatever's between his hands right now, I won't embarrass myself by trying to name it.

Wyatt hears my footsteps, the way the gravel and the crunchy leaves are displaced by the same heels I've worn since this morning, and he looks over in a way that stops my breath. He stands, using a rag to wipe at his hands, cleaning each finger individually as he thoroughly eye-fucks me on my approach.

"Don't tell me you're here to finally let me pick out a better car for you?"

I shake my head at him as I keep walking, eyes roving his tall frame.

"You need to be serviced?" The words shouldn't sound so sexy, but from him? My nipples pebble, cheeks heat at the implication.

"You do lube jobs?" I toss out the best joke I can think of, flustered like this.

He tosses the rag onto the side of the hood he was just under and widens his stance as I get closer.

"You need your system serviced, your pipes need attention, Hellcat, I'll give you a special deal."

"I'm listening."

"I'll get ya good and lubed up, make sure you have a smooth ride, and I'll send you on your way, free of charge."

My eyes glide along his muscled, lean build, up and down, and decide I need to have a ride on this man, and soon. "What if I told you I was here to service ... you?" I let the last word fall from my lips as I finally reach the space right in front of him.

"That it was you I couldn't stop thinking of all day? That it was —" My hand trails down the front of his pants, right over his fly as I speak. "—this cock I kept imagining in my mouth as I was logging billable hours at eight hundred dollars a pop." The material beneath my hand twitches, and I feel him wake up. "That I watched the time tick down until your day was over, and I could race over here and show you what I've been wet over for hours."

Wyatt pulls his lower lip through his teeth with a tight expression on his face. His eyes don't give away his next move, so all the air whooshes out of me when one of his rough hands abruptly comes up to the opening of my dress and works its way inside, flattening against one lace-covered breast. His thumb rubs the hardened bud there, while his fingers press into the soft flesh surrounding it.

I let my hand rub up and down his hardening length through the material, in time with what he's doing to my nipple.

"You've been sitting still, dripping for me, and didn't think to text me to come fuck you?"

I don't tell him how I wanted to come to *him* for once. To do something for *him*. To bridge that gap only he's been willing to so far. That I wanted to thank him for being the only one here who doesn't hate me for what I did all those years ago. Instead, I say silkily, "The anticipation is half the fun, don't you think? Getting all worked up over the possibilities, visualizing the perfect ... outcome?"

I peer around the shop behind him until I spot what I was looking for. I strut over to it, his hand falling out of my dress as I go, walking carefully through the shop in these heels, until I come to a car that looks clean enough to sit on. Turning to face him, I lean back, ass resting against the hood and cock my head at him.

"Wanna fuck my face while I sit on one of your favorite cars?"

He follows, striding across the garage in less than half the time it took me, steely promise painted across his stony features.

"I have a better idea," he says roughly. His strong hands band around my waist and he lifts me off the car, hoisting me in the air to somewhere back in the far corner of the shop. To another car covered in a drop cloth that looks like it hasn't been touched since MTV played music.

He rests me down on the ground momentarily while he rips the drop cloth off, revealing a hot orange car (or one that used to be hot orange) with black racing stripes, an old one, from the looks of it.

"I wanna fuck your mouth on Weston's favorite car. Fuck up his paint. Let you make a mess all over it. He'll never be back for it anyway, and if he ever is, well, only you and I will know what *great* care we took of his precious 1970 Charger."

"Oh God, don't make this weird, Wyatt. If you're getting hard over pissing off your brother, I don't think I want to do this."

He comes back to stand in front of me, grabs my hand in his and places it over his distended fly again. "This dick *only* gets hard for you. You've goddamn jinxed it. Don't get any other ideas, okay, Hellcat?"

That shouldn't be a romantic line, but here I am swooning anyway.

He continues in that low voice that has my heartbeat fluttering between my legs. "The fact it'll piss Weston off is just the cherry on top. Fucking your mouth is enough to get me off anytime, anywhere, Hellcat. Shit, all I had was the thought of it for long enough, the real thing will spoil me."

He hoists me up again, plopping me down on the flat trunk of the Charger, but instead of unzipping his pants, pulling my head forward and putting me to work, he presses me back, lays me down flush on top of the car. My legs are bent, heels resting on the trunk, and I'm sure that can't be good for it, but he doesn't seem to mind. My noises of protest are shushed as he rounds the car, reemerging in my line of sight right above me.

Wyatt leans forward, hands wrapping around my wrists, and he yanks, pulling me further across the car, until I'm stretched completely flat out, my head falling off of the other side, neck curving with the car, and the rest of me on display for him. The way I've been pushed and pulled around, the skirt of my dress has ridden up, too, and my need for this man is enough that I'm not even going to complain about my bare ass being on a gross *car* like I normally would. If I move another inch or two, he'll see the rest of me is bare and ready too.

He unbuttons the rest of my dress until the material is wide open, top of my tits spilling out of this lacy bra at this angle, and he can see it all from where he stands above me.

"How many times have you gotten yourself off thinking of this moment?" Wyatt's gruff voice scrapes against my nipples, just like the rough lace would beneath his touch, and I hum.

"This week? Or ever?" I purr.

"Tell me, Hellcat," he says, unbuttoning his pants and lowering the zipper. He pulls his thick cock out of his boxer briefs, stroking it a couple times before pausing to pull his pants and underwear down so I have a clear view of everything I need. "In your fantasy, do I come on your face? Your tits? Or down your throat?"

He wraps his fist around the base of his cock again, and steps forward to guide the tip to my lips. I open eagerly, and Wyatt smears the head across my mouth, dragging my lower lip with it and then releasing so it bounces back into place. The way he watches, the fascination roiling in his gaze, it's intoxicating.

"You tell me," I breathe out. "Because in my fantasy, it's you doing whatever the fuck you want to me."

The burn that flickers to life in those endless green depths sets off a need low in my body. So do his next words. "That's a dangerous offer, Hellcat."

Instead of answering him, I simply open my mouth as wide as it'll go, and I wait.

A primal sort of growl leaves his chest as he positions himself, lining up his crown with my mouth, and pushes forward. My hands search for purchase on the car's slippery surface as his head passes over my tongue, but there's nowhere for me to grab. I do my best, digging my fingertips in to steady myself as he drives in for the first time. There's no stopping the moan I make around his length, the way it stretches out my mouth in the most beautiful way. I can't help but feel the pinch and sting of a burn in my pussy from the last time he got to do whatever he wanted to me, and I'm desperate to feel it again, stat.

"Nowhere to hold on tight, hmm?" I swear I can feel the vibration of the bass in his voice in my mouth as he speaks, connected the way we are. "Guess I'll just have to hold onto you then," he says and even though my line of vision is slightly obscured at this exact moment, I can still picture the smirk on his face, the way one side of his lightly bearded mouth will be twitched up, the evil glint in his eye. It's enough to make me squirm with need.

Wyatt doesn't give me time to ponder what he means, as he withdraws his length from my mouth and pushes back in, his hands come down on my breasts, roughly, and he squeezes, holding me for purchase as his hips piston forward roughly. He hits the back of my throat and a small scream sounds at the intrusion, the invasion, but it's muffled by his girth.

"Come on, Hellcat, open up for me," he urges. His fingers

start to pluck and play with my nipples, my breasts, through the scratch of the fabric. My eyes flutter shut and the pool of wetness between my legs grows as my thighs fall open, heels scraping the surface of the car beneath me, but it must not be a priority for him right now.

I plead with my jaw to loosen up, unlock, and make more space for him. For my throat to calm down, to open wide and let him in.

"That's it," he praises me. "That's my girl. Just like that."

One of his hands leaves the breast it's been worshiping, and he uses his fingers to stroke down the column of my throat, wholly exposed to him like the rest of me, encouraging it to open up and not keep him out. It works.

"Mmm, you're taking me like a goddamn pro, Aurora."

I moan around him and he pulls back, taking some of my spit with him, which drips down the corner of my mouth and across my face.

"Take a deep breath now, Hellcat. It's the last one you're going to get for a bit."

Like I've been possessed, taken over by the spirit of someone compliant, I follow his orders for once, breathing in deeply through my nose as he leans forward, filling my mouth entirely, and not stopping as he breaches my throat. I gag, but he doesn't stop. He pulls back what can't be more than halfway, just enough that I can almost take a breath, but not quite enough, and then he's pushing forward again, and again.

"Ah, fuck. That's it," he rumbles, continuing to murmur an assortment of curses, praise, and crude demands.

That one hand keeps stroking my throat, loosening me for him, before he circles my throat instead and tightens his grip, as his other hand continues playing with my nipple, and every part of me is his. He can fuck my throat, my soaking wet pussy, or anything he wants. I'd give him all of me. More than he ever had before.

I wonder if he can feel the way he's driving into my throat with his hand, if it feels or looks like he's fucking his fist. I wish I could see it.

"You're a wet dream like this, you know that?" he murmurs the question, not expecting an answer, but I moan around him anyway, wanting him to hear my response.

Wyatt brings both hands back to my hardened nipples, paying them enough attention that I'm a squirming mess beneath him, pussy probably soaking this poor classic car, and I'll never be able to look Weston in the eyes again if he ever finds out about this.

Wyatt pulls back, letting me gasp in a much-needed breath, and I relish in his salty taste on my tongue. I can feel the mess on my face, but all I do is lick my lips and open my mouth again, ready for more.

"You like sucking me off, don't you?"

I nod, mouth still open for him, despite the complaints from my lower jaw. It's been an age since I've had something as big as Wyatt's cock in it. Or someone that lasted more than a couple of sucks. If I end up sticking around, I'm gonna have to enroll in some sort of training regimen so my poor mouth can keep up with his giant cock. Do you think there is some sort of Jane Fonda-esque workout tape for sucking massive dicks? That's a Google search for a later time, and an incognito browser window, maybe on a burner phone. Or Alexis's stupid Android when she isn't looking.

Wyatt distracts my train of thought by pushing back in, rubbing his head up and down on my lips, then forcing more of himself into my waiting mouth. He puts those fingers to use again, strumming, plucking, and tweaking my nipples, and I swear to God, if this man makes me come from nipple play alone, I'll get a new journal to write about him in it at thirty-three. Shit, maybe I'll write an ode to him and put it up on Wattpad, call it fanfic. He'd deserve every possible sexual accolade and then some.

"Last chance," he says in that husky tone he uses when he's high on me.

Last chance for what? Breath? Not falling for this man all over again? Because I think it's too late for both with how deep into my throat he is right now, and how deep into the rest of me, for that matter.

"Pinch my leg if you want me to pull out, otherwise you're swallowing every drop you suck out of me."

I bring my hands up to his thighs, run my fingers through the coarse hair there, but I don't pinch. It's more of a caress, silent consent to do whatever the fuck he wants to me and more. It might be more like begging for that, actually.

He growls in response and leans forward so suddenly it's probably better classified as a lunge. Hands still gripping my breasts, he dives forward, burying his face in between my legs, the dress that's pulled up there and revealing exactly how into this blowjob I am. His cock lodged deeper in my throat than it's ever been, Wyatt takes one long, dirty, deep lick, from clit to crack, and my legs start to shake from the first contact. He pulls back up, standing, and looks down at me, starting to fall apart from a single touch. Or really, more accurately, from the buildup of so many other touches, the need that's got me so worked up, bubbling over to the point where a single touch could have me splitting at the seams.

"Damn, Hellcat. You're fucking soaked."

I can't even get air, don't stand a chance to answer him, but I mumble incoherently around the intrusion in my mouth all the same.

"You should've told me how much you needed a little attention. Should've asked me to help you out with this," he says, swiping at his several-day-old scruff and pulling away a handful of my need. "When are you going to learn that I don't mind what a needy cunt you have? What a dirty fucking girl I fell for all those years ago?" He pulls back, letting me take a large gasp of air, then he fills my mouth again.

I'm so close to crumbling, to breaking under his form of teasing, of torture. My nerve endings feel like they're on fire, every inch of my skin a pleasure receptor at the moment. I think if he touched so much as my cheek right now, I might come. But he doesn't. He continues driving into my mouth, watching me from above, and I whimper, not caring that I have slobber on my face, that I'm writhing on top of this car like I'll burn up if he doesn't give me more.

"In fact," he whispers the words so I have to strain to hear them, "it gets me off how fucking nasty you are. The fact that you crave this filth as much as I do." My whole body starts to shake now, delirious in my need, this state of hyper-awareness, where I'm a breath away from combustion, and I need his release in my mouth to feel whole. I want to make him feel the way he makes me feel. Safe. Needed. Enough. And I want every last fucking drop for myself.

"How bad have you been, Hellcat?" Wyatt continues teasing me, pushing in and out of my mouth, not letting me answer him. "Fantasizing about my cum in your mouth when you were supposed to be working for your hotshot clients, hmm? Were you thinking about my cum in other places too? Maybe me filling your ass? You liked that preview the other night, I know you did."

My eyes slam shut at the visual, unwilling to admit how much I like the sound of that. Of him exploring every inch of my body. Using all of me, making a mess of every part of me.

"It's okay, Hellcat. You can be yourself with me. Every

bratty, dirty impulse you have, you can do that shit with me. I'm not gonna judge you for it. Everyone else can tell you what a bad girl you are for what you like, but I get it. I'll give you what you need, no matter how depraved. Because all your kinks are mine too."

I give in, groaning and rolling my head along the side of the car, tears pooling in my eyes at how *much* he's making me feel. Like he sees all of me, and he *likes* it all. The dirty part of me that wants to be used in any way he wants to use me. The over-achiever who lives inside of me that needs to be perfect on the job. Even the overthinker who struggles with getting her mind to still. There's no part of me that scares him away.

"Let's make a deal," Wyatt says almost playfully. He's drag-ging this out when he could give it a few strong pumps and we'd both be done. He's *enjoying* stretching this out. "The harder you suck on my cock, the harder I'll go on your tits here, just the way I know you like it. Enough to hurt, enough to push you over that edge. That thrill you've been chasing since you first found what you like. What I give you. Go ahead. Show me how hard you want it from me."

I groan around him, and my cheeks and tongue start pulling on his cock more firmly, sucking and stroking him in tandem, as hard as I'm capable of in this position. My moans are muffled, but he hears them and knows exactly what they mean, what to do with the response.

As the pressure in my mouth ramps up, so does the intensity on my breasts. What starts out as a light pull turns into a firm tweak and then pinching as it hits the scale of pain, and takes a big fucking jump up it. Just when I think he's gone too far, fresh tears stinging the backs of my eyes, an unspent scream lodged in my throat, he releases my nipples, and the sensation swiftly changes to a massive rush of pleasure, straight through my bloodstream. It feels like every blood cell in my body is headed toward my clit right now, it's so swollen I can feel the air against it like a caress from Wyatt's tongue. A stiff breeze blows through this place and I might come.

"Get ready to swallow, dirty girl," Wyatt gets out through strained breaths. "In three ... two ..." and on *one* I feel a sharp slap on my pussy, right on my clit. He *slapped* my pussy, and moreover, I liked it. I scream at the contact, but I know I liked it because it sent me spiraling over the edge, topping into a kind of pleasure I've never felt with anyone but him. The kind that's so whole, so complete, it scrapes the edges of your soul as it takes you over, fills you up and ebbs, leaving you somehow more full than you were before the experience.

At my garbled scream, his dick grows thicker and pulses against my tongue, ropes of cum shooting out, spilling up and back onto my tongue as I struggle to swallow it, suck down everything he's giving me as my own waves of release course through my entire body and I'm choked by his girth, upside down. My legs shake, my arms go numb, my entire midsection is on fire in the best possible way as I ride out the orgasm, wracking my entire body as it detonates.

There's never been anything more satisfying. That deep of a release for me, the taste of his own in my mouth, proof that I give it just as good as I get it, the two of us intertwined, still connected in this way, nothing awkward between us despite the filthy things we just did together.

This might be as close to perfection as I've ever found.

And I'm the idiot who threw it away.

But I'm seeing a different path now. One where I've seen I was wrong to run. Where we've both grown since then. And where maybe it's possible to let ourselves want more again.

Wyatt pulls himself out of me, rights himself and puts his clothes back on, then helps me sit up, wiping my mouth and entire lower face with the bottom of his Henley and pulling my skirt down. And as he does, I think my newfound softness is showing. I can feel it radiating out of my face, but I can't stop my eyes from giving me away to him. I never could and why would I start now? Now that I finally see how we've both evolved, how this could really work.

His eyes harden, narrowed on my gaze. "Don't look at me like that, Aurora."

"Like what?" I ask him demurely.

"Like this is more than sex for you. Like you're getting feelings here."

"And what if I am?" I ask him, testing the waters, ready to start negotiating.

"Then I'm not going to fuck you again," he says plainly. "We had a deal here, and you need to hold up your end of it. Sex, and nothing more. Can you do that, *Aurora*? Or are we done?"

24
Wyatt

The ultimatum ripped me open to lay out there, but it has to be said. I had to call her out on the way she's looking at me, all soft and pliant, a lot more than lust in those earthen brown eyes.

The *only* way I've survived having her back in my life, having her in the way I just did, is knowing it's just sex. Losing her once ruined me. Having her back and losing her again? I might not have all her degrees, but I'm smart enough to know I wouldn't survive it.

This emotional minefield is the dangerous territory our little pact was supposed to protect us from.

"Are you saying I can't be honest with you about my feelings changing?" The way she pops a hip as she asks it says there's a lot more sass to her words than shone through in that soft tone she used.

My voice is unmistakably bitter when my words come out. No way to confuse *me* for sweet. "If we're going to be honest, let's start from the beginning. I'll go first. You left. We were together for five years, you were my entire future, Rory, and you left. In the middle of the goddamn night. You didn't even tell me to fuck off, not even a thanks for a couple thousand nights together. Definitely not the courtesy of a breakup, some fucking closure or a fucking goodbye kiss."

Her lower lip trembles and something inside me splits open when her eyes drop to the ground, unable to hold my own. This headstrong, brave, brilliant woman has never met an opponent she can't face down, but apparently it's me. Me and my shitty truths are too much for her.

Throw my arms up in the air, run a hand through my hair before I get out the rest of that thought. "Spent all my best years with you, planning out another seventy of them, and you leave me a one-paragraph note that broke my fucking heart."

I spin on a foot, turn away from her and get a few steps of space, some air that doesn't smell like her and sex, some fresh goddamn perspective. Grease, old metal, and all the things my life have looked like without her in it. Now even that's tainted by her scent, her taste, her image too.

"What?" I taunt her, the cracked silence she's choosing to grace me with. "Too much honesty for you?"

"Stop," she whispers the plea. The way her shoulders hunch in on herself, so rare for her, should be my warning to take heed, but she's always been reckless with my heart, why can't I return the favor for once?

"You want some more honesty? Huh? Or are you still running from the truth, like you've been doing since you were twenty-one?"

Head down, her shoulders shake, and I'm not sure if it's a silent sob, or fear that's making her quake.

"Here's another one. It should've been us. It should *still* be us."

Her eyes don't look up to meet mine, body trembling, but she's opened this can of worms, and my filter can't stop the rest of my ugly truths at this point.

"Ask me," I insist.

She shakes her head.

"Ask me why I got it done."

Rory shakes her head again and I can see tears forming in those brown depths, but not spilling.

"Aren't you curious? How I went from dreaming of our kid together, to not being able to have any? Fucking ask me, Rory." That last part comes out way too loud, but the volume isn't what makes her flinch.

"Why." She whispers the word, because she doesn't want to ask, and she doesn't want to know. She's gonna hear it anyway. I wait until her eyes come back to mine before I give her the answer.

"If it wasn't you, it wasn't anyone."

Tears spill over her lash line, and I don't look away. I track every single one as it maps a path down her cheeks, and I memorize them, because I need to remember why she doesn't belong here, not fall for her pretty lies another time. But I'm not done with my ugly truths yet.

"It should've been us, in the end. You were it for me, Aurora. You were all I ever wanted, but I wasn't enough for you. You're the one that wanted more from life."

She shakes her head, not even wiping the tears away, but she doesn't fight me with her words for once in her damned life, so I keep talking.

"It was your choice to do this to what we had. I didn't get a say in it. Well, I'm having one this time. If you're not for real, if you're still leaving at the end of this, don't do this to me again." Now I'm the one pleading.

Truthfully, this is going to ruin me either way. I'm already too far gone for this girl. But she left for a reason, and she's found what she was looking for, and I won't be the reason she throws it all away. She wasn't happy here then, she won't be happy here now. Can't let her make the mistake of believing she could be.

And for once, when it comes to her, I need to stand up for what *I* need. She's always been my priority, always been the one I've fought to protect. Now, I need to fight to protect me too.

Besides, this is what's best for both of us. If we can't keep things purely physical, we need to stop. Doesn't matter that nothing about this feels like *the best* when she runs off, wobbling in her heels on the uneven surface, clutching her open dress to hold it together as she goes, and I don't chase after her.

Feels like the worst, truthfully.

And one more piece of honesty here, just for me, myself, and I. There isn't a day that's gone by since I was a teenager that I haven't loved her.

Even when I should've hated her.

And I know I always will, even when she breaks my heart by leaving again, but that's my burden to bear. I'm trying to keep *her* heart safe this time. Mine's always been fucked.

25
Aurora

Finding a kickboxing gym that's open all hours within fifty miles of the Heights wasn't easy. Actually, it was impossible. The one I found was in the closest thing the Smokies has to a big city, it was closer to a hundred miles away, and I drove straight to it.

Stopped at the first mall I found, went into Lululemon and bought a few days' worth of clothes, changed into some in the dressing room. Walked around barefoot, mascara on my cheeks until I found a store that sold acceptable footwear and grabbed some white sneakers and socks.

Unlike New York, where people won't stop to ask if you're okay even if you're bleeding out—they'll just move you out of their way if you're blocking traffic and keep on going—I forgot how damned hospitable people are in the South. Even my bitchiest face didn't keep at least three different women and one kind older man from checking in on me. When I snarled at them, though, that did the trick. My mouth might've been foaming, which probably helped my case.

After a quick stop at the drugstore for essentials, I check into the nearest hotel that doesn't scream *cockroaches* (I couldn't find one that screamed *mimosas and massages* or I would've gone there), drop off my new bags and my old clothes, then scrub my face until all evidence of the tears are gone. Just a red, raw face, and one absolutely ruined woman remain. The remnants of the woman I used to be. Both Rory and Aurora have been shattered in one day.

I've forgotten what it's like to be a prisoner in your own mind.

Not even two months here and I'd gotten used to the peace that has crept up and blessed me. It was so gradual, I hardly noticed the shift until it all came slamming back into me, first with Lexi, then the dressing down my mother gave me, realigning the last decade and a half of my life, and then again with Wyatt's words tonight.

Like when you never knew you'd had a headache for all those years, until it's gone?

I think this was the opposite. The effect Wyatt had on me was so gentle, so subtly pervasive, I didn't even realize that my cruelest thoughts have hardly barraged me at all until they erupted at full force again.

Tonight, they're so vivid, so sharply penetrating, they ram past my usual barriers. No amount of stimulation, of attempting to distract myself with my surroundings seems to be helping. In fact, they rage louder with the new, firsthand knowledge of how badly I hurt everyone I used to care about.

It's all I can do to make it to the kickboxing gym, fill out a membership form, and buy the gear I didn't bother bringing with me from New York. I couldn't tell you how long passes once I find an open corner and get a bag to myself. I'd say it was minutes, but when I get a glimpse at myself in the mirror after a concerned employee suggests I go home and sleep, I'm pretty sure it's been hours.

My hair is drenched, matted to my skull, and the ponytail to my upper back. My face isn't red, it's drained of all color. I look like I've been in a sauna instead of a gym. I look like I belong in *The Walking Dead*. And I don't realize how tired my muscles are until I try to move my limbs to get back to the hotel and they don't cooperate.

The Cutlass picks this time, tonight, to decide it's done with my shit, too, just like everyone else in my life. I leave it in the parking lot and get an Uber to take me to the hotel, where I don't bother showering, and cry out whatever moisture remains in my body until it finally shuts down on me too.

ALMOST TWO DAYS OF SLEEP. Another kickboxing workout. Force myself to eat something, because Wyatt isn't here to do it. Then another twelve hours of sleep, another couple workouts. Ignore my phone through all of it, not even bothering to charge it, or look at it, beyond the initial email I sent off to the firm that I wouldn't be available for some time.

Eventually, my mind quiets. I think it's day three of being here. Or maybe week three?

I'd be worried about my mom, about something happening to her, if I didn't know she has Duke, she has Lexi, and she probably has the entire town behind her now.

And if I didn't know that I'm the biggest asshole in her life, in Lexi's, and in Wyatt's. In fact, there's no one I've ever loved whose life I haven't fucked up. Whose future I haven't darkened. Which is why I stayed away.

I may have left out of self-preservation, but I stayed away out of the one small part of my heart that's good. The part of me that knows I'm bad news, and none of them deserve my selfishness inflicted on them any more than they've already been subjected to.

And when I got overly optimistic? Forget what my past behavior has done to them? That's when my hopes finally made an appearance. Until all three of them made it incredibly clear to me the type of effects I've had on their lives, and I remembered where I belong. Away from them.

And if the landline in my hotel room hadn't rung, I might never have gone back to the Heights.

"'Lo?" I tried to say *hello*, but I think my vocal cords got buried under some cobwebs after all this disuse.

"Aurora, hon? Oh, thank fuck." Trevor's voice goes from panicked to relieved when he recognizes mine.

"Trevor?"

"When you get back, we're going to have words about you dropping off the face of the earth. Where is your phone? Is it okay? Are *you* okay?"

"I dunno." I'm not sure which of his questions I answered, I think all of them. "What's going on, why are you calling me?"

"What, I don't get a 'wow, how'd you find me' moment to showcase my glorious PI skills? You could at least give me that much." Been a while since I've heard that Eastern seashore accent.

"Fine," I say, a begrudging chuckle freeing itself from the shackles of my misery. I put on an affected tone to participate. After all, he's what's waiting for me back in New York, no need to burn that bridge too. "How ever did you find me, Trevor?"

"Shit, Aurora." He whistles, either really impressed, or really *un*impressed. "All that enthusiasm, you're lucky you don't get the Keynote presentation on it. Tell ya what. For your overzealous interest in how I tracked you down, I'll give you three options, and let you believe whichever one makes you feel safe at night. One, I got IT to ping the IP address you sent the last email from. Two, I tracked the GPS chip in your laptop to a location near the hotel you're in and had to call eight others before I found you there. Or three, I'm psychic."

Even my Eeyore-channeling ass can't not give him a small laugh at that. "Fuck, Trevor, what do you want? Can't a girl take personal time?"

He pauses for a moment before asking, "Is your mom okay?"

"I think so."

"Are *you* okay?"

"Been better."

"Will good news cheer you up?"

"Better be some great fucking news."

"Would I have tracked you down just to say the muffin guy started bringing extra banana nut?"

"What the fuck is your news, Trevor? Jesus Christ, you're acting like you're billing me by the damn minute, here. And don't even think about trying that shit on me."

He chuckles, but quickly stops when he presumably picks up on my icy demeanor through the phone. "So. Our pet project. Turns out there's a lot more they've fucked with in that town you claim not to love than just that bar, and the senior partners have a strategy in mind ..."

I MIGHT BE GOING BACK to the Heights one more time, but it's to do what's right. To bad bitch up and help Duke, and hopefully my mom, and to stick to my original promise I made to her.

All it took was my mother, my sister, *and* my ex all letting loose on me in one day with how they really feel to see that I was delusional to think I could build a life in this town after I left it the way I did. But me, my firm, and this new plan? We can help some folks out *majorly*.

However long I have left in the Heights, I'll do what I can for my mom, do what I can to get this motion underway, and then I'll get back to New York, where I'll finish this out from there.

Where everyone I care about here will be safe from me and the tornado of destruction I apparently bring with me. And if I get to improve their quality of life, restitute the wrongs done to them by this one colossal fuckwad of a corporation—the bank that services most of the residents of Smoky Heights, this reverse Robin Hood thing they've got going on—hopefully that's some lasting positivity I can leave in my wake this time. One final attempt to right the ways I've wronged so many people here.

For the first time since that night at the garage my head isn't spinning. I've had the time and space to reflect, to see the ways I've hurt Wyatt, my mom, my sister, probably others I used to be close to, and I know what I'm walking back into this time. I'm not the martyr in their story, I'm the one with the scarlet letter. I earned every bit of shame and contempt these people hold for me, that I hold for myself. But I'm determined to do what's in my power to help all of them.

I grab an apple crisp macchiato—giving cider vibes with the best coffee has to offer—before I hit the road in my newly acquired rental, wrapped up in a new zip-up and matching yoga pants to give me a little warmth in the rapidly dropping temperatures.

Looking out my hotel window this morning, the grass wasn't dewy, it was frosty. And the open windows on this drive confirm that fall is well and truly here. We're past the sixty-degree days and the fifty-degree nights. This unseasonable chill tells me the first snow might be here before Christmas this year, a rare treat in the Smokies. In fact, the only place prettier than New York in the winter just might be Smoky Heights, as the seasons change from crisp air to nippy nights in front of a fire.

It's just about an hour-long drive once I'm off the interstate as I come back from my hideout, a gorgeous path on winding roads, the passing trees doing their best to hold onto their last leaves, in auburn, maroon, gold, and the final greens, as the wind tries to carry them away.

Crossing through the southern Welcome to Downtown Smoky Heights arch, I see downtown is what I think the locals might call *bustling*. A handful of people on either side of Main, in and out of the brick storefronts (at least the ones that are still open), including Ernie who's sat himself in front of the hardware shop and looks like he's decided to start telling stories on the side of the road now, because the folks in the bar have heard 'em enough, I guess. Mrs. Dixon is holding court at a table in the front window of the coffee shop, Foamy Heights, an audience of other old biddies hanging onto her every word. It might not be the Upper West Side, but it's got charm, I'll admit that much.

I park in the lot at the end of Main Street and when I get to Suds I don't think to use the left-hand door, using the one on the right out of habit and smiling to myself when I feel the smooth underside of the carved wooden handle.

Something about the brisk air, the lingering taste of apples on my tongue, the rustling of the trees that line Main Street, and walking into this place makes me want a beer, so I head over to Dallas behind the empty bar and order two. Is it three o'clock on what my phone (and Trevor) told me is a Wednesday? Sure. But Duke and I have something to celebrate, finally.

Set the beers down and track the old man down in his office. When I lean against the doorjamb, he barely looks up before making a derisive sound.

"So you are alive."

"Sure am."

"Your mother wasn't so sure. Neither was Grady, from what I hear. Would it have killed you to check in with someone?"

"It might have, and I'm sorry for that, but I'm back now."

"For how long?"

"Jeez, what do you think, you're my father already? I'm here for as long as Mom will have me, okay? But that's not what I'm here to talk to you about right now. Can you come out here?"

Duke eyes me wearily but stands anyway, joining me at the high-top in the corner by the pool table that I chose for us. His brows shoot up when he sees the beers, and when I take a seat on the stool and down half of it in one go, like I belong here or something, he gives me an impressed nod.

"Damn that's good," I say, smacking my lips.

He moves to follow suit, but I stop him with a look. "We should really be toasting first."

Those heavy brows of his climb up his forehead again.

"I'd ask if you're pregnant, but ..." Those expressive gray eyes of his fall down to the drink in my hand.

"Hardy har har."

I clink his glass with mine and let him take a hearty draw before I hit him with the news.

"We got 'em."

His stare is hopeful, but not ready to assume, so I put his mind at ease.

"Brown Stone. I have it confirmed that we have what we need to get them off your back. And then some."

"What does that mean?" he asks, that hope expanding out and leaking into his voice now.

I tell him what I can, not everything is ready to be shared publicly yet, not even with family. Nothing is worth risking the integrity of this case we're building for the people of the Heights.

The next months will contain an extensive discovery period, and hearing this evidently prompts Duke to confirm a fear that's been developing in me since finding out about his relationship with my mother.

"You know I refinanced the bar," he says, twirling the empty pint glass between his hands. "Well, I didn't tell you why. It was paid off years ago. But I took out a new loan on it to help pay for Laura Lee's medication and treatments. One of those pills she takes is over a thousand dollars each, and that's just one of a ton of prescriptions she's got. Even with insurance, we can't keep up with the costs."

The tip of my nose wriggles, trying to stop that stinging from spreading, but I fail once again.

"She also refinanced her house, and the adjustable rate on the mortgage got so high she can't pay it without working again, so I'm helping her as much as I can, but the same thing is happening to me here, plus her hospitalization, the pain management regimen, and ..." His somber voice dies out after it breaks for a second time.

"Please let me help in the meantime. If you won't take my money outright, let me invest in the bar. Something, anything, while we get the paperwork filed to halt their harassment on you here and get this in front of a judge who can stop it for good. It'll be months before we get our case submitted and get a preliminary hearing scheduled for the residents' suit, which might be able to do a lot more for you both long-term, but please don't keep me from helping when I can, Duke."

My eyes aren't the only wet ones by the end of my plea. Our conversation lasts a long time—my educated guess would be at least 10 increments, or $800 were I on the clock—and it's one that refills my cup.

"Do you know how much documentation is required to present a consumer protection suit of this magnitude to the attorney general?" I ask him, and he watches me with something like pride as he shakes his head no. "This is going to be a civil suit bigger than this neck of the woods has ever seen. The partners have assigned a significant amount of resources to this project back in New York, but I'll be boots on the ground for now, and more may come out to gather evidence and statements as needed. Especially after I go back." Neither of us comment on the elephant in the room, on what has to happen for me to go back.

Duke has a few questions, but mostly he just wants to hear as much as I can share, guffawing in disbelieving laughter at what the initial investigation found, what this means for Suds, and for the entire town.

"You gonna be okay here for however long this takes?" he asks me.

I look down at the table, swirl the last of my beer in the glass before tossing it back and draining it.

"Sure gonna try to be."

"You're a great person, Aurora. You hurt a lot of people a long time ago, but you don't have to hate yourself over it forever. There's nothing in life you can't come back from. We all have pasts. We can't separate ourselves from them. They're a part of us. Maybe you need to make peace with your past instead of pretending it doesn't exist. No good person is going to hold it against you when you take accountability for what you did and show you've changed. Especially not ones who love you."

My eyes water again, but he kindly pretends not to notice and keeps talking. "Besides, the only reason it could hurt them so deep in the first place was because they loved you so much to start with. Give them the chance to fall in love with who you are now, while you still have time with them, okay? You're surrounded by people who have big hearts, let them use them on you. Even if you're not ready to forgive yourself, they are."

I hug the man my mother's always deserved, the one she got many years too late.

I don't let myself wonder what all of our lives would've looked like if they'd found each other sooner, or torture myself emotionally by picturing him as the father figure Lexi and I could've used. But I do let his words sink in, healing the first part of that damage I caused in myself when I ran. Restoring the belief that there's still something good in me, that I might be capable of more than inflicting hurt on the ones that I love.

Forgiveness of self might be a foreign concept for me, that might take years of work, but I'm going to get to work a lot faster on gaining forgiveness from the rest of the people I hurt.

I think this case might be the perfect place to start. For my mom, for the man she loves, and this town they call home.

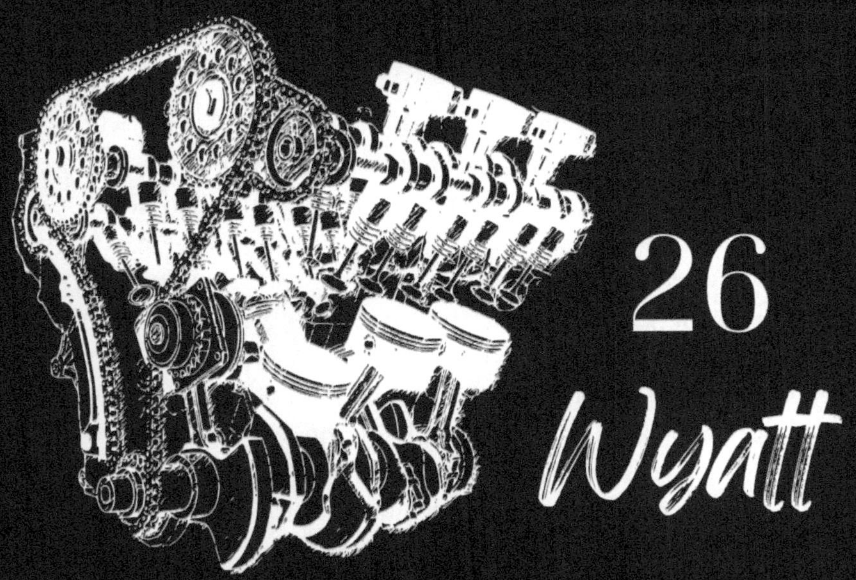

26
Wyatt

Ever since the town's staple diner closed, when Rory and Lexi's dad—the owner and cook—left the Heights, we've had a real lack of decent food options here. A couple people have tried to open places, but nothing has stuck. The entire downtown isn't what it used to be, truthfully. Barely a shadow of the vibrant community we once had.

Economy isn't my specialty, but something is off with ours in this town. I dunno if we just don't have enough people, if they don't have enough money, or maybe everyone is still in the mindset of a home-cooked supper around the table with their family every night, but for a bachelor like me, the lack of restaurants, cafés, or diners means my stomach is rumbling with not much to do about it. My fridge has nothing left in it but the rest of that cider, and I'm not ready to go to the corner market to pick up groceries and have every person I run into talk to me about Laura Lee dying. The garage has been my hideout since that news broke, and even there Gonzo and every single customer that's come by have all tried to talk my ear off about it. Like it might not be a painful subject for me, the guy who should've been her son-in-law.

I've been trying to avoid Suds since the explosion with Aurora. I've been honoring the bar as her turf, but looks like I'm gonna have to give in and head over if I want to survive the night. Plus, it's been, like, a week since that day at the garage and I haven't seen or heard from her. She hasn't even read my text asking if we could talk.

All that to say, I don't know what I'm walking into when I arrive at the bar for the first time in days, but I didn't expect it to be Rory and Duke sitting at a high-top in the far corner, both wiping their eyes, smiling, and sharing in a hug.

He walks away from the table first, spotting me as he steps away from her, and heads my way. All he gives me is a pat on the shoulder and a slight nod, but it feels like he's directing me to take his seat. Jerk my chin at Dallas and mouth my order at him as I pass him, going to the high-top by the games, right by the billiards table where I have a new top ten memory with her. They're all of her, really. The only ones in color, at least. Bright spots in a half a lifetime of dark fog.

Her eyes sparkle more than usual, glittering topaz instead of the usual chocolate, evidence of the conversation—the tears— she just shared. Aurora meets my gaze as I move in her direction and tilts her head to the open seat in invitation.

No time to second-guess this now, eh, Grady?

Even the crowd of rowdy regulars, even Ernie himself, must sense not to fuck with the vibe in here tonight, because when I sit down at the table with her, nobody catcalls, shouts anything inappropriate at us, or tries to tell the same story about a trout that never existed for the millionth night in a row. They all just carry on with their conversations at respectful volumes, even if I do feel curious eyes darting over to us at regular intervals. It's the closest thing to privacy I've ever gotten in this town.

"Can we ... ?" Aurora asks tentatively.

Something is different about her from the last time I saw her, and I guess I should be thankful for that. Never wanna see her that way again.

If I had to guess, I'd say it's clarity, determination in her features, brightening her eyes, beyond what the remnants of tears are doing.

"Yeah, of course."

"Just wanted to clear the air." She sets the expectations for this conversation, like a good attorney. I half expect her to outline some bullet points to discuss next. "Not just about the other day," she adds on.

"I'm sorry," I reply automatically. Because making her run away crying was never what I wanted. I just wanted her to see why we can't pretend it's safe to let feelings get involved when all that's here for her is her past. Her future is almost a thousand miles away.

"You shouldn't be," she says, just as quickly. "I want to apologize to you."

"It's okay." I'm still trying to reassure her, even after the way I broke her the last time we tried to talk things out.

"It's not." It might be a whisper, but it's firm.

My chin dips in a nod, hearing her. "Then tell me, Aurora."

"It's a cliché, really. But humor me, anyway." She sniffs a laugh, but it's not a joyful one. "My dad ... *leaving*," she chooses the word carefully, "really shook me. My mom and I have always been so similar, I'm just the Wish dot com version of her, I think." That gets an actual laugh from both of us, her because she thinks it's funny and me because it's laughable that she thinks she isn't an original, an absolute work of art of a human being, a masterpiece, and completely one-of-a-kind. "But if the man I grew up worshiping could do that to her, what did my future look like here? What was I in for if I stayed? You know I always had my eye on more, but that?" She blows out a big breath and meets my eyes. "That made me *scared* to stay. It destroyed my trust and made me fear my own future. It would probably take years of therapy to unpack it in a way that makes sense, so I don't know what to tell you right now other than I'm so sorry. You deserved better."

My head twists to the side, rejecting her statement. "No, Aurora, you did. Like you said before, we had our issues back then. I had my head up my ass. I wasn't even aware you were struggling, beyond the surface level bullshit. I wasn't there for you the way you needed. I've never been the man you deserve."

Her eyes brighten again, and she shakes her head a bit, but tears don't fall.

"I've been coming to terms with the damage I did for the first time. You were right. I've been scared of the truth. Having to face how deeply I hurt everyone here, it hasn't been easy. I don't know how to make up for the way I left and what that did to you, but I'm starting by telling you I'm sorry. I'm sorry for not trying to fix what we had, for not giving you the chance to try, and ... I'm sorry you can't have kids because of me."

One shoulder pops up toward my ear. I only ever wanted them with her. Seems fair to me if you ask me.

"That part has its perks," I say, trying to lighten that load on her shoulders.

Her brows raise and that beautiful mouth quirks. "Sure does."

Truthfully, I don't need any more of an apology from her. I don't have some groveling kink, as much as I like to see her on her knees. All I wanted was us on the same page, and her head on straight about what's waiting for her when she's done in the Heights. No false hope for either of us.

Would I have done anything to give her what she needed back then? I'd like to think the answer is yes, but she's got a point. Neither of us were ready to do the things it took to be the best partner we could be back then. In fact, I'm pretty damn sure that if I hadn't gotten the fresh perspective of how miserable life is without her in it, I may never have grown into someone who appreciates every chance to have her like I do now. And if we're back on track, if we both know what this is, that it's got a time limit on it, and we have the rules of our pact to keep us on track, am I naïve for hoping we can keep that going? So I *can* have more of her before she's gone?

"So does that mean we can go back to our *arrangement*?" I float the question with a tilt of my lips.

That gets a half a smile out of her. "Sorry for violating your terms. I can appreciate this for what it is while I'm still here if you can."

Don't think I didn't catch what she did there. Absolutely no mention of not letting feelings enter the chat. That makes it easier for me, though. Not as direct of a lie I'll have to tell.

"I'm good with that."

You're gonna tell me I can have a sliver of the best I'll ever have or nothing at all, that's the easiest fucking choice I've ever made.

She's the only woman I'll ever love. Twelve years apart has proven that.

Aurora Weiss is the only thing I've ever wanted for myself, and I'm going to take whatever I can get, while I can.

A double ding of a sharp bell rings out from the window to the kitchen before Dallas drops off my food and fresh beers for us both, and we spend the evening catching up on her family, the case against the bank while we play darts and down beer like we're at a kegger.

When we finally head upstairs and I push into her, raw, it's me that looks away this time, unable to meet her gaze when I know we both lied tonight, and neither of us are getting out of this unscathed, but I'm not strong enough to stay away while she's here and wants me.

Every thrust is digging my own grave, but I don't stop. No way I'll be okay after she leaves again, but I'm too far gone in her to care.

27
Aurora

I wish I could say Alexis forgave me as easily as Wyatt did. It took a lot of wordsmithing, a lot of taking the jabs and cheap shots she had to lash out with before we finally got somewhere. Mom may have helped referee (who was, by the way, actually quick to forgive, just like Duke promised).

Maybe I can't say Lexi's forgiven me, but I think we're on our way.

One stipulation she had was for me to not be "too good" for the Heights. I tried to argue that I'm not, but the looks I got from four eyes that look just like mine stopped me cold.

To help on all fronts, between Lex, Mom, and myself, we came up with the plan for Lexi and I to spend a girls' day together, strolling through downtown and "getting back in touch with my roots" while our mother has more visitors at home today.

Apparently, me making a snippy comment about Lexi's charger not fitting my phone as we drive downtown didn't help my case, though.

"You're so fucking judgy, Rory, God! This is what I mean when I say you're too good for us."

"She says *judgingly*," I say pointedly. "Besides, an Android isn't synonymous with the Heights, just so you know." I continue to lecture Lexi as we get out of her car in the parking lot off Main Street. "Wyatt has an iPhone. Mom is willing to get one. You could have one too, you're choosing to have an inferior product at this point. Is it spite that keeps you on team green? You're better than this, come on. Think of how much fun we could have in group chats if you upgraded." Though, I guess the point is that she doesn't know what she's missing, so how could she imagine it?

"It's not an upgrade, it's conforming," she says resolutely.

"Because a shitty phone is what differentiates you from the masses?" I roll my eyes at her. "It's called convenience, Lex. Luxury. It'll change your life, just let me—" But I don't get to finish my sentence because she swats me into silence with both hands. A cat fight, if a cranky kitten hadn't figured out how to use its claws yet. Nothing but fluff and padding, and a lot of attitude. It ends with the two of us cackling, laughing all the way into the lone coffee shop on the main strip downtown. It's not Starbucks, but I've come to like it even more. Plus, the owner-operator learned how to make an apple crisp macchiato for me, and it's absolutely everything.

I treat Lexi to the coffee she orders, but when she realizes it's on me, she adds in three baked goods (one for now, two go in her purse, the wench), and all I can do is laugh at her and flip her off. We both say hi to Mrs. Dixon when we cross paths with her on the way to our table, as she's headed to make the daily rounds and keep the town up to date on the latest. Which is probably the fact that Alexis and I were seen in public together, not pulling one another's hair out. Unless she saw that catfight on the walk from the parking lot, in which case, she has a juicier tale to tell.

Our coats (hers a puffer, mine a trench) on the backs of our chairs, we sit at a small table near the windows that overlook Main Street, and watch more leaves float by the window than people as we sip our drinks and spend an afternoon together. Our first since high school, probably.

We discuss ways to give Mom more great experiences, more memories for us to cherish when that's all that's left of her, and I ask Lexi's opinion on something I've been trying to plan for our mom the last few days. Her squeal of delight at being included, at what we're now going to plan together, it spreads a balm of rightness over my insides and starts to repair the deeper cracks between us.

It's not lost on me as we watch familiar faces drift in and out of the open shops along Main, how I used to wonder where the life was in the Heights. Now I see it everywhere, now that I know where to look. In every interaction, every hug, every smile that lights up someone's face when they run into someone they adore. It might not be as *busy* as the city, but it's got more genuine love sewn in the fabric of this small town than anything I've seen back in New York.

A fresh leaf shower greets us when we make our way back outside, and I stop to take it in, arms spread, face to the sky, soaking in what it feels like to be home, with my sister (!), on this gorgeous day.

"God, you're such a nerd," she teases me, shoving my shoulder as she passes me on the street. "I thought you were supposed to be the sophisticated one of us."

I narrow my eyes at her and scowl. "I'm cerebral, not nerdy."

"Wow, real fucking Ravenclaw of you to be standing there like Leo in Titanic right now."

"I can be highbrow and also enjoy the simple things, you know. I'll take that over being a Slytherin," I shoot back at her.

"Whatever you say, nerd. Hey, let's go visit Gracie!"

She doesn't give me a chance to respond or object, Lexi is pushing through the glass door into the one salon we have in town, Mane on Main. The same place I've been having to get my nails done by the lone tech who favors neons and doesn't seem to understand the concept of subtle elegance. Gracie is a hairstylist there, I can see her sweeping up some hair in the back corner, the furthest chair in the row for hairstylists. The row is two chairs long, by the way.

Lex holds the door open for me (progress), but before I can make it in the door, two girls I grew up with but haven't seen since the bonfire months ago come through it, and we come face to face. Neither of us acknowledged the other at the bonfire, so I expect this to be awkward, but they both surprise me.

"Sophia," I say dipping my head in greeting to the one on the right.

"Ro—Aurora!" Sophia says in a chipper—and not entirely false—voice. Then her face falls in realization, I can see it hit her when she remembers. "I'm so sorry about your mom. You too, Lexi." She turns to look at Lexi, who nods in thanks, then she shifts back to me. "It's so good to see you back home though, you look great, girl." She pairs it with a touch to the arm, which surprises me. Last time I had the distinct impression nobody was willing to come too close and catch whatever I had. The smiles from both women are genuine, if not sympathetic, as they bid me farewell, pass me by, and walk down the street toward the other end of downtown.

"Well, if it isn't the Weiss sisters!" Gracie, Ronnie's wife and Lexi's lifelong bestie, puts away the broom and dustpan and greets us at the door, the little bell on it jangling as it closes. "What brings you by, gorgeous?" She kisses Lexi's cheek and gives me a bright smile.

"Would you believe that we were in the neighborhood? And I remembered how you texted me this morning that you had no clients booked this afternoon, and Aurora has just been *begging* me to help her get her in to get her hair done." Lexi shoots me a lethal glare and it takes all of my hard-won composure to keep my face from showing my thoughts right now.

The hairstylist I go to in New York is booked for six months in advance and only accepts payment in crypto or potentially illegal favors from well-connected individuals. I once saw him take a poodle for a cut and color. Missing my last appointment with him put me on a blacklist I'm actually scared to find out the ramifications of. But I don't trust these locks to just anyone. Even if she is Lexi's best friend. I have touchy hair, perfecting the exact shade of blonde took a master in his craft. Most people turn me a brassy orange when they try. Whatever is going on with my hair, it's as hard-headed as the rest of me, apparently.

I use every sisterly telepathy gift I've ever had and promise Lexi to kill her in her sleep, to kill her while she's awake, or even *be nice* to her if she just doesn't do what I think she's about to do.

Lexi's grin spreads wider, reaching both of her eyes, when she looks back at Gracie, and then to me once more. "Weren't you just saying you wanted to be bleach blonde again? 'Like the rays of the sun were painted onto your scalp,' that's what she said!" She nods effusively, selling the story.

I feel like Gracie should know me well enough to know there's not a single snowflake's chance in hell of ever wishing for such a look, not since 1997, at least. But that beatific smile on her face makes me think she bought every word Lexi was selling.

There's no way for me to get out of this without acting like I'm "too good" for the town, as Lexi says. So that's how I spend two hours in the second chair at Mane, my sister sitting next to me, happiest I've ever seen her yet as she watches the foils get applied in my hair, both my scalp and eyes on fire from the strong mixture. All Lexi needs is some popcorn for this scene to be complete.

I try not to think about what I'm going to look like walking out of here and let my mind wander to the talk with Wyatt to distract me.

You deserved better.

No, Aurora, you did.

His words keep replaying, but they still make no sense.

Fucking ridiculous. There *is* no one better for me than that man. *He's* the one who deserves better. But if I'd said that out loud, he would've known I was lying when I agreed to continue our *arrangement*, as he called it. That I can't keep my heart out of the equation, but I'm done trying. I just want as much to remember him by as I can get before I can't have anything else from him again.

Taking Duke's advice, letting them get to know the Aurora I am now doesn't mean they deserve to be saddled with the selfish, difficult person I grew into. Make good memories, help Mom navigate this time period, and go back when it's all over. Even if I no longer hate it here. Even if that future I saw with Wyatt for one whole day still glimmers in the corner of my mind's eye when I recall that look on his face as we renewed the terms of our agreement.

I can appreciate this for what it is while I'm still here if you can.

I'm good with that.

For someone who deals in the fine print day in and day out, I left an awful lot of specificity out of my words. I wasn't sure if I could lie to his face, tell him there's no feelings involved on my end, but I can't not make the most of these months I have left here. He didn't seem to catch it, or maybe he just let me get away with it.

And speaking as that woman whose living relies heavily on

keeping track of time, I'm embarrassed to say daydreaming of Wyatt Grady makes me lose all sense of it completely. Recalling the way we'd reconnected up in my apartment after that talk, the way he let me be on top, yet was still the one taking me, fucking me senseless even from below, it gets me hot all over again. How he commanded the entire night, even when I was the one riding him. His finger on my clit, cock spearing me, mouth on my breast, and my head thrown back as I came. My cheeks flush and thighs clench, and I realize this is a dangerous line of thought when I'm in public, next to my sister who won't hesitate to call me out on it when she realizes the reactions I'm having. She's well-accustomed to the faces I make when I'm thinking about Wyatt Andrew Grady when I shouldn't be.

And let's thank whatever guardian angel is looking out for me today, that's the time Gracie is sweeping the cape off of me, a proud, "Take a look," as she beams at me.

It's all I can do not to squint when I take in my reflection. Lexi comes over to lean on my shoulder, the side Gracie isn't standing on, and she looks tickled fuchsia at the me that's staring back at her in the mirror.

It's full skunk hair. My natural brown turned a highly unattractive rusty apricot color that I *cannot* pull off, streaked with thick, chunky highlights in a shade of platinum that should never be paired with my coloring or aesthetic.

I look like the cream cheese pumpkin roll in my sister's purse right now.

"My God, you could be Ginger Spice, Ror," Lexi says, delighted.

"You know I always wanted to be Posh," I scowl at her.

"It was Baby for me," says Gracie, diplomatically. "Is it blonde enough for you?" she asks me seriously, concern dripping from her features. "I didn't expect it to go so ... orange, but I think it's really pretty for this time of year!"

"It does like to turn orange," I say as politely as I can through clenched teeth, eyes searing into Lexi's laughing face.

"It looks great, Gracie, you nailed it! I think it's *just* blonde enough for Aurora, here," Lexi says, before snapping her fingers and pointing at me. "No! You know who you look like? You look like 2002 Kelly Clarkson, that's who!"

"That's *very* specific," I mutter. "What are you, falling asleep to *American Idol* reruns?"

But the insult doesn't land, because hers was too spot on. She pulls up the Google search to show Gracie and me, and now that she's said it, I'll never unsee it. And I might love my sister, but, dammit, right now I hate her for what she's done to my head.

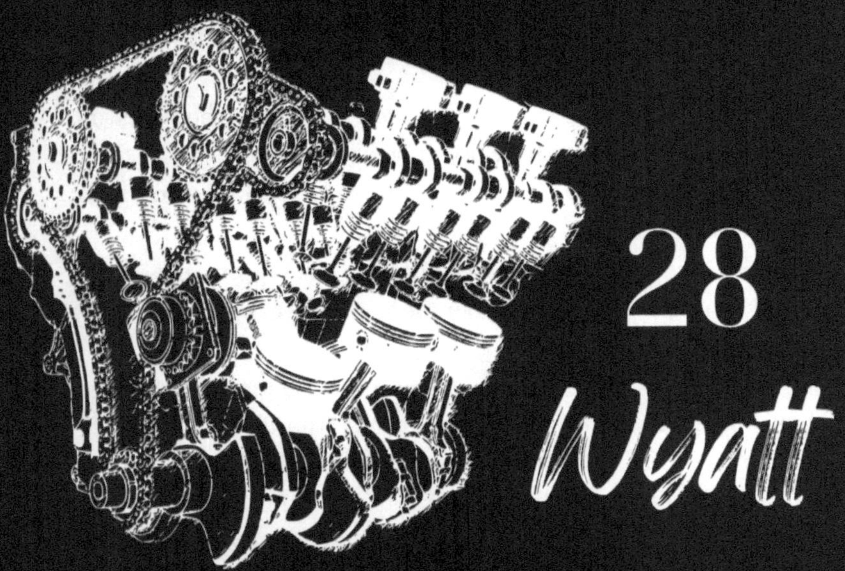

28
Wyatt

When her text came in, I didn't know what the fuck to think.

Now that I'm here, pulling up to the old bowling alley that had a tradition of playing records while patrons gamed, Pins + Needles—the big "DO NOT ENTER" sign across the door, the "Property of Brown Stone Bank" sign across the exterior wall facing the road—I have more questions than I did when she sent the text.

Aurora and Laura Lee are around the back, by the old employee entrance. I know, 'cause I was one in high school. Had a lot of fun sneaking Rory in this door and keeping quiet in the back corners, behind the lanes, when I was supposed to be working.

It was kind of a local ritual, actually. Sneak in, fool around, carve your initials in the wall to the side of the mechanical area.

You'd add a / for spare if you fooled around without getting caught, and an X for a strike if you went all the way.

I bet our initials are still there. Probably several sets of them. With a lot of Xs.

Not sure what to make of that same girl tapping her foot at me as I approach them now, her mom seated on a walker as they wait.

Shame this place got closed down not too long ago. Not too many other places for people to hang out around here.

"Was a B&E on that list of yours, Ms. Weiss?"

But then the sun glints on Aurora's hair, blinding me, and I lose the train of thought I was on. It's like a spotlight is on me in an interrogation. I throw an arm over my eyes and stagger backward. "Whoa."

"Don't you dare say a word," she threatens me, finger in my face as I step closer.

"About how your head looks like a safety vest a litter crew would wear on the side of the highway, or something else?"

"I told you!" Aurora scowls at her mother, like the hair is her fault, and Laura Lee just chuckles breathily.

"And I told *you*, that hair's not going to keep him away, dove."

Aurora leans her head back, pulling her hair together in her hands in some sort of ponytail that looks fancier than the ones I'm used to seeing around here before tying it up with a band she pulls off her wrist, and then glares at me angrily.

One hand holds the back of her head as I lean forward and kiss her on the top of it, right on that hair that's nothing like her, and let her know her mom was right.

"You look as gorgeous as ever, Hellcat," I reassure her. "From the forehead down."

She punches my shoulder, and, good for her, it hurts.

"If Duke wasn't working right now, I'd send you right back

where you came from, Grady, and do this without your ass." Well, damn. Some of her twang came out on that little vent. I thought it was gone for good.

"Well, sucks for you, I'm all you got. So why don't you show me what law we're breaking today and maybe tell me why? Or do I not want to know? Am I supposed to have deniability or whatever the official word for that is."

"Not sure we can argue plausible deniability when you're the one that brought us the gear to break in with, but if you stay on the only lawyer you know's good side, maybe you'll get lucky," Aurora shoots at me.

"I already got lucky," I whisper the words in a growl against her ear with a tap to her ass, and I think we're both going to pretend her mom didn't catch both of those things from a few feet away. I watch Aurora's cheeks heat, and it gives me satisfaction to know I can affect her like that with a single line, one touch.

My eyes flick to the camera on the corner of the building. "We worried about that?"

Laura Lee pipes up, vehemently. "They should be worried about a lot bigger matters than an abandoned building they forced a foreclosure on and did nothing with after that. Scum, these people. Scum!" she shouts the word at the camera, and I expect her to spit, or maybe a shake a fist or something.

"We've been here for an hour already. Thanks for that, by the way," Rory says, cutting a harsh glance at me again. "And nobody has shown up or anything, so here's to hoping this place is unmonitored and we're safe. Either way, what are they going to do? The violation calls for a minor fine at best. All she wants to do is retrieve an earring she lost here, they can suck a fat one if they call that a crime."

She leans in close to whisper so only I can hear her, "This is the second-to-last major thing on her list, getting this earring back." Excited eyes, wide and full of that untamed passion I'm obsessed with are locked on mine and for a second I forget about anything else, heart in my throat as I let her exhilaration sweep through me.

"Can you two hurry up already? I'm freezing to death out here." Laura Lee wraps her giant jacket around herself tighter and then lets out a dry laugh. "That's not far from the truth, is it?" She laughs again, and Rory stares on, horrified at first. But the longer she watches her mom laugh, sees her double over in the walker, legs crossed and howling, she eventually cracks, joining in.

"You're ... so ... fucking ... morbid!" Aurora gets the words out between cries of laughter, and it just makes Laura Lee laugh even harder.

Rory's mom tries to talk, tries to explain why it's funny, but she can't get out a single word without laughing harder, and I'd be lying if I said watching this entire exchange didn't pull some rare laughter out of me too.

"I'm gonna pee!" Laura Lee howls, tears streaming down her cheeks. "Please stop!"

"I told you I'd end up wiping your ass while I was here!" Rory crows, and it sets off a fresh round.

"Over my dead body!" her mom quips back, and they're just done for. Neither woman can stand up, Aurora is leaning against the wall, staggering as she tries to get herself upright again, but these women are just making each other laugh harder every time they make eye contact, or even look at the other.

Eventually, the cackles turn into heavy sighs, and they (even more eventually) quiet down.

"My cheeks hurt," Aurora says, touching them gingerly, testing them out.

"Not used to taking me yet?"

I whisper it, but Aurora's eyes go completely round as her

mouth thins into a line. Damn, am I glad looks can't actually kill. She'd be toasting her mom over my casket right now.

"Are you gonna get us in this damn building, or are you just here as eye candy?"

Didn't expect that from Ms. Weiss, give her a small chuckle at that sass I normally see primarily from her daughter, but I take the hint.

"All right, what's the issue here?"

Aurora shows me the door, the various padlocks they have on it (three feels excessive for a town with so little crime and no vagrancy to speak of, but then again, here we are about to pop them all off anyway, so maybe they were right to be overprotective). I grab what we need from my truck—thankful she didn't really want me to bring a battering ram or anything—and make quick work of getting the locks out of our way.

The door looks a little crusty from disuse, but when I go to kick it open for the girls, Laura Lee stops me.

"Allow me," she says, chin held high, as she stands from the walker on shaky legs and pushes the door forward with both hands. It looks like it takes all her waning strength, but her triumphant smile says it was worth it.

Once she steps through the door, she seems to lose her balance, wobbling a bit, and Aurora catches her, swooping in behind her with gentle arms that steady her, and placing the walker there so she can rest on it again. "Easy does it there, SEAL Team Six. Take a breather, get your balance back, and then we'll go get your earring back in the name of justice."

I step in behind Aurora and place a hand on her low back after closing the door behind us. My thumb traces a circle on the small of her back and she leans into me ever so slightly. Try not to be too obvious about how I inhale her scent when she does.

"All right, let's blow this popsicle stand," Laura Lee says, standing back up and marching forward, phone acting as a flashlight to lead our way in the blackness.

"I still don't know how you think you're going to find this earring, Mom. Where do you think it would be at this point?"

"Oh, there's no earring, don't be gullible, Aurora," Laura Lee spits out over her shoulder.

I hear the breath leave Aurora in surprise at that.

"Well, what the hell are we here for then?"

"Unfinished business," she says simply.

Rory and I follow her, she seems to know where she's going, which is the back route to that wall I mentioned earlier. Sure enough, when we pass it by, Aurora's hand comes out to trace some of the carved initials we go by.

RW + WG X

I smirk when I spot it and sneak the tips of my fingers in the waistband of the burnt orange pants she's got on, skim them along her delicate skin there until I see her shiver and shoot me a look to cool it over her shoulder. Give her a wink that promises to get much, *much* hotter later, and withdraw my hand after one final pinch for good luck. She squeaks, and her mom doesn't miss a beat.

"What is it?"

"I think I saw a mouse," Rory says, clearing her throat.

"Must be the same mouse that visited your bedroom late at night all throughout your teen years," Laura Lee says knowingly.

"Mom!" Rory yelps, and I can't help it. I let out a laugh, a hearty one.

"You ever get that infestation taken care of, Aurora?" I ask her.

"Pretty sure Duke's seen that mouse still sneaking into her room at the bar," Laura Lee muses, coming to a stop at a spot close to the end of the wall in question. "She must have the cheese that particular mouse is after."

"Okay, *stop*," Rory orders, holding up her hands. "There's been a lot of weird euphemisms for my vagina in our household, but *cheese* has to be the worst of them. Please, just stop."

"Hand me your pocketknife, Wyatt." Laura Lee holds her hand out to me expectantly, eyes still on the wall in front of her.

Dig around in my front pocket, hand it over to her and watch in astonishment as she opens up the screwdriver with ease and begins carving into the wall.

"What—?" For once, Rory seems to be knocked speechless.

I lean forward, pressed in against Aurora's back to look more closely at what her mom is doing.

LW + DE

"Laura Lee?" I say. "I'm not trying to get too personal here, but you *do* know what this wall is, right?"

"A little late to say you don't wanna get too personal when you've been as personal as one can be with my youngest child. I'd say we're pretty close by extension at this point, wouldn't you, Wyatt?"

"Yes, ma'am."

Without moving her head she eyes me out of the corners of her eyes, cutting me a warning glare.

"Sorry, ma'am," I mutter.

"Of course I know what this wall is," she says flippantly.

"So why are your initials on it?" Aurora asks her.

"You think you kids are the only ones who get to have a good time?"

Aurora sputters, mouth open, as she watches on in disbelief.

"You and *Duke?*"

"What other 'DE' do you know?"

I blow out a long whistle. "Damn, Mama Weiss. Respect."

Laura Lee finishes carving the slash, for spare, into the wall right next to the initials that were already there, but takes the knuckles I'm holding out to her and indulges me in a pound. She turns back to the wall and puts the tip of the screwdriver back to it, starting to cross over her slash to turn it into an X.

"MOM!" Rory yells. "No, an X means you went all the way back here."

Her mom looks at the girl I've always loved and smirks at her. "I know." She goes back to scratching at the wall.

"Oh my God, I did *not* need to be here for this." Aurora covers her eyes, then her ears, then her eyes once more, before finally speaking again. "If you knew all this, why didn't you carve your initials in back then?"

"We were about to get caught, we had to run," Laura Lee says with a shrug. "Never thought to go back before the place closed, but while we're in the spirit of wrapping up unfinished business, as you're so fond of saying, seemed like my only chance."

"And you didn't want Duke with you when you did this?" Aurora presses her for more.

"It's gonna be my little surprise for him," Laura Lee says with a wicked smile that is scarily similar to her daughter's. "Wyatt, snap a picture, honey." She poses next to the carving, and I take a picture that turns out surprisingly well in this dim lighting. Damn, I'm impressed with my phone.

But all of a sudden it gets *super* bright in here, and I know that's not from my screen.

The beam of light bounces around the dark space, and I hear a door slam in the distance. Laura Lee turns off her flashlight.

"Put your hands where I can see them and make yourself known!" Wow, even the guy's voice sounds douchey. That's not one of our sheriffs, I know all our boys by name. Grew up with most of 'em, under the watch of the rest of 'em. Whoever the fuck this shitstain is, he's got something major up his ass, but he's about to get my foot up there too.

Aurora must come to the same conclusion I do, that there's no path out of here we won't run into this guy, and we won't be able to do it in the pitch black. Plus, he's probably already written down our plate numbers, and we're likely on camera, anyway.

"Don't say another word to my clients," Aurora bluffs. She doesn't practice criminal defense. She's a corporate attorney specializing in contract law, and I bet that's never gotten her in a situation like this before, but it doesn't stop her from trying to protect us. "They've invoked their right to an attorney."

"He's not a cop," I tell her, and say it loud enough for this jackass to hear.

"I'm a security guard," he says, pompous as can be, but he's breathing heavily, like the fifty-yard walk was a hike through the Smokies in the height of summer. "And you're in violation of the no trespass sign on these premises." He finally makes it to us, shining his flashlight in our faces, one by one, causing us to shut our eyes and jerk our heads away from the light. Aurora steps in front of her mom, to protect her eyes and her head from the discomfort of that light. Probably doesn't want to risk triggering another seizure. Yep, this guy's even shittier than he sounded when he first opened his mouth. An ugly fucker too. Like a bulldog gained a few hundred pounds and learned to walk upright.

"How about you stop playing Paul Blart and we'll leave, then," I say, shoulders back and back straight.

"What are you doing here in the first place?" he asks, instead of moving for us to pass him by.

"Looking for an earring," I reply drolly.

"Right," he scoffs. "You broke into the premises to get an earring."

"Yep," I answer quickly. "And now we found it, so if you'll move out of our way, we'll be on our way."

"We're going to wait right here," the asshole says, thumbs in his front belt loops, beneath his sagging stomach.

"Are you keeping my clients here?" Rory goes full attorney on him, and, fuck, I'm half hard for her for it. "One of my clients has a health condition that I'm not required to disclose to you, but keeping her here when she needs medical care and her scheduled medications, is not going to work out well for you. Believe me when I say you do not want to be on my bad side."

"You really don't," I pipe up, and her mom nods from behind her.

"We can step outside," he says, like he's doing us a favor. "But you're not going anywhere until the deputies arrive."

"Mmkay, lead the way," Aurora clips. She can tell when the intelligence of her opponent doesn't register on the same scale as hers, and there's no point in arguing further.

Me? I'm not as smart as her, I wanna destroy this prick, even if that doesn't accomplish much more than satisfaction for me.

"That 'earring' must've been mighty important," the wannabe says, complete with air quotes because he sucks. "Took y'all long enough to get in here."

"Took y'all long enough to show up," I retort to his back.

He reaches the door, pulls it toward us to open it, and steps outside, but bars our path to leave beyond that, arms crossed over his massive chest.

Rory helps her mom out of the dark building and then gets her settled in on the seat of the walker along the outside wall, wrapped up in a couple layers to keep her warm enough as I face off with King Dong.

"Took me forty-five minutes to get to your shithole of a town," he says, sneering down his nose at me. Guess it'll be a bit easier when our outpost opens up here next year. We'll be able to keep an eye on the miscreants here up close."

"Why the hell would you need a location *here*?"

I narrow my eyes on his gold nametag that glints in the last sun of golden hour. *Bubba.*

"Faster response time when our client needs us to keep their properties secure." He somehow made *response* into four syllables, while popping his lips, *and* he said it while fingering the edge of his badge, like a fucking creep.

I step into his personal space, closer than I'd care to, but he needs to get the point. "You get yourself off with that plastic Temu badge, don't you, you fucking rent-a-cop?"

"What did you just say to me?" Bubba breathes the words out around his underbite.

"Wyatt," Aurora snaps my name. I feel like the Rory I grew up with would be right here by my side, taking this motherfucker's legs out from beneath him, but I guess Aurora picks and chooses her battles. To be fair, I do, too, and I picked this one. I think we take turns these days.

Before anything can escalate further, a patrol vehicle, a Crown Victoria, rolls into the lot, a familiar face behind the wheel. One of those childhood friends I mentioned, Carlos. Once he's out of the car and by our sides, Bubba opens his mouth again.

"Good. Another officer of the peace is here. Cameras caught these folks breaking and entering into this here property. When I apprehended them, they said they were 'getting a lost earring.'" He uses air quotes on the words.

"Okay, well, they're out of the building. I trust you helped them find that earring, so you can secure the property now, and I'll make sure these ragamuffins skeedaddle." Carlos stifles the smallest of smirks as he tries not to make eye contact with any of us.

Bubba isn't happy with that. "Our client would like to press charges."

Carlos glances at me, Laura Lee, and Aurora, uncertain. "Against these three?"

"Against anyone who breaks into their properties, yes."

"Did they take anything valuable?"

"Not as far as I can tell."

"Did you find spray paint? Did they deface the property?"

"Nope."

"So you want me to book them for ... walking into a building and *not* hurting anything or anyone, and being perfectly willing to vacate the premises when asked?"

"Yep." This fuckwad's fly is probably tight from the boner his micropenis is getting over this display of massive power he wields.

"As far as I can tell, there was no crime committed, no intention to commit a crime beyond trespassing, so that doesn't qualify as breaking and entering."

"Is your body cam recording?" Bubba asks Carlos.

The deputy does his best not to laugh directly in the other man's face, but I can tell it's a struggle. "Body cam? We don't have body cams here, we don't even have *crime*."

"Well, our camera showed the crime of our property being broken into, and I'm asking you to hold the responsible parties accountable."

"Trespassing is only a criminal offense when the persons don't leave upon request, and we tried to leave," Aurora says with more authority in her voice than anyone else in this parking lot. "This 'guard,'" she uses his air quotes against him, "prevented us from leaving."

"Are you going to do your job or not, Deputy?" A little speck of spit flies out when Bubba pops that *p*, and I cringe for Carlos's poor face.

"It's fine," I jump in. "I'll head over to the station, you can book me, and my lawyer will be right behind us to bail me out." My eyes catch Rory's, just to be sure, and hers soften in silent thank you.

Bubba's definitely gonna jerk it the second he's back in his Chevy Aveo, judging by the look on his face when he speaks again. "According to the video surveillance, this woman is the one who forced entry and opened the door." He jerks a thumb at Ms. Weiss.

"You've got to be kidding me." Aurora's jaw actually falls down.

"I think it'll be enough of a message to the other dirtbags of this town if she's held accountable for her crime. I'll let you take it from here, Deputy." Bubba lets a meaty hand fall on Carlos's uniformed shoulder, thunking him more than patting him, and he steps back to watch, and probably fondle himself.

"I'm sorry about this," Carlos whispers. "If you'll just get in the car, I'll drop you off at home, Laura Lee."

"Are you kidding?" Laura Lee stands up off her walker and steps over to him. "I didn't think I'd have a chance to get arrested too. I didn't even bother to put that on my bucket list, but this is worth at least triple points, wouldn't you say? Aurora, get a picture, will ya? Your old woman is wanted!"

Aurora covers her mouth with both hands to hide her laugh from the jerk off to the side, but I don't bother hiding my smile from him. Let him know he didn't defeat shit here. We're making memories with her mom, having a day for the mental scrapbook, despite his best efforts to ruin it.

The theme song from the James Bond movies sounds from somewhere in the parking lot and Bubba answers his phone. "Yeah, I'm still in Smoky Farts." He laughs at his own joke, belly and chins jiggling. "No problem, boss." He stands straight, snapping to. "Be right there. About an hour. Okay, I'll try." He ends his call and puts the phone back in a holster on his belt that looks like the closest thing he'll ever get to wearing a pistol for his job and gives us one final stink eye. "I trust you'll keep this place on your patrol from now on, until the locks get replaced."

Carlos rolls his eyes and turns his back on the guy, but my girl isn't having it.

"Hey," Aurora calls out, snapping her chin up toward him. "For the record, I hope every time you think you have to shit, nothing comes out. And then as soon as you get in a public place, it hits. And you never make it to the toilet in time. Ever." She wriggles her fingers at him in goodbye and turns her back on him again. The view is better than he deserves, and I step in front of her to glare at him until he's gone.

Laura Lee looks like she's having the time of her life as Carlos loads her in the back of his Crown Vic, and Aurora documents the whole thing, letting her mom pose for funny shots, and ones that make her look like she's been picked up on the lam after a crime spree, very mafia heyday.

Aurora makes sure her mom's walker and cardigans go with them in case she needs them, and we agree to pick her up from the building that triples as city hall, the police station, and the fire department, then Carlos carts her away, Laura Lee cackling in the back. Aurora turns to wave at her the entire time, me at her back, watching as they go.

The second they're out of sight, Rory's on the phone with someone back at her firm in New York. "I want you to find every single offense they could be held accountable for. Not just the ones we've been focusing our efforts on. Every single violation we can nail them for. I want to drown them in legal fees, fines, and penalties. Rip their proverbial fingernails out one by fucking one. Let's give them ten thousand cuts and let them gurgle and choke on their own blood until they pass out from the blood loss and never wake up again."

I might be ten kinds of fucked up for getting a semi at that, but damn, I've always had a thing for this feisty woman bringing out her claws (metaphorical *and* literal). I call her Hellcat, after all.

She ends the call, slipping her phone in the small purse slung across her body, and I yank on her hair, pull her by the ponytail until her head is leaned all the way back, and I have full access to that gorgeous face. My other hand comes up to cup her chin, and then I claim her mouth, tongue sweeping in and showing her how much I need this woman, her determination, the fire she brings to everything she touches.

I'm with her. I'll help however I can, and so will the rest of the Heights when they hear about this. Which, they probably already have.

"When this is all taken care of, I think it's time you spent a night at my house for once," I murmur against her lips.

"Maybe after I get my hair fixed. I think we'll be relegated to quickies until I can bear for you to look at it."

I chuckle, then nip at her lips with a tap to her ass.

"Hellcat, you could come over bald and I'd still want you."

She hums against my mouth, and I pull back so she can look me in the eye.

"Kind of ironic, no?"

"What is?"

"That I left because I was scared to become my mom, or follow in her footsteps."

"Why's that ironic?"

"Did you see her today? If I end up like her, I'll be one lucky bastard."

29
Aurora

"Careful!" I gripe at Lexi.

She turns to steady the painting that's still swaying on Mom's living room wall from where she bumped it. The one my mom finished a few weeks back when I had the instructor come to her house for her, Lexi, and I to all do an at-home paint and sip together.

Lex glares at me over her shoulder once it's steady, a classic scowl on her face, then chucks the lighter she was using at my head. "*You* light the candles, then," she says, wild hair bobbing with every erratic motion of her head. I catch it, but it hurts, so I glare at her.

"Bet I can do it without knocking anything over," I taunt her.

She mocks me, singsonging nonsense back at me, and we both laugh.

It *is* tricky to step between everything we have set up and get the candles lit so the experience is fully ready for Mom. Duke gave us the final warning, so now is our chance.

Lemongrass wafts toward my nose as my hand circles the air in front of me, pulling it forward, and as I move one step over, a spicy blend greets my nostrils, and then a strong hit of jasmine permeates as well.

It might not *be* Thailand, but it's the closest we could get for her.

Lex and I step back, right in front of the TV that's cued up and ready to go, and we admire our handiwork, shoulder-to-shoulder.

It was weeks of planning, of shopping online, of coordination between the two of us and Duke, but I think we might have nailed it.

There's a path through the center of the room so we can navigate, but virtually every other surface is covered.

Just about every wall in the house has been covered in giant, oversized poster prints of the landscape and skyline you'd see were you in Bangkok. No hint of the house we grew up in remains.

The dining room has been turned into one of Thailand's floating markets, or as close as we could get, being on land. All four chairs were pushed back against the wall, and we've balanced child-sized kayaks on each seat, chock full of baskets of different exotic fruits and vegetables in each, bundles of tropical florals nestled in the open spaces so the entire thing is completely covered. Her antique wooden table is buried in the feast Lex and I prepared, courtesy of Goldbelly. The best LA, New York, and Chicago had to offer, every dish she could want to taste, nibble, or sip, and then some.

We moved all of the furniture out of the living room and into our old bedrooms and turned the main space into a silk market. Racks of clothing, of raw material in every color and pattern imaginable, are lined up along one wall, with an entire wall of authentic options set up on the other, all imported for her to browse and peruse. Then there's also another several hundred samples folded in precise stacks that line the available spaces around the racks.

Our matching robes I had custom made and flown in are on hangers at the end of the display, a shiny moss green with tan and pink florals artfully adorning the sides, a thick trim all down the inside hem, and a coordinating silk tie around the waist.

Lexi and I change into ours, along with the vibrant, hand-made slip-on shoes I also ordered for each of us, and wait for that door to open. When we hear the car door close, she hits play on the TV, completing the ambience with a video of scenery and sounds from the place my mom will never get the chance to go. Now it will look, smell, taste, and *sound* like Bangkok in here. As close as we can get to her feeling like she's experiencing the real thing.

The back door opens, a frigid wind rushing in with it, and there's my mom, frailer by the day but still holding strong, in her wheelchair, Duke pushing her from behind. The door closes behind them and the daylight that was framing them disappears.

It took all three of us teaming up on her for a while, but eventually she caved. Her balance has gotten bad enough that it was safer and more comfortable for her to use a wheelchair to get around when she leaves the house, and I don't want to think about how bad she must be feeling if she finally agreed to make the swap. Getting her to accept using a walker was hard enough.

Her care team say the prognosis stands, still another five months at best, but they won't be pretty ones. As the tumor grows, the cancer progresses, her body will be going through hell, and so will everyone who loves her. I've had months to ponder the circumstances, and I still don't know what's better. Is it easier to lose someone suddenly, have to live with a lifetime of wishing you got to say goodbye, got just one more day with them, one more *hour*, or is it easier to watch them suffer, to know the inevitable is hanging in the balance, a pendulum waiting to drop at any moment, but at least you have the selfish chance to make the most of the time you get with them? I don't think there is a right answer. They're all wrong answers. There's nothing right losing someone you love, period. Preparing for it, or dealing with the shock of it, grief is grief, either way. I'm not sure anything could make it better.

Watching her suffering ratchet up week by week, it makes me wish for nothing more than this to not happen to her. To take her place. For some way to make this easier for her. But we're past the bargaining stage now. We're in this shitty phase called acceptance, where we know what our options are, they all suck, and we're going to make the best of it while we can—in between the tears that come with acceptance—because that's all we can fucking do.

So when her face lights up, when she takes in the way her home has been transformed, what's waiting for her there, I know she figures it out on her own, but Lex and I can't help ourselves from giving her the welcome speech we'd practiced anyway.

"Welcome to Bangkok," I start off.

"Your all-inclusive, one-day visit includes an all-you-can-eat buffet, a trip to the silk markets, the floating markets, a trip to the Grand Palace, as well as an authentic Thai massage, an exclusive ethical elephant experience, and a tuk tuk tour," Lexi says proudly, sweeping her arm toward everything we have set up for Mom to enjoy.

"Please, enjoy your stay in Thailand," I tell her, bowing.

Duke's face has been less stressed for weeks, ever since he let me start helping on some of the financial aspects, and seeing the joy there now, his eyes glassy as he watches my mother, I'm right-clicking and saving this one in a mental folder called Best Moments. He leans down and kisses the top of her head, a lot like Wyatt does to me sometimes, and steps away. "Have a great time, love. I'll be back after girls' day is over. Don't let that masseuse's hands get near anywhere that's just for me, okay, no frisky business while I'm gone." That last warning was to me and Lex, and we both promise. Lexi even mock solutes him.

"Let's get you changed," I say to her once Duke is gone.

Lexi grabs the robe and shoes for her, and I'll never forget the look on Mom's face when she sees how all three of us will be matching. I hate myself for robbing her of more moments like this. For not giving her more memories of the three of us together, but I'll make tonight the best I possibly can, another in the first set of as many memories as we can fit in before it's too late.

Our at-home paint and sip and Thanksgiving should be filed in that same folder too. We made it through that day fairly unscathed as a family of four, and Wyatt even stopped by for a bit after he couldn't take being home with Weston any longer. Felt a lot like the best holidays of my life used to, just with a better male role model present.

"How did you—when—what?" Mom stutters, unable to form a complete question, but just the way she's gawking in appreciation is enough to make this entire thing worth it.

Our masseuses show up right on time, having driven the hundred or so miles from the city, and they set up the tables in the walkway in the living room while we start our agenda off with hot green tea.

An hour later, I can't speak for the others, but I'm feeling loose and refreshed. Based on the noises Mom was making, I'd say she enjoyed the hell out of hers too. Once the ladies have left, Lex and I take Mom to the table, where the chafing dishes and burners have kept the food warm until we were ready for it. Cost a fortune to have a catering company set up these dishes for us, but it was worth it after all the effort Lex and I put into the food, and we wanted it to stay ready all day, for whenever any of us might want it.

Mom has a blast selecting flowers and sifting through the fresh produce for goodies to try. And while she doesn't have the appetite she used to, she picks and nibbles at every single thing we made her, tasting each dish at least once, while Lexi and I shove our faces full of our favorites after we tried it all. Her alarm goes off during our meal and she downs another small handful of pills, but she doesn't take a nap like usual. She manages to milk every second out of our day together.

Later, we go through the silk market, and Mom *oohs* and *aahs* at the variety available, and I insist that she picks out a few materials to have a couple of new pieces made out of. She chooses a bright teal with a bold floral design, and another that's a subtle rosy color, with gold woven throughout it. When she says they remind her of the two of us, I get a little misty eyed. We set those to the side to have more robes made out of, souvenirs for her from today.

The next portion of the itinerary requires a VR headset that Wyatt helped me set up and prep after it arrived in the mail.

"What the heck is that thing?" Mom asks as I approach her with it.

"This is what's going to let you visit the Grand Palace," I tell her, fitting it over her head.

It takes a few adjustments to get it set up right for her, and then she's cackling, waving her arms out in front of her, swiping at something she can see on the headset that the rest of us can't. Until I open the app on my phone, and her display is mirrored on my screen, so Lex and I can see what she's seeing.

"Move your head, Mom," I tell her, and watch the scenery change on my phone as she looks up, then down, turns her head from one side to the other, and faces back to front.

The sky, the ground, tourists all around, and the beautiful Grand Palace right in front of us.

"It's beautiful," Mom whispers. "It's like I'm right there."

"Take a step forward," I tell her.

She does, and then lets out a tiny scream, which makes Alexis and me laugh. We come around either side of her and hold an arm each, stabilizing her so she can walk freely, the headset reacting in real-time, like she was there and not in her living room.

"When you're ready, we can take you to the sanctuary so you can have an ethical experience with the elephants from here," I tell her.

Mom's face turns toward me, like she's looking at me, but she's got the headset on, which looks like a giant set of goggles you'd wear snorkeling, but neither of us can see through the screen in front of her face, so it just looks ridiculous.

"Elephants?" she asks in a choked voice.

"Up close and personal," Lexi confirms.

Mom turns her head to "look" at her eldest daughter, and I see the smile spread on Lexi's face.

We cue it up through the phone and sit her down so she can feel like she's sitting in the field of elephants all around, watching them toss their heads around, ears tumbling with the motion.

I lose track of how many times Mom laughs, how many times Lexi and I look at each other, grinning, or how many times one of them squeezes my hand when words aren't good enough.

As busy as the bank case has kept me, I couldn't be more thankful I prioritized planning and pulling today off. All of my other workload has been reassigned to other associates, the senior partners having seen what a massive opportunity we have with the case against Brown Stone Bank, the things I have planned on that front, and I managed to balance keeping up with heading *that* while still doing *this*. Even managed to fit in some boring things from Mom's list in the meantime, like helping her organize her financial matters and her will.

Fit in a few nights with Wyatt, too, though none at his place, yet. (Even though the only box dye I was willing to trust arrived from NYC shortly after Mom's arrest, and my hair is back to my natural brown—as good as it's gonna get for now—*technically* fulfilling my stipulation on a sleepover with him.) He's been visiting me at the bar whenever we can both swing it, but tonight might finally be that night for more.

I have to say, though, seeing the result of these past weeks, the joy present on these women's faces, it makes me want to be the Rory who can do it all again. The working badass and the one who makes her family a priority too.

"Is it the drugs I'm on, did I hallucinate it, or did y'all say there was gonna be a tuk tuk ride?" Mom asks, once we've finished with the elephants and she's resting after the adventure we've had today.

Lex and I look at each other, and she stands first. "Let me grab your chariot," Alexis says, while I help Mom stand.

"Close your eyes," I tell her.

Lexi pushes the wheelchair up quietly behind Mom, and I guide her back into it, eyes closed. "Keep 'em closed," we say together.

I cue up the right option on the VR headset and put it back on her head.

"You can open now," I say, watching both her face and the phone in my hand to see what she's seeing.

"Are you ready?" Lexi asks.

Mom nods, and the view in the headset moves with her head.

I hand the phone to Lexi and take hold of the handles on the back of the wheelchair as she pushes play, and the experience begins. I push Mom's wheelchair forward, through the path we left in the house, as the VR tour starts on the headset. Lexi holds the phone up so I can see what Mom sees, walking next to us, and I push our mother through the house, narrating as we go.

"On the right here, you'll see the Emerald Temple of Buddha, constructed in 1783. Fun fact, this temple was constructed specifically to house the Emerald Buddha that is believed to have been carved in the year 43 B.C. Oh, and it looks like next we'll be taking a shortcut to the Flower Market," I say, swinging her though the kitchen and looping her around so we can come out to the dining room again, in time with the video.

When I say *flower market*, Lexi hands Mom some of the florals from the setup we'd prepped, and Mom takes hold of them, putting her nose in deep and taking a big whiff. As we pass by each area of the house, Lex grabs different items and blows on them to get the scents to Mom—food, flowers, candles —making it an immersive experience.

I run at full speed when we reach an open stretch in the main living space, and Mom's laughter hitting my ears is a sound I'll cherish forever. "Oh, and now we're already to Wat Arun, one of the most mesmerizing landmarks in all of Bangkok," I say, breathing heavily.

Lexi and I keep it going, up and down the path we'd laid out in the house until the video tour ends and we come to a stop. Mom takes the headset off, and we help her out of the chair and onto some cushions we laid out on the floor earlier, plopping down on either side of her. She's gotta be exhausted, but I'm impressed at how well she's done.

"How on earth did you pull this off?" she asks us.

Alexis and I look at each other, and she shrugs while I pop a shoulder.

"This must've cost a fortune," Mom breathes out, still reeling in the best way.

"Eh, believe it or not, it wasn't much more than our trip would've been," I tell her.

"I don't know what to say, girls."

"You don't have to say anything," I assure her, a hand on her knee.

This is one of those moments where words just won't do.

But this feeling? I'll keep it with me forever.

30
Laura Lee

I don't have the words for what today has been.

Seeing my girls like this.

I've had a lot of good moments in my life. A *lot*.

I don't think any of them top today.

The knowledge that they're in good hands.

Each other's.

They've finally got *each other* when they haven't for so long.

And Duke. I know he'll be there for them, whatever comes next.

And Wyatt, regardless of what Rory's telling herself when it comes to that man.

Alexis will find someone who loves her just as much, I know she will.

It lifts a weight that I've had in my chest since I first saw the look on the doctor's face, before they even got the words out and told me my fate.

I realize what my heart's filled with. It's a feeling I've spent more than twelve years chasing.

Peace.

31

Aurora

It's nearing dusk when I pull up to the address Wyatt texted me. His house.

I would've loved to stay with Mom longer, but she was tuckered out after today. We ended up watching a chick flick, the three of us cuddled together in the cushions on the floor, under some blankets. That's where she fell asleep, a smile on her face, each of our hands in one of hers.

Duke came home and told us he'd take it from there, and to have a good night. So that's what I'm here to do. Something I'm long overdue for.

Pull up the driveway, marveling at the beauty of this land. I think this might be his family's property, it looks a lot like where they used to go camping sometimes, if memory serves. It's a long way to get through the woods and into the clearing where his house is. Tucked deep into a forest that's a mix of evergreens and deciduous, there's a carpet of leaves along the driveway as I go, but still enough greenery left in the woods to provide a healthy dose of privacy.

Glad I made it in daylight, this is secluded enough it'd be tricky to do for the first time in the dark. When I get up to the house, Wyatt is standing there, waiting for me, fine as ever. Tanned skin, dark hair, green eyes glinting, that black ink on his skin that I can only see a hint of, because for once, his sleeves aren't pushed up. It's cold enough out now that he should be in a jacket, but maybe the fact that I'm wearing his favorite hoodie —the one he put on me when we were hiking and I never gave back—is the problem. I paired it with some of the additional jeans I bought after he asked me if I owned any, and it's as comfy as I remember being.

At least *I'm* toasty as I step out of the car and press my lips to his.

"Damn, you look good," he says, bringing a hand up to twirl some of my hair that's fallen loose. "I'm not over this hair color yet. It's fucking gorgeous on you."

"It's my natural hair color," I deflect. "It's not that exciting."

"Tell that to my dick," he says with another peck to my mouth.

"I'd love to have a chat with the big guy," I say, twisting on a foot and spinning to take in the scenery. "But you owe me a tour first."

"Right," he says, and blows out a breath. "Now or never, huh?"

"Mmhmm," I say, because when else would I get a tour?

Wyatt points to the house, which I finally look at now that he's not distracting me with his tantalizing masculinity, and he starts to tell me about it.

It's cozy, a rustic-modern cottage that's deceptively simple in design, until you look closer and realize how complex the details really are. It's smaller than I would've expected, but it's so perfectly *him* that I smile.

Stone exterior, black metal trim, stunning natural wooden beams to accent the entrance, and a black metal gabled roof.

The front door is really just a large pane of glass, edged in black metal. Striking.

It's one story, but the ceilings are clearly taller than the standard. A porch wraps around one side of the house, from the front to the back, as does a stone walkway, and I marvel at the craftsmanship displayed, even in just the exterior of the house. I can't wait to see what it looks like on the inside.

I follow Wyatt around the back and listen to him talk as we go. "Took me about seven years to build, but I've been here almost four years now."

"Wow, you had this custom built?" I'm impressed.

Floor-to-ceiling windows overlook the backyard, which is really more accurately classified as a meadow, I would say. At least a small field. It extends well beyond the size of a normal yard, edged by more woodland, the iconic Smoky Mountains a distant backdrop. I'd be willing to bet in a season when the temperature isn't playing jump rope with the point of freezing, wildflowers would be springing up all around the edges.

The windows on the back of the home lead all the way to the gabled roof, black metal running down all the joints, giving it a modern vibe that screams Wyatt. Sophisticated, edgy, a little industrial, just enough masculinity without being too much. Gorgeous, a little wild, nothing you'd mistake for soft.

The windows hide nothing about the interior from this view out back. The living space that's visible behind the giant translucent panes, a small dining table in one corner, next to a kitchen that's maybe small by modern standards, but it's bigger than anything I've seen in NYC for under ten grand a month. Perfectly workable. And the living room, so cozy I could curl up in the sofa in front of the stone fireplace there forever if I wasn't careful, that chair by the window along the side wall, it would be perfect for a chilly day like today. I could crack the window open, probably even catch a snowflake from that seat while I sipped a cider beneath a blanket and read the newest Theo Carter book.

Wyatt clears his throat. "Actually, built most of it myself. Had a little help." He tilts his head side to side with each name he says. "Ronnie, Gonzo, my stepdad. Had to hire a couple things out. But most of it, this project was my baby."

The way he's looking at me, it's trepidation and worry and like he's waiting for the other shoe to drop. Like I'm liable to run on him at any minute. And here I thought we were really getting somewhere.

The bite of the icy wind picks up as the clouds blow in and I shiver. It's gotta be below freezing now. "Well, let's head inside," I say, still struck, dumbfounded by the beauty of this place. "Why don't you show me the rest of it. I think the bathroom and bedrooms are the only rooms I can't see from outside, but show me all of it."

One side of his stubbled mouth tilts up and he nods, putting a hand on my low back as we go.

If I thought the inside was gorgeous from outside, I had no idea what I was in for. Plush furniture, simple but perfect, in darks and neutrals. Like the colors found in the woods around us, and the shadows they live in beneath the canopy of the tree-tops. No one could call it a large home, two modest bedrooms, each with a simple bathroom, but the primary en suite has a soaking tub that overlooks the forest, and I think I got wet just looking at it.

When we make it back to the living room, I turn to face him, unable to voice my thoughts just yet.

It's so *homey*, tears spring to my eyes, making everything in my line of vision hazy, even more than usual where he's concerned. But it's clear enough that I realize this is what I could've had if I hadn't run away. If I'd been brave enough to tell him my fears, what I was struggling with, and tried to weather the storm together.

We could've had the cottage in the meadow, with the cozy seat by the window where I can watch the snow—

The thought is interrupted by movement in my peripheral vision.

Snow falls outside the windows. As I turn in place, I can see it no matter where I look. Flakes drifting down past the beautiful front door, the giant windows with that clear view out to the yard in the back, even the side of the house, that chair that's calling my name beneath the window there. I rush over to it and open the window, cranking it to open outward, squealing in delight as I reach a hand through it and catch a snowflake. I spin around to show Wyatt, and he's closer than I expected him to be, watching me with so much focus it takes my breath away.

"This is what I used to dream about," I tell him, holding the melting snowflake up on my fingertips for his inspection.

"I know," he says softly, and my blinders come off. The high I've been riding after the day with my mom and sister, the haze it cast over my vision, it peels back, allowing me to see what's right in front of me clearly. It all starts to click, faster than I'm ready for.

"Wyatt," I breathe out.

"Aurora," he says in a dangerously low voice.

It's the snowflake melting on my fingertips that acts as the neon sharpie, connecting the dots in a way that there's no way to miss them, even when I've been blinded by the emotion of the day.

"You built our dream house?" I whisper.

"Build it and they'll come, right?" He shrugs a shoulder lazily, but he can't downplay this.

This isn't keeping my scarf in a drawer as a memento and thinking of me fondly from time to time.

He took *the* thing we always dreamed about and spent seven years dedicating his energy, money, time, and labor to it. He built this house with his own hands, when I left without even telling him goodbye.

I don't deserve him—I may never have—but I need him all the same.

I leap forward, colliding into him, and wrap myself in his arms, bringing his face down to mine to kiss him deeply.

"I came," I whisper against his lips in between kisses. "Show me, Wyatt. Show me what we should've had all this time."

His hands close around me, steadying me as I move against him. One large palm holds the back of my head, the other frames my ass as he holds me to him, letting our lips do all the talking we need right now.

He presses kisses to my face, my jawline, my neck, trailing teases that make my pussy flutter at the feel of them.

I reach down for the hem of the hoodie and pull it upward, and he takes over, removing it for me. We undress as we go, a new article of clothing dotting our path every few steps, like some sort of Hansel and Gretel retelling, the adult version. We leave a trail in our wake as we walk through his cottage in the woods, and it's straight out of my own personal fairytale.

The hoodie of his I'm so fond of.

His Henley.

My long-sleeved shirt.

His boots.

My Uggs.

His Dickies.

My jeans.

Until we're in his bedroom. What should've been our bedroom. And we're in nothing but our underwear. I push him back until he's sitting on the edge of the bed, one arm extended behind him, one on my side. One of my knees comes up to rest on the side of his body, and then the other does the same on his other side. I straddle him, his hands running up and down my back, as his lips explore my neck, my chest, my breasts.

The feel of him, hard between my legs, nothing but two layers of thin material separating us, it's the most delicious sort of anticipation, and I'm living for it. Yeah, I'm here for the main event, but when what comes first is so damn good, what's the rush?

"Wyatt?" I ask, panting as his tongue traces the skin above my nipple, tormenting me in my favorite way possible.

"Mmm?" His lips don't even close, he doesn't break the contact from my skin, and I think that deserves recognition. I force myself to pull back, and look him in the eye, even if my hips grind a little bit on top of his lap automatically.

"How long have you had hope for us?" I ask him, not sure if I'm ready for the answer, but needing to know.

"Since I asked you out," he says, breaths coming heavily.

I trace a finger down his chest, the patch of short hair there, and keep running it down.

"Are you counting that as the bonfire or the ATV disaster? Or was it the night we played pool?"

"Not sure anything we did that night could be considered playing pool, Hellcat. But the first time. When you were sixteen, in history class."

My breath falters. "All this time?"

"I've never not loved you. If there's anyone on this plane for me, it's you, Aurora."

Tears build, but something is off about this moment. That name, it twinges, something like discomfort echoing inside me. It doesn't fit with him, with us, with this reality we're in. "Don't call me that," I breathe.

His hand smooths over the top of my head, down the back of

it, until it rests on the nape of my neck, fingers tracing delicate shapes there as he stares in my eyes.

"Okay, Rory," he whispers a breath away from my lips. The name, all the emotion behind it from this man, sends chills skittering along my spine. "You ready for more truth from me?"

I nod, and mean it.

"I still love you. More than ever, now that I've seen how strong you've become, how incredibly brilliant and badass you are, despite the burden you've been carrying all alone. You're the most terrifying woman I've ever met, your enemies need all the help they can get, and the highlight of my life has been every chance I've had to love you."

His words fill me with a kind of serenity I haven't known without him in all this time. The belief that even as messed up as I am, the ways I've done wrong in my life, a man like this can still love me ... That elusive forgiveness of self feels that much closer, because of him and the good he sees in me, even when I can't see it myself.

If my eyes aren't wet, another part of me definitely is, and I lean back in, closing my mouth around his again, ramping up the kiss from zero to at least a hundred on the dash in record time.

I let my body talk for me, hips circling over his hardness, lips on his body while his fingers trail my spine, his touch lighting me up and sending fresh goosebumps sizzling across the surface of my skin. His mouth closes around that spot beneath my ear that turns me into a puddle, and I whimper, grinding down harder on him.

Wyatt stands, holding me to him as he does, and he turns and drops me on the bed, letting me fall from his arms and bouncing with the impact. He smiles down at me, then follows me, one knee on the bed as he covers my body with his. Kisses dot my stomach as he works his way down, and the spark of need fans into a burn of desire, a physical need, like air, or your first love's touch to heal all your invisible wounds.

"Please," I whimper.

"I got you, Rory," he says against my skin.

Wyatt makes quick work of removing my underwear, and he doesn't tease me this time. He dives straight in, licking me from my center to my clit, with the kind of pressure that makes my legs jolt off the bed. I can feel his mouth twitch up, the burn of his scruff shifting against my sensitive skin, and his palms come down on my thighs to hold them in place as he takes another lick. Long, sensuous, deep. He's getting his fill, but he's not making me wait for what I need, either. I think this is what compromise looks like.

His tongue parts me, circling my clit like a homing beacon that's calling to him, and then slipping down, lapping as fresh juices spill out of me.

"You've never tasted better," he groans into my thigh, and it makes me writhe against the bed, against his hold, the way his face is pressed into me. It's obnoxious. I hope he never stops.

"More," I plead with him, softer than a demand, being open with him for once on what I need. Letting him respond how he wants to.

"I'll give you everything you need," he promises, and then his mouth is busy again, flush against my core.

The man eats me like his survival depends on it, like it's me alone that's giving him life, and the way his eyes barrel into me as his tongue is doing the same, it's got me hurtling toward the finish line. He feels it, too, upping the intensity and pushing me further and further toward that bright light.

"Fuck," I cry out. "Wyatt!"

His fingers grip my thighs, pressing into the skin there, and with nothing but his tongue inside of me, his truth nestled somewhere deep that makes me warm and safe and like I can finally stop running, it's enough for me. I shatter.

He groans against my center as he licks it up, everything my body gives him, he takes it greedily, leaving nothing behind. His eyes darken as his tongue moves, then he swallows and my insides tumble, a path straight from my low belly down to my core lighting up already, while the rest of me still trembles in the aftershocks.

My head thrown back, chest heaving, I feel the mattress shift with him as he prowls up my body and open my eyes when he's above me again. I watch as he leans down, taking my mouth and letting me taste what's got his cock so hard, pressed up against my thigh.

It's dirty, it's personal, it's something I've only done with him, and I groan when he does it. I'm already wet again, already needy to feel all of him. My hand seeks him out, running down the carved planes of his body until I reach his boxer briefs. I slip my hand in the waistband and twist my wrist so I can encircle him in my hold, and pump. He jerks his head when I make contact, breaking his mouth off of mine, and withdraws his hips so I'm left empty-handed.

"Later." It's gruff, and the need in his voice speaks volumes.

I nod at him, perfectly willing to feel him inside me now, and play with him later.

Wyatt pulls off his underwear and parts my thighs, holding them wide so he can look as long as he wants. "Forgot how beautiful this pussy was after it just came, Rory. Pink and swollen, still dripping, rubbed raw from my beard. Fucking perfect." He waits until those words hit me, the noise I make in response before he adds, "Can't wait to see how it looks when it's my cum pouring out of it."

The use of my name, the truths he shared, how bare I feel with him—not just physically, but how he knows all of my truths and wants me anyway—and that heat burning in his deep green eyes as he watches the emotion swim in my gaze, it all makes me need him in a way I've never needed anyone.

"Take it," I beg him.

"Mine," he vows.

I nod at him, back of my head pressed into the pillow, and that's all he needed from me. A promise my lips still won't give him. But I hope he feels it just the same.

Wyatt leans forward, holding himself up with one arm as he uses the other hand to bring his thick head to my entrance. Once he's notched in, he drags that hand up to cup my cheek as he pushes in.

My breath catches, but I don't let my eyes close as he sinks inside of me. For the first time, neither of us looks away. And I find his gaze more interesting than even watching his cock would be right now. Feeling him stretch me, shape my walls to his girth, the way his hard length fills me, there's nothing like it, but having him pierce me, scale all the way to my inner depths with those irises, the color of pine needles and all my best memories as he does? How am I supposed to hold out against feelings like this?

My mouth pops open when the promise of another orgasm starts, low in my core. The pressure coils, delicious heat spreading, pleasure starting to ripple through me.

Wyatt's jaw tics as he feels it too. "That's it, Rory, squeeze my cock when you come."

If my walls weren't already clenching, they are now.

"Mmm," he groans, watching me, rapt.

"Do you need more?" he asks, pumping his hips into me slowly, so deep, letting me slowly crest this high and milk it.

"More," I echo, not because I need it, but just because I want everything from him. It's what I'll give him too.

He tilts his head down, bringing his mouth to mine and

kissing me as deeply as he's fucking me. One hand comes to my breast and he rolls my nipple, riding that line between what makes me sweat and what makes me scream.

The combo tips me over, triggering another onslaught that has me convulsing, mindless from bliss as I ride it out. Wyatt moans in my mouth as he feels my orgasm hit, the way I'm so tight around him he struggles to pull out and push back in, and he pulses his hips against mine to keep the rhythm going instead of those deep thrusts. His pelvic bone presses into my clit, it sends my eyes rolling back in my head, my nails digging into his back.

Wyatt shows me how much he enjoys that by biting down on my lip, dragging it up, and then releasing it with something like a growl.

Staring at him, panting as I come down while he still moves inside of me, I can't hide from the fact that what made me come that time was how much I love this man.

For once, I'm not running from the voice in my head.

I'm done running, period.

I think I'm home.

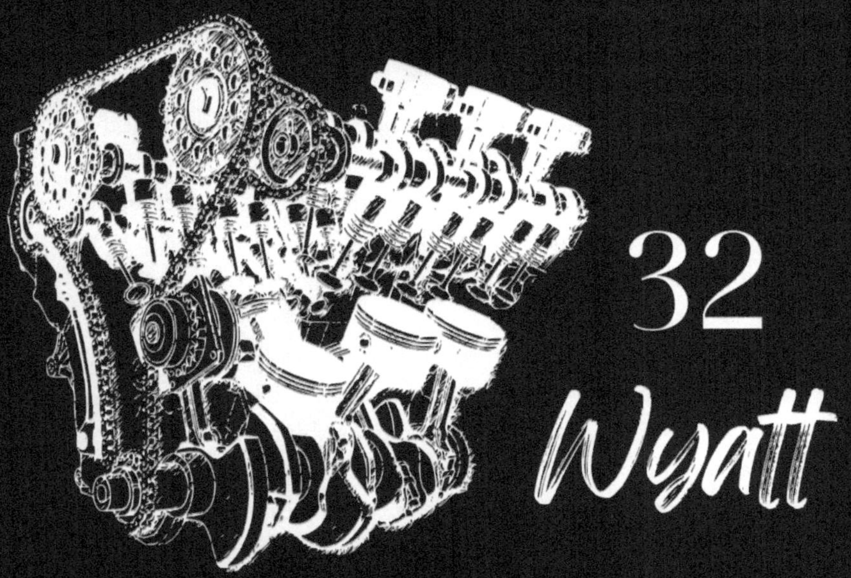

32
Wyatt

The way she's looking at me, it's everything I've spent the last twelve years waiting for. My cock jerks inside of her at the recognition of that particular expression and the sentiment behind it, and I pull out so I don't blow already.

Spent seven years building this house, another four wishing it had her in it. Not gonna fuck up my first night with her in here with a rookie move like that.

But this time between us is different, and I'm not the only one who knows it. It's not just her eyes that are softer, I can feel it in every kiss, every time her hips move to meet mine. This isn't just fucking anymore, if it ever was.

"Sit up," I tell her, and I pull her forward, onto my lap as I sit down, legs extended.

We work together to get her situated on top of me, legs wrapped around my back, and then she's sliding down my cock, such a tight fit that early tremors of pleasure hit me, and I tell them to fuck off.

Rory wraps her arms around my neck, bracing herself on my shoulders with a groan, and I wrap my hands around her waist. We lift her and let her drop back down slowly a couple of times to adjust to the position, the feel of our bodies working together in this new angle. She's so worked up, her pussy is bright pink and so fucking hot to watch as she slides down my dick again. This time, she takes me all the way, sinking down to the base, and she gasps, humming in satisfaction when I hit that spot that's so deep inside her.

I watch her for a few thrusts, her cheeks flushed like that, silky brown hair thrown back in a ponytail. I bring my hands down to her hips and keep her steady as she rotates her pelvis, testing out some moves we haven't gotten to try together. She might be turning me into a believer of yoga if that's what it's done for her flexibility. Plus, the way her pussy is gripping me right now, it's like her hand is squeezing me, pumping me, trying to coax the cum out of me. I'm not gonna stand a chance at making this last if she keeps this up.

One hand stays on her hip, gripping her tightly while the other skims over her side and climbs up her back, taking hold of her ponytail and wrapping it around my fist once, then twice, and tugging. Her head falls back with a moan, and my mouth closes over her throat, working my way up to her ear and back down to her nipple, giving it some overdue attention with lips, tongue, and teeth.

She starts to grind on me faster, and I feel it brewing for both of us. I slide my hands down her body until they're gripping her ass cheeks, and I pull on them, spreading her for me. Her eyes widen when I do, and I watch, reading her better than she knows herself when it comes to what she needs from me, at least on a physical level. Here's hoping my confession earlier wasn't too much too soon, and I didn't scare her away again.

I bring this back to a physical connection, where I know she needs me most. Our eyes stay on one another's as one hand has a firm grasp on one cheek, and a finger on the other comes out to play. My finger rims her asshole, and she bucks, moaning, clenching *everywhere*. I press against the puckered flesh, just pressure, not breaching the ring just yet, and her noises get louder.

"You gonna let me play with you soon?" I ask against her lips, then kiss her.

She nods against my mouth, not breaking the kiss, and I smile against her flesh.

"There's a lot I wanna do with you, Ror," I tell her, bringing my hands back to her front. My clean hand comes back to pinch her nipple, pull on it, roll it in the way that sends her skyrocketing.

"Do it," she pleads.

"I'm gonna," I promise her. "If you stay."

That same hand slides down her stomach, over her pussy and I flick her clit. Her cunt clenches around my length, and I smirk up at her, before circling the swollen nub with my thumb, watching her react to every change in pressure, angle, and pattern I use on her.

It doesn't take long to find what's going to do the job for the third time tonight, and I start talking to her as her pleasure builds and she chases that high, bouncing on my lap. "I'll do anything you want me to, Rory. You spend all day fantasizing, you come home to me, and I'll make it happen. You want me to worship you, disrespect you, I'll fucking do it. That dirty mind gets any ideas in it at all, you bring them to me, okay? You need me to fuck you like I hate you, I can do that. But know that just you is enough for me."

Rory's eyes flutter shut on a moan, but then she opens them again, heavy lidded stare on mine. "Wyatt?" Her breathing is labored, and it looks like it's taking effort to keep her eyes open against the pleasure that's taking over her system right now.

"Yeah, Rory?"

"I've never not loved you too."

And would you look at that, looks like my mouth isn't the only one that knows how to spit out what the other one needs to finish.

My balls tighten, the high of release coursing through my veins as she bears down on me, walls tightening as we come together, bodies flush, both naked hearts and truths bared.

My orgasm tears through me, shot after shot of hot cum leaving me, and her grade A pussy sucks it all out of me as she shudders, breaking. I feel her heels dig into my ass, toes curled into my back as her whole body stiffens with the assault of her own.

We come down slowly, not rushing to break apart, but when we finally do I make her stay in bed while I run some warm water and bring a cloth back to clean her up with.

I was right, her cunt looks even better like this.

A sight I'll never get tired of, this girl in the bed that was always meant to be ours, spent, both of our releases leaking out of her, sweat and satisfaction all over that perfect face.

Her, in this house at all, really. It was always meant to have her in it.

We spend the evening doing the simple shit. I heated up a late dinner for us, warmed some cider for her so she could keep watching the first snowfall from that window of hers. It's too early for the snow to stick to the ground, but she ate up watching those flakes drift down while it lasted.

At one point we made it back to the bedroom, where I toyed with her clit lazily until her back bowed, her legs shook, and my hand was soaked. Then she grabbed that hand, wrapped it around my cock, and kept her own hand circled around my wrist. She jerked me off with my own fucking hand, wet with her release, all under her control. It was slow, unhurried, unlike anything I've done with anyone else, and she kept it going until I covered her stomach in cum. What we did after that, I'll keep between her and me.

We've since brushed our teeth (she used a spare toothbrush that's been here since I moved in), plugged in our phones (apparently she never leaves home without her charger, the most Rory shit I ever heard), set alarms for the morning, and are now savoring one another's company as we cuddle in bed.

"I can't believe you did it. You built it," she says, a bit of disbelief in that voice and on that flawless face.

"Yeah, I still can't believe it some days, and it's been done for four years now." A small smile tugs up the corner of my mouth, and one of my hands reaches out to tuck some hair behind her ear.

"Although," she says thoughtfully. "I guess it's my fault one part of that dream can't ever come true."

"Which part?"

"The little boy who's supposed to be playing in that yard out there. Axle." The smile she returns is sad, but it doesn't need to be.

I guess now's as good a time as any to tell her the rest.

"Actually ..." I start.

Her eyes meet mine.

"When I went for the procedure, they encouraged me to save a sample in case I ever changed my mind."

She sucks in a sharp breath, waiting for me to say more before she lets hope sink in.

"I thought if there was any chance you'd come back, any chance of that future we wanted together ... I had to do it. And later that year I started building this place." I gesture with my eyes to the roof above us. "Just in case."

"Are you saying what I think you're saying?" She's practically vibrating with apprehension.

"You're telling me you can devour a two-hundred-page document written in legalese and know every instance of when to use who and whom, or whereby and henceforth, but you can't understand when I'm telling you I have some of my sperm frozen?"

"Grady!" It's somewhere between a squeal and a reproach.

"We have options, Hellcat," I tell her, bringing one of her hands to my mouth and kissing her knuckles. "If you want them. That's what I'm saying."

Some time later we're drifting off in the dark room, her tucked into my side, head nestled beneath my chin, tickling me with strands of loose hair that dive for my nose with every inhale, and those small hands on my chest.

"Rory?" I ask.

"Yes?" she says sleepily.

"I never got the chance to ask you last time, but I'm asking you this time. Stay. Stay with me. Or ask me to go with you. Just don't leave me again."

Her head nods against my chest, but before I can get a verbal response from her, I hear those tiny noises she makes that mean she's asleep.

THE ALARM GOES OFF, and for once it pulls up one side of my mouth a fraction of an inch. Waking up with Rory is how I wanna start every morning. A reason to open my eyes. A reason to come home at night, instead of hide out at the bar.

I fumble around the nightstand, reaching for the phone, and find the drawer is open. Probably forgot to close it after grabbing the lube at some point last night. Get the alarm silenced and reach out with the other arm to stroke whatever I can reach of

Rory, wake her up gently, and pull her in close before we have to get up.

My hand finds nothing but covers and sheets. This bed has exactly as many people in it now as it has every other morning I've woken up in it. Just me and the ghost of the girl who always haunts me in it.

Eyes popping open I sit up and throw my legs over the side of the bed, scrub my face.

"Rory?" I call out, voice starting to shake.

Last time I woke up without her she was gone for good. Waking up alone that morning was the worst thing that's ever happened to me. She's probably in the kitchen this time, starting her coffee with the expensive beans I've kept here for three months, but it's a little too similar for me to feel comfortable.

That's probably why my heart pounds as my feet slap on the wooden floors when I walk from the primary bedroom to the kitchen. She's not there, but I can't say there's no sign of her.

A familiar piece of paper is on the counter, and when I recognize it, that's when the full-body tremors start.

I pick it up, wrinkled and ruffled with time, and force my eyes to read it once more even though I could recite it word for word a hundred years from now. The lines are burned into my soul. The hand holding the paper shaking doesn't make it easier, but I already know what it says.

> *Wyatt,*
> *There's no easy way to say this. There's no way to make this suck less. If I don't go now, I never will. I hope you find a way to be happy in the Heights, but I need to go.*
> *I'm so sorry.*
> *Rory*

This can't be happening again.

I run back to my nightstand, searching the drawer for what I know I won't find. The lube was returned, but the note is (obviously) missing.

I drop onto the bed, palms pressed into my eyes, and try to run through the likely outcomes. Try not to jump to conclusions.

Check the cameras, the voice of reason says.

Tap to pull up the app I use to monitor my security cameras on the perimeter of the house. Normally don't see anything other than deer or the occasional black bear, now I'm hoping to spot a Hellcat.

Scroll through the activity log, the recordings that were triggered by motion sensors, and sure enough, there's one from four-thirty in the morning. Hold my breath as I click on it and wait.

It's dark, it's grainy, but it's unmistakably Rory, running away from me. Getting in her rental car and peeling out, probably halfway back to New York by now.

Decide to make one last effort before I accept the truth.

I call her. It goes straight to voicemail.

I wonder if she left this phone in a trashcan on her drive, like she did the other one. Start completely fresh when she gets back to the city.

The sinking in my gut is for more than just me this time. Scaring her off hurts more than just me. I guess her seeing the house, me asking her to stay, seeing the reminders of why she left last time, it shook her so bad she couldn't even stay through her mom's passing.

Maybe she'll come back and forth over the coming months?

Maybe she'll come back just at the end?

Maybe she can't deal with any of it anymore.

I hate that I cost her that time with her mom, the only time she has left.

But if it's me she wants to avoid, if I'm what makes her want to stay away from the Heights, I'll make that easier on her, starting now.

Everything in this town reminds me of her anyway.

The bar, where every corner of it holds a memory of her from this fall.

The shop, where I watched her come, back bowed on a classic car, mouth full of my cock.

This house, built for her memory, for the dream of her, it's always screamed her. But now it smells like her too. I can still hear her laugh, her moans, her confession to me in it.

I need out of it.

I can think of one place where I have the fewest memories of her, where I have a chance of finding peace. The place she'd never go on her own. Where, even if she were in the Heights, she'd never go looking, we'd never run into each other, so she'll be safe from me.

While I shower—I have to get her smell off me if I have any chance of surviving this again—the thoughts swirl.

I guess at least I know now. I don't have to spend the next twelve years wondering what if.

What if I got to ask her to stay.

What if I offered to go with her.

I knew I'd regret it if I didn't try to keep her this time. With what we've gone through apart, the ways we've both grown, and what I've come to realize since she's been back in my life. I know she deserves more than I can give her, but I'd happily spend the rest of my life giving her everything I'm capable of, pampering her, spoiling her, and it still wasn't enough. I was willing to do long distance, or go to New York, whatever she wanted.

All I wanted was for her to stay with me. And she still said no.

I got the chance to put myself on the line this time, like I never got to last time, and I guess I should be thankful for that.

Because at least now I know.

There was never a reality where I'm good enough for Rory Weiss.

I'm the one who said I wanted ugly truths. Got my wish.

Opening the text thread with Gonzo, I grimace when I see his last message to me.

GONZO

Good luck with the missus.

Throwing my own words back in my face, a teasing reminder of how lucky I am and not to fuck it up. Too fucking late. Type my response and then throw my phone on the bed.

ME

I won't be around for a while.

Won't be long before that makes it through the rumor mill, and at least I won't be the thing that keeps her from seeing Laura Lee. She can have the Heights. I don't think I want it anymore.

I pack a bag with the bare essentials and take off.

CHILLY, crisp air and this view can cure a lot.

It can't cure me, but I think this is as close as I'll find to peace ever again.

This land was my grandfather's. Grew up camping on it, so I knew exactly where to go with my tent, sleeping bag, and the necessities. The old man passed down a couple dozen hectares, and I think Weston will hold it against me forever that it went to me and not him. Fine by me, there's plenty of shit I hold against him too.

Makeshift campsite down by the creek, an offshoot of the river that's overlooking the Smokies—burrowed between the evergreens and the bare branches of the birch, maple, and hickory trees—a simple breakfast and dinner over the fire, hikes to clear my mind. That's been my last couple days.

I wouldn't say life is *good*. I can't think about the reason I'm out here. The girl that isn't back at home waiting for me. Every time I do, my meager meals come back up. But I'm still in one piece, as far as I can tell. That's gotta be worth something, right?

All that solitude, the hard-won stillness gets fractured when I hear a male voice hollering my name.

Within minutes loud footsteps accompany the voice, branches snapping and breaking under the steps, like they're *trying* to scare all the wildlife away. Ronnie should know better, he's acting like he's not even a Southern boy with those clunky footfalls.

Then the voice is *in* my campsite. "Thank God."

You've gotta be fucking kidding me.

How far does a guy have to go to get privacy around here?

If I open that tent flap, and Ronnie's fucking face is peering in here again—no regard for my privacy, *again*—I'll lose it. Whatever shred of *it* I even have left.

But it's not Ronnie's face that greets me when I unzip and open the tent flap.

It's Weston's.

Does he even know how much I've gone through to find him?

I have a life of my own. But when your mom calls you and says no one has seen or heard from your only sibling in days, there's been an emergency and you're the only one who can probably tap into his psyche and find him ... Well, we might have a strained relationship, but I'm not a heartless dick. That's more his thing.

Dropped everything, made the five-hour drive out to Smoky Heights overnight, and spent the entire day in the woods we grew up camping in, searching for the spot I knew he'd be.

It's been almost twenty years since I was here, and I was just a kid then, but I kept going, determination leading the way. And lo and behold. Here's the grumpy fucker now.

Fuzzy, overgrown face glaring at me through a small opening in the tent flap, looking like he doesn't recognize me, or maybe he just can't figure out why the *fuck* I'm here. Why I tracked him down and why I'm invading his precious alone time. Like I'm encroaching on his territory and ruining his life by daring to interrupt his solo camping sesh on our family's land. Like I'm here to mess with his plans, the tagalong little brother he can't stand, rather than tell him something important, something he wants to hear.

I don't seem like a great choice for this mission, considering Wyatt's never taken me seriously. He doesn't even listen when I talk. And if he does, he sure as fuck doesn't *hear* what I have to say.

But he needs to hear this.

I start out strong, with a wry, "I know, I'm who you blame for everything, the reason anything in your life sucks, but this time, hold that thought and listen to what I'm here to say."

His eyes narrow, but at least he unzips the flap the rest of the way. "What do you want, Weston?"

"It's Rory," I say solemnly, a rare tone for me. "Well," I clarify, "it's her mom."

34
Wyatt

It's Rory. Well, it's her mom.

Cotton fills my ears, making everything around me sound like it's happening a hundred yards away. No sound is discernible, I see Weston's lips moving, but nothing comes out. Though maybe that's not new. The trees behind him spin, and that's definitely not what they normally do. I have to grasp the fabric opening of the tent door for the closest thing I can get to purchase. Something to steady me as the whole world tilts right off its axis.

The sound comes rushing back at once, three times louder than it usually is. The rushing of the creek, the wind through the branches all around me, the voice of my brother.

"She passed on Friday night. Saturday morning, I guess, technically. Seizure when she was in the bathroom. She fell and hit her head on the tub, and ... It was fast, Wyatt. A blessing if you ask me. But no one has been able to reach you, Mom asked me to help find you. Rory needs you, brother."

He should've started with *Rory needs you*, I'd be halfway back to the house already.

As it is, I'm up and racing to get my shit together, literal and metaphorical, spinning in a circle in the campsite, trying to figure out where to start and how to get there *now*.

"Where is she?" I ask him.

He pulls his phone out of his pocket and opens it up.

"WHERE?" I bellow.

"I'm checking. Jesus, man."

Rory didn't *leave* me. Rory left to go *to* her mom. Her mom who's gone. It still isn't sinking in, that feeling that I'm going to puke is coming back fast, but for a whole different reason than the last seven times it hit since I've been out here.

"Yeah, I found him," Weston is saying into his phone. "He's fine." His amber eyes cut over to me again, assessing me. "Well, maybe not *fine*, but he's uninjured. He could use a fucking shower. Probably a bourbon. Definitely a shave." West nods his head at whatever Mom is telling him. "Yeah, I'll tell him. He'll be there in an hour or so." He hangs up and faces me again. "Mom's taking her to your place."

I can make it there in thirty.

"Don't do something stupid on the way and break your ankle, Wyatt. She needs you. Just get back to her safely, man."

Is that gnats buzzing in my ear? I swear, when Weston talks, it doesn't even register for me.

West places a hand on my shoulder, and it brings me back to the moment. "I'll take care of your campsite. Just go."

I give him a single nod, the closest thing I can spare to thanks, turn, and take off to get back to her.

THE TREK ISN'T that long as the crow flies, but when you're going up and down foothills next to the Smokies, winding in and out of the woods without any real established path to speak of, it takes a lot longer than I wish it did when I have her to get back to.

My mind races the entire time.

She had to go through it alone. I should've been there for her.

Does this mean she really was planning on staying? She didn't try to leave town again?

Or the letter on the counter, did that change her mind? Did she remember all the reasons she left before, realize she really can't do this again?

Or did losing her mom cut her last tie to Smoky Heights?

Between her mother and I, is this place too painful for her now?

By the time I get back to the cabin even my veins are vibrating, bouncing with unspent energy, the need to see her, hold her, try to help her be okay in whatever way I can. Whatever okay might even look like right now.

As I jog through the field at the back of the clearing, I see my mom coming toward me on the north side of the house, by the driveway. Not a chance in hell I'm going to divert my path to go see her before Rory, but I can see the disapproval in her gaze all the way from here. It's pinging me, like she can channel that shit and send it long distance while she shakes her head at me, watching me go to where I should've been all along, before she sets off for her car now that I'm back. Giving us privacy. I know that after this, I'll have amends to make with more than Rory, but she's where it starts. She's where everything starts for me.

I'm out of breath when I make it inside, sweating from the exertion of running this far in the near-freezing weather, lungs stinging, like shards of ice are peppering them with each inhale. Every breath hurts worst than the last, but it's all worth it when I see her in her chair.

Face taut, rife with nerves, everything changes when she looks at me. Her face clears, eyes water, and all of that stress is replaced with relief. Sorrow, yes, but she's not suffering alone anymore. I'm going to take as much of that burden as she'll let me. If she'll let me.

Rory pushes herself up from the chair as I run across the room to her, and she collapses in my arms as soon as I'm within reach. I don't count the minutes she spends shaking, sobbing in my arms, I just hold her and let her get it out. Try to keep my own emotion at bay, because she needs me to be strong for her.

When the sobs turn to sniffles and then hiccups, she straightens up and I pull back to look at her.

"You were gone." Her voice is so small. I wasn't there for her when she needed me. I'm the one who left her on her own this time.

"I'm so sorry. I'm here."

My hands clutch each side of her face, holding her tight as I kiss every inch of her face I can reach. Her cheeks, her nose, her forehead, her lips.

"I heard what happened," I say quietly, against her temple.

She nods, head still in my hands.

"I'm so sorry you were alone for this, Rory."

She shakes her head this time, and I watch in wait, puzzled.

"I wasn't alone. Lex was with me."

Something clenches tight in my chest, and I shut my eyes against the swell of emotion.

"Thank God you have her," I say, and press another kiss to the side of her head, where she's tucked into my chin.

"She wasn't alone, either. Duke was with her when it happened."

I feel the tears hit my hand where it still frames her cheek, a drop of liquid pain against the one who should've been there.

"He said she was so happy right before it happened." Her

chest shakes with silent sobs, and I hold her tighter. At some point, she breathes a bit easier, stepping back and walking over to the couch, sitting down on it, so I follow her.

Rory plays with her hands, fiddling with her fingers, hidden in the sleeves of that black hoodie of mine she's wearing. "In a way, it seems better almost. She won't have to go through all the stages of her body shutting down. She got to go before the cancer took away her dignity." Her palm comes up to wipe away another tear that spilled over. "But we were supposed to have five more months."

"You were supposed to have *years*," I insist.

She nods, head falling down and taking a deep breath before bringing her watery eyes to mine again.

"What am I supposed to do now?" Her voice cracks as her heart does, all over her face. "Where do I go from here?"

I take one of her hands with both of mine and stroke my thumbs over the back of it.

"Take it one day at a time. An hour at a time, if you need to. Minute by fucking minute. I won't hold you to anything, Rory. You do whatever is best for you, and take all the time you need to figure out what that looks like."

I wouldn't blame her if she needed away from the Heights after this. I just hope she knows she doesn't have to leave me behind too. But I'm not putting that on her now. I'll stay on her back burner another half my life if she needs me to. We both know there's no one else for me. If there's even a chance I'm what she wants, too, when all this settles, I'll be here whenever she's ready.

But her face, it's all screwed up when she jerks her head back to look at me like I'm insane. I seem to be getting that look from everyone in my life today.

"What?" I ask her.

"Are you seriously telling me, after I just lost years with my mom, that you're willing to lose years with me too?"

I stutter for a second but come up with a response. "I can't even imagine what you're going through, the road you have ahead of you, but I'll be here for anything I can be, Rory." Seems like the most honest answer I can give her without putting any expectations on her, without tying her down to anything she can't commit to with what she's only just begun going through. She'll need time to process, to respond, and I can't begin to fathom what her healing is going to look like.

Her eyes burn into mine and that hand of hers I'm holding squeezes mine. "Wyatt, I'll *never* get the time back I wasted and lost with my mom. I can't do that again."

My mouth opens, then closes. Do I want to waste any of my time with her? No. But she made the most of her life. She went out and did the shit she was meant to do. I don't want her to waste that, either. To wake up and regret any decisions she makes in the wake of a disaster.

"Rory, don't rush into anything, okay? We have time."

"But we're wasting it, that's my point, Wyatt." She turns her body on the sofa so she's facing me. "Time is the most precious thing we have. We don't know how much of it we're going to get. And I'm not doing this again, not with you, or with my sister, or anyone else." She shakes her head side to side, resolutely.

"I thought you were gone." It's my turn for my voice to crack.

"I'm not leaving you again, Wyatt." She sounds so sure, so certain, but all she had to do was tell me what was happening and I would've gone with her. Just like last time.

"I found the note. And I tried to call you," is all I say. After days of thinking of nothing but that morning, it's still bothering me that she didn't wake me up, she didn't think to tell me. "I would've gone with you. Twelve years ago, and the other morning. But you didn't ask me to."

She nods, another tear slipping down her cheek. "Oh God, I'm sorry. Fuck, that must've been so awful for you. I didn't even think of that."

I try not to react, give her time to talk to me, the thing I wished for so many years she'd done for me, but my stomach is trying to spill its meager contents all over the both of us here if she doesn't hurry up.

"I woke up to pee." She scrubs her face with both hands, then takes mine back in hers. "That fucking cider, I had to pee in the middle of the night." I almost laugh because she always used to complain about that. It always made her get up overnight, but she never stopped drinking it anyway. "And I put the lube back in the nightstand on my way to the bathroom, and I found the note." She shakes her head, eyes on the fireplace as she recalls it, and then her gaze is back on mine. "It shocked me. It was awful to see, it woke up some terrible feelings, and it kills me that you've had it all this time. I'm sure you're more familiar with it than I am by now. But while I was reliving that, my phone rang. Duke called, and I panicked, Wyatt. I ran out the door. I should've woken you up, should've gotten you to come with me, but I was out of my mind. And I must've screwed up plugging my phone in for the two hours I did sleep, I don't know. It died at the hospital, and I left my charger here, and by the time we figured it out, Duke tried to call you, and Lexi had Gracie and Ronnie trying to reach you, but nobody could."

All I can do is nod, as the picture is painted for me.

She takes a big breath before she speaks again. "Look. I tried to get away from my problems before by running, but they stayed with me because the problem wasn't the Heights. It wasn't you, or my family. It was *me*, and the way I needed to grow. I still need to grow, Wyatt. But I see the horizon now. I see a life where we're healthy with one another, where I'm not running from my issues, but I'm going to get there *with* you. Here with you, and my sister, and Duke."

"You don't want to go back to New York?" I can't even get a breath in, the way she's got my hopes up right now.

Rory shakes her head slowly, eyes never leaving mine. "New York was my escape. It was supposed to be my dream, and there's a lot I love about it. But it doesn't have the things that are most important to me. I want to see this case through. I want to help the people of this town get restitution. Live up to my mom's legacy. I want to live the life you and I should've always had. Because this is where I belong. *You're* where I belong. This cottage. Our kid in that backyard. I'm not losing another chance at the life I was meant to have with you." She gives me a smile, a real fucking smile, and then she adds, "But maybe we can visit the city once in a while? Order in some of the things I'll miss most?"

"Sounds like we need to make some amendments to our little arrangement," I say. "Point one, if you order that Korean barbecue again, it gets shipped to the bar, not to our cabin. No memories of other men are allowed in our home, sorry."

"What, like you don't have memories of other women here?" She tosses it back to me like she already knows the answer.

I give her a look that says it all. This place has always screamed her, and only her. Of course I haven't brought any other woman to it.

Rather than get mushy on me, she switches to another lane of conversation, one that tries to rile me up, her usual MO. This woman can make my heart beat faster for the rest of our lives, any way she chooses to do it, and it'll be fine by me. But she'd better be ready to get back exactly what she gives.

"Are we calling this place a cabin? It's really more of a cottage, I'd say."

"Point two, if you're gonna stay, I'm really gonna need you to start calling it a cabin. There's a big difference in connotation between cottage and cabin, surely you're aware of that, Ms. Who Versus Whom."

She laughs and leans in close, where I meet her halfway. "Can we worry about the fine print later?" Rory asks against my lips.

"We have the rest of forever to negotiate workable terms," I promise her, and seal it with a kiss.

She snickers when we break apart. "Good luck finding a better lawyer than me to represent your interests."

"You *are* my interests, Rory Weiss. My sole interest, as a matter of fact. And I have just one more question for you, about our future. Point three, and it's kind of the biggest one."

I slide off the couch to one knee in front of her, still holding her hand. Her eyes go round and sparkly as she watches me.

"Will you," I ask, looking her in those gorgeous warm brown eyes, "let me pick you out a decent car now?"

She laughs, shoving at my shoulder until I fall over on the ground, but I take her with me, wrapped in my arms so I cushion her short plummet, Rory landing on top of me with a small whoosh of breath. Her deep chestnut ponytail swings around one side of her face, tickling my beard where it hangs down.

"Only if it comes with a giant fucking ring."

Doesn't take me a half a second to answer her. "Deal."

"You're a sucker." She cackles, head tilted back, then looks back down at me. "I would've settled for a small one that sparkles a lot."

"You're the sucker," I tell her against her lips. "I would've settled for no car, no terms, just you."

The dogwood trees are in full bloom, our yard flowering in vivid white buds that look like cherry blossoms. The meadow has dots of yellow, purple, and pink as other flowers stretch their petals in this gorgeous weather, testing their spring wardrobe ahead of the new season. I breathe in the smell of it, taking a second to enjoy the simple things.

The sun is close to setting behind our favorite backdrop to the paradise we live in, those picturesque Smokies that line our view, now back to a vibrant green that screams of new life.

The mountains aren't the only sign of it.

"Rory!" Wyatt calls my name from the south side of the house.

"Coming!" I shout back and make my way over.

"Henrietta won't get in her coop. She keeps running away from me and—" Wyatt dives for the feisty bird and she dodges him like she's in the NFL.

She might be past her egg-laying years, but she's still with our flock. My mom's flock, that live with us now.

I block her off at the pass, stopping her path to freedom so Wyatt can catch her and put her back in the run he made for them. Call me crazy, but I think that look on her face when my husband finally closes his hands around her body, wings, and neck is a look of satisfaction. I think that was all she wanted all along. And honestly? Same, sister. I can relate. My feathers get ruffled when he hasn't touched me in a while, myself. The man's got magic hands, what do you want from me?

As soon as she's through her little chicken door, she bolts, running through what might as well be a playground for birds to be with her sisters for the night, clucking to probably tell them all about how she tricked Wyatt into picking her up yet again.

We made good on our promise to Henrietta the Eighth and her gal pals. If other coops are Androids—no, Nokias—they have the iPhone 30 of chicken housing. In the shoe store of life as a chicken, they have the equivalent to Italian, hand-stitched leather heels.

As I look down, I realize mine might be getting a little muddy, and I slip them off, placing my Valentino Garavanis on the stone walkway where they're safer, and stand barefoot in the grass watching Wyatt come back to me. I gotta say, he's gotten even finer with time. Dark hair trimmed just short enough that he can push it back and have that effortless look that most have to try for. Face like he forgot to shave just a couple days too many. Mouth that doubles as a hell of a seat. Eyes that melt my insides.

"Was she the last one?" I ask him.

"She was the holdout," he confirms. When he's close enough to, he sweeps me in his arms and dips me backward, kissing me. I lose my breath more from the depth of emotion than the intensity of the kiss, but we break apart and keep it from getting out of hand when we hear a husky voice.

"Keep it PG out here, you've got young, impressionable eyes around, you two."

Duke rounds the corner from the front of the house, a baby in his arms. Our baby in his arms. His grandchild.

Turns out, we didn't have Axle.

We had a little girl, Laura Lee Ellis Grady.

"I swear, she's grown about a foot since I last saw her," he says, holding her out in front of him for inspection.

He's got her in an outfit I don't recognize. Something colorful, is that real silk? Hard to tell from this far away.

"It's not even a couple of pounds she's gained since you last saw her, now you're starting to sound like Ernie, just exaggerating for the hell of it," Wyatt calls out to him.

Duke takes a seat at the table, Laura Lee in his lap, bouncing her on his knee as he relishes the moment, playing with her, giant hearts popping out of his eyes every time he makes her giggle.

"I mean it, son," he calls over. "You go to Thailand for a month, and your own granddaughter has doubled in size by the time you're back. No way is this a couple o' pounds! If I'd extended my trip any longer, she probably would've had her driver's license by the time I got back."

A warm smile breaks out across my face. It's good to see him again.

Took him a while to be willing to live out that trip for Mom. The last thing on her bucket list. He said he was ready to go on the one-year anniversary of her death, but with the baby on the way, he decided to wait until we were settled in as new parents before he went. Didn't want to miss any part of that journey, he said.

Today's the first time we've seen him since he got back from his trip yesterday.

Our weekly family dinner. Finally warm enough for us to

host it out here in the backyard after a winter of squeezing the five of us around the small dining table. Spring has finally sprung. And tonight, there's going to be six of us.

"You owe me!" My sister's piercing voice cuts through the yard before she does. "If I ever have kids, you owe me one dirty, dirty diaper duty."

"You got it, Lex!" She scowls at me, but there's no heat behind it as she plops down next to Duke at the picnic-style table and joins him in playing with her niece.

"You're safe from that one," Wyatt says out of the side of his mouth, so only I hear him. "She is *not* gonna settle down with anyone in this town."

He's not wrong about that last part. Lexi has a long history with everyone in this town, enough to keep her away from dating any of them seriously, and she's so cemented here she'll never leave it, either. But I'm not so sure I'd take that bet that she's never gonna find her person or start a family. She's approaching her late thirties now, but look at my mom and Duke. They didn't find each other until much later in life, but we're all thankful they did.

Plus, with all the growth I'm anticipating in Smoky Heights with my New Heights project, you just never know. We're rebuilding it into the kind of place anyone would love to live. Attracting not just new residents for labor, with all the construction and development, but talent, young entrepreneurs with great ideas who needed the right place, a vibrant economy to bring them to life.

The Brown Stone settlement did more than just make right the wrongs they did on a personal level to most of our town. After a long, long two years of thorough discovery and prep, the suit we presented to the state attorney general was remarkably smooth, and the AG decided to make a statement to any other financial institutions looking to suck the life out of an entire community through illegal and immoral practices by awarding a settlement fund to go to the betterment of the town as restitution, just like we were pushing for.

Guess who's been put in charge of overseeing and executing that, dispensing the approved grants and filing all the necessary paperwork with the AG's office? Yours truly. My firm set up a satellite office for me here, happy to let me continue on this project until its eventual completion.

It's been a *lot* of work, but we're finally seeing the changes happen to our small town on more than paper. Buildings downtown, restored. New ones being built. An influx of new residents. Not enough to disrupt our tiny infrastructure, but enough to breathe new life into this place. To make it the stunning small town it used to be, a healthy economy, beautiful views, the perfect place to live, work, and raise your family, for generations to come.

Brown Stone Bank may have sapped the life out of us for a while with their unfair business practices, but we're making it right.

And who did I recruit to come paint all of the interiors of these new businesses, so close to ready to open?

"Weston." I think Wyatt was just trying to say his name, but it came out more like a snarl.

So look, there's more progress to be made, but we all start somewhere, right?

Weston slams his car door closed and starts to trek across our grass to shortcut getting back here.

"Do I need to give you the speech again?" I ask him through clenched teeth, a smile plastered to my face for West's sake as I wave to him.

"No."

"Remind me," I tell him, jabbing an elbow into his side.

"Time is precious." Why does that sound like a threat

coming out of his mouth? "We're not wasting the time we have with the ones we love." His mouth is all but entirely closed, jaw clenched, lips barely moving with the words.

"And we're willing to try to mend those bridges we let get a little singed along the way, right?" I ask him pointedly.

He doesn't answer and I dig in deeper with my words. "Or are you telling me if you watched Weston die tomorrow, you wouldn't regret all the years you've lost with your brother?"

"Fine, just don't pull that card on me, you know it's not fair."

"What isn't fair is that I'll never get to talk to my mom again, but you still have the chance to talk to him. He's right there, Wyatt."

It's been a tough battle with the grieving process. I don't think losing someone you love is something you're ever over, but you do eventually learn to live again. You have to. Because you still can, and you owe it to that person you lost to do something that makes all this worthwhile. To have enough good in your life that it makes the suffering they went through, that we all went through, worth it.

Wyatt's helped me through every step of it, which is why he knows exactly what I mean. We both know he'd hate himself for the rest of *his* life if he didn't get that relationship back. And now that Weston's going to be spending some time in the Heights, he just might have no excuse not to do it.

"I hate that you're right so much of the time, I hope you know that," Wyatt grumbles at me as we walk over to the table.

"I've had my moments of being very wrong," I say, nose in the air, the closest I can get to anything approximating humble. "But I'm happy to report that someone got me back on the right path a couple years ago, and they didn't let me stay lost."

"That person sounds like they deserve a pretty big thank you."

"I thank him every day."

"I think today you thanked me twice, actually," he says with a filthy smirk, slapping my ass.

Self-forgiveness has been a slower journey for me, but as we step up to the table, greeting his brother, my sister, the closest thing I have to a father, and the daughter Wyatt and I named after both my mother and the love of her life, I have hope for our future. Because I'm surrounded by the people who make our lives great.

After searching for so long, it feels like I've finally found the meaning to the mess we call life.

I've finally made a home.

AUTHOR'S NOTE

Did you enjoy this book? If so, would you be willing to take a few seconds to leave a review on Amazon and/or Goodreads?

Your word of mouth makes all the difference for brand new indie authors like me. ♡

Keep reading for a sneak peek of The Roommate Syndrome, available to read for free on Kindle Unlimited.

XOXO,
Maddie

ACKNOWLEDGMENTS

Writing four debut novels at once, then putting them out back-to-back is not for the faint of heart. I wrote this book concurrent to editing, publishing, and marketing the first four, which was a new sort of terrifying "fun" for me. There were a lot of times I struggled with the process, but there were people who made it easier for me, and who I'd like to thank.

To Kaymie, my writing partner and bitchstie, because we both know this book wouldn't be here without you. Any one of the countless days you brought me back to life over the year I worked on this book would be enough to thank you for, but all of them? Leaves me speechless. Counting down to the mountain, where maybe we'll have our own Waka Flocka Flame Oh, and now we all know it's canon that Rory's favorite author is Theo, and she was fangirling *hard* to get to work on that merger.

To my best friend since Kindergarten, the best chicken mama I know, who spent a weekend nursing one of her hens back to health with honey water in a bathtub, who may have inspired a particular scene, and who Rory would be lucky to learn a few things from, as I have been over the past three decades.

My boo thang, T.L. Martin, for being unfailing in the hope + encouragement you share with me when I need it most.

My adventure buddy for being down for all the things together, even when most of those things are just rambling voice notes about my books and the current issues I'm facing with them. Thanks for nodding and smiling along through it all.

My alpha readers, @_danireads, @addisonreads_ & @bookish.bri16, who read the roughest versions of this story and kept me encouraged and moving on it, cheered me on and saw the best in me and these characters. And most especially, my one and only beta reader on this one, Sophie Hamilton, who gave the most insightful and valuable feedback when I needed it most.

The ARC reviewers who are giving a shot to this brand-new author most of you have never even heard of before, and gifting me your time and enthusiasm, thank you for spreading the word about Rory, Wyatt, and Smoky Heights.

The Madison Myers Street Team for helping get the word out about me and my books to the world of readers. So, so thankful for each of your posts, shares, and everything you do to support the dream!

My editor, proofreader, and ally, Juli Burgett, for your insight and inspiration, and putting up with my long ass sentences.

Sam of Ink and Laurel Designs for this gorgeous freaking cover.

My PA, Cortney of Anti-Hero Author Services + What the Smut Are You Talking About podcast fame, for helping me turn my creative insanity into order. If I get up to doing more than a book or two a year, I'm giving you all the credit, babe.

My hubby for the ridiculous level of belief and support you give me, taking care of our entire household while I write from dark to dark, and being my ear for literally everything. For pulling a Wyatt and feeding me when I forget to take care of myself, and making things that much less worse every time you do. I dream of hiring you one day, so at least you get paid for all the shit you put up with from me. Oh, also thanks for coming up with the bowling alley scene idea. Maybe you should write dirty romance, too?

Everyone who's given my books a shot, told their friends, left a kind review, spread the word on social media or (gasp) irl. You're a pioneer of indie romance and though this book puts me past a half a million words published so far, I lack the words to tell you how much I appreciate you and your support!

P.S.

Fuck cancer + those who profit off of it.

This book is in loving memory to my family and friends who have lost their battles with cancer, and to all those who've lost someone too soon to its cruelty.

SNEAK PEEK OF THE ROOMMATE SYNDROME

ONE

CHRISSY

Right there. *God, yes!*

It's been *way* too long since I've had a decent orgasm.

I owe myself this, um, *self-care* session of epic proportions.

Just one ... more ... second ... I'm so *close.*

"MOM!" a little voice yells from outside my bedroom door.

Aaaand it's gone. This can't be happening.

What happened to giving me a break, Chance? What happened to watching the kids for ten fucking *minutes, Chance?*

"Mommy?" the voice tries again, quieter this time. I sigh, about to get up to see what he needs that only Mom can solve. Let me guess ...

His sippy cup is only half full and he can't drink from it unless it's exactly two-thirds full?

Maybe his chicken nuggets are too dinosaur-shaped.

Or his cheese isn't yellow enough?

Somehow these are all problems I've had to deal with in the past week, and they were all problems that the little bastards insisted Daddy couldn't solve, Mom only. Ugh. Even the voice in my head sounds sarcastic and bitter. I'm not always so bitter, especially not toward my own children, but it's been ... tough lately. Having kids is a *hoot*, y'all.

"Preston!" I hear my husband whisper-hiss, likely while he grabs our second youngest and carries him away. I relax back down onto the mound of pillows and listen to be sure he has it under control.

"Remember what I told you? *Mami* is resting, we can't wake her up. Come here, buddy."

His voice grows quieter as he moves farther down the hallway, back to the kids' playroom, and I hear the door close over Preston's murmured response.

I sigh. Like it isn't hard enough to find time for us to *be together*, now I can't even find five minutes to handle my own needs in between cartoons, clean-ups, and playdates? Not to mention, you know, my own work and career and *life*. Not that I have much of one anymore. That's kind of how it goes when you have four kids under the age of ten.

Not that I'm complaining. They're the loves of my life. But sometimes I miss *me*. And I definitely miss spending one-on-one time with Chance.

Okay, so maybe I am complaining *just a little*. But bear with me.

Well, if I can't get time with my husband, at least I can clock in an O or two with my favorite vibrator, whom I have lovingly dubbed Ranger, after one of my favorite book boyfriends. He always gets the job done, he's tactical, precise, and never fails to accomplish his mission objectives. *Operation Long-Overdue-O is back underway.*

I focus my attention back to my own needs (highly rare as a mother), and work myself back up to where I left off within just a minute or two. *Finally.*

But then, the rhythm stutters, the suction slows, and the

vibrator gives one last shudder and dies in my hand, leaving me on the brink of a very promising release.

"FUCK!" I whisper-shout, now frustrated in more ways than one.

Now this is probably the time to give up, chalk it up to a bad round, and move on with my life. But it's been *weeks* since Chance and I have had sex, and after my last pregnancy ... I just can't go that long anymore.

My libido has been hyped up for three years now (not that it was low before that—it wasn't), and I don't see it coming down anytime soon.

I *need* a release.

I start to turn into even more of a feisty bitch if I go more than a few days, and I'm going to blame my recent irritability on this dry spell.

Yeah. Sure. That's all it is. Biology.

It has nothing to do with the fact that your husband has practically become your roommate instead of the love of your life, the salty voice in my head chides.

Sensitive topic, let's not go there and kill my vibe. Let's get back to that release I'm so desperate for ...

Instead of giving up, or selecting another toy from our little collection, I decide to finish with Ranger. His moves are what I've been craving, dammit.

I pull my robe closed and quietly (yet still somewhat dramatically, I'll admit), stomp my way through the single-story house to the kitchen, opening the junk drawer to grab replacement batteries. After rifling through the Ds, Cs, and AAs, I discover an empty package of AAAs.

Great. I'm sure one of the kids grabbed the last of them for their remote-control car or some shit.

Glancing around the room, my eyes are drawn to the

random battery that is sitting miserably at the bottom of our fishbowl. Yep, you guessed it, AAA.

Awesome. At least it went to good use.

Not.

I give a mental snort.

Oh no! Topanga!

Topanga isn't looking quite so hot, if goldfish can even look hot to begin with.

I let my head fall and shake it for a moment, a chuckle escaping my lips. Can't help but to laugh at my own misfortune. I guess it's just not in the cards for me today.

I pull out my cell phone and quickly order the largest pack of AA batteries Amazon has to offer. (Do they sell 100 packs? They should. I'd definitely invest in them. Or maybe I should invest in a decent rechargeable toy? Mental note to get back to that later.)

Luckily, they'll be here tomorrow. Unluckily, my mood for today is long gone.

Sorry, libido. And sorry anyone who has to put up with me until then. I highly doubt my salty demeanor is going to improve until I work some of this tension out of my system.

Grabbing the empty package (No, but seriously, would it have been that hard to add it to the stupid list on the fridge? Or at least tell me we were getting low or had already run out? Or, at the bare minimum, could they really not have just thrown the fucking package away?), I head down the main hallway to the kids' playroom and poke my head in the door, nostrils still flared.

Despite the irritation I felt not ten seconds ago, the sight that greets me warms my heart, and I take in Chance's features as he sits on the colorful interlocking foam flooring with Preston and our youngest (the only daughter of our brood) on his lap. He's reading them a book about a hungry caterpillar, while our two oldest lie on the foam tiles all the way on the other side of the room, facing off with Beyblades in some sort of battle royale, complete with their own sound effects and all.

The kids all stay focused on their activities, but Chance looks up to me with a gentle, knowing smile on his face. "Feeling better, Di?" he asks huskily, his deep blue eyes twinkling.

I narrow my gaze at him, and his little nickname for me, as I hold up the empty package, and I can't help the accusatory note in my voice. "Not quite. Did you know we were out of batteries? I could use some more to really help me *feel better*."

Before we first became parents, I thought it would be harder to talk in code around the kids, but it's really not. When you've been with someone for as long as Chance and I have been together (thirteen years and counting), it gets pretty easy to tell what the other one is thinking, or what the meaning is behind their child-friendly words.

His face falls in understanding. "No, baby, I would've put them on the list if I used the last of them." He sounds so earnest, I believe him. "One of the boys must've used them. I'm sorry."

At that, Preston lifts his head to look at me, eyes wide. "I gave 'Panga a battery to give him extra juice, Mommy. He didn't look so good."

My expression morphs into one of amusement and appreciation for this caring little dude who always has the best of intentions, even if they're poorly executed ninety percent of the time. "That's okay, buddy, thanks for telling me. Next time he's not looking so good, will you tell Daddy or me so we can try to help him, too?"

He nods vigorously, eyes still wide, and turns his attention back to the book in his dad's hands.

Chance shoots a glance at the big clock on the wall that is shaped like crayons, sees that it's a quarter to eight, almost the kids' bedtime, and then brings his gaze back to me, one side of his mouth moving upward as he rakes those gorgeous eyes over my body.

"Let me take care of bath time, and then maybe I can come take care of you for once," he says, quietly and full of intent, with another of his trademark winks. I try to maintain my indignance, but dammit, that smirk gets me every time.

Fuck him for still looking so hot after eleven years of marriage and a whole brood of children. I'll be honest, I never got the appeal of a dad bod until Chance lost his not-quite-six-pack and softened up a little with time, but damn if he doesn't pull it off. And when he adds a backward hat, like he's got on now? Whoo-ey, I swear to Fendi, I don't stand a chance.

And how is he in such a good mood? He hasn't been laid in weeks, either, right? Ugh.

It's been way too long, Christina. Get the kids to bed early tonight and steal some time with your husband. You deserve it.

"A modern fairy tale," I reply sardonically, rolling my eyes, as if his offer hasn't completely melted me. It's not like he doesn't already know what he does to me. I don't need to add to his ego in that regard.

"Hey, what kind of Prince Charming would I be if I didn't take care of my princess, Di?" he teases, eyes still on mine, that damned smirk still lingering on his lips.

A shiver runs through me at his words, pictures flashing through my mind of all of the times he's more than taken care of me, and a thrill shoots through me straight to my downstairs.

Hey, what do you know, my libido is still hanging around after all.

"Daddy! We can do princess story?" Eleanor asks, looking up at him eagerly.

"Anything you want, my darling," he tells her as he kisses the top of her head, winking at me.

I don't miss the double meaning behind his words, and I can't help but grin as I back out of the room, eyes still on him.

He turns his attention back to the book and the two children he is entertaining. "What do you say, kiddos? You guys gonna go to sleep on time for once tonight? Hmmm?" He tickles them on the last word, and they break out in laughter, promising him they'll be good.

I shake my head, trail down the hallway to the kids' bathroom to start the bathwater, mind racing.

Maybe tonight we can get back on track, back to the us we were before this ... chaos that became our daily life. Finally fit in some time for each other, instead of nothing but work and kids. The voice in my head is surprisingly hopeful, optimistic, rather than the usual pessimistic side of myself that resides there. Weird, but I'll go with it.

Once the water is running, I lay out all the toys, towels, and jammies we'll need for two showers and two baths, and wait for the tub to fill. The nighttime routine has gotten fairly easy over the years, and luckily, our kids are actually pretty great at listening (which I am very thankful for when I *do* get the chance to catch up with my other mommy friends and hear their horror stories).

With the hellhound I was growing up, I was sure Fate was gonna get me back, but so far, we've been blessed.

It's probably Chance. He's always been one of those people who can smooth rough waters, bring calm to just about any situation, and ease tensions when they build.

Parenting comes naturally to him. The negotiating, bartering, and diplomatic skills he's been wielding his whole life really come in handy for more than his sales job at my bestie's family's marketing company.

Who knew those same skills would translate so well to parenting?

I mean, in both cases, it's basically someone talking about their problems, figuring out what they need, and reaching an agreement on how to best provide a solution. He was born for this role.

Hell, he was acting as a peacekeeper between his parents even as a young thing, and maybe our kids being half-saints is the payback he's earned for his good deeds over the years?

Me, on the other hand? We are truly fortunate we aren't reaping what I sowed in my youth. But that was before Chance. And when I was without my best friend Ellie. I've come around since then. Mostly.

⁕

Wetness leaks out from the corner of my mouth, and I use a finger to wipe it away, a smile forming as I swallow.

I slowly open my eyes and attempt to form a conscious thought, forcing my brain to put two and two together.

Drool?

Did I fall asleep?

Shit. Real sexy, Christina. At least that dream was hot ...

The thoughts are coming a little more readily now, and I check the time on my phone—almost ten PM. *Ugh, I can't believe I passed out before he got back from putting Lea to bed. I* roll over to see if Chance is in bed with me.

His side of the bed is empty, but the covers are thrown back, so I can tell he's been here. I sit up, putting my left tit back in my robe where it had worked itself free during my impromptu nap, and tying the robe closed once again. *Damn, this thing really isn't meant for lying down in.*

As my eyes adjust to the low light in the room, I quickly scan to see if he's in the closet undressing or something, but I can hear slight noises coming from the bathroom, where light leaks out from beneath the mostly closed door.

Call it a wife's intuition, but I have to check on him.

Two months ago, he got food poisoning and didn't even tell me he was throwing up *all* night, until four AM when I woke up to find him asleep on the floor in front of the toilet and got him some nausea medicine and Gatorade.

I swear, men won't ask for help until they're on their damn deathbed. At least mine doesn't.

My friend Lola's ex-husband apparently wouldn't get out of bed if he had so much as a tickle in his throat. He made her wait on him hand and foot when he was under the weather, but not my man.

I peek my head around the edge of the door, and what I see is so much worse than Chance passed out in his own vomit.

My husband, sitting on the toilet.

My husband, with his dick in his right hand.

My husband, with his phone in his other hand.

My stomach drops when I see what's on his screen.

Another girl on his phone.

I can't even call her a woman. She looks early twenties, at the most. Definitely no crow's feet like I'm getting. She's tiny, like I used to be. Perky tits, like I used to have.

She looks like she knows how hot she is.

She definitely doesn't look like she's long past her best years, or like she's brought four of his children into this world.

He is furiously jerking the hand gripping his cock, making soft noises as he obviously tries to remain quiet, staring intently at the photo in his hand before he closes his eyes and continues his ministrations to his own shaft, moving faster with each stroke, completely unaware of his wife watching on in horror as her entire world shatters with each pump of his fist.

I can't make a noise. I'm not sure my body is even functioning. My stomach is still in the region of my knees.

My creaky, thirty-three-year-old knees.

Far below my thirty-three-year-old ass and hips that will never be as small as they were before I got pregnant with Bradshaw, our firstborn.

Never as small as the ass on the chick he is currently pleasuring himself to the sight of.

I slowly back away from the bathroom, not making a sound. I can't even form a coherent thought other than *my husband doesn't want me. My husband wants that tight little thing, not the woman he brought four new lives into the world with.*

I guess for better or worse didn't mean when life gets too busy for regular sex?

Or when your wife gains some baby weight?

I can't help the callous thoughts flooding my mind right now, but I wish I could. My usual pessimism is back with a bite I haven't heard in so damn long. *If I wasn't what you wanted, Chance, maybe you shouldn't have knocked me up four times in six years.*

I'm not proud of what I'm thinking right now, but I've never claimed to be perfect. I'm salty and quick to defend myself and my family on the best of days, and I would *not* call this the best of my days.

As I head back to bed, crawling up to my pillow and underneath the covers again—my back toward his side of the bed, pretending I never saw anything—one thought won't leave my mind above all the others. It's on repeat, like a fucked-up chant, a morbid mantra to the demise of my marriage.

My husband wants someone else.

My husband doesn't want me.

That's my only thought as I somehow, eventually, drift off to sleep, long after Chance came back to bed, oblivious to his wife silently crying into her pillow with her back to him, no more than ten inches and a world apart.

KEEP READING FOR FREE ON KINDLE UNLIMITED

ABOUT THE AUTHOR

Maddie is an elder millennial who writes contemporary romance books for other overworked, undersexed millennials.

Her books focus on relatable characters you'll fall for, journeys you'll root for and spice you'll melt for. She's awful at social media and talking in the third person, but she's slightly less terrible at writing romance and spice.

When she isn't writing from dark to dark, she's usually blasting music that hasn't been cool for fifteen years, or curling up with a spicy book, her pups and the book boyfriend of the day, or her very real (and very understanding) husband of over a decade.

You can see her current and upcoming books on her website: madisonmyersauthor.com

Connect with Maddie on social:

instagram.com/madisonmyersauthor

tiktok.com/@madisonmyersauthor

bookbub.com/profile/madison-myers

9 798348 383961